Praise for *INKHEART*

. . . a breathtakingly fast-moving tale.
INDEPENDENT

. . . one of the outstanding children's novels of the year.
THE TIMES

*I don't think I've ever read anything that conveys so
well the joys, terrors and pitfalls of reading.*
DIANA WYNNE JONES, GUARDIAN

*. . . the ideas about the relationship of author, characters and
reader are so fascinating and resonant that it has to be
a favourite for any bibliophile.*
SUNDAY TIMES

*. . . a story that celebrates books, and the conclusion is
especially satisfying.*
HORN BOOK

*A complex . . . tale of life and literature,
creating almost 600 pages of endless delight.*
IRISH TIMES

*Suspenseful, darkly comic tale of 12-year-old Meggie, who
discovers the perils of fictional characters coming to life.*
TIME MAGAZINE

As beguiling as the trompe l'oeil painting on its cover.
NEW YORK TIMES

A MESSAGE FROM CHICKEN HOUSE

I've always loved books and dreamt of what would happen if I could join the characters who fire up my imagination. But getting what you want can sometimes be dangerous. Those heroes might be pretty unreliable in real life – and the villains? Well, they could be even more scary if you met them face to face.

Inkheart is a novel for everyone who loves to read and dares to dream about stories that can come to life in more ways than one.

BARRY CUNNINGHAM
Publisher
Chicken House

CORNELIA FUNKE

Translated from the German by **Anthea Bell**

2 PALMER STREET, FROME, SOMERSET BA11 1DS

For Anna, who even put The Lord of the Rings *aside
for a while to read this book. Could anyone ask more
of a daughter?*

*And for Elinor, who lent me her name, although I
didn't use it for an elf queen.*

Published in Germany as *Tintenherz* by Cecilie Dressler Verlag 2003
Original text copyright © Dressler Verlag 2003
English translation copyright © The Chicken House 2003

First paperback edition published in Great Britain in 2004
This edition published in 2020
Chicken House
2 Palmer Street
Frome, Somerset BA11 1DS
United Kingdom
www.chickenhousebooks.com

Chicken House/Scholastic Ireland, 89E Lagan Road, Dublin Industrial Estate,
Glasnevin, Dublin D11 HP5F, Republic of Ireland

Cover design by Steve Wells
Cover illustration © Karl James Mountford
Designed and typeset by Dorchester Typesetting Group Ltd
Printed and bound by CPI Group (UK) Ltd, Croydon, CR0 4YY

FSC
www.fsc.org
MIX
Paper from
responsible sources
FSC® C020471

3 5 7 9 10 8 6 4

British Library Cataloguing in Publication data available.

ISBN 978-1-912626-84-7
eISBN 978-1-906427-97-9

If you are a dreamer, come in
If you are a dreamer, a wisher, a liar,
A Hope-er, a Pray-er, a Magic Bean buyer,
If you're a pretender, come sit by my fire
For we have some flax-golden tales to spin
Come in!
Come in!

Shel Silverstein

A Stranger in the Night

The moon shone in the rocking horse's eye, and in the mouse's eye, too, when Tolly fetched it out from under his pillow to see. The clock went tick-tock, and in the stillness he thought he heard little bare feet running across the floor, then laughter and whispering, and a sound like the pages of a big book being turned over.

L.M. Boston, *The Children of Green Knowe*

Rain fell that night, a fine, whispering rain. Many years later, Meggie had only to close her eyes and she could still hear it, like tiny fingers tapping on the windowpane. A dog barked somewhere in the darkness, and however often she tossed and turned Meggie couldn't get to sleep.

The book she had been reading was under her pillow, pressing its cover against her ear as if to lure her back into its printed pages. 'I'm sure it must be very comfortable sleeping with a hard, rectangular thing like that under your head,' her father had teased, the first time he found a book under her pillow. 'Go on, admit it, the book whispers its story to you at night.'

'Sometimes, yes,' Meggie had said. 'But it only works for children.' Which made Mo tweak her nose. Mo. Meggie had never called her father anything else.

That night – when so much began and so many things changed for ever – Meggie had one of her favourite books under her pillow, and since the rain wouldn't let her sleep she sat up, rubbed the drowsiness from her eyes, and took it out. Its pages rustled promisingly when she opened it. Meggie thought this first whisper sounded a little different from one book to another, depending on whether or not she already knew the story it was going to tell her. But she needed light. She had a box of matches hidden in the drawer of her bedside table. Mo had forbidden her to light candles at night. He didn't like fire. 'Fire devours books,' he always said, but she was twelve years old, she could surely be trusted to keep an eye on a couple of candle flames. Meggie loved to read by candlelight. She had five candlesticks on the windowsill, and she was just holding the lighted match to one of the black wicks when she heard footsteps outside. She blew out the match in alarm – oh, how well she remembered it, even many years later – and knelt to look out of the window, which was wet with rain. Then she saw him.

The rain cast a kind of pallor on the darkness, and the stranger was little more than a shadow. Only his face gleamed white as he looked up at Meggie. His hair clung to his wet forehead. The rain was falling on him, but he ignored it. He stood there motionless, arms crossed over his chest as if that might at least warm him a little. And he kept on staring at the house.

I must go and wake Mo, thought Meggie. But she stayed put, her heart thudding, and went on gazing out into the night as if the stranger's stillness had infected her. Suddenly, he turned his head, and Meggie felt as if he were looking straight into her eyes. She shot off the bed so fast the open book fell to the floor, and she ran barefoot out into the dark corridor. This was the end of May, but it was chilly in the old house.

There was still a light on in Mo's room. He often stayed up reading late into the night. Meggie had inherited her love of books from her father. When she took refuge from a bad dream with him, nothing could lull her to sleep better than Mo's calm breathing beside her and the sound of the pages turning. Nothing chased nightmares away faster than the rustle of printed paper.

But the figure outside the house was no dream.

The book Mo was reading that night was bound in pale blue linen. Later, Meggie remembered that too. What unimportant little details stick in the memory.

'Mo, there's someone out in the yard!'

Her father raised his head and looked at her with the usual absent expression he wore when she interrupted his reading. It always took him a few moments to find his way out of that other world, the labyrinth of printed letters.

'Someone out in the yard? Are you sure?'

'Yes. He's staring at our house.'

Mo put down his book. 'So what were *you* reading before you went to sleep? *Dr Jekyll and Mr Hyde?*'

Meggie frowned. 'Please, Mo! Come and look.'

He didn't believe her, but he went anyway. Meggie tugged him along the corridor so impatiently that he stubbed his toe on a pile of books, which was hardly surprising. Stacks of books were piled high all over the house – not just arranged in neat rows on bookshelves, the way other people kept them, oh no! The books in Mo and Meggie's house were stacked under tables, on chairs, in the corners of the rooms. There were books in the kitchen and books in the lavatory. Books on the TV set and in the wardrobe, small piles of books, tall piles of books, books thick and thin, books old and new. They welcomed Meggie down to breakfast with invitingly opened pages, they kept boredom at bay when the weather was bad. And sometimes you fell over them.

'He's just standing there!' whispered Meggie, leading Mo into her room.

'Has he got a hairy face? If so, he could be a werewolf.'

'Oh, stop it!' Meggie looked at him sternly, although his jokes made her feel less scared. Already, she hardly believed any more in the figure standing in the rain – until she knelt down again at the window. 'There! Do you see him?' she whispered.

Mo looked out through the raindrops running down the pane, and said nothing.

'Didn't you promise burglars would never break into our house because there's nothing here to steal?' whispered Meggie.

'He's not a burglar,' replied Mo, but as he stepped back from the window his face was so grave that Meggie's heart thudded faster than ever. 'Go back to bed, Meggie,' he said. 'This visitor has come to see me.'

He left the room before Meggie could ask what kind of visitor, for goodness' sake, turned up in the middle of the night? She followed him anxiously. As she crept down the corridor she heard her father taking the chain off the front door, and when she reached the hall she saw him standing in the open doorway. The night came in, dark and damp, and the rushing of the rain sounded loud and threatening.

'Dustfinger!' called Mo into the darkness. 'Is that you?'

Dustfinger? What kind of a name was that? Meggie couldn't remember ever hearing it before, yet it sounded familiar, like a distant memory that wouldn't take shape properly.

At first, all seemed still outside except for the rain falling, murmuring as if the night had found its voice. But then footsteps approached the house, and the man emerged from the darkness of the yard, his long coat so wet with rain that it clung to his legs. For a split second, as the stranger stepped into the light spilling out of the house, Meggie thought she saw a small furry head over his shoulder, snuffling as it looked out of his rucksack and then quickly disappearing back into it.

Dustfinger wiped his wet face with his sleeve and offered Mo his hand.

'How are you, Silvertongue?' he asked. 'It's been a long time.'

Hesitantly, Mo took the outstretched hand. 'A very long time,' he said, looking past his visitor as if he expected to see another figure emerge from the night. 'Come in, you'll catch your death. Meggie says you've been standing out there for some time.'

'Meggie? Ah yes, of course.' Dustfinger let Mo lead him into the house. He scrutinised Meggie so thoroughly that she felt quite embarrassed and didn't know where to look. In the end she just stared back.

'She's grown.'

'You remember her?'

'Of course.'

Meggie noticed that Mo double-locked the door.

'How old is she now?' Dustfinger smiled at her. It was a

strange smile. Meggie couldn't decide whether it was mocking, supercilious, or just awkward. She didn't smile back.

'Twelve,' said Mo.

'Twelve? My word!' Dustfinger pushed his dripping hair back from his forehead. It reached almost to his shoulders. Meggie wondered what colour it was when it was dry. The stubble round his narrow-lipped mouth was gingery, like the fur of the stray cat Meggie sometimes fed with a saucer of milk outside the door. Ginger hair sprouted on his cheeks, too, sparse as a boy's first beard but not long enough to hide three long, pale scars. They made Dustfinger's face look as if it had been smashed and stuck back together again. 'Twelve,' he repeated. 'Of course. She was . . . let's see, she was three then, wasn't she?'

Mo nodded. 'Come on, I'll find you some dry clothes.' Impatiently, as if he were suddenly in a hurry to hide the man from Meggie, he led his visitor across the hall. 'And Meggie,' he said over his shoulder, 'you go back to sleep.' Then, without another word, he closed his workshop door.

Meggie stood there rubbing her cold feet together. Go back to sleep. Sometimes, when they'd stayed up late yet again, Mo would toss her down on her bed like a bag of walnuts. Sometimes he chased her round the house after supper until she escaped into her room, breathless with laughter. And sometimes he was so tired he lay down on the sofa and she made him a cup of coffee before she went to bed. But he had never *ever* sent her off to her room so brusquely.

A foreboding, clammy and fearful, came into her heart as if, along with the visitor whose name was so strange yet some- how familiar, some menace had slipped into her life. And she wished – so hard it frightened her – that she had never fetched

Mo, and Dustfinger had stayed outside until the rain washed him away.

When the door of the workshop opened again she jumped.

'Still there, I see,' said Mo. 'Go to bed, Meggie. Please.' He had that little frown over his nose that appeared only when something was really worrying him, and he seemed to look straight through her as if his thoughts were somewhere else entirely. The foreboding in Meggie's heart grew, spreading black wings.

'Send him away, Mo!' she said as he gently propelled her towards her room. 'Please! Send him away. I don't like him.'

Mo leaned in her open doorway. 'He'll be gone when you get up in the morning. Word of honour.'

'Word of honour – no crossed fingers?' Meggie looked him straight in the eye. She could always tell when Mo was lying, however hard he tried to hide it from her.

'No crossed fingers,' he said, holding both hands out to show her.

Then he closed her door, even though he knew she didn't like that. Meggie put her ear to it, listening. She could hear the clink of china. So the man with the sandy beard was getting a nice cup of tea to warm him up. I hope he catches pneumonia, thought Meggie . . . though he needn't necessarily die of it. Meggie heard the kettle whistling in the kitchen, and Mo carrying a tray of clattering crockery back to the workshop. When that door closed she forced herself to wait a few more seconds, just to be on the safe side. Then she crept back out into the passage.

There was a notice hanging on the door of Mo's workshop, a small metal plaque. Meggie knew the words on it by heart. When she was five she had often practised reading the old-fashioned, spindly lettering:

Some books should be tasted
some devoured,
but only a few
should be chewed and digested thoroughly.

Back then, when she still had to climb on a box to read the plaque, she had thought the chewing and digesting were meant literally and wondered, horrified, why Mo had hung on his workshop door the words of someone who vandalised books. Now, she knew what the plaque really meant, but tonight she wasn't interested in written words. Spoken words were what she wanted to hear, the words being exchanged in soft, almost inaudible whispers by the two men on the other side of the door.

'Don't underestimate him!' she heard Dustfinger say. His voice was so different from Mo's. No one else in the world had a voice like her father's. Mo could paint pictures in the empty air with his voice alone.

'He'd do anything to get hold of it.' That was Dustfinger again. 'And when I say anything, I can assure you I mean *any-thing*.'

'I'll never let him have it.' That was Mo.

'He'll still get his hands on it, one way or another! I tell you, they're on your trail.'

'It wouldn't be the first time. I've always managed to shake them off before.'

'Oh yes? And for how much longer, do you think? What about your daughter? Are you telling me she actually likes moving around the whole time? Believe me, I know what I'm talking about.'

It was so quiet behind the door that Meggie scarcely dared

14

breathe in case the two men heard her.

Finally her father spoke again, hesitantly, as if his tongue found it difficult to form the words. 'Then what do you think I ought to do?'

'Come with me. I'll take you to them.' A cup clinked. The sound of a spoon against china. How loud small noises sound in a silence. 'You know how much Capricorn thinks of your talents. He'd be glad if you took it to him of your own free will, I'm sure he would. The man he found to replace you is useless.'

Capricorn. Another peculiar name. Dustfinger had uttered it as if the mere sound might scorch his tongue. Meggie wriggled her chilly toes and wrinkled her cold nose. She didn't understand much of what the two men were saying, but she tried to memorise every single word of it.

It was quiet again in the workshop.

'Oh, I don't know,' said Mo at last. He sounded so weary that it tore at Meggie's heart. 'I'll have to think about it. When do you think his men will get here?'

'Soon!'

The word dropped like a stone into the silence.

'Soon,' repeated Mo. 'Very well. I'll have made up my mind by tomorrow. Do you have somewhere to sleep?'

'Oh, I can always find a place,' replied Dustfinger. 'I'm managing quite well these days, although it's still all much too fast for me.' His laugh was not a happy one. 'But I'd like to know what you decide. May I come back tomorrow? About midday?'

'Yes, of course. I'll be picking Meggie up from school at one-thirty. Come after that.'

Meggie heard a chair being pushed back, and scurried back

to her room. When the door of the workshop opened she was just closing her bedroom door behind her. Pulling the covers up to her chin, she lay there listening as her father said good-bye to Dustfinger.

'And thank you for the warning anyway,' she heard him add as Dustfinger's footsteps moved away, slowly and uncertainly as if he were reluctant to leave, as if he hadn't said everything he'd wanted to say. But at last he was gone, and only the rain kept drumming its wet fingers on Meggie's window.

When Mo opened the door of her room she quickly closed her eyes and tried to breathe as slowly as you do in a deep, innocent sleep. But Mo wasn't stupid. In fact, he was sometimes terribly clever.

'Meggie, put one of your feet out of bed,' he told her. Reluctantly, she stuck her toes out from under the blanket and laid them in Mo's warm hand. They were still cold.

'I knew it!' he said. 'You've been spying. Can't you do as I tell you, just for once?' Sighing, he tucked her foot back underneath the nice warm blankets. Then he sat down on her bed, passed his hands over his tired face and looked out of the window. His hair was as dark as moleskin. Meggie had fair hair like her mother, who she knew only from a few faded photographs. 'You should be glad you look more like her than me,' Mo always said. 'My head wouldn't look at all good on a girl's neck.' But Meggie wished she did look more like him. There wasn't a face in the world she loved more.

'I didn't hear what you were saying anyway,' she murmured.

'Good.' Mo stared out of the window as if Dustfinger were still standing in the yard. Then he rose and went to the door.

16

'Try to get some sleep,' he said.

But Meggie didn't want to sleep. 'Dustfinger! What sort of a name is that?' she asked. 'And why does he call you Silvertongue?'

Mo did not reply.

'And this person who's looking for you – I heard what Dustfinger called him. Capricorn. Who is he?'

'No one you want to meet.' Her father didn't turn round. 'I thought you didn't hear anything. Goodnight, Meggie.'

This time he left her door open. The light from the passage fell on her bed, mingling with the darkness of the night that seeped in through the window, and Meggie lay there waiting for the dark to disappear and take her fear of some evil menace away with it. Only later did she understand that the evil had not appeared for the first time that night. It had just slunk back in again.

2

Secrets

'What do these children do without storybooks?' Naftali
asked.

And Reb Zebulun replied: 'They have to make do.
Storybooks aren't bread. You can live without them.'

'I couldn't live without them,' Naftali said.

Isaac Bashevis Singer,
Naftali the Storyteller and his Horse Sus

It was early dawn when Meggie woke up. Night was fading
over the fields as if the rain had washed the darkness out of
the hem of its garment. The alarm clock said just before five,
and Meggie was going to turn over and go back to sleep when
she suddenly sensed someone else in the room. Startled, she
sat up and saw Mo standing by her open wardrobe.

'Hello,' he said, putting her favourite sweater in a case. 'I'm
sorry, I know it's very early, but we have to leave. How about
cocoa for breakfast?'

Still drowsy with sleep, Meggie nodded. Outside, the birds
were twittering loudly as if they'd been awake for hours. Mo

put two more pairs of jeans in her case, closed it and carried it to the door. 'Wear something warm,' he said. 'It's chilly outside.'

'Where are we going?' asked Meggie, but he had already disappeared. She looked out of the window, feeling confused. She almost expected to see Dustfinger, but there was only a blackbird in the yard hopping over the stones, which were wet after the rain. Meggie put on her jeans and stumbled into the kitchen. Two suitcases, a travelling bag and Mo's toolbox stood out in the hall.

Her father was sitting at the kitchen table making sandwiches for the journey. When she came into the kitchen he looked up briefly and smiled at her, but Meggie could see he was worried about something. 'Mo, we can't go away now!' she said. 'The school holidays don't start for another week!'

'Well, it won't be the first time I've had to go away on business in your term-time.'

He was right about that. In fact, he went away quite often, whenever an antique dealer, a book collector or a library needed a bookbinder and commissioned Mo to restore a few valuable old books, freeing them of dust and mould or dressing them in new clothes, as he put it. Meggie didn't think the word 'bookbinder' described Mo's work particularly well, and a few years ago she had made him a notice to hang on his workshop door saying 'Mortimer Folchart, Book Doctor'. And the book doctor never called on his patients without taking his daughter too. They had always done that and they always would, never mind what Meggie's teachers said.

'How about chicken-pox? Have I used that excuse already?'

'Yes, last time. When we had to go and see that dreary man with the Bibles.' Meggie scrutinised her father's face.

'Mo. Is it . . . is it because of last night we have to leave?'

For a moment she thought he was going to tell her every-thing – whatever there was to tell. But then he shook his head. 'No, of course not,' he said, putting the sandwiches he had made in a plastic bag. 'Your mother has an aunt called Elinor. We visited her once, when you were very small. She's been wanting me to come and put her books in order for a long time. She lives beside a lake in the north of Italy, I always forget which lake, but it's a lovely place, a day's drive away.' He did not look at her as he spoke.

Meggie wanted to ask: but why do we have to go now? But she didn't. Nor did she ask if he had forgotten that he was meeting someone at midday. She was too afraid of the answers – and she didn't want Mo to lie to her again.

'Is this aunt as peculiar as the others?' was all she said. Mo had already taken her to visit various relations. Both he and Meggie's mother had large families whose homes, so far as Meggie could see, were scattered over half of Europe.

Mo smiled. 'Yes, she is a bit peculiar, but you'll get on with her all right. She has some really wonderful books.'

'So how long are we going to be away?'

'It could be quite some time.'

Meggie sipped her cocoa. It was so hot that she burned her lips, and had to quickly press the cold blade of a knife to her mouth.

Mo pushed his chair back. 'I have to pack a few more things from the workshop,' he said. 'It won't take long. You must be very tired, but you can sleep once we're in the van.'

Meggie just nodded and looked out of the kitchen window. It was a grey morning. Mist drifted over the fields at the foot of the nearby hills, and Meggie felt as if the shadows of the night were still hiding among the trees.

'Pack up the food and take plenty to read!' Mo called from the hall. As if she didn't always! Years ago he had made her a box to hold her favourite books on all their journeys, short and long, near and far. 'It's a good idea to have your own books with you in a strange place,' Mo always said. He himself always took at least a dozen.

Mo had painted the box poppy-red. Poppies were Meggie's favourite flower. They pressed well between the pages of a book, and you could stamp a star-shaped pattern on your skin with their pepper-pot seed capsules. He had decorated the box and painted *Meggie's Treasure Chest* in lovely curly lettering on the lid. The box was lined with shiny black taffeta, but you could hardly see any of the fabric because Meggie had a great many favourite books, and she always added another whenever they travelled anywhere. 'If you take a book with you on a journey,' Mo had said when he put the first one in her box, 'an odd thing happens: the book begins collecting your memories. And forever after you have only to open that book to be back where you first read it. It will all come into your mind with the very first words: the sights you saw in that place, what it smelled like, the ice-cream you ate while you were reading it . . . yes, books are like flypapers. Memories cling to the printed page better than anything else.'

He was probably right, but there was another reason why Meggie took her books whenever they went away. They were her home when she was somewhere strange – familiar voices, friends that never quarrelled with her, clever, powerful friends, daring and knowledgeable, tried and tested adventurers who had travelled far and wide. Her books cheered her up when she was sad, and kept her from being bored while Mo cut leather and fabric to the right size, and re-stitched old pages that over countless years had grown fragile from the many fingers leafing through them.

Some of her books always went away with Meggie. Others were left at home because they weren't right for where she was going, or to make room for new, unknown stories that she hadn't yet read.

Meggie stroked their curved spines. Which books should she take this time? Which stories would help to drive away the fear that had crept into the house last night? I know, thought Meggie, why not a story about telling lies? Mo told her lies. He told terrible lies, even though he knew that every time he told one she looked hard at his nose. *Pinocchio*, thought Meggie. No, too sinister. And too sad. But she wanted something exciting, a story to drive all other thoughts out of her head, even the darkest. *The Witches*, yes. She'd take the bald-headed witches who turn children into mice – and *The Odyssey*, with the Cyclops and the enchantress who transforms his warriors into pigs. Her journey could hardly be more dangerous than his, could it?

On the left-hand side of the box there were two picture books that Meggie had used when she was teaching herself to read – five years old, she'd been, and you could still see where her tiny forefinger had moved over the pages – and right at the bottom, hidden under all the others, were the books Meggie had made herself. She had spent days sticking them together and cutting up the paper, she had painted picture after picture, and Mo had to write what they were underneath them. *An Angel With a Happy Face, from Meggi for Mo*. She had written her name herself, although back then she always left the 'e' off the end. Meggie looked at the clumsy lettering and put the little book back in the box. Mo had helped her with the binding, of course. He had bound all her home-made books in brightly patterned paper, and he had given her a stamp for the others so that she could print her name and the head of a unicorn on the title page, sometimes in black ink and sometimes in red, depending how she felt. But Mo had never read aloud to her from her books. Not once.

He had tossed Meggie up in the air, he had carried her round the house on his shoulders, he had taught her how to make a bookmark of blackbird's feathers. But he had never read aloud to her. Never once, not a single word, however often she put books on his lap. Meggie just had to teach herself how to decipher the black marks and open the treasure chest.

She straightened up. There was still a little room in the box. Perhaps Mo had a new book she could take, a specially big, fat, wonderful book . . .

The door to his workshop was closed.

'Mo?' Meggie pressed the handle down. The long table where he worked had been swept clean, with not a stamp, nor a knife in sight. Mo had packed everything. Had he been lying after all?

Meggie went into the workshop and looked around. The door to the Treasury was open. The Treasury was really just a lumber-room, but Meggie had given the little cubby-hole that name because it was where her father stored his most precious materials: the finest leather, the most beautiful fabrics, marbled paper, stamps to print patterns in gold on soft leather . . . Meggie put her head round the open door and saw Mo covering a book with brown paper. It was not a particularly large book, and not especially fat. The green linen binding looked worn, but that was all Meggie could see, because Mo quickly hid the book behind his back as soon as he noticed her.

'What are you doing here?' he snapped.

'I—' For a moment Meggie was speechless with shock, Mo's face was so dark. 'I only wanted to ask if you had a new book for me. I've read all the ones in my room, and . . .'

Mo passed his hand over his face. 'Yes, of course. I'm sure I can find something,' he said, but his eyes were still saying: go away, go away, Meggie. And the brown paper crackled behind his back. 'I'll be with you in a moment,' he said. 'I have a few more things to pack. OK?'

A little later he brought her three books, but the one he had been covering with brown paper wasn't one of them.

An hour later, they were taking everything out into the yard. Meggie shivered when she stepped out of doors. It was a chilly morning after the night's rain, and the sun hung in the sky like a pale coin lost by someone high up in the clouds.

They had been living in the old farmhouse for just under a year. Meggie liked the view of the surrounding hills, the swallows' nests under the roof, the dried-up well that yawned darkly as if it went straight down to the Earth's core. The house itself had always been too big and draughty for her liking, with all those empty rooms full of fat spiders, but the rent was low and Mo had enough space for his books and his workshop. There was a hen-house outside, and the barn, which now housed only their old camper van, would have been perfect for a couple of cows or a horse. 'Cows have to be milked, Meggie,' Mo had said when she suggested keeping a couple. 'Very, very early in the morning. Every day.'

'Well, what about a horse?' she had asked. 'Even Pippi Longstocking has a horse, and she doesn't have a stable.'

She'd have been happy with a few chickens or a goat, but they too had to be fed every day, and she and Mo went away too often for that. So Meggie had only the ginger cat who sometimes came visiting when it couldn't be bothered to compete with the dogs on the farm next door. The grumpy old farmer who lived there was their only neighbour. Sometimes his dogs howled so pitifully that Meggie put her hands over her ears. It was twenty minutes by bike to the nearest village, where she went to school and where two of her friends lived, but Mo usually took her in the van because it was a lonely ride along a narrow road that wound past nothing but fields and dark trees.

'What on earth have you packed in here? Bricks?' asked Mo as he carried Meggie's book-box out of the house.

'You're the one who says books have to be heavy because the whole world's inside them,' said Meggie, making him laugh for the first time that morning.

The camper van, standing in the abandoned barn like a solid, multicoloured animal, was more familiar to Meggie than any of the houses where she and Mo had lived. She never slept more deeply and soundly than in the bed he had made in it for her. There was a table too, of course, a kitchen tucked into a corner and a bench to sit on. When you lifted the seat of the bench there were travel guides, road maps and well-worn paperbacks under it.

Yes, Meggie was fond of the van, but this morning she hesitated to get in. When Mo finally went back to the house to lock the door, she suddenly felt that they would never come back here, that this journey was going to be different from any other, that they would drive further and further away, in flight from something that had no name. Or at least none that Mo was about to tell her.

'Very well, off we go south,' was all he said as he got behind the steering wheel. And so they set off, without saying goodbye to anyone, on a morning that still seemed much too early and smelled of rain.

But Dustfinger was waiting for them at the gate.

3

Going South

'Beyond the Wild Wood comes the Wild World,' said the Rat. 'And that's something that doesn't matter, either to you or to me. I've never been there, and I'm never going, nor you either, if you've got any sense at all.'

Kenneth Grahame, *The Wind in the Willows*

Dustfinger must have been waiting in the road beyond the wall. Meggie had picked her precarious way along the top of that wall hundreds of times, up to the rusty hinges of the gate and back again, eyes tightly closed so that she could get a clearer view of the tiger she'd imagined waiting in the bamboo at the foot of the wall, his eyes yellow as amber, or the foaming rapids to her right and her left.

Only Dustfinger was there now, but no other sight could have made Meggie's heart beat faster. He appeared so suddenly that Mo almost ran him down. He wore only a sweater, and he was shivering, with his arms folded over his chest. His coat was probably still damp from last night's rain, but his hair was dry now – a ruffled, sandy mop above his scarred face.

Mo swore under his breath, switched off the engine and got out of the van.

Smiling his strange smile, Dustfinger leaned back against the wall. 'Where are you going in such a hurry, Silvertongue? Didn't we have a date?' he asked. 'You stood me up like this once before, remember?'

'You know why I'm in a hurry,' replied Mo. 'For the same reason as last time.' He was still standing by the open door of the van, looking tense, as if he couldn't wait for Dustfinger to get out of the way. But Dustfinger pretended not to notice Mo's impatience.

'Then may I know where you're going?' he enquired. 'It took me four years to find you last time, and if luck hadn't been on your side Capricorn's men would have got to you first.' When he glanced at Meggie she stared back icily.

Mo was silent for a while. 'Capricorn is in the north,' he answered at last. 'So we're going south. Or has he taken up residence somewhere else now?'

Dustfinger looked down the road. Last night's rain shone in the potholes. 'No, no,' he said. 'No, he's still in the north. Or so I hear, and since you've obviously made up your mind to go on refusing him what he wants I'd better go south myself as fast as I can. Heaven knows I don't want to be the one to give Capricorn's men the bad news. So, if you'd give me a lift part of the way? . . . I'm ready to leave.' The two bags he picked up from where they stood by the wall looked as if they'd been all round the world a dozen times. Apart from the bags, Dustfinger had nothing but his rucksack with him.

Meggie compressed her lips.

No, Mo, she thought, no, let's not take him! But she had

only to look at her father to know that his answer would be different.

'Oh, come on, Silvertongue!' said Dustfinger. 'What am I going to tell Capricorn's men if I fall into their hands?'

He looked lost, standing there like a stray dog. And hard as Meggie tried to see something sinister about him she couldn't, not in the pale morning light. All the same, she didn't want him to go with them. Her face showed that very clearly, but neither of the two men took any notice of her.

'Believe me, I couldn't keep the fact that I've seen you from them for very long,' Dustfinger continued. 'And anyway . . .' he hesitated before completing his sentence, 'you still owe me, don't you?'

Mo bowed his head. Meggie saw his hand closing more firmly round the open door of the van. 'If you want to look at it like that,' he said, 'yes, I suppose I do still owe you.'

The relief was plain to see on Dustfinger's scarred face. He quickly hoisted his rucksack over his shoulders and came over to the van with his bags.

'Wait a minute!' cried Meggie, as Mo moved to help him. 'If he's coming with us then I want to know why we're running away. Who is this man called Capricorn?'

Mo turned to her. 'Meggie,' he began in the tone she knew only too well: Meggie, don't be so silly, it meant. Come along now, Meggie.

She opened the van door and jumped out.

'Meggie, for heaven's sake! Get back in! We have to leave!'

'I'm not getting back in until you tell me.'

Mo came towards her but Meggie slipped away, and ran through the gate into the road.

'Why won't you tell me?' she cried.

The road was deserted, as if there were no other human beings in the world. A slight breeze had risen, caressing Meggie's face and rustling in the leaves of the lime tree that grew by the roadside. The sky was still wan and grey, and refused to clear.

'I want to know what's going on!' cried Meggie. 'I want to know why we had to get up at five o'clock, and why I don't have to go to school. I want to know if we're ever coming back, and I want to know who this Capricorn is!'

When she spoke the name Mo looked round as if the man with the strange name, the man he and Dustfinger obviously feared so much, might step out of the empty barn next moment as suddenly as Dustfinger had emerged from behind the wall. But the yard was empty, and Meggie was too furious to feel frightened of someone when she knew nothing about him other than his name. 'You've always told me everything!' she shouted at her father. 'Always.'

But Mo was still silent. 'Everyone has a few secrets, Meggie,' he said at last. 'Now, come along, do get in. We have to leave.'

Dustfinger looked first at Mo, then at Meggie, with an expression of incredulity on his face. 'You haven't told her?' Meggie heard him ask in a low voice.

Mo shook his head.

'But you have to tell her something! It's dangerous for her not to know. She's not a baby any more.'

'It's dangerous for her to know too,' said Mo. 'And it wouldn't change anything.'

Meggie was still standing in the road.

'I heard all that!' she cried. 'What's dangerous? I'm not getting in until you tell me.'

Mo still said nothing.

Dustfinger looked at him, uncertain for a moment, then put down his bags. 'Very well,' he said. 'Then I'll tell her about Capricorn myself.'

He came slowly towards Meggie, who involuntarily stepped back.

'You met him once,' said Dustfinger. 'It's a long time ago, you won't remember, you were so little.' He held his hand at knee-height in the air. 'How can I explain what he's like? If you were to see a cat eating a young bird I expect you'd cry, wouldn't you? Or try to help the bird. Capricorn would feed the bird to the cat on purpose, just to watch it being torn apart, and the little creature's screeching and struggling would be as sweet as honey to him.'

Meggie took another step backwards, but Dustfinger kept advancing towards her.

'I don't suppose you'd get any fun from terrifying people until their knees were so weak they could hardly stand?' he asked. 'Nothing gives Capricorn more pleasure. And I don't suppose you think you can just help yourself to anything you want, never mind what or where. Capricorn does. Unfortunately, your father has something Capricorn has set his heart on.'

Meggie glanced at Mo, but he just stood there looking at her.

'Capricorn can't bind books like your father,' Dustfinger went on. 'In fact, he's not much good at anything except terrifying people. But he's a master of that art. It's his whole life. I doubt if he himself has any idea what it's like to be so paralysed by fear that you feel small and insignificant. But he knows just how to arouse that fear and spread it, in people's homes and their beds, in their heads and their hearts. His men spread fear abroad like the Black Death, they push it under doors and through letterboxes, they paint it on walls and stable doors until it infects everything around it of its own accord, silent and stinking like a plague.' Dustfinger was very close to Meggie now. 'Capricorn has many men,' he said softly. 'Most have been with him since they were children, and if Capricorn were to order one of them to cut off your nose or one of your ears he'd do it without batting an eyelid. They like to dress in black like rooks – only their leader wears a white shirt under his black jacket – and should you ever meet any of them then make yourself small, very small, and hope they don't notice you. Understand?'

Meggie nodded. Her heart was pounding so hard that she could scarcely breathe.

'I can see why your father has never told you about Capricorn,' said Dustfinger, looking at Mo. 'If I had children I'd rather tell them about nice people too.'

'I know the world's not just full of nice people!' Meggie couldn't keep her voice from shaking with anger, and more than a touch of fear.

'Oh yes? How do you know that?' There it was again, that mysterious smile, sad and supercilious at the same time. 'Have you ever had anything to do with a real villain?'

'I've read about them.'

Dustfinger laughed aloud. 'Yes, of course that almost comes to the same thing!' he said. His mockery hurt like stinging nettles. He bent down to Meggie and looked her in the face. 'All the same, I hope reading about them is as close as you ever get,' he said quietly.

Mo was stowing Dustfinger's bags in the back of the van.

'I hope there's nothing in there that might come flying round our heads,' he said as Dustfinger got in the back seat behind Meggie. 'With your trade I wouldn't be surprised.'

Before Meggie could ask what trade that was, Dustfinger opened his rucksack and carefully lifted out an animal. It was blinking sleepily. 'Since we obviously have quite a long journey ahead of us,' he told Mo, 'I'd like to introduce someone to your daughter.'

The creature was almost the size of a rabbit, but much thinner, with a bushy tail now draped over Dustfinger's chest like a fur collar. It dug its slender claws into his sleeve while inspecting Meggie with its gleaming beady black eyes, and when it yawned it bared teeth as sharp as needles.

'This is Gwin,' said Dustfinger. 'You can tickle him behind the ears if you like. He's very sleepy at the moment, so he won't bite.'

'Does he usually?' asked Meggie.

'Yes,' said Mo, getting back behind the wheel. 'If I were you I'd keep my fingers away from that little brute.'

But Meggie couldn't keep her hands off any animal, however sharp its teeth. 'He's a marten or something like that, right?' she asked.

'Something of that nature.' Dustfinger put his hand in his trouser pocket and gave Gwin a piece of dry bread. Meggie stroked his little head as he chewed – and her fingertips found something hard under the silky fur: tiny horns growing beside his ears. Surprised, she took her hand away. 'Do martens have horns?'

Dustfinger winked at her and let Gwin climb back into the rucksack. 'This one does,' he said.

Bewildered, Meggie watched him do up the straps. She felt

as if she were still touching Gwin's little horns. 'Mo, did you know that martens have horns?' she asked.

'Oh, Dustfinger stuck them on that sharp-toothed little devil of his. For his performances.'

'What kind of performances?' Meggie looked enquiringly, first at Mo, then at Dustfinger, but Mo just started the engine and Dustfinger, who seemed to have come far, judging by his bags, took off his boots and stretched out on Mo's bed in the van with a deep sigh. 'Don't give me away, Silvertongue,' he said before he closed his eyes. 'I have my own secrets, you know. And for those I need darkness.'

They must have driven fifty kilometres, and Meggie was still trying to work out what he could possibly have meant.

'Mo?' she asked, when Dustfinger began snoring behind them. 'What does this Capricorn want from you?' She lowered her voice before she spoke the name, as if that might remove some of the menace from it.

'A book,' replied Mo, without taking his eyes off the road.

'A book? Then why not give it to him?'

'I can't. I'll explain soon, but not now, all right?'

Meggie looked out of the van window. The world they were passing outside already looked unfamiliar – unfamiliar houses, unfamiliar roads, unfamiliar fields, even the trees and the sky looked unfamiliar – but Meggie was used to that. She had never really felt at home anywhere. Mo was her home, Mo and her books, and perhaps the camper van that carried them from one place to the next.

'This aunt we're going to see,' she said, as they drove through an endless tunnel. 'Does she have any children?'

'No,' said Mo, 'and I'm afraid she doesn't particularly like children either. But as I said, I'm sure you'll get on well with her.'

Meggie sighed. She could remember several aunts, and she hadn't 'got on' particularly well with any of them.

They were driving through mountains now, the slopes on both sides of the road rose ever more steeply, and there came a point where the houses looked not just unfamiliar but really different. Meggie tried to pass the time by counting tunnels, but when the ninth swallowed them up and the darkness went on and on she fell asleep. She dreamed of martens in black jackets and a book in a brown-paper cover.

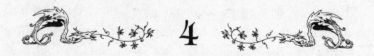

A House Full of Books

There is a sort of busy worm,
That will the fairest book deform.
Their tasteless tooth will tear and taint
The poet, patriot, sage or saint,
Nor sparing wit nor learning.
Now, if you'd know the reason why,
The best of reasons I'll supply:
'Tis bread to the poor vermin.

J. Doraston, quoted by W. Blades

Meggie woke up because it was so quiet. The regular sound of the engine that had lulled her to sleep had stopped. The driver's seat beside her was empty. It took Meggie a little while to remember why she wasn't in bed at home. Tiny dead flies were stuck to the windscreen, and the van was parked outside an iron gate. It looked alarming, with sharp ashen-grey spikes, a gate made of spearheads just waiting to impale anyone who tried to clamber over. It reminded Meggie of one of her favourite stories, the tale of the Selfish

Giant who wouldn't let children into his garden. This was exactly how she had imagined his garden gate.

Mo was standing in the road with Dustfinger. Meggie got out and went over to them. On the right of the road a densely wooded slope fell steeply to the bank of a wide lake. The hills on the other side rose from the lake like giants emerging from the depths. The water was almost black, and pale twilight, darkly reflected in the waves, was already spreading across the sky. The first lights were coming on in the houses on the bank, looking like glow-worms or fallen stars.

'A lovely place, isn't it?' Mo put his arm round Meggie's shoulders. 'I know you like stories about robbers. See that ruined castle? A notorious robber band once lived there. I must ask Elinor about them. She knows everything about this lake.'

Meggie just nodded and rested her head against his shoulder. She was so tired that she felt quite dizzy, but for the first time since they had set off Mo's face wasn't looking grim with anxiety. 'Where does she live, then?' asked Meggie, stifling a yawn. 'Not behind that spiky gate?'

'Actually, yes. This is the entrance to her property. Not very inviting, is it?' Mo laughed and led Meggie across the road. 'Elinor is very proud of this gate. She had it specially made. It's copied from a picture in a book.'

'A picture of the Selfish Giant's garden?' murmured Meggie, peering through the intricately twining iron bars.

'*The Selfish Giant*?' Mo laughed. 'No, I think it was another story. Although that one would suit Elinor pretty well.'

Tall hedges grew on both sides of the gate, their thorny branches hiding any view of what lay beyond. But even through the iron bars Meggie could see nothing promising except for tall rhododendron bushes and a broad gravel drive that soon disappeared between them.

'Looks like you have rich relations,' Dustfinger whispered in her ear.

'Yes, Elinor is quite rich,' said Mo, drawing Meggie away from the gate. 'But she'll probably end up poor as a church mouse because she spends so much money on books. I think she'd sell her soul to the Devil without thinking twice if he offered her the right book for it.' He pushed the heavy gate open with a single movement.

'What are you doing?' asked Meggie in alarm. 'We can't just drive in.' For there was a notice beside the door, still clearly legible even if some of the letters were partly hidden by the leaves of the hedge:

PRIVATE PROPERTY.

NO UNAUTHORISED ENTRY.

Meggie didn't think it sounded very inviting.

Mo, however, only laughed. 'Don't worry,' he said, opening the gate wider. 'The only thing Elinor guards with a burglar alarm is her library. She couldn't care less who walks through this gate. She's not what you'd call a nervous woman, and she doesn't have many visitors anyway.'

'What about dogs?' Dustfinger peered anxiously into the strange garden. 'That gate suggests at least three ferocious dogs to me. Big ones, the size of calves.'

But Mo just shook his head. 'Elinor hates dogs,' he said, going back to the van. 'Right, get in.'

Elinor's grounds were more like a wood than a garden. Once they were through the gateway the drive curved, as if taking a deep breath before going on up the slope, then lost itself among dark firs and chestnut trees which grew so close together that their branches made a tunnel. Meggie was just thinking it would never end when the trees suddenly receded, and the drive brought them to an open space covered with gravel and surrounded by carefully tended rose beds.

A grey estate car stood on the gravel in front of a house that was bigger than the school Meggie had been attending for the last year. She tried to count the windows, but soon gave up. It was a very beautiful house but looked just as uninviting as the iron gate. Perhaps it was only the evening twilight that made the ochre-yellow of the plaster look so dirty. And perhaps the green shutters were closed only because night was already falling over the surrounding mountains. Perhaps. But Meggie would have bet her last book they were seldom open even in the daytime.

The dark wooden front door looked as forbidding as a tightly closed mouth, and Meggie involuntarily reached for Mo's hand as they approached it.

Dustfinger followed warily, with his battered rucksack over his shoulder. Gwin was probably still asleep inside it. When Mo and Meggie went up to the door he kept a couple of steps behind them, looking uneasily at the closed shutters as if he suspected that the mistress of the house was watching them from one of the windows.

There was a small barred window beside the front door, the only one not hidden behind green shutters. Below it was another notice:

IF YOU INTEND TO WASTE MY TIME
ON TRIVIA, YOU'D BETTER GO AWAY **NOW**!

Meggie cast Mo an anxious glance, but he only made an encouraging face at her and pressed the bell.

Meggie heard it ringing inside the big house, but nothing

happened for quite a while. A magpie fluttered out of one of the rhododendron bushes growing near the house, and a couple of fat sparrows pecked busily at invisible insects in the gravel, but that was all. Meggie was just throwing them the breadcrumbs she had found in her jacket pocket – left over from a picnic on some long-forgotten day – when the door suddenly opened.

The woman who came out was older than Mo, quite a lot older – although Meggie could never be quite sure how old grown-ups were. Her face reminded Meggie of a bulldog, but perhaps that was more her ferocious expression than its features. She wore a mouse-grey sweater and an ash-grey skirt, with a pearl necklace round her short neck and felt slippers on her feet, the kind of slippers Meggie had once had to wear when she and Mo had visited an historic castle. Elinor's hair was grey too. She had pinned it up, but strands were hanging down everywhere as if she had done it impatiently and in a hurry. She didn't look as if she spent much time in front of a mirror.

'Good heavens, Mortimer! What a surprise!' she said, without wasting time on further greetings. 'Where did you spring from?' Her voice sounded brusque, but her face couldn't entirely hide the fact that she was pleased to see Mo.

'Hello, Elinor,' said Mo, putting his hand on Meggie's shoulder. 'Do you remember Meggie? As you can see, she's grown up quite a bit now.'

Elinor cast Meggie a brief, irritated glance. 'Yes, so I see,' she said. 'It's only natural for children to grow, wouldn't you say? As far as I remember, it's been some years since I last set eyes on either you or your daughter, so to what do I owe the unexpected honour of your visit today? Are you finally going to take pity on my poor books?'

'That's right.' Mo nodded. 'One of my library commissions has been postponed – you know how libraries are always short of money.'

Meggie looked at him uneasily. She hadn't realised he could lie quite so convincingly.

'And because it was so sudden,' Mo continued, 'I couldn't find anywhere for Meggie to go, so I brought her with me. I know you don't like children, but Meggie won't leave jam on your books or tear out pages to wrap up dead frogs.'

Elinor muttered something suspicious, and scrutinised Meggie as if she thought her capable of any kind of disgraceful conduct, whatever her father might say. 'When you last brought her we could at least put her in a playpen,' she remarked coldly. 'I don't suppose that would do now.' Once again, she looked Meggie up and down as if she were being asked to admit a dangerous animal to her house.

Meggie felt her anger make the blood rise to her face. She wanted to go home, or get back in the camper van and go somewhere else, anywhere, so long as she didn't have to stay with this horrible woman whose cold pebble eyes were boring holes in her face.

Elinor's gaze moved from Meggie to Dustfinger, who was still standing in the background looking awkward. 'And who's this?' She looked enquiringly at Mo. 'Do I know him?'

'This is Dustfinger, a . . . a friend of mine.' Perhaps only Meggie noticed Mo's hesitation. 'He wants to go on south, but maybe you could put him up for a night in one of your many rooms?'

Elinor folded her arms. 'Only on condition his name has nothing to do with the way he treats books,' she said. 'And he'll have to put up with rather Spartan accommodation in the attic, because my library has grown a great deal over the last few years. Nearly all my guest bedrooms are full of books.'

'How many books do you have?' asked Meggie. She had grown up among piles of books, but even she couldn't imagine there were books behind *all* the windows of this huge house.

Elinor inspected her again, this time with unconcealed contempt. 'How many?' she repeated. 'Do you think I count them like buttons or peas? A very, very great many. There are probably more books in every single room of this house than you will ever read – and some of them are so valuable that I wouldn't hesitate to shoot you if you dared touch them. But as you're a clever girl, or so your father assures me, you wouldn't do that anyway, would you?'

Meggie didn't reply. Instead, she imagined standing on tiptoe and spitting three times into this old witch's face.

However, Mo just laughed. 'You haven't changed, Elinor,' he remarked. 'A tongue as sharp as a paper-knife. But I warn you, if you harm Meggie I'll do the same to your beloved books.'

Elinor's lips curled in a tiny smile. 'Well said,' she answered, stepping aside. 'You obviously haven't changed either. Come in. I'll show you the books that need your help, and a few others as well.'

Meggie had always thought Mo had a lot of books. She never thought so again, not after setting foot in Elinor's house.

There were no haphazard piles lying around as they did at home. Every book obviously had its place. But where other people have wallpaper, pictures, or just an empty wall, Elinor had bookshelves. The shelves were white and went right up to the ceiling in the entrance hall through which she had first led them, but in the next room and the corridor beyond it the shelves were as black as the tiles on the floor.

'These books,' announced Elinor with a dismissive gesture as they passed the closely-ranked spines, 'have accumulated over the years. They're not particularly valuable, mostly of mediocre quality, nothing out of the ordinary. Should certain fingers be unable to control themselves and take one off the shelf now and then,' she added, casting a brief glance at Meggie, 'I don't suppose the consequences would be too serious. Just so long as once those fingers have satisfied their curiosity they put every book back in its right place again and don't leave any unappetising bookmarks inside.' Here, Elinor turned to Mo. 'Believe it or not,' she said, 'I actually found a dried-up slice of salami used as a bookmark in one of the last books I bought, a wonderful nineteenth-century first edition.'

Meggie couldn't help giggling, which naturally earned her another stern look. 'It's nothing to laugh about, young lady,' said Elinor. 'Some of the most wonderful books ever printed were lost because some fool of a fishmonger tore out their pages to wrap his stinking fish. In the Middle Ages, thousands of books were destroyed when people cut up their bindings to make soles for shoes or to heat steam baths with their paper.' The thought of such incredible abominations, even if they had occurred centuries ago, made Elinor gasp for air. 'Well, let's forget about that,' she said, 'or I shall get overexcited. My blood pressure's much too high as it is.'

She had stopped in front of a door which had an anchor with a dolphin coiled around it painted on the white wood. 'This is a famous printer's special sign,' explained Elinor, stroking the dolphin's pointed nose with one finger. 'Just the thing for a library door, eh?'

'I know,' said Meggie. 'Aldus Manutius. He lived in Venice and printed books the right size to fit into his customers' saddlebags.'

'Really?' Elinor wrinkled her brow, intrigued. 'I didn't know that. In any case, I am the fortunate owner of a book that he printed with his own hands in the year 1503.'

'You mean it's from his workshop,' Meggie corrected her.

'Of course that's what I mean.' Elinor cleared her throat and gave Mo a reproachful glance, as if it could only be his fault that his daughter was precocious enough to know such things. Then she put her hand on the door handle. 'No child,' she said, as she pressed the handle down with almost solemn reverence, 'has ever before passed through this door, but as I assume your father has taught you a certain respect for books I'll make an exception today. However, only on condition you keep at least three paces away from the shelves. Is that agreed?'

For a moment Meggie felt like saying no, it wasn't. She would have loved to surprise Elinor by showing contempt for her precious books, but she couldn't do it. Her curiosity was too much for her. She felt almost as if she could hear the books whispering on the other side of the half-open door. They were promising her a thousand unknown stories, a thousand doors into worlds she had never seen before. The temptation was stronger than Meggie's pride.

'Agreed,' she murmured, clasping her hands behind her back. 'Three paces.' Her fingers were itching with desire.

'Sensible child,' said Elinor, so condescendingly that Meggie almost went back on her decision. But then they entered Elinor's holy of holies.

'You've had the place renovated,' Meggie heard Mo say. He added something else, but she wasn't listening any more. She was just staring at the books. The shelves on which they stood smelled of freshly sawn wood. They went all the way up to a sky-blue ceiling with tiny lights in it, hanging there like stars. Narrow wooden stepladders on castors stood by the shelves, ready to help any reader up to the top shelves. There were reading desks with books lying open on them, held in place by brass chains that shone like gold. There were glass display cases containing books with pages stained by age but showing the most wonderful pictures. Meggie couldn't resist moving closer. One step forward, a quick glance at Elinor, who luckily had her back turned, and she was right beside the display case. She bent lower and lower over the glass until her nose was touching it.

Prickly leaves twined around pale brown letters. A tiny red dragon's head was spitting out flowers over the stained paper. Riders on white horses looked at Meggie as if scarcely a day had passed since someone painted them with tiny marten-hair brushes. A man and woman stood beside them, perhaps a bridal couple. A man with a bright red hat was looking angrily at them.

'You call that three paces?'

Meggie spun round in alarm, but Elinor didn't seem too angry. 'Yes, the art of illumination,' she said. 'Once only rich people could read, so the pictures painted round the letters were to help the poor to understand the stories too. Of course no one planned to give them pleasure – the poor were put into the world to work, not to have a nice time or look at pretty pictures. That kind of thing was only for the rich. No, the idea was to instruct the poor. Usually the stories came from the

Bible and everyone knew them anyway. The books were put in churches, and a page was turned every day to show a new picture.'

'What about this book?' asked Meggie.

'I shouldn't think this one was ever in a church,' replied Elinor. 'More likely it was made for a very rich man to enjoy. It's almost six hundred years old.' There was no missing the pride in her voice. 'People have committed murder for such a book. Luckily, I only had to buy it.'

As she spoke these last words she turned abruptly and looked at Dustfinger, who had followed them into the library, soundless as a prowling cat. For a moment Meggie thought Elinor would send him back into the corridor, but Dustfinger stood in front of the shelves looking so impressed, with his hands behind his back, that he gave her no reason to turn him out, so she just cast him a final distrustful glance and turned back to Mo.

He was standing at one of the reading desks with a book in his hand. Its spine hung only by a couple of threads. He held it very carefully, like a bird with a broken wing.

'Well?' asked Elinor anxiously. 'Can you save it? I know it's in terrible shape, and I'm afraid the others aren't in a much better way, but . . .'

'Oh, that can all be put right.' Mo put the book down and inspected another. 'But I think it will take me at least two weeks. If I don't have to get hold of more materials, which could mean I need more time. Will you put up with us that long?'

'Of course.' Elinor nodded, but Meggie noticed the glance she cast at Dustfinger. He was still standing beside the shelves near the door and seemed entirely absorbed in looking at the books, but Meggie sensed that he had missed none of what was said behind his back.

There were no books in Elinor's kitchen, not one, but they ate an excellent supper there at a wooden table that came, so Elinor assured them, from the scriptorium of an Italian monastery. Meggie doubted it. As far as she knew, the monks had worked at desks with sloping tops in the scriptoria of their monasteries, but she kept this information to herself. Instead, she took another slice of bread, and was just wondering how nice the cheese standing on the supposed scriptorium table would be when she noticed Mo whispering something to Elinor. Since Elinor's eyes widened greedily, Meggie concluded that they could only be discussing a book, and she immediately thought of brown paper, a pale green linen binding, and the anger in Mo's voice.

Beside her, Dustfinger surreptitiously slipped a slice of ham into his rucksack for Gwin's supper. Meggie saw a round nose emerge from the rucksack, snuffling in the hope of more delicacies. Dustfinger smiled at Meggie when he noticed her looking at him and gave Gwin some more ham. He didn't seem to find anything odd about Mo and Elinor's whispering, but Meggie was sure the two of them were planning something secret.

After a short time Mo rose from the table and went out. Meggie asked Elinor where the bathroom was – and followed him.

It was a strange feeling to be spying on Mo. She couldn't remember ever doing it before – except last night, when Dustfinger had arrived. And the time when she had tried to find out whether Mo was Father Christmas. She was ashamed of stealing after him like this, but it was his own fault. Why was he hiding the book from her? And now he might be going to give it to this Elinor – a book Meggie wasn't allowed to see! Ever since Mo had hurriedly hidden it behind his back, Meggie hadn't been able to get it out of her head. She had even looked for it in Mo's bag before he loaded his things into the van, but she couldn't find it.

She just had to see it before it disappeared, maybe into one of Elinor's display cases! She had to know why it meant so much to Mo that, for its sake, he would drag her all the way here.

He looked round once more in the entrance hall before leaving the house, but Meggie ducked down behind a chest just in time. The chest smelled of mothballs and lavender. She decided to stay in hiding there until Mo came back. He'd be sure to see her if she went out of doors. Time passed painfully slowly, as it always does when you're waiting for something with your heart thumping hard. The books in the white bookcases seemed to be watching Meggie, but they said nothing to her, as if they sensed that there was only one book Meggie could think about just now.

Finally, Mo came back carrying a package wrapped in brown paper. Perhaps he's just going to hide it here, thought Meggie. Where could you hide a book better than among ten thousand others? Yes, Mo was going to leave it here and then they'd drive home again. But I *would* like to see it, thought Meggie, just once, before it's put on one of those shelves I'm supposed to stay three paces away from.

Mo passed her so close that she could have touched him, but he didn't notice her. 'Meggie, don't look at me like that!' he sometimes told her. 'You're reading my thoughts again.'

Now he looked anxious – as if he wasn't quite sure he was doing the right thing. Meggie counted slowly to three before following her father, but a couple of times Mo stopped so suddenly that Meggie almost ran into him. He didn't return to the kitchen but went straight to the library. Without looking back once, he opened the door with the Venetian printer's mark on it, and closed it quietly behind him.

So, there stood Meggie among all the silent books, wondering whether to follow him and ask him to show her the book. Would he be very angry? She was just about to summon up all her courage and go after him when she heard footsteps – rapid, firm footsteps, quick and impatient. That could only be Elinor. Now what?

Meggie opened the nearest door and slipped through it. A four-poster bed, a wardrobe, silver-framed photographs, a pile of books on the bedside table, a catalogue lying open on the rug, its pages full of pictures of old books. She was in Elinor's bedroom. Heart thudding, she listened for noises outside; she could hear Elinor's energetic footsteps and then the sound of the library door closing for the second time. Cautiously, she slipped out into the corridor again. She was still standing outside the library, undecided, when she felt a hand suddenly laid on her shoulder from behind. Another hand stifled her cry of alarm.

'It's only me!' breathed Dustfinger into her ear. 'Keep quiet or we're both in trouble, understand?'

Meggie nodded, and Dustfinger slowly took his hand away from her mouth. 'Your father's going to give the old witch that book, right?' he whispered. 'Has he taken it out of the van? Tell me. He did have it with him, didn't he?'

Meggie pushed him away. 'I don't know!' she snapped.

'Anyway, what business is it of yours?'

'What business is it of mine?' Dustfinger laughed quietly. 'Well, perhaps I'll tell you some time. But just now all I want to know is whether you've seen it.'

Meggie shook her head. She didn't know herself why she was lying to Dustfinger. Perhaps because he had pressed his hand over her mouth a little too hard.

'Meggie, listen to me!' Dustfinger looked at her intently. His scars were like pale lines that someone had drawn on his cheeks: two slightly curved marks on the left cheek, a third and longer line on the right cheek running from ear to nostril. 'Capricorn will kill your father if he doesn't get that book!' hissed Dustfinger. 'Kill him, do you understand? Didn't I tell you what he's like? He wants the book, and he *always* gets what he wants. It's ridiculous to believe it will be safe from him here.'

'Mo doesn't think so!'

Dustfinger straightened up and stared at the library door. 'Yes, I know,' he murmured. 'That's the trouble. And so,' he said, putting both hands on Meggie's shoulders and propelling her towards the closed door, 'so now you're going to go in there, the picture of innocence, and find out what the pair of them are planning to do with that book. OK?'

Meggie was about to protest, but before she knew it Dustfinger had opened the door and pushed her into the library.

Only a Picture

For him that stealeth, or borroweth and returneth not,
this book from its owner, let it change into a serpent in his
hand and rend him.
Let him be struck with palsy, and all his members blasted.
Let him languish in pain, crying aloud for mercy, and let
there be no surcease to this agony till he sing in dissolution.
Let bookworms gnaw his entrails . . . and when at last he
goeth to his last punishment, let the flames of hell consume
him for ever.
Curse on book thieves, from the monastery of San Pedro,
Barcelona, Spain

They had unwrapped the book. Meggie saw the brown
paper lying on a chair. Neither of them noticed that she
had come in; Elinor was bending over one of the reading desks
with Mo beside her. They both had their backs to the door.

'Amazing. I thought there wasn't a single copy left,' Elinor
was saying. 'There are strange stories about this book going
around. A second-hand dealer from whom I buy quite often

told me that three copies were stolen from him a few years ago. All on the same day too. And I've heard much the same story from two other booksellers.'

'Really? Yes, very strange,' said Mo, but Meggie knew his voice well enough to know that he was only pretending to be surprised. 'Well, anyway, even if this wasn't a rare book it means a lot to me, and I'd like to be sure it's in safe hands for a while. Just till I come back for it.'

'All books are in safe hands with me,' replied Elinor, sounding cross. 'You know that. They're my children, my inky children, and I look after them well. I keep the sunlight away from their pages, I dust them and protect them from hungry bookworms and grubby human fingers. This one shall have a place of honour, and no one will see it until you want it back. I don't really welcome visitors to my library. They just leave fingerprints and stray hairs in my poor books. Anyway, as you know, I have a very expensive burglar alarm system.'

'Yes, that's extremely reassuring!' Mo's voice sounded relieved. 'Thank you, Elinor! I really am most grateful. And if anyone comes knocking at your door in the near future asking about the book, please will you make out you've never heard of it, all right?'

'Of course. I'd do anything for a good bookbinder, and anyway you're my niece's husband. I really do miss her sometimes, you know. I expect you feel the same. Your daughter seems to be getting on all right without her, though.'

'She hardly remembers her mother,' said Mo quietly.

'Well, that's a blessing, wouldn't you say? Sometimes it's a good thing we don't remember things half as well as books do. But for them we probably wouldn't know anything for very long. It would all be forgotten: the Trojan War, Columbus, Marco Polo, Shakespeare, all the amazing kings and gods of the past . . .' Elinor turned round – and froze.

'Did I fail to hear you knock?' she asked, staring so angrily that Meggie had to summon up all her courage not to turn round and slip quickly back out into the passage.

'How long have you been there, Meggie?' asked Mo.

Meggie stuck her chin out. '*She* can see it, but you hide it away from *me!*' she said. Attack, she knew, is the best form of defence. 'You never hid any book from me before! What's so special about this one? Will I go blind if I read it? Will it bite my fingers off? What terrible secrets are there in it that I mustn't know?'

'I have my reasons for not showing it to you,' replied Mo. He looked very pale. Without another word he went over and tried to lead her to the door, but Meggie tore herself away.

'Pig-headed, isn't she?' remarked Elinor. 'It almost makes me like her! Her mother was just the same, I remember. Come here.' She stepped aside and beckoned Meggie over. 'Look, you can see there's nothing very exciting about this book, at least not to you. But see for yourself. We're always most likely to believe the evidence of our own eyes. Or doesn't your father agree?' She cast Mo an enquiring glance.

Mo hesitated, then resigned himself and nodded.

The book was lying open on the reading desk. It didn't seem particularly old. Meggie knew what really old books looked like. She had seen books in Mo's workshop with their pages spotted like leopard-skin and almost as yellow. She remembered one with a binding that had been attacked by woodworm. The traces of their jaws had looked like tiny bullet holes, and Mo had got out his book block, carefully fixed the pages back together, and then, as he put it, gave them a new dress. Such a dress could be made of leather or linen, it might be plain, or Mo might imprint a pattern on it with his tiny decorative stamps.

This book was bound in linen, silvery green like willow leaves. The edges of the pages were slightly roughened, and the paper was still so pale that every letter stood out clear and black. A narrow red bookmark lay between the open pages. The right-hand page had an illustration on it, showing women in magnificent dresses, a fire-eater, acrobats, and a man who looked like a king. Meggie turned the pages. There weren't many illustrations, but the first letter of each chapter was itself a little decorative picture. Animals sat on some of these initial letters, plants twined round others, one 'F' burned bright as fire. The flames looked so real that Meggie touched them with one finger to make sure they weren't hot. The next chapter began with an 'N'. An animal with a furry tail sat perched in the angle between the second and third strokes of the letter. *No one saw him slip out of town*, read Meggie, but before she could get any further with the story Elinor closed the book in her face.

'I think that'll do,' she said, tucking it under her arm. 'Your father's asked me to put this book somewhere safe for him, and so I will.'

Mo took Meggie's hand again, and this time she followed him. 'Please forget that book, Meggie!' he whispered. 'It's an unlucky story. I'll get you a hundred others.'

Meggie just nodded. Before Mo closed the door behind them, she caught a last glance of Elinor standing there look-ing at the book lovingly, the way Mo sometimes looked at her when he put her to bed in the evening.

Then the door was closed.

'Where will she put it?' asked Meggie as she followed Mo down the corridor.

'Oh, she has some very good hiding-places for such things,' replied Mo evasively. 'But they're secret, as hiding-places ought to be. Suppose I show you your room now?' He was trying to sound carefree, and not succeeding particularly well. 'It's like a room in an expensive hotel. No, much better.'

'Sounds good,' murmured Meggie, looking round, but there was no sign of Dustfinger. Where had he gone? She had to ask him something. At once. That was all she could think of while Mo was showing her the room and telling her that everything was all right now; he just had to do his bookbinding work, then they'd go home. Meggie nodded and pretended to be listening, but her mind was full of the question she wanted to ask Dustfinger. It burned on her lips so fiercely that she was surprised Mo didn't see it there.

When Mo left her to go and fetch their bags from the camper van Meggie went into the kitchen, but Dustfinger wasn't there either. She even looked for him in Elinor's bedroom, but however many doors in the huge house she opened there was no sign of him. Finally, she was too tired to go on searching. Mo had gone to bed long ago, and Elinor had disappeared into her own bedroom. So Meggie went to her room and lay down in the big bed. She felt very lost in it, like a dwarf, as if she had shrunk. Like *Alice in Wonderland*, she thought, patting the flowered bed linen. Otherwise she liked the room. It was full of books and pictures, and there was even a fireplace, although it looked as if no one had used it for at least a hundred years. Meggie swung her legs out of bed again and went over to the window. Outside, night had fallen long ago, and when she pushed the window shutters open a cool breeze blew on her face. The only thing she could make out in the dark was the gravel forecourt in front of the house. A lamp cast pale light over the grey and white pebbles. Mo's stripey van stood beside Elinor's grey estate car like a zebra lost in a horse's stable. Meggie thought of the house they had left in such a hurry, and her room there, and school, where her desk would have been empty today. She wasn't sure whether she felt homesick or not.

She left the shutters open when she went back to bed. Mo had put her book-box beside her. Wearily, she took a book out and tried to make herself a nice nest in its familiar words, but it was no good. Again and again the thought of that other book blurred the words, again and again Meggie saw the big initial letters before her – large, colourful letters surrounded by figures whose story she didn't know because the book hadn't had time to tell it to her.

I must find Dustfinger, she thought sleepily. He must be here somewhere. But then the book slipped from her fingers and she fell asleep.

The sun woke her next morning. The air was still cool from the night before, but the sky was cloudless, and when Meggie leaned out of the window she could see the lake gleaming in the distance beyond the branches of the trees. The room Elinor had given her was on the first floor. Mo was sleeping only two doors further along, but Dustfinger had to make do with an attic room. Meggie had seen it when she was looking for him yesterday. It held nothing but a narrow bed surrounded by crates of books towering up to the rafters.

Mo was already sitting at the table with Elinor when Meggie came down to the kitchen for breakfast, but Dustfinger wasn't there. 'Oh, he's had breakfast already,' said Elinor sharply, when Meggie asked about him. 'Along with some animal like a Pomeranian dog. It was sitting on the table and it spat at me when I came into the kitchen. I wasn't expecting anything like that. I made it clear to your peculiar friend that flies are the only animals I'll allow anywhere near my kitchen table, and so he took the furry creature outside.'

'What do you want him for?' asked Mo.

'Oh, nothing special. I – I just wanted to ask him something,' said Meggie. She hastily ate half a slice of bread, drank some of the horribly bitter cocoa Elinor had made, and went out.

She found Dustfinger behind the house, standing on a lawn of short, rather rough grass where a solitary deckchair stood next to a plaster angel. There was no sign of Gwin. A few birds were quarrelling among the red flowers of the rhododendron, and there stood Dustfinger looking lost to the world, and juggling. Meggie tried to count the coloured balls – four, six, eight. He plucked them out of the air so swiftly that it made her dizzy to watch him. He stood on one leg to catch them, casually, as if he didn't even have to look. Only when he spotted Meggie did a ball escape his fingers and roll at her feet. Meggie picked it up and threw it back.

'Where did you learn to do that?' she asked. 'It looked – well, wonderful.'

Dustfinger made her a mocking bow. There was that strange smile of his again. 'It's how I earn my living,' he said. 'With the juggling and a few other things.'

'How can you earn a living that way?'

'At markets and fairs. At children's birthday parties. Did you ever go to one of those fairs where people pretend they're still living in Medieval times?'

Meggie nodded. Yes, she had once been to a fair like that with Mo. There had been wonderful things there, so strange that they might have come from another world, not just another time. Mo had bought her a box decorated with brightly coloured stones, and a little fish made of shiny green and gold metal, with its mouth wide open and a jingle in its hollow body that rang like a little bell when you shook it. The air had smelled of freshly baked bread, smoke and damp clothes, and Meggie had watched a smith making a sword, and had hidden behind Mo's back from a woman in witch's costume.

Dustfinger picked up his juggling balls and put them back in his bag which was standing open on the grass behind him. Meggie went over to it and looked inside. She saw some bottles, some white cotton wool and a carton of milk, but before she could see any more Dustfinger closed the bag.

'Sorry, trade secrets,' he said. 'Your father's given the book to this Elinor, hasn't he?'

Meggie shrugged her shoulders.

'It's all right, you can tell me. I know anyway. I was listening. He's mad to leave it here, but what can I do?' Dustfinger sat down on the deckchair. His rucksack was on the grass next to him, with a bushy tail spilling out of it.

'I saw Gwin,' said Meggie.

'Did you?' Dustfinger leaned back, closing his eyes. His hair looked even paler in the sunlight. 'So did I. He's in the rucksack. It's the time of day when he sleeps.'

'I mean I saw him in the book.' Meggie didn't take her eyes off Dustfinger's face as she said this, but it didn't move a muscle. His thoughts couldn't be read on his brow, in the same way as she could read Mo's. Dustfinger's face was a closed book, and Meggie had the feeling that if anyone tried reading it he would rap their knuckles. 'He was sitting on a letter,' she went on. 'On a capital N. I saw his horns.'

'Really?' Dustfinger didn't even open his eyes. 'And do you know which of her thousands of shelves that book-mad woman put it on?'

Meggie ignored his question. 'Why does Gwin look like the animal in the book?' she asked. 'Did you really stick those horns on him?'

Dustfinger opened his eyes and blinked up at the sun.

'Hm, did I?' he enquired, looking at the sky. A few clouds were drifting over Elinor's house. The sun disappeared behind one of them, and its shadow fell across the green grass like an ugly mark.

'Does your father often read aloud to you, Meggie?' asked Dustfinger.

Meggie looked at him suspiciously. Then she knelt down beside the rucksack and stroked Gwin's silky tail. 'No,' she said. 'But he taught me to read when I was five.'

'Ask him *why* he doesn't read aloud to you,' said Dustfinger. 'And don't let him put you off with excuses.'

'What do you mean?' Meggie straightened up, feeling cross. 'He doesn't like reading aloud, that's all.'

Dustfinger smiled. Leaning out of the deckchair, he put one hand into the rucksack. 'Ah, that feels like a nice full stomach,' he commented. 'I think Gwin had good hunting last night. I hope he's not been plundering a nest again. Perhaps it's just Elinor's rolls and eggs.' Gwin's tail twitched back and forth almost like a cat's.

Meggie looked at the rucksack with distaste. She was glad she couldn't see Gwin's muzzle. There might still be blood on it.

Dustfinger leaned back in Elinor's deckchair. 'Shall I give you a performance this evening – show you what the bottles, the cotton wool and all the other mysterious things in my bag are for?' he asked without looking at her. 'It has to be dark for that, pitch dark. Are you scared to be out of doors in the middle of the night?'

'Of course not!' said Meggie, offended, although really she was not at all happy to be out in the dark. 'But first, tell me why you stuck those horns on Gwin! And tell me what you know about the book.'

Dustfinger folded his arms behind his head. 'Oh, I know a lot about that book,' he said. 'And perhaps I'll tell you some time, but first the two of us have a date. Here at eleven o'clock tonight. OK?'

Meggie looked up at a blackbird singing its heart out on Elinor's rooftop. 'OK,' she said. 'Eleven o'clock tonight.' Then she went back to the house.

Elinor had suggested that Mo set up his workshop next door to the library. There was a little room where she kept her collection of old books about animals and plants (for there seemed to be no kind of book that Elinor didn't collect). She kept this collection on shelves of pale, honey-coloured wood. On some of the shelves the books were propping up glass display cases of beetles pinned to cardboard, which only made Meggie dislike Elinor all the more. By the only window was a handsome table with turned legs, but it was barely half as long as the one Mo had in his workshop at home. Perhaps that was why he was swearing quietly to himself when Meggie put her head round the door.

'Look at this table!' he said. 'You could sort a stamp collection on it but not bind books. This whole room is too small. Where am I going to put the press and my tools? Last time I worked up in the attics, but now they're filled with crates of books too.'

Meggie stroked the spines of the books crammed close together on the shelves. 'Just tell her you need a bigger table.' Carefully, she took a book off the shelf. It contained pictures of the strangest of insects: beetles with horns, beetles with probosces, one even had a proper nose. Meggie passed her forefinger over the pastel-coloured pictures. 'Mo, why haven't you ever read aloud to me?'

Her father turned round so abruptly that the book almost fell from her hand. 'Why do you ask me that? You've been talking to Dustfinger, haven't you? What did he tell you?'

'Nothing. Nothing at all.' Meggie herself didn't know why she was lying. She put the beetle book back in its place. It felt almost as if someone were spinning a very fine web around the two of them, a web of secrets and lies closing in on them all the time. 'I think it's a good question, though,' she said as she took out another book. It was called *Masters of Disguise*. The creatures in it looked like live twigs or dry leaves.

Mo turned his back to her again. He began laying out his implements on the table, even though it was too small: his folding tool on the left, then the round-headed hammer he used to tap the spines of books into shape, the sharp paperknife . . . He usually whistled under his breath as he worked, but now he was perfectly quiet. Meggie sensed that his thoughts were far away. But where?

Finally, he sat on the side of the table and looked at her. 'I just don't like reading aloud,' he said, as if it was the most uninteresting subject in the world. 'You know I don't. That's all.'

'But why not? I mean, you make up stories. You tell wonderful stories. You can do all the voices, and make it exciting and then funny . . .'

Mo crossed his arms over his chest as if hiding behind them.

'You could read me *Tom Sawyer*,' suggested Meggie 'or *How the Rhinoceros Got His Skin*.' That was one of Mo's favourite stories. When she was smaller they sometimes played at having crumbs in their clothes, like the crumbs in the rhino's skin.

'Yes, an excellent story,' murmured Mo, turning his back to her again. He picked up the folder in which he kept his endpapers and leafed absent-mindedly through them. 'Every book should begin with attractive endpapers,' he had once told Meggie. 'Preferably in a dark colour: dark red or dark blue, depending on the binding. When you open the book it's like going to the theatre. First you see the curtain. Then it's pulled aside and the show begins.'

'Meggie, I really do have to work now,' he said without turning round. 'The sooner I'm through with Elinor's books the sooner we can go home again.'

Meggie put the book about creatures who were masters of disguise back in its place. 'Suppose he didn't stick the horns on?' she asked.

'What?'

'Gwin's horns. Suppose Dustfinger didn't stick them on?'

'Well, he did.' Mo drew a chair up to the table that was

not long enough for him. 'By the way, Elinor's gone shopping. If you feel faint with hunger before she gets back, just make yourself a couple of pancakes, OK?'

'OK,' murmured Meggie. For a moment she wondered whether to tell him about her date with Dustfinger that night, but then she decided against it. 'Do you think I can take some of these books to my room?' she asked instead.

'I'm sure you can. So long as they don't disappear into your box.'

'Like that book thief you once told me about?' Meggie put three books under her left arm and four under her right arm. 'How many was it he stole? Thirty thousand?'

'Forty thousand,' said Mo. 'But at least he didn't kill the owners.'

'No, that was the Spanish monk whose name I've forgotten.' Meggie went over to the door and opened it with her toe. 'Dustfinger says Capricorn would kill you to get hold of that book.' She tried to make her voice sound casual. 'Would he, Mo?'

'Meggie!' Mo turned round with the paper-knife, pretending to point it at her threateningly. 'Go and lie in the sun or bury your pretty nose in those books, but please let me get some work done. And tell Dustfinger I shall carve him into very thin slices with this knife if he goes on telling you such nonsense.'

'That wasn't a proper answer!' said Meggie, making her way out into the passage with an armful of books.

Once in her room, she spread the books out on the huge bed and began to read. She read about beetles who moved into empty snail-shells as we might move into an empty house, about frogs shaped like leaves and caterpillars with brightly coloured spines on their backs, white-bearded monkeys, stripy anteaters, and cats that dig in the ground for sweet potatoes. There seemed to be everything here, every creature Meggie could imagine, and even more that she could never have dreamed existed at all. But none of Elinor's clever books said a word about martens with horns.

6

Fire and Stars

So along they came with dancing bears, dogs and goats, monkeys and marmots, walking the tightrope, turning somersaults both backwards and forwards, throwing daggers and knives and suffering no injury when they fell on their points and blades, swallowing fire and chewing stones, doing tricks with magic goblets and chains under cover of cloak and hat, making puppets fence with each other, trilling like nightingales, screaming like peacocks, calling like deer, wrestling and dancing to the sound of the double flute . . .

Herzt, *Book of Minstrelsy*

The day passed slowly. Meggie saw Mo only in the afternoon, when Elinor came back from doing her shopping and half an hour later gave them spaghetti with some kind of ready-made sauce. 'I'm afraid I've no patience with toiling over a stove,' she said as she put the dishes on the table. 'Perhaps our friend with the furry animal can cook?'

Dustfinger merely shrugged his shoulders apologetically.

'Sorry, I'm no use to you that way.'

'Mo cooks very well,' said Meggie, stirring the thin, watery sauce into her spaghetti.

'Mo's here to restore my books, not to cook for us,' replied Elinor sharply. 'What about you, though?'

Meggie shrugged. 'I can make pancakes,' she said. 'Why don't you get some cookery books? You have books of every other kind. I'm sure you'd find cookery books a help.'

Elinor didn't even deign to reply to this suggestion.

'And by the way, there's a rule for night-time,' she said, when they had all been eating in silence for a while. 'I won't have candlelight in my house. Fire makes me nervous. It's far too greedy for paper.'

Meggie gulped. She felt caught in the act, for of course she had brought candles with her. They were on her bedside table upstairs, where Elinor must have seen them. However, Elinor was looking not at Meggie but at Dustfinger, who was playing with a box of matches.

'I hope you'll take that rule to heart,' she said to him. 'Since we're obviously going to have the pleasure of your company for another night.'

'Yes, if I may impose on your hospitality a little longer. I'll be off first thing in the morning, I promise.' Dustfinger was still holding the matches. He didn't seem bothered by Elinor's distrustful gaze. 'I'd say someone here has the wrong idea about fire,' he added. 'It bites like a fierce little animal, admittedly, but you can tame it.' And with these words he took a match out of the box, struck it, and popped the flame into his open mouth.

Meggie held her breath as his lips closed around the burning matchstick. Dustfinger opened his mouth again, took out the spent match, smiled and left it on his empty plate.

'You see, Elinor?' he said. 'It didn't bite me. It's easier to tame than a kitten and almost as easy as a dog.'

Elinor just wrinkled her nose, but Meggie was so amazed that she could hardly take her eyes off Dustfinger's scarred face. She looked at Mo. The little trick with the burning match didn't seem to have surprised him. He shot a warning glance at Dustfinger, who meekly put the box of matches away in his trouser pocket.

'But of course I'll keep the no-candles rule,' he was quick to say. 'That's no problem. Really.'

Elinor nodded. 'Good,' she said. 'And one more thing: if you go out again as soon as it's dark this evening, the way you did last night, you'd better not be back too late, because I switch the burglar alarm on at nine-thirty on the dot.'

'Ah, then I was in luck yesterday evening.' Dustfinger slipped some spaghetti into his bag. Elinor didn't notice, but Meggie did. 'Yes, I do enjoy walking at night. The world's more to my liking then, not so loud, not so fast, not so crowded and a good deal more mysterious. But I wasn't planning to walk this evening. I have other plans for tonight, and I'll have to ask you to switch this wonderful system of yours on a bit later than usual.'

'Oh, indeed. And why, may I ask?'

Dustfinger winked at Meggie. 'Well, I've promised to put on a little show for this young lady,' he said. 'It begins about an hour before midnight.'

'Oh yes?' Elinor dabbed some sauce off her lips with her napkin. 'A little show. Why not in daylight? After all, the young lady's only twelve years old. She should be in bed at eight o'clock.'

Meggie tightened her lips. She hadn't been to bed as early as eight since her fifth birthday, but she wasn't going to the trouble of explaining that to Elinor. Instead, she admired the casual way Dustfinger reacted to Elinor's hostile gaze.

'Ah, but you see the tricks I want to show Meggie wouldn't look so good by day,' he said, leaning back in his chair. 'I'm afraid I need the black cloak of night. Why don't you come and watch too? Then you'll understand why it all has to be done in the dark.'

'Go on, accept his offer, Elinor!' said Mo. 'You'll enjoy the show. And then perhaps you won't think fire's so sinister.'

'It's not that I think it's sinister. I don't like it, that's all,' remarked Elinor, unmoved.

'He can juggle!' Meggie burst out. 'With eight balls.'

'Eleven,' Dustfinger corrected her. 'But juggling is more of a daylight skill.'

Elinor retrieved a string of spaghetti from the tablecloth and glanced first at Meggie and then at Mo. She looked cross. 'Oh, very well. I don't want to be a spoilsport,' she said. 'I shall go to bed with a book at nine-thirty as usual and put the alarm on first, but when Meggie tells me she's going out for this private performance I'll switch it off again for an hour. Will that be time enough?'

'Ample time,' said Dustfinger, bowing so low to her that the tip of his nose collided with the rim of his plate.

Meggie bit back her laughter.

It was five to eleven when she knocked at Elinor's bedroom door.

'Come in!' she heard Elinor call, and when she put her head round the door she saw her aunt sitting up in bed, poring over a catalogue as thick as a telephone directory. 'Oh, too expensive, too expensive!' she murmured. 'Take my advice, Meggie: never develop a passion you can't afford. It'll eat your heart away like a bookworm. Take this book here, for instance.' Elinor tapped her finger on the left-hand page of her catalogue so hard that it wouldn't have surprised Meggie if she had bored a hole in it. 'What a fine edition – and in such good condition too! I've been wanting it for fifteen years, but it just costs too much money. Far too much.'

Sighing, she closed her catalogue, dropped it on the rug and swung her legs out of bed. To Meggie's surprise, she was wearing a long, flowered nightdress. She looked younger in it, almost like a girl who has woken up one morning to find her face wrinkled. 'Ah, well, you'll probably never be as crazy as I am!' she muttered, putting a thick pair of socks on her bare feet. 'Your father's not inclined to be crazy, and your mother never was either. Quite the opposite – I never knew anyone with a cooler head. My father, on the other hand, was at least as mad as me. I inherited over half my books from him, and what good did they do him? Did they keep him alive? Far from it. He died of a stroke at a book auction. Isn't that ridiculous?'

With the best will in the world, Meggie didn't know what to say to that. 'My mother?' she asked, instead. 'Did you know her well?'

Elinor snorted as if she had asked a silly question. 'Of course I did. It was here that your father met her. Didn't he ever tell you?'

Meggie shook her head. 'He doesn't talk about her much.'

'Well, probably better not. Why probe old wounds? And you're not particularly like her. She painted that sign on the library door. Come on, then, or you'll miss this show of yours.'

Meggie followed Elinor down the unlit corridor. For a moment she had the odd feeling that her mother might step out of one of the many doors, smiling at her. There was hardly a light on in the whole vast house, and once or twice Meggie bumped her knee on a chair or a little table that she hadn't seen in the gloom. 'Why is it so dark everywhere here?' she asked as Elinor felt around for the light switch in the entrance hall.

'Because I'd rather spend my money on books than unnecessary electricity,' replied Elinor, looking at the light she had turned on as if she thought the stupid thing should go easy on the power. Then she made her way over to a metal box fixed to the wall near the front door and hidden behind a thick, dusty curtain. 'I hope you switched your light off before you knocked on my door?' she asked, as she opened the box.

'Of course,' said Meggie, although it wasn't true.

'Turn round!' Elinor told her before setting to work on the alarm system. She frowned. 'Heavens, all these knobs! I hope I haven't done something wrong again. Tell me as soon as the show's over – and don't even think of seizing your chance to slink into the library and take a book off the shelves. Remember that I sleep right next door, and my hearing is keener than a bat's.'

Meggie bit back the answer on the tip of her tongue. Elinor opened the front door. Without a word, Meggie pushed past her and went outside. It was a mild night, full of strange scents and the chirping of crickets. 'Were you always as nice as this to my mother?' she asked as Elinor was about to close the door behind her.

Elinor looked at her for a moment as if turned to stone. 'Oh yes, I think so,' she said. 'Yes, I'm sure I was. And she was always as cheeky as you, too! Have fun with your fire-eater!' Then she shut the door.

As Meggie was going through the dark garden behind the house she suddenly heard unexpected music. It filled the night air as if it had been only waiting for Meggie's footsteps: strange music, a carnival mixture of bells, pipes and drums, both boisterous and sad. Meggie wouldn't have been surprised to find a whole troop of fairground entertainers waiting for her on the lawn behind Elinor's house, but only Dustfinger stood there.

He was waiting where Meggie had found him that afternoon. The music came from a cassette recorder on the grass beside the wooden deckchair. Dustfinger had placed a garden bench on the edge of the lawn for his audience. Lighted torches were stuck into the ground to the right and left of it, and two more were burning on the lawn, casting quivering shadows in the night. The shadows danced across the grass like servants conjured up by Dustfinger from some dark world for this occasion. He himself stood there bare-chested, his skin as pale as the moon, which was hanging in the sky right above Elinor's house as if it too had turned up especially for Dustfinger's show.

When Meggie emerged from the darkness Dustfinger bowed to her. 'Sit down, pretty lady!' he called over the music. 'We were all just waiting for you.'

Shyly, Meggie sat down on the bench and looked around her. The two dark glass bottles she had seen in Dustfinger's bag were standing on the deckchair. Something whitish shimmered in the bottle on the left, as if Dustfinger had filled it with moonlight. A dozen torches with white wadding heads were wedged between the wooden rungs of the chair, and beside the cassette recorder stood a bucket and a large, big-bellied vase, which if Meggie remembered correctly came from Elinor's entrance hall.

For a moment, she let her eyes wander to the windows of the house. There was no light in Mo's bedroom – he was probably still working – but one floor below Meggie saw Elinor standing at her lighted window. The moment Meggie looked her way she drew the curtain, as if she had felt Meggie watching her, but she still stayed at the window. Her shadow was a dark outline against the pale yellow curtain.

'Do you hear how quiet it is?' Dustfinger switched the recorder off. The silence of the night fell on Meggie's ears, muffled as if by cotton wool. Not a leaf moved; there was nothing to be heard but the torches crackling and the chirping of the crickets.

Dustfinger switched the music back on. 'I had a private word with the wind,' he said. 'There's one thing you should know: if the wind takes it into its head to play with fire then even I can't tame the blaze. But it gave me its word of honour to keep still tonight and not spoil our fun.'

So saying, he picked up one of the torches from Elinor's deckchair. He sipped from the bottle with the moonlight in it and spat something whitish out into the big vase. Then he dipped the torch he was holding into the bucket, took it out again, and held its dripping head of wadding to one of its burning sisters. The fire flared up so suddenly it made Meggie jump. However, Dustfinger put the second bottle to his lips, filling his mouth until his scarred cheeks were bulging. Then he took a deep, deep breath, arched his body like a bow, and spat whatever was in his mouth out into the air above the burning torch.

A fireball hung over Elinor's lawn, a bright, blazing globe of fire. It ate away at the darkness like a living thing. And it was so big, Meggie felt sure everything around it would go up in flames: the grass, the deckchair, and Dustfinger himself. But he just spun round and round on the spot, exuberant as a dancing child, breathing out more fire. He made the fire climb high in the air, as if to set the stars alight. Then he lit a second torch and ran its flame over his bare arms. He looked as happy as a child playing with a pet animal. The fire licked his skin like something living, a darting, burning creature that he had befriended, a creature that caressed him and danced for him and drove the night away. He threw the torch high in the air where the fireball had just been blazing, caught it as it came down, lit more, juggled with three, four, five torches. Their fire whirled around him, danced with him but never hurt him: Dustfinger the tamer of flames, the man who breathed sparks, the friend of fire. He made the torches disappear as if the darkness had devoured them, bowed to the speechless Meggie with a smile, before once more spitting fire out into the night's black face.

Afterwards, she could never say what had distracted her attention from the whirling torches and the showers of sparks, making her look up once more at the house and its windows. Perhaps you feel the presence of evil on your skin like sudden heat or cold . . . or perhaps it was just that the light now seeping through the library shutters caught her eye, the light falling on the rhododendron bushes where their leaves pressed close to the wood. Perhaps.

She thought she heard voices rising above Dustfinger's music, men's voices, and a terrible fear rose inside her, as dark and strange as the terror she had felt on the night when she first saw Dustfinger standing out in the yard. As she jumped up, a burning torch slipped from his hands and fell on the grass. He quickly trod the fire out before it could spread any further, then followed the direction of Meggie's eyes, and he too looked at the house without a word.

Meggie began to run. Gravel crunched under her feet as she raced towards the house. The front door stood ajar, there was no light in the entrance hall, but Meggie heard loud voices echoing down the corridor that led to the library. 'Mo?' she called, and there was the fear back again, digging its curved beak into her heart, taking her breath away.

The library door was open too. Meggie was about to rush in when two strong hands grasped her by the shoulders.

'Quiet!' breathed Elinor, pulling her into her bedroom. Meggie saw that her fingers were shaking as she locked the door.

'Don't!' Meggie dragged Elinor's hand away, and tried to turn the key. She wanted to shout that she must help her father, but Elinor put a hand over her mouth and pulled her away from the door, hard as Meggie struggled, hitting and kicking. Elinor was strong, much stronger than Meggie.

'There are too many of them!' Elinor whispered as Meggie tried to bite her fingers. 'About four or five, big strong men, and they're armed.' She hauled the struggling Meggie over to the wall by the bed. 'I've told myself a hundred times – oh, a thousand times! – I ought to buy a revolver!' she muttered, pressing her ear to the wall.

'Of course it's here!' The voice carried through the wall

without Meggie's having to strain to hear it, rasping like a cat's tongue. 'Shall we fetch your little daughter from the garden to show us just where? Or would you rather find it for us yourself?'

Meggie tried to pull Elinor's hand away from her mouth. 'Stop it, for goodness' sake!' Elinor hissed in her ear. 'You'll only put him in more danger, do you understand?'

'My daughter! What do you know about my daughter?' That was Mo's voice.

Meggie sobbed aloud, and Elinor's fingers were instantly back over her face. 'I tried to call the police,' she whispered in Meggie's ear. 'But the lines are all down.'

'Oh, we know all we need to know.' The other voice again. 'So where's the book?'

'I'll give it to you!' Mo's voice sounded weary. 'But I'm going with you, because I want that book back as soon as Capricorn has finished with it.'

Going with them? What did he mean? He couldn't leave just like that! Meggie tried making for the door again, but Elinor held her fast. Meggie did her best to push her away, but Elinor simply wrapped her strong arms around her and pressed her fingers to Meggie's lips once more.

'All the better. We were told to bring you anyway,' said a second voice. It had a broad, coarse accent. 'You've no idea how Capricorn longs to hear your voice. He's got great faith in your abilities, Capricorn has.'

'That's right – the replacement Capricorn found for you makes a terrible hash of it.' The rasping voice again. 'Look at Cockerell there.' Meggie heard feet scraping on the floor. 'He's limping, and Flatnose's face has seen better days. Not that he was ever much of a beauty.'

'Don't just stand there talking, Basta, we haven't got for ever. How about it – do we take the kid as well?' Another voice. That one sounded as if the speaker's nose were being pinched.

'No!' Mo snapped at him. 'My daughter stays here or I won't give you the book!'

One of the men laughed. 'Oh yes, Silvertongue, you'd give it to us all right, but don't worry. We weren't told to bring her. A child would just slow us down, and Capricorn's been waiting for you long enough already. So where's that book?'

Meggie pressed her ear against the wall so hard that it hurt. She heard footsteps, and then a sound like something being pushed aside. Elinor, beside her, held her breath.

'Not a bad hiding-place!' said the cat-like voice. 'Wrap it up, Cockerell, and take good care of it. After you, Silvertongue. Let's go.'

They left the library. Meggie tried desperately to wriggle out of Elinor's arms. She heard the sound of the library door closing, and then steps moving away, getting fainter and fainter. After that, all was still. Quite suddenly, Elinor let go of her. Meggie rushed to the door, unlocked it, sobbing, and ran down the corridor to the library. It was deserted. No Mo. The books stood ranged tidily on their shelves, except in one place where there was a wide, dark gap. Meggie thought she saw a hinged flap, well hidden, standing open among the books.

'Incredible!' she heard Elinor saying behind her. 'They really were after just that one book.' But Meggie pushed her aside and ran along the corridor.

'Meggie!' Elinor called after her. 'Wait!'

But what was there to wait for? For the strangers to take

her father away? She heard Elinor running after her. Elinor's arms might be stronger, but Meggie's legs were faster.

There was still no light in the entrance hall. The front door stood wide open, and a cold wind blew in Meggie's face as she stumbled breathlessly out into the night.

'Mo!' she shouted.

She thought she saw car headlights come on where the drive disappeared into the trees, and an engine started. Meggie ran that way. She tripped and fell, grazing her knee on the gravel, which was wet with dew. Warm blood trickled down her leg, but she took no notice. She ran on and on, limping and sobbing, until she had reached the big wrought iron gate. The road beyond it was empty. Mo was gone.

What the Night Hides

A thousand enemies outside the house
are better than one within.

Arab proverb

Dustfinger was hiding behind a chestnut tree when Meggie ran past him. He saw her stop at the gate and look down the road. He heard her calling her father's name in a desperate voice. Her cries, as faint as the chirping of a cricket in the vast black night, were lost in the darkness. And when she gave up it was suddenly very quiet, and Dustfinger saw Meggie's slim figure standing there as if she would never move again. All her strength seemed to have forsaken her, as if the next gust of wind might blow her away.

She stood there so long that Dustfinger eventually closed his eyes so as not to have to look at her, but then he heard her weeping and his face turned hot with shame. He stood there without a sound, his back to the tree trunk, waiting for Meggie to go back to the house. But still she didn't move. At last, when his legs were quite numb, she turned like a marionette with some of its strings cut and went back towards the house. She was no longer crying as she passed Dustfinger, but she was wiping the tears from her eyes, and for a terrible moment he felt an urge to go to her, comfort her, and explain why he had told Capricorn everything. But Meggie had already passed him, and had quickened her pace as if her strength were returning. Faster and faster she walked, until she had disappeared among the black trees.

Only then did Dustfinger come out from behind the tree, put his rucksack on his back, pick up the two bags containing all his worldly goods, and stride off towards the gate, which was still open.

The night swallowed him up like a thieving fox.

8

Alone

'My darling,' she said at last, 'are you sure you don't mind
being a mouse for the rest of your life?'

'I don't mind at all,' I said. 'It doesn't matter who you are
or what you look like so long as somebody loves you.'

Roald Dahl, The Witches

Elinor was standing in the brightly lit doorway of the house
when Meggie came back. She had put a coat on over her
nightdress. The night was warm, but a cold wind was blowing from the lake. How desperate the child looked – and lost.
Elinor remembered the feeling. There was nothing worse.

'They've taken him away!' Meggie's voice almost choked in
her helpless rage. She glared angrily at Elinor. 'Why did you
hold me back? We could have helped him!' Her fists were
clenched as if she wanted to hit out blindly.

Elinor remembered that feeling too. Sometimes you wanted to lash out at the whole world, but it did no good, none at
all. The grief remained. 'Don't talk such nonsense!' she said
bluntly. 'How could we have helped him? They'd just have

taken you too, and how would your father have liked that? Would it have done him any good? No. So don't stand around out here any longer – come indoors.'

But Meggie didn't move. 'They're taking him to Capricorn!' she whispered, so softly that Elinor could hardly make out what she was saying.

'Taking him where?'

Meggie just shook her head and wiped her sleeve over her tear-stained face.

'The police will be here any minute,' said Elinor. 'I called them on your father's mobile. I never wanted one of those, but now I think I'd better get one after all. They simply cut my phone line.'

Meggie still hadn't moved. She was trembling. 'They'll be well away by now anyway,' she said.

'Good heavens, I'm sure no harm will come to him!' Elinor wrapped her coat more closely around her. The wind was getting up. There would be rain soon, she felt sure.

'How do you know?' Meggie's voice was trembling with anger.

Heavens, thought Elinor, if looks could kill I'd be pushing up the daisies. 'Because he went with them of his own free will,' she said crossly. 'You heard him too, didn't you?'

Meggie bowed her head. Of course she'd heard him.

'Yes,' she whispered. 'He was more worried about the book than me.'

Elinor had no answer to that. Her own father had been firmly convinced that books deserved more attention than children, and when he suddenly died she and her two sisters had barely noticed his absence. It was as if he was just sitting in the library as usual, dusting his books. But Meggie's father wasn't like that.

'Nonsense, of course he was worried about you!' she said. 'I don't know any father who's more besotted with his daughter than yours. You wait and see, he'll soon be back. Now, do come in!' She reached out her hand to Meggie. 'I'll make you some hot milk with honey. Isn't that what children get when they're really miserable?'

But Meggie ignored the hand. She turned suddenly and ran away as if something had occurred to her.

'Here, wait a minute!' Muttering crossly, Elinor slipped her feet into her gardening shoes and stumbled after her. The silly girl was running round behind the house to the place where the fire-eater had given his performance. But of course there was no one on the lawn now, just the burnt-out torches still stuck in the ground.

'Well, well, so Master Matchstick-Swallower seems to be gone too,' said Elinor. 'At least, he's not in the house.'

'Perhaps he followed them!' The girl went up to one of the burnt-out torches and touched its charred head. 'That's it! He saw what happened and followed them!' She looked hopefully at Elinor.

'Of course. That's what must have happened.' Elinor really did try hard not to sound sarcastic. How do you think he followed them she added silently in her mind. On foot? But instead of saying so out loud she put a hand on Meggie's shoulder. Heavens above, the girl was still shaking. 'Come on!' she said. 'The police will soon be here, and there's nothing we can do just now. Your father will surely turn up again in a few days' time, and perhaps your fire-breathing friend will be with him. You'll just have to put up with me in the meantime.'

Meggie merely nodded, and unresistingly let Elinor lead

her back to the house.

'On one condition, though,' said Elinor, as they reached the front door.

Meggie looked at her suspiciously.

'While we're here on our own, do you think you could stop looking at me as if you wanted to poison me all the time? Could that be arranged?'

A small, sad little smile stole over Meggie's face. 'I should think so,' she said.

The two policemen whose car drew up on the gravel forecourt a little later asked a lot of questions, to which neither Elinor nor Meggie had many answers. No, they had never seen the men before. No, they hadn't stolen money or anything else of value, just a book. The two men exchanged amused glances when Elinor said that. She immediately gave them an angry lecture on the value of rare books, but that only made things worse. When Meggie finally said they'd be sure to find her father if they tracked down a bad man called Capricorn, they looked at each other as if she had seriously claimed that Mo had been carried off by the big bad wolf. Then they drove away again, and Elinor took Meggie to her room. The silly child had tears in her eyes once more, and Elinor hadn't the faintest idea how you set about comforting a girl of twelve, so she just told her, 'Your mother always slept in this room,' which was probably the worst thing she could have said. She quickly added, 'Read a story if you can't get to sleep,' cleared her throat twice, and then went back through the dark, empty house to her own room.

Why did it suddenly strike her as so big and so empty? In all the years she had lived alone here it had never troubled her to know that only her books awaited her behind all the doors. It was a long time since she and her sisters had played hide-and-seek in the many rooms. How quietly they always had to slip past the library door . . .

Outside, the wind rattled the shutters of the windows. Heavens, I won't be able to sleep a wink, thought Elinor. And then she thought of the book waiting beside her bed, and with a mixture of anticipation and a very guilty conscience she disappeared into her bedroom.

9

A Poor Exchange

A strong and bitter book-sickness floods one's soul. How ignominious to be strapped to this ponderous mass of paper, print and dead man's sentiment. Would it not be better, finer, braver to leave the rubbish where it lies and walk out into the world a free untrammelled illiterate Superman?

Solomon Eagle

Meggie didn't sleep in her own bed that night. As soon as Elinor's footsteps had died away she ran to Mo's room. He hadn't unpacked yet, and his bag stood open beside the bed. Only his books were on the bedside table, and a partly eaten chocolate bar. Mo loved chocolate. Even the mustiest old chocolate Santa Claus wasn't safe from him. Meggie broke a square off the bar and put it in her mouth, but it tasted of nothing. Nothing but sadness.

Mo's quilt was cold when she crept under it, and the pillow didn't yet smell of him either, only of washing powder. Meggie put her hand under the pillow. Yes, there it was: not a book, a photograph. Meggie drew it out. It was a picture of her mother; Mo always kept it under his pillow. When she was little she believed that Mo had simply invented a mother for her one day because he thought she'd have liked to have one. He told wonderful stories about her. 'Did I like her?' Meggie always asked. 'Yes, very much.' – 'Where is she?' – 'She had to go away when you were just three.' – 'Why?' – 'She just had to go away.' – 'A long way away?' – 'Yes, a very long way.' – 'Is she dead?' – 'No, I'm sure she isn't.' Meggie was used to the strange answers Mo gave to many of her questions. By the time she was ten she no longer believed in a mother made up by Mo, she believed in one who had simply gone away. These things happened. And as long as Mo was there she hadn't particularly missed having a mother.

But now he was gone, and she was alone with Elinor and Elinor's pebble eyes.

She took Mo's sweater out of his bag and buried her face in it. It's the book's fault, she kept thinking. It's all that book's fault. Why didn't he give it to Dustfinger? Sometimes, when you're so sad you don't know what to do, it helps to be angry. But then the tears came back again all the same, and Meggie fell asleep with the salty taste of them on her lips.

When she woke all of a sudden, her heart pounding and her hair damp with sweat, it all came back to her: the men, Mo's voice, the empty road. I'll go and look for him, thought Meggie. Yes, that's what I'll do. Outside the sky was just turning red. Not long now and the sun would rise. It would be better if she was gone before it got really light. Mo's jacket was hanging over the chair under the window, as if he'd only just taken it off. Meggie took his wallet out of it – she'd need the money. Then she crept back to her room to pack a few things, only the essentials: a change of clothing and a photograph of herself and Mo, so that she could ask people if they'd seen him. Of course she couldn't take her book-box. She thought of hiding it under the bed, but she decided to write Elinor a note instead:

Dear Elinor, she wrote, although she didn't really think that was the correct way to address an aunt. *I have to go and look for my father,* she went on. *Don't worry about me.* Well, Elinor wasn't likely to do that anyway. *And please don't tell the police I've gone or they'll be sure to bring me back. My favourite books are in my box. I'm afraid I can't take them with me. Please look after them. I'll come and fetch them as soon as I've found my father. Thank you. Meggie.*

P.S.: I know exactly how many books there are in the box.

She crossed out that last sentence. It would only annoy Elinor, and who knew what she might do with the books then? Sell them, probably. After all, Mo had given them all particularly nice bindings. None of them was bound in leather, because Meggie didn't like to think of a calf or a pig losing its skin for her books. Luckily, Mo understood how she felt. Many hundreds of years ago, he had once told Meggie, people made the bindings for particularly valuable books from the skin of unborn calves, *charta virginea non nata,* a pretty name for a terrible thing. 'And those books,' Mo had told her, 'were full of the most wonderful words about love and kindness and mercy.'

While Meggie was packing her bag she did her best not to think, because if she did she knew she'd have to ask herself where she was going to search for Mo. She kept pushing the thought away, but all the same her hands slowed down, and at last she was standing beside her packed bag, no longer able to ignore the cruel little voice inside her. 'Well then, where *are* you going to look, Meggie?' it whispered. 'Are you going to turn left or right when you reach the road? You don't even know that. How far do you think you'll get before the police pick you up? A twelve-year-old girl carrying a bag, with a wild story about a father who's disappeared, and no mother they can take her back to.'

Meggie put her hands over her ears, but what use was that when the voice was inside her head? She stood like that for quite a long time. Then she shook her head until the voice stopped, and dragged her bag out into the corridor. It was heavy. Much too heavy. Meggie opened it again and put almost everything back in her room. She kept only a sweater, a book (she had to have at least one), the photo and Mo's wallet. Now she could carry the bag as far as she had to.

She slipped quietly downstairs with the bag in one hand and the note for Elinor in the other. The morning sunlight was already filtering through the cracks of the shutters, but it was as silent in the big house as if even the books on the shelves were sleeping. Only the sound of quiet snoring came through Elinor's bedroom door. Meggie really meant to push the note under the door, but it wouldn't fit. She hesitated for a moment and then pressed the door-handle down. It was light in Elinor's bedroom, even though the shutters were closed. The bedside lamp was switched on, so obviously Elinor had gone to sleep while she was reading. She was lying on her back with her mouth slightly open, snoring at the plaster angel on the ceiling above her. And she was clutching a book to her chest. Meggie recognised it at once.

She was beside the bed in an instant. 'Where did you get that?' she shouted, tugging the book out of Elinor's arms, which were heavy with sleep. 'That's my father's!'

Elinor woke as suddenly as if Meggie had tipped cold water over her face.

'You stole it!' cried Meggie, beside herself with rage. 'And *you* brought those men here, yes, that's what happened. You and that Capricorn are in this together! You had my father taken away, and who knows what you did with poor Dustfinger? You wanted that book from the start! I saw the way you looked at it – like something alive! It's probably worth a million – or two million or three million . . .'

Elinor was sitting up in bed, staring at the flowers on her nightdress and saying not a word. She didn't move until Meggie was struggling to get her breath back.

'Finished?' she asked. 'Or are you planning to stand there yelling your head off until you drop dead?' Her voice sounded as brusque as usual, but it had another note in it too – a touch of guilt.

'I'm going to tell the police!' cried Meggie. 'I'll tell them you stole the book and they ought to ask *you* where my father is.'

'I *saved* you – and this book!'

Elinor swung her legs out of bed, went over to the window and opened the shutters.

'Oh yes? And what about Mo?' Meggie's voice was rising again. 'What's going to happen when they realise he gave them the wrong book? It's all your fault if they hurt him. Dustfinger said Capricorn would kill him if he didn't hand over the book. He'll kill him!'

Elinor put her head out of the window and took a deep

breath. Then she turned round again. 'What nonsense!' she said crossly. 'You think far too much of what that matchstick-eater says. And you've obviously read too many bad adventure stories. Kill your father? Heavens above, he's not a secret agent or anything dangerous like that! He restores old books! It's not exactly a life-threatening profession! I just wanted to take a look at the book in peace. That's the only reason I swapped it round. How could I guess those villains would come here in the middle of the night to take your father away along with their precious book? All he told me was that some crazy collector had been badgering him for that book for years. How was I to know this collector wouldn't shrink from breaking and entering, not to mention kidnapping? Even *I* wouldn't think up an idea like that. Well, maybe for just one or two books in the world I might.'

'But that's what Dustfinger said. He said Capricorn would kill him!' Meggie was clutching the book tightly, as if that were the only way of preventing yet more misfortunes from creeping out of it. It was as if she suddenly remembered Dustfinger's voice again. 'And the little creature's screeching and struggling,' she whispered, 'would be as sweet as honey to him.'

'What? Who are you talking about now?' Elinor perched on the edge of the bed and made Meggie sit down beside her. 'You'd better tell me everything you know about this business. Begin at the beginning.'

Meggie opened the book and leafed through the pages until she found the big 'N' with the animal that looked so like Gwin sitting on it.

'Meggie! I'm talking to you!' Elinor shook her roughly by the shoulders. 'Who were you talking about just now?'

'Capricorn.' Meggie just whispered the name. Danger seemed to cling to it – to every single letter of it.

'Capricorn. Go on. I've heard you mention that name a couple of times before. But who, for goodness' sake, *is* this Capricorn?'

Meggie closed the book, stroked the binding, and looked at it from all sides. 'It doesn't give the title on the cover,' she murmured.

'No, not on the cover or inside.' Elinor rose and went to her wardrobe. 'There are a good many books where you can't find the title straight away. After all, it's a relatively modern habit to put it on the cover. When books were still bound so that the spines curved inwards the title might be on the side, if anywhere, but in most cases you found it out only when you opened the book. It wasn't until bookbinders learned to make rounded spines that the title moved to the front of the book.'

'Yes, I know!' said Meggie impatiently. 'But this isn't an old book. I know what old books look like.'

Elinor looked at her ironically. 'Oh, I apologise! I was forgetting you're a real little expert. But you're right, yes, this book isn't very old. It was published almost exactly thirty-eight years ago. Ridiculously young for a book!' She disappeared behind her open wardrobe door. 'But of course it has a title all the same. It's called *Inkheart*. I suspect your father intentionally bound it so that no one could identify it just from looking at the cover. You don't even find the title on the first page, and when you look carefully you see that he's removed it – the title page.'

Elinor's nightdress landed on the carpet, and Meggie saw a pair of tights being put on over her bare legs.

'We have to go to the police again,' said Meggie.

'What for?' Elinor threw a sweater over the wardrobe door. 'What are you going to tell them? Didn't you notice the way those two policemen looked at us last night?' Elinor imitated them: '"Oh yes, what was that again, Signora Loredan? Someone broke into your house after you'd been kind enough to switch off the burglar alarm? And then this amazingly cunning burglar stole just one book, although there are books worth millions in your library, and they took this girl's father away after he'd offered to go with them in any case? Yes, very interesting. And it seems that these men were working for a man called Capricorn. Doesn't that mean goat or something?" Heavens above, child!' Elinor emerged from behind the wardrobe door. She was wearing an unattractive check skirt and a caramel-coloured sweater that made her look as pale as dough. 'Everyone living around this lake thinks I'm crazy, and if we go back to the police with this story, then the news that Elinor Loredan has finally flipped will be all over the place. Which just goes to show that a passion for books is extremely unhealthy.'

'You dress like an old granny,' said Meggie.

Elinor looked down at herself. 'Thank you very much,' she said, 'but comments on my appearance are uncalled-for. Anyway, I *could* be your granny. With a little stretch of the imagination.'

'Have you ever been married?'

'No, why would I want to? And could you now kindly stop making personal remarks? Hasn't your father ever taught you that it's bad manners?'

Meggie did not reply. She wasn't sure herself why she had asked the question. 'This book is very valuable, isn't it?' she asked.

'What, *Inkheart*?' Elinor took it from Meggie's hand, stroked the binding and then gave it back. 'I think so. Although you won't find a single copy in any of the catalogues or lists of valuable books. But I'm sure that many collectors would offer your father a very great deal of money if word got around that he has what may be the only copy. Actually, I found out quite a lot about it, and I believe it's not just a rare book but a good one too. I can't give an opinion on that. I scarcely managed a dozen pages last night. When the first fairy appeared I fell asleep. I never was particularly keen on stories full of fairies and dwarves and all that stuff.'

Elinor went round behind the wardrobe door again, obviously to look at herself in a mirror. Meggie's comment on her clothes seemed to be bothering her after all. 'Yes, I think it *is* very valuable,' she repeated thoughtfully. 'Although it's almost forgotten now. Hardly anyone seems to remember what it's about, hardly anyone seems to have read it. You can't even find it in libraries. But now and then these strange stories about it do crop up: they say it's been forgotten only because all the copies that still existed were stolen. I expect that's nonsense. Although it's not just plants and animals that die out, so do books. Quite often, I'm sorry to say. I'm sure you could fill a hundred houses like this one to the roof with all the books that have disappeared for ever.' Elinor closed the wardrobe door again, and pinned up her hair with clumsy fingers. 'As far as I know the author's still alive, but obviously he's never done anything about getting his book reprinted – which strikes me as odd. I mean, you write a story so that people will read it, don't you? Well, perhaps he doesn't like his own story any more, or perhaps it just sold so badly that no publisher was willing to bring it out again. How would I know?'

'All the same, I don't think they stole it just because it's valuable,' muttered Meggie.

'You don't?' Elinor laughed out loud. 'My word, you really are your father's daughter! Mortimer could never imagine people doing something bad for money, because money has never meant much to him. Do you have any idea what a book can be worth?'

Meggie looked at her crossly. 'Yes, I do. But I still don't think that's the reason.'

'I do. And Sherlock Holmes would think so too. Have you ever read those books, by the way? Wonderful stuff. Specially on rainy days.' Elinor slipped her shoes on. She had strangely small feet for such a sturdily built woman.

'Perhaps there's some kind of secret in it,' murmured Meggie, thoughtfully caressing the close-printed pages.

'You mean something like invisible messages written in lemon juice, or a map hidden in one of the pictures showing where to find treasure?' Elinor sounded so sarcastic that Meggie felt like wringing her short neck.

'Why not?' Meggie closed the book again and put it firmly under her arm. 'Why else would they take Mo too? The book would have been enough.'

Elinor shrugged her shoulders.

Of course she can't admit she never thought of that, Meggie told herself scornfully. She always has to be right!

Elinor looked at Meggie as if she had guessed her thoughts. 'Listen, I tell you what, why don't you read it?' she said. 'You really might find something that you don't think belongs in the story. A few extra words here, a couple of unnecessary letters there – and there's your secret message. The signpost pointing to the treasure. Who knows how long it will be before your father comes back? You'll have to do something to pass the time here.'

Before Meggie could answer that one, Elinor bent to pick up a piece of paper lying on the carpet beside her bed. It was Meggie's goodbye note. She must have dropped it when she saw the book in Elinor's arms.

'What on earth's this?' asked Elinor, when she had read it, frowning. 'You were planning to go and look for your father? Where, for heaven's sake? You're even more foolish than I thought.'

Meggie pressed *Inkheart* close to her. 'Who else is going to look for him?' she said. Her lips began to tremble, and there wasn't a thing she could do about it.

'Well then, we'll just have to go and look for him together!' replied Elinor, sounding annoyed. 'But first let's give him a chance to come back. Do you think he'll be pleased to get back here only to find you've disappeared, gone looking for him in the big wide world?'

Meggie shook her head. Elinor's carpet was swimming before her eyes. A tear ran down her nose.

'Right, that's all settled, then,' growled Elinor, offering Meggie a cotton handkerchief. 'Blow your nose and then we'll have breakfast.'

She wouldn't let Meggie out of the house before she had eaten a roll and swallowed a glass of milk.

'Breakfast is the most important meal of the day,' she announced, buttering her own third slice of bread. 'And what's more, when your father gets back I don't want you telling him I've been starving you. Like the wicked stepmother in the fairy tale, you know.'

An answer sprang to the tip of Meggie's tongue, but she swallowed it along with the last of her roll, and took the book outside.

10

The Lion's Den

Look. (Grown-ups skip this paragraph.) I'm not about to tell you this book has a tragic ending, I already said in the very first line how it was my favourite in all the world. But there's a lot of bad stuff coming.

William Goldman, *The Princess Bride*

Meggie sat on the bench behind the house. Dustfinger's burnt-out torches were still stuck in the ground beside it. She didn't usually hesitate so long before opening a book, but she was afraid of what was waiting for her inside this one. That was a brand-new feeling. She had never before been afraid of what a book would tell her. Far from it. Usually, she was so eager to let it lead her into an undiscovered world, one she had never been to before, that she often started to read at the most unsuitable moments. Both she and Mo often read at breakfast and, as a result, he had more than once taken her to school late. And she used to read under the desk at school too, and late at night in bed until Mo pulled back the covers and threatened to take all the books out of her room so that she'd get enough sleep for once. Of course he would never have done such a thing, and he knew she knew he wouldn't, but for a few days after such a threat she would put her book under her pillow around nine in the evening and let it go on whispering to her in her dreams, so that Mo could feel he was being a really good father.

She wouldn't have put this book under her pillow, for fear of what it might whisper to her. For the very first time in her life Meggie wasn't sure that she wanted to enter the world waiting for her between the covers of a book. All the bad things that had happened over the last three days seemed to have come out of this book, and perhaps they were only a faint reflection of what still awaited her inside it.

All the same, she had to begin. Where else was she to look for Mo? Elinor was right; there was no point in simply running off at random. She had to look for Mo's trail among the printed letters in *Inkheart*. But she had hardly opened it at the first page when she heard footsteps behind her.

'You'll get sunstroke if you carry on sitting in the full sunlight,' said a familiar voice.

Meggie spun round.

Dustfinger made her a bow. Of course his face wore its usual smile. 'Well, what a surprise!' he said, leaning over her shoulder and looking at the open book on her lap. 'So it's here after all. *You've* got it.'

Meggie was still looking uncomprehendingly at his scarred face. How could he stand there acting as if nothing had happened? 'Where've you been?' she snapped. 'Didn't they take you too? And where's Mo? Where have they taken him?' She couldn't get the words out fast enough.

But Dustfinger took his time over answering. He examined the bushes all around as if he had never seen anything like them before. He was wearing his coat, although the day was so hot that perspiration stood out in gleaming little beads on his forehead. 'No, they didn't take me too,' he said at last, turning to face Meggie again. 'But I saw them drive off with your father. I ran after them, right through the undergrowth, a couple of times I thought I'd break my neck going down that wretched slope, but I got to the gate just in time to see them driving off south. Naturally I recognised them at once. Capricorn had sent his best men. Even Basta was with them.'

Meggie was staring at his lips as if she could make the words come out of them faster. 'Do you know where they've taken Mo?' Her voice shook with impatience.

'To Capricorn's village, I think. But I wanted to be sure,' said Dustfinger, taking off his coat and draping it over the bench, 'so I ran after them. I know it sounds silly to run after a car,' he added, when Meggie frowned in disbelief, 'but I was so furious. It had all been for nothing – me warning you, the three of us coming here . . . Well, I managed to hitch a lift to the next village. They'd filled up the fuel tank there, four men in black, not very friendly. And they hadn't been gone long. So I . . . er . . . borrowed a moped and tried to go on after them. Don't look at me like that – you can set your mind at rest – I took the moped back later. It wasn't particularly fast, but luckily the roads are very, very winding here, and I eventually saw them again far down in the valley, while I was still making my way round the bends above them. Then I was sure they were taking your father to Capricorn's headquarters. Not to one of his hideouts further north, but straight to the lion's den.'

'The lion's den,' Meggie repeated. 'Where is it?'

'About three hundred kilometres south of here, I'd say.' Dustfinger sat down on the bench beside her and blinked as he peered at the sun. 'Not far from the coast.' Once again, he looked at the book still lying on Meggie's lap. 'Capricorn's not going to be pleased when his men bring him the wrong book,' he said. 'I only hope he doesn't take his disappointment out on your father.'

'But Mo didn't know it was the wrong book! Elinor swapped them round in secret.' There they came again, those infuriating tears! Meggie wiped her eyes on her sleeve. Dustfinger wrinkled his brow, looking at her as if he wasn't sure whether to believe her.

'She says she just wanted to look at it! She had it in her bedroom. Mo knew the secret place where she'd hidden it, and because the book they took was wrapped in brown paper he never noticed it was the wrong one! And Capricorn's men didn't check either.'

'Of course not. How could they?' Dustfinger's voice was full of scorn. 'They can't read. One book is much like any other to them, just printed paper. Anyway, they're used to being given anything they want.'

Meggie's voice was shrill with fear. 'You must take me to that village! Please!' She looked pleadingly at Dustfinger. 'I'll explain everything to Capricorn, and give him the book, and then he'll let Mo go. All right?'

Dustfinger blinked up at the sun again. 'Yes, of course,' he said, without looking at Meggie. 'That's probably the only solution . . .'

But before he could say any more they heard Elinor's voice

calling from the house. 'Well, well, what have we here?' she cried, leaning out of her open window. Its pale yellow curtain flapped in the wind as if a ghost were caught in it. 'If it isn't our friend the matchstick-swallower!'

Meggie jumped up and ran over the lawn towards her. 'Elinor, he knows where Mo is!' she cried.

'Does he indeed?' Elinor leaned on the windowsill and scrutinised Dustfinger through narrowed eyes. 'Put that book down!' she snapped at him. 'Meggie, take the book away from him.'

Taken aback, Meggie turned round. Dustfinger really was holding *Inkheart*, but when Meggie looked at him he quickly put it back down on the bench. Then, with a nasty glance in Elinor's direction, he beckoned her over. Hesitantly, Meggie went to him.

'Yes, all right, I'll take you to your father, even though it may be dangerous for me,' whispered Dustfinger when she was beside him. 'But *she* stays here, understand?' He slyly nodded his head in Elinor's direction.

Meggie looked uncertainly at the house.

'Like me to guess what he whispered to you?' called Elinor across the lawn.

Dustfinger cast Meggie a warning glance, but she ignored it. 'He's going to take me to Mo!' she called back.

'A good idea,' called Elinor, 'but I'm coming too. Even if the pair of you might prefer to do without my company!'

'We certainly might!' muttered Dustfinger, smiling guilelessly at Elinor. 'But who knows, perhaps we can swap her for your father? I dare say Capricorn could do with another maidservant. I know she's no good at cooking, but perhaps she can do the laundry – even if that's not something you learn from books.'

Meggie had to laugh – although she couldn't tell from Dustfinger's face if he was joking or meant it seriously.

11

A Coward

Home! That was what they meant, those caressing appeals,
those soft touches wafted through the air, those invisible little hands pulling and tugging, all one way.
                    Kenneth Grahame, *The Wind in the Willows*

Dustfinger did not steal into Meggie's room until he was
quite sure she was asleep. She had locked her door.
Undoubtedly Elinor had persuaded her to do that, because she
didn't trust him and because Meggie had refused to give
Inkheart back to her. Dustfinger couldn't help smiling as he
inserted the thin wire into the lock. What a stupid woman she
was, in spite of all those books she'd read! Did she really think
such an ordinary lock was any obstacle? 'Well, perhaps it
might be for fat fingers like yours, Elinor!' he whispered to
himself as he opened the door. 'But my fingers play with fire,
and it's made them quick and skilful.'

His liking for Silvertongue's daughter was a more serious
obstacle, and his guilty conscience didn't make matters any
easier. Yes, Dustfinger did have a guilty conscience as he crept

into Meggie's room, although he hadn't come to steal the book. Naturally Capricorn still wanted it – the book and Silvertongue's daughter too, those were his new orders. But that must wait. Tonight, Dustfinger was there for a different reason. Tonight, something that had been gnawing at his heart for years drove him to Meggie's room.

He stood thoughtfully beside the bed, looking at the sleeping girl. Betraying her father to Capricorn had not been particularly difficult, but with her it would be different. Her face reminded Dustfinger of another one, although no grief had yet left dark shadows on Meggie's childish features. Strange, every time the girl looked at him he felt a wish to show her that he *didn't* deserve the distrust he always saw in her eyes, even when she was smiling at him. She looked at her father in a very different way – as if he could protect her from all the dark and evil in the world. What a stupid, stupid idea! No one would be able to protect her from that.

Dustfinger stroked the scars on his face and frowned. Enough of such useless thoughts. He would take Capricorn what he wanted: the girl and the book. But not tonight.

Gwin moved on his shoulder, trying to wriggle out of his collar, which he liked as little as he liked the dog's leash Dustfinger always carried with him. He wanted to go hunting, but Dustfinger wasn't letting him out. Last night the marten had run away from him while he was talking to Basta. The furry little devil was still afraid of Basta. Dustfinger couldn't blame him.

Meggie was sleeping soundly, her face buried in a grey sweater, probably her father's. She murmured something in her sleep but Dustfinger couldn't make out what. Once again his guilty conscience stirred, but he pushed the tiresome feeling away. He couldn't do with that kind of thing, not now and not later. The girl was nothing to do with him, and he was quits with her father now. Yes, quits. He had no reason to feel like a miserable double-dealing villain.

He looked round the dark room, in search of something. Where would Meggie put the book? There was a red box beside her bed. Dustfinger lifted the lid. Gwin's chain clinked softly as he leaned forward.

The box was full of books – wonderful books. Dustfinger took out the torch from under his coat and shone it on them. 'Look at that!' he murmured. 'What beauties! Like a party of ladies dressed in their best to go to a prince's ball.' Silvertongue had probably rebound them after Meggie's little fingers had worn out the old bindings. Yes, of course, there was his sign, the unicorn's head. Each book bore it, and each was bound in a different colour. All the hues of the rainbow were gathered together in that box.

The book Dustfinger was looking for was right at the bottom. With its silvery green binding it looked plain, a poor thing among all the other grand and lordly volumes.

It didn't surprise Dustfinger that Silvertongue had given this book such a plain dress to wear. Very likely Meggie's father hated it as much as he loved it. Dustfinger carefully extracted it from the other books. It was almost nine years since he last had it in his hands. At the time it had still had a cardboard binding and a torn paper dust-jacket.

Dustfinger raised his head. Meggie sighed, and moved until her sleeping face was turned his way. How unhappy she looked. She must be having a nightmare. Her lips quivered, and her hands clutched the sweater as if she were looking for something – or someone – to give her security. But you are usually alone in nightmares, dreadfully alone. Dustfinger remembered many of his own bad dreams and, for a moment, he was tempted to put out his hand and wake Meggie. What a soft-hearted fool he was!

He turned his back to the bed. Out of sight, out of mind. Then he opened the book hastily before he could think better of it. His breathing was heavy – as if he had filled his mouth with liquid in preparation for breathing fire. He leafed through the first few pages, and began to read, slowly turning page after page after page. But with every page his fingers hesitated a little longer, until suddenly he closed the book. Moonlight was seeping through the cracks in the shutters. He had no idea how long he had been standing there, his eyes lost in the labyrinth of letters. He had always been a very slow reader . . .

'Coward!' he whispered. 'Oh, what a coward you are, Dustfinger!' He bit his lips until they hurt. 'Come on!' he told himself. 'This may be your last chance, you fool! Once Capricorn has the book he'll never let you look at it again.' Once more, he opened the book, leafed rapidly through to about the middle – and closed it again, with a sound loud enough to make Meggie give a little start in her sleep and bury her head under the covers. Dustfinger waited motionless beside the bed until she was breathing regularly again, then leaned over her treasure chest with a deep sigh and put the book back under the others.

Soundlessly, he closed the lid.

'Did you see that, Gwin?' he whispered to the marten. 'I just dare not look. Wouldn't you rather find a braver master? Think it over.' Gwin chattered softly in his ear, but if that was an answer Dustfinger didn't understand it.

For a moment he went on listening to Meggie's quiet breathing, then stole back to the door. 'Well, what does it matter?' he muttered when he was out in the corridor. 'Who wants to know the end of a story in advance?'

He climbed up to the attic bedroom Elinor had given him and lay down on the narrow bed with the crates of books towering around it. But he could not sleep until morning came.

12

Going Further South

The Road goes ever on and on
Down from the door where it began.
Now far ahead the Road has gone,
And I must follow, if I can,
Pursuing it with weary feet,
Until it joins some larger way
Where many paths and errands meet.
And whither then? I cannot say.

J.R.R. Tolkien
The Lord of the Rings: The Fellowship of the Ring

After breakfast next morning Elinor spread a crumpled road map out on the kitchen table.

'Right, three hundred kilometres south of here,' she said with a wary glance at Dustfinger. 'So show us exactly where we have to look for Meggie's father.'

Meggie looked at Dustfinger, her heart thudding. There were dark shadows round his eyes, as if he had slept very badly. Hesitantly, he came over to the table, rubbing his stubbly chin. He bent over the map, scrutinised it for what seemed an eternity, and finally pointed with his finger.

'There,' he said. 'Capricorn's village is just there.'

Elinor looked over his shoulder. 'Liguria,' she said. 'Aha. And what is the name of this village, if I may ask? Capricornia?' She was examining Dustfinger's face as if tracing his scars with her eyes.

'It doesn't have a name.' Dustfinger responded to her gaze with unconcealed dislike. 'I expect it had one once, but the name was already forgotten before Capricorn settled there. You won't find it on this map, or any other either. To the rest of the world the village is just a collection of tumbledown houses reached along what can hardly be called a road.'

'Hmm.' Elinor bent closer to the map. 'I've never been in that region. I was in Genoa once. I bought a very fine edition of *Alice in Wonderland* there, in good condition and for half what it was worth.' She looked enquiringly at Meggie. 'Do you like *Alice in Wonderland*?'

'Not particularly,' said Meggie, staring at the map. Elinor shook her head at such childish folly, and turned back to Dustfinger.

'What does this Capricorn do when he's not stealing books and abducting people's fathers?' she asked. 'If I understand Meggie correctly, you know him pretty well.'

Dustfinger avoided her eyes and ran his finger along a blue river winding its way through the green and pale brown of the map. 'We come from the same place,' he said. 'But apart from that we don't have much in common.'

Elinor looked at him so penetratingly that Meggie would not have been surprised to see a hole suddenly appear in his forehead. 'There's one thing that strikes me as strange,' she said. 'Meggie's father wanted to keep *Inkheart* safe from this Capricorn. So why bring the book here to me? He was practically running into Capricorn's arms!'

Dustfinger shrugged his shoulders. 'Well, perhaps he just thought your library would be the safest hiding-place.'

A memory stirred in Meggie's mind. At first, she couldn't identify it, but then it all came flooding back to her, perfectly clearly, as vivid as a picture in a book. She saw Dustfinger standing beside their camper van at the gate of the farmhouse, and it was almost as if she heard his voice again . . .

She looked at him in horror. 'You told Mo that Capricorn was in the *north!*' she said. 'He specially asked, and you said you were sure of it.'

Dustfinger examined his fingernails.

'Well, yes . . . yes, that's right,' he admitted, without looking at Meggie or Elinor. He just went on staring at his nails. Finally, he rubbed them on his sweater as if to remove an ugly mark. 'You don't trust me,' he said hoarsely, still without looking at them. 'Neither of you trust me. I— I can understand that, but I wasn't lying. Capricorn has two main headquarters, and several smaller hideouts in case things get too hot for him, or one of his men needs to disappear for a while. He usually spends the summer months in the north and doesn't come south until October, but this year he's obviously spending the summer down in the south. How would I know why? Perhaps he had trouble with the police in the north? Perhaps he has business of some kind in the south and wants to see to it personally?' His voice sounded injured, like the voice of a child unjustly accused. 'In any case, his men drove south with Meggie's father, I saw them go myself, and when Capricorn is in the south he always does anything of importance in that village. He feels safe in it, safer than anywhere else. He's never had any trouble with the police there, he can act like a king, as if the whole world belonged to him. He makes the laws, he decides what happens, he can do or not do anything he likes. His men take care of that. Believe you me, I understand these things.' Dustfinger smiled. It was a bitter smile. It seemed to be saying: if only you knew! But you don't know anything. You don't understand anything.

Meggie felt unease spread through her again. It was not caused by what Dustfinger said, but by what he wasn't saying. Nothing is more frightening than a fear you cannot name.

Elinor seemed to be feeling the same. 'For heaven's sake, don't make such a mystery of it!' she snapped. 'I'm asking you again, what does this Capricorn do? How does he earn his money?'

Dustfinger crossed his arms. 'You won't get any more information out of me. Ask him yourself. Even taking you to his village could cost me dear, so am I going to tell you about Capricorn's business? Not likely!' He shook his head. 'I warned Meggie's father. I advised him to take Capricorn the book of his own free will, but he wouldn't listen. If I hadn't warned him, Capricorn's men would have found him much sooner. Ask Meggie! She was there when I warned him. Right, I didn't tell him everything I knew. So what? I talk about Capricorn as little as possible, I try not even to think of him, and you take my word for it, once you know him you'll feel the same.'

Elinor wrinkled her nose as if such an idea were too ridiculous for her to waste a single word on it. 'So I assume you can't tell me why he's so keen to get hold of this book?' she asked, folding up the road map. 'Is he some kind of collector?'

Dustfinger ran his finger along the edge of the table. 'All I'm going to tell you is that he wants this book. And that's why you'd better give it to him. I once knew his men to stand outside a man's house for four nights running just because Capricorn took a fancy to the man's dog.'

'Did he get the dog?' asked Meggie quietly.

'Of course,' replied Dustfinger, looking at her thoughtfully. 'Believe me, no one sleeps soundly with Capricorn's men standing outside the door looking up at their window – or their children's window. Capricorn usually gets what he wants within a couple of days, maximum.'

'Disgusting!' said Elinor. 'He wouldn't have got *my* dog.'

Dustfinger examined his fingernails again, smiling.

'Stop grinning like that!' snapped Elinor. And, turning to Meggie, she added, 'You'd better pack a few things! We set off within the hour. It's about time you got your father back. Even if I don't like having to leave the book with this Capri-what's-his-name. I hate to see books fall into the wrong hands.'

They were going in Elinor's estate car, although Dustfinger would have preferred to travel in Mo's camper van.

'Nonsense, I've never driven anything like that,' said Elinor, dumping in Dustfinger's arms a cardboard box full of provisions for the journey. 'Anyway, Mortimer's locked the van.'

Meggie saw that Dustfinger had an answer on the tip of his tongue, but chose to keep it to himself. 'Suppose we have to spend the night somewhere?' he asked, carrying the box over to Elinor's car.

'Heavens above, who said anything about that? I intend to

be back here tomorrow morning at the latest. I hate leaving my books on their own for more than a day.'

Dustfinger rolled his eyes up at the sky, as if more sense might be expected there than in Elinor's head, and began clambering into the back seat, but Elinor stopped him. 'No, wait, you'd better drive,' she said, handing him her car keys. 'You're the one who knows where we're going.'

But Dustfinger gave her back the keys. 'I can't drive,' he said. 'It's bad enough sitting in a car, never mind driving it.'

Elinor got behind the steering wheel, shaking her head. 'Well, you're an oddity and no mistake!' she said as Meggie climbed into the passenger seat beside her. 'And I hope you really do know where Meggie's father is, or you'll find out that this Capricorn of yours isn't the only person to be frightened of around here!'

Meggie wound down her window as Elinor started the engine. She looked back at Mo's van. It felt bad leaving it behind here, worse than leaving a house, even this one. Strange as a place might be, the camper van meant that Mo and she always had a bit of home with them. Now that was gone too, and nothing was familiar any more except the clothes in her travelling bag in the boot of the estate car. She had also packed a few things for Mo – and two of her books.

'Interesting choice!' Elinor had commented when she lent Meggie a bag for the books, an old-fashioned one made of dark leather that you could sling over your shoulder. 'These stories about the ill-made knight, and people with hairy feet going on a long journey to dark places. Have you read them both?'

Meggie had nodded. 'Lots of times,' she smiled at Elinor's descriptions, stroking the bindings before she put the books in the bag. She could remember every detail of the day when Mo had rebound them.

'Oh dear, don't look so dismal!' Elinor had said, looking at her with concern. 'You just wait – our journey isn't going to be half as bad as those hairy-footed people's quest. It will be much shorter too.'

Meggie would have been glad to feel as sure of that herself. The book that was the reason for their own journey was in the boot, under the spare tyre. Elinor had put it in a plastic bag. 'Don't let Dustfinger see where it is!' she urged Meggie, before putting it into her hands. 'I still don't trust him.'

But Meggie had decided to trust Dustfinger. She wanted to trust him. She needed to trust him. Who else could lead her to Mo?

Capricorn's Village

> 'But to the last question,' Zelig replied, 'he probably flew to beyond the Dark Regions, where people don't go and cattle don't stray, where the sky is copper, the earth iron, and where the evil forces live under roofs of petrified toadstools and in tunnels abandoned by moles.'
>
> Isaac Bashevis Singer, *Naftali the Storyteller*

The sun was already high in the cloudless sky when they set off. Soon the air was so hot and muggy in Elinor's car that Meggie's T-shirt was sticking to her skin with sweat. Elinor opened her window and passed a bottle of water round. She herself was wearing a knitted jacket buttoned up to her chin, and when Meggie wasn't thinking of Mo or Capricorn she wondered whether Elinor might melt away inside it.

Dustfinger sat on the back seat, so silent that you could almost have forgotten he was there. He had put Gwin on his lap. The marten slept while Dustfinger's hands restlessly stroked his fur, passing over it again and again. Now and then Meggie turned to look at him. He was usually gazing out of the window indifferently, as if he were looking straight through the mountains and trees, houses and rocky slopes passing by outside. His expression seemed perfectly empty, as if he were thinking of something far away, and once, when Meggie glanced round, there was such sadness on his scarred face that she quickly turned to look out of the windscreen ahead of her.

She would have liked to have an animal on her own lap during this long, long journey. Perhaps it would have driven away the dark thoughts that insisted on coming into her mind. Outside, the world was a place of gently unfolding mountains rising higher and higher. Sometimes it seemed as if they would crush the road between their grey and rocky sides. But worse than the mountains were the tunnels. Pictures seemed to lurk in them that not even Gwin's warm body could have kept at bay. They seemed to be hiding there in the darkness, waiting for Meggie: pictures of Mo in some dark, cold place, and of Capricorn . . . Meggie knew it must be Capricorn, although his face was different every time.

She tried reading for a while, but soon noticed that she wasn't taking in a word of what she read, so she gave it up and stared out of the window like Dustfinger. Elinor chose minor roads without much traffic on them. 'Otherwise the driving gets so boring,' she said. It made no difference to Meggie. She just wanted to arrive. She looked impatiently at the mountains, and the houses where other people lived. Sometimes, through the window of a car coming the other way, she caught a glimpse of a stranger's face, and then it was gone, like a book you open then close at once. When they were driving through one village she saw a man by the roadside sticking a plaster on the grazed knee of a tearful little girl. He was stroking her hair comfortingly, and Meggie couldn't help remembering how often Mo had done that for her, how he sometimes chased all round the house, cursing when he couldn't find a plaster in time. The memory brought tears to her eyes.

'Heavens above, it's quieter in here than in a Pharaoh's burial chamber!' said Elinor at some point. (Meggie thought she said 'Heavens above' rather a lot.) 'Couldn't one of you at least say something now and then? "Oh, what a lovely landscape!", for instance, or, "That's a very fine castle!" If you keep as deathly quiet as this I'll be falling asleep at the wheel any minute now.' She still hadn't undone a single button of her knitted jacket.

'I don't see any castle,' muttered Meggie, but it wasn't long before Elinor spotted one. 'Sixteenth century,' she announced as the ruined walls appeared on a mountainside. 'Tragic story. Forbidden love, pursuit, death, grief and pain.' And as they passed between the strong and silent rock walls Elinor told the tale of a battle that had raged in this very place over six hundred years ago. 'To this day, if you dig among the stones you'll still find bones and dented helmets.' She seemed to know a story about every church tower. Some were so unlikely that Meggie wrinkled her brow in disbelief, and Elinor, without taking her eyes off the road, always responded, 'No, really, that's just what happened!' She seemed to be particularly fond of bloodthirsty stories: tales of the beheading of unhappy lovers, or princes walled up alive. 'Yes, everything looks very peaceful now,' she remarked when Meggie turned a little pale at one of these stories. 'But I can tell you there's always a sad story somewhere. Ah, well, times were more exciting a few hundred years ago.'

Meggie didn't know what was so exciting about times when, if Elinor was to be believed, your only choice was between dying of the plague or getting slaughtered by invading soldiers. But Elinor's cheeks glowed pink with excitement at the sight of some burnt-out old castle, and whenever she told tales of the warrior princes and greedy bishops who had once spread terror and death abroad in the very mountains through which they themselves were now driving on modern paved roads, a romantic gleam lit her usually chilly pebble eyes.

'My dear Elinor, you were obviously born into the wrong story,' said Dustfinger at last. These were the first words he had spoken since they set out.

'The wrong story? The wrong period, you mean. Yes, I've often thought so myself.'

'Call it what you like,' said Dustfinger. 'Anyway, you should get on well with Capricorn. He likes the same kinds of stories as you.'

'Is that supposed to be an insult?' asked Elinor, offended. The comparison seemed to trouble her, for after that she kept quiet for almost an hour, which left Meggie with nothing to distract her from her miserable thoughts and the frightening pictures they conjured up for her in every tunnel.

Twilight was beginning to fall when the mountains drew back from the road and the sea suddenly appeared beyond green hills, a sea as wide as another sky. The sinking sun made it glisten like the skin of a beautiful snake. It was a long time since Meggie had seen the sea, and then it had been a cold sea, slate-grey and pale from the wind. This sea looked different, very different.

It warmed Meggie's heart just to see it, but all too often it disappeared behind the tall, ugly buildings covering the narrow strip of land that lay between the water and the encroaching hills. Sometimes, the hills reached all the way down to the sea, and in the light of the setting sun they looked as if they were giant waves that had rolled up on to the land.

As they followed the winding coastal road Elinor began telling stories again: tales of the Romans who, she said, had built the road they were on, and how they feared the savage inhabitants of this narrow strip of land. Meggie was only half listening. Palm trees grew beside the road, their fronds dusty and sharp-edged. Giant agaves flowered among the palms, looking like spiders squatting there with their long spiny leaves. The light behind them turned pink and lemon-yellow as the sun sank further down towards the sea, and dark blue trickled down from the sky like ink flowing into water. It was so beautiful a sight that it almost hurt to look at it. Meggie had thought the place where Capricorn lived would be quite different. Beauty and fear make uneasy companions.

They drove through a small town, past houses as bright as if a child had painted them. They were colour-washed orange and pink, red and yellow. A great many were yellow: pale yellow, brownish yellow, sandy yellow, dirty yellow, and they had green shutters and red-brown roofs. Even the gathering twilight couldn't drain them of their brightness.

'It doesn't seem so very dangerous here,' remarked Meggie, as they drove past another pink house.

'That's because you keeping looking to your left,' said Dustfinger behind her. 'But there's always a light side and a dark side. Look to your right for a change.'

Meggie did as he said. At first she saw nothing but the brightly coloured houses there too. They crowded close to the roadside, leaning against each other as if they were arm in arm. But then the houses were suddenly left behind, and steep hills with the night already settling among their folds lined the road instead. Yes, Dustfinger was right. It looked sinister over there, and the few houses left seemed to be drowning in the gathering dusk.

It quickly grew darker, for night falls fast in the south, and Meggie was glad that Elinor was driving along the well lit coastal road. But all too soon Dustfinger told her to turn off along a minor road leading away from the coast, away from the sea and the brightly coloured houses, and into the dark.

The road wound further and further into the hills, going up and down as the slopes by the roadside grew steeper and steeper. The light of the headlamps fell on gorse, on vines run wild, and olive trees crouching like bent old men beside the road.

Only twice did they meet another vehicle coming towards them. Now and then the lights of a village emerged from the darkness. But the roads along which Dustfinger guided Elinor led away from the lights and deeper and deeper into the night. Several times the beam of the headlights fell on ruined houses, but Elinor didn't know stories about any of them. No princes had lived in those wretched hovels, no red-robed bishops, only farmers and labourers whose stories no one had written down, and now they were lost, buried under wild thyme and fast-growing gorse.

'Are we still going the right way?' asked Elinor in a muted voice, as if the world around her were too quiet for anyone to speak out loud. 'Where on earth do we find a village in this God-forsaken wilderness? We've probably taken at least two wrong turnings already.'

But Dustfinger only shook his head. 'We're going the right way,' he replied. 'Once we're over that hill you'll be able to see the houses.'

'I certainly hope so!' muttered Elinor. 'I can hardly make out the road. Heavens above, I had no idea anywhere in the world was still so dark. Couldn't you have told me what a long way it was? Then I'd have filled up the tank again. I don't even know if we have enough fuel to make it back to the coast.'

'So whose car is this?' Dustfinger snapped back. 'Mine? I told you I don't know the first thing about cars. Now, keep your eyes on the road. We'll be coming to the bridge any moment.'

'Bridge?' Elinor drove round the next bend and suddenly stamped on the brake. Right across the road, lit by two builders' lamps, was a metal barrier. It looked rusty, as if it had stood there for years.

'There!' said Elinor, clapping her hands on the steering wheel. 'We *have* gone the wrong way. I told you so.'

'No, we haven't.' Dustfinger took Gwin off his shoulder and got out of the car. He looked round, listening intently as he approached the barrier, then dragged it over to the side of the road.

Elinor's look of disbelief almost made Meggie laugh out loud. 'Has the man gone right out of his mind?' she whispered. 'He doesn't think I'm going to drive down a closed road in this darkness, does he?'

All the same, she started the engine when Dustfinger impatiently waved her on. As soon as she was past him he pulled the barrier back across the road.

'No need to look at me like that!' he said, climbing back into the car. 'The barrier's always there. Capricorn had it put up to keep unwanted visitors away. Not that people often venture up here. Capricorn spreads stories about the village that keep most of them at a distance, but—'

'What sort of stories?' Meggie interrupted him, although she didn't think she really wanted to know.

'Blood-curdling stories,' said Dustfinger. 'Like most folk, the locals round here are superstitious. The most common tale is that the Devil himself lives on the far side of that hill.'

Meggie was cross with herself for being scared, but now she just couldn't take her eyes off the dark hilltop. 'Mo says human beings invented the Devil,' she said.

'Well, maybe.' Dustfinger's mysterious smile was hovering round his mouth again. 'But you wanted to know about the stories. They say no bullet can kill the men who live in that village, they can walk through walls, they kidnap three boys every month when the moon is new, and Capricorn teaches them to commit theft, arson and murder.'

'Good heavens, who thought all that up? The folk of these parts or this man Capricorn himself?' Elinor was leaning right over the steering wheel. The road was full of potholes, and she had to drive very slowly so as not to get stuck.

'Both.' Dustfinger leaned back and let Gwin nibble his fingers. 'Capricorn rewards people who think up new stories. The one man who never joins in that game is Basta. He's so superstitious himself he even goes out of his way to avoid black cats.'

Basta. Meggie remembered the name, but before she could ask any more questions Dustfinger was speaking again. He seemed to enjoy telling these tales. 'Oh yes, I almost forgot!

Of course everyone living in the village of the damned has the
Evil Eye, even the women.'

'The Evil Eye?' Meggie looked at him.

'That's right. One glance and you fall mortally ill. Three
days after that, at the latest, and you're dead as a doornail.'

'Who'd believe a thing like that?' murmured Meggie, turning to look ahead of her again.

'Idiots would.' Elinor stamped on the brake again. The car
skidded over gravel on the road. The bridge Dustfinger had
mentioned lay ahead, its grey stone pale in the headlights.

'Go on, go on!' said Dustfinger impatiently. 'It'll hold,
though you might not think so.'

'It looks as if the ancient Romans built it,' muttered Elinor.
'But for donkeys, not cars.'

All the same, Elinor drove on. Meggie squeezed her eyes
tight shut, and didn't open them until she could hear the
gravel under the car tyres once more.

'Capricorn likes this bridge a lot,' said Dustfinger quietly.
'A single well-armed man is enough to make it impassable.
But luckily he doesn't post a guard here every night.'

'Dustfinger.' Meggie turned hesitantly to look at him as
Elinor's car laboured up the last hill. 'What are we going to
say when they ask us how we found the village? I mean, it's
not going to be a good idea for Capricorn to know that you
showed us the way, is it?'

'No, you're right,' muttered Dustfinger, avoiding Meggie's
eyes. 'Although we are bringing him the book.' He picked up
Gwin, who was clambering around the back seat, held him so
that he couldn't snap, and then lured him into the rucksack
with a piece of bread. The marten had been restless ever since
darkness fell. He wanted to go hunting.

They had reached the top of the hill. The world around them had disappeared from view, swallowed up by the night, but not far away a few pale rectangles glowed in the dark. Lighted windows.

'There it is,' said Dustfinger. 'Capricorn's village. Or the Devil's village, if you prefer.' He laughed softly.

Elinor turned to him crossly. 'For heaven's sake, will you stop that!' she snapped at him. 'You really seem to like these stories. Who knows, perhaps they're all your own invention, and this Capricorn is just a rather eccentric book collector!'

Dustfinger made no reply, but only looked out of the window with the strange smile that Meggie sometimes wanted to wipe off his face. Yet again it seemed to be saying: how stupid you two are!

Elinor had switched off the engine. The silence surrounding them was so absolute that Meggie hardly dared to breathe. She looked down at the lighted windows. Usually, she thought brightly lit windows were an inviting sight in the dark, but these seemed far more menacing than the darkness all around.

'Does this village have any normal inhabitants?' asked Elinor. 'Harmless old grannies, children, people who don't have anything to do with Capricorn?'

'No. Nobody lives there but Capricorn and his men,' whispered Dustfinger, 'and the women who cook and clean and so on for them.'

'"And so on" . . . oh, wonderful!' Elinor snorted with distaste. 'I like the sound of this Capricorn less and less! Right, let's get this over and done with. I want to go home to my books, proper electric light and a nice cup of coffee.'

'Really? I thought you were longing for a little adventure?'

If Gwin could speak, thought Meggie, he'd do so in

Dustfinger's voice.

'I prefer adventures in the sunlight,' replied Elinor curtly. 'Heavens, how I hate this darkness! Still, if we sit around here until dawn my books will be mildewed before Mortimer can do anything about them. Meggie, go round to the back of the car and fetch that bag. You know the one.'

Meggie nodded, and was just about to open the passenger door when a glaring light blinded her. Someone whose face she couldn't make out was standing beside the driver's door, shining a torch into the car. He tapped it commandingly against the pane.

Elinor jumped in such alarm she hit her knee on the steering wheel, but she quickly pulled herself together. Cursing, she rubbed her hurt leg and opened the window.

'What's the idea?' she snapped at the stranger. 'Do you have to frighten us to death? A person could easily get run over, skulking about in the dark like that.'

By way of answer the stranger pushed the barrel of a shotgun through the open window. 'This is private property!' he said. Meggie thought she recognised the rasping cat's-tongue voice from Elinor's library. 'And a person can very easily get shot trespassing on private property at night.'

'I can explain.' Dustfinger leaned over Elinor's shoulder.

'Well, well, who have we here? If it isn't Dustfinger!' The man withdrew the barrel of his gun. 'Do you *have* to turn up in the middle of the night?'

Elinor turned and cast Dustfinger a glance that was more than suspicious. 'I'd no idea you were on such friendly terms with these people!' she commented. 'You called them devils!'

But Dustfinger was already out of the car. And Meggie didn't like the familiar way the two men were talking. She remembered exactly what Dustfinger had said to her about Capricorn's men. How could he talk to one of them like this? However hard Meggie strained her ears, she couldn't make out what the pair were saying. She caught only one thing. Dustfinger called the stranger Basta.

'I don't like this!' whispered Elinor. 'Look at the pair of them. They're talking to each other as if our matchstick-eating friend can come and go here as he likes!'

'He probably knows they won't hurt him because we're bringing them the book!' Meggie whispered back, never taking her eyes off the two men. The stranger had a couple of dogs with him. German shepherds. They were sniffing Dustfinger's hands and nuzzling him in the ribs, wagging their tails.

'See that?' hissed Elinor. 'Even those dogs treat him as an old friend. Suppose—'

But before she could say any more Basta opened the driver's door. 'Get out, both of you,' he ordered.

Reluctantly, Elinor swung her legs out of the car. Meggie got out too and stood beside her. Her heart was thudding. She had never seen a man with a gun before. Well, on TV she had, but not in real life.

'Look, I don't like your tone!' Elinor informed Basta. 'We've had a strenuous drive, and we only came to this God-forsaken spot to bring your boss or whatever you call him something he's been wanting for a long time. So let's have a little more civility.'

Basta cast her such a scornful glance that Elinor drew in a sharp breath, and Meggie involuntarily squeezed her hand.

'Where did you pick *her* up?' enquired Basta, turning back to Dustfinger, who was standing there looking as unmoved as if none of this had anything at all to do with him.

'She owns that house – you know the one I mean.' Dustfinger had lowered his voice. but Meggie heard him all the same. 'I didn't want to bring her, but she insisted.'

'I can imagine that.' Basta scrutinised Elinor once again, then turned to Meggie. 'So this is Silvertongue's little daughter? Doesn't look much like him.'

'Where's my father?' asked Meggie. 'How is he?' These were the first words she had managed to utter. Her voice was hoarse, as if she hadn't used it for a long time.

'Oh, he's fine,' replied Basta, glancing at Dustfinger. 'Although he's saying so little at the moment that *Leadentongue* would be more like it.'

Meggie bit her lip. 'We've come for him,' she said. Now her voice was high and thin, although she was trying as hard as she could to sound grown-up. 'We have the book, but we won't give it to Capricorn unless he lets my father go.'

Basta turned to Dustfinger again. 'Something about her does remind me of her father after all. See her lips tighten? And that look! Oh yes, anyone can see they're related.' His voice sounded as if he were joking, but there was nothing funny about his face when he looked at Meggie again. It was thin, sharply angular, with close-set eyes. He narrowed them slightly as if he could see better that way. Basta was not a tall man, and his shoulders were almost as narrow as a boy's, but Meggie held her breath when he took a step towards her. She was afraid of him. She had never been so afraid of anyone before, and it wasn't because of the shotgun in his hand. He had an aura of fury about him, of something keen and biting—

'Meggie, get the bag out of the boot.' As Basta was about to grab Meggie, Elinor pushed herself between them. 'There's nothing dangerous in it,' she said crossly. 'Just what we came here to hand over.'

By way of answer, Basta pulled the dogs aside, pulling so harshly on their leashes that they yelped out loud.

'Meggie, listen to me!' whispered Elinor, as they left the car and followed Basta down a steep pathway leading to the lighted windows. 'Don't hand over the book until they let us see your father, understand?'

Meggie nodded, clutching the plastic bag firmly to her chest. How stupid did Elinor think she was? On the other hand, how was she going to hang on to the book if Basta decided to take it away from her? She preferred not to follow this line of thinking through to its conclusion.

It was a hot, sultry night. The sky above the black hills was sprinkled with stars. The path down which Basta was leading them was stony, and so dark that Meggie could hardly see her own feet, but whenever she stumbled there was a hand to catch her. The hand belonged either to Elinor, walking beside her, or to Dustfinger, who was following as silently as if he were her shadow. Gwin was still in his rucksack, and Basta's dogs kept raising their noses and sniffing, as if they had picked up the sharp scent of the marten.

Slowly, they came closer to the lighted windows. Meggie saw old houses of grey, rough-hewn stone, with a pale church tower rising above the rooftops. Many of the houses looked empty as they passed, going down alleys so narrow that Meggie felt they could close in on her. Some of the houses had no roofs, others were little more than a couple of walls partly fallen in. It was dark in Capricorn's village. Only a few lamps were on in the streets, hanging from masonry arches above the alleyways. At last they reached a small square. The church with the tower they had seen from a distance stood on one side of the square, and not far away, divided from it by a narrow passage, there was a large, two-storey house which did not look at all derelict. This square was better lit than the rest of the village, with four lanterns casting menacing shadows on the paving stones. Basta led them straight to the big house, where more light showed behind three windows on the upper floor. Was Mo in there? Meggie listened to herself as if she could find the answer there, but all her heart would tell her was a tale of fear. Fear and grief.

A Mission Accomplished

'The reason there's no use looking,' said Mr Beaver, 'is that we know already where he's gone!' Everyone stared in amazement.

'Don't you understand?' said Mr Beaver. 'He's gone to her, to the White Witch. He has betrayed us all.'

C.S. Lewis, *The Lion, the Witch and the Wardrobe*

Hundreds of times since Dustfinger had first told her about him, Meggie had tried to picture Capricorn's face. She'd thought about it on the way to Elinor's house when Mo was sitting beside her in the van, and in the huge bed there, and finally on the drive here. Hundreds of times? No, she had tried to imagine it thousands of times, drawing on her ideas of all the villains she had ever read about in books: Captain Hook, crooked-nosed and thin; Long John Silver, a false smile always on his lips; Injun Joe, who had haunted so many of her bad dreams with his knife and his greasy black hair . . .

But Capricorn looked quite different.

Meggie soon gave up counting the doors they passed before

Basta finally stopped outside one. But she did count the black-clad men. Four of them were standing in the corridors, looking bored. Each man had a shotgun propped against the whitewashed wall beside him. Dustfinger had been right: in their close-fitting black suits they really did look like rooks. Only Basta wore a snow-white shirt, just as Dustfinger had said, with a red flower in the buttonhole of his jacket, a red flower like a warning.

Capricorn's dressing gown was red too. He was seated in an armchair when Basta entered the room with the three new arrivals, and a woman was kneeling in front of him cutting his toenails. The chair seemed too small for him. Capricorn was a tall man, and gaunt, as if the skin had been stretched too tight over his bones. His skin was pale as parchment, his hair cut short and bristly. Meggie couldn't have said if it was grey or very fair.

He raised his head when Basta opened the door. His eyes were almost as pale as the rest of him, as if the colour had drained out of them, but bright as silver coins. The woman at his feet glanced up when they came in, then bent over to resume her work.

'Excuse me, but the visitors we were expecting have arrived,' said Basta. 'I thought you might want to speak to them at once.'

Capricorn leaned back in his chair and cast a brief glance at Dustfinger. Then his expressionless eyes moved to Meggie. She was clutching the plastic bag containing the book to her chest, her arms firmly wrapped around it. Capricorn stared at the bag as if he knew what was in it. He made a sign to the woman at his feet. Reluctantly, she straightened up, smoothed down her black dress, and glared at Elinor and Meggie. She looked like an old magpie, with her grey hair scraped back and a pointed nose that didn't seem to fit her small, wrinkled face. Nodding to Capricorn, she left the room.

It was a large room, only sparsely furnished: a long table with eight chairs, a cupboard and a heavy sideboard. There were no lamps in the room, only candles, dozens of them in heavy silver candlesticks. It seemed to Meggie that they filled the room with shadows rather than light.

'Where is it?' asked Capricorn. When he scraped back his chair Meggie flinched involuntarily. 'Don't tell me you've only brought the girl this time.' His voice was more impressive than his face. It was dark and heavy, and the moment she heard him speak Meggie hated it.

'She's got it with her. In that bag,' replied Dustfinger before Meggie could say so herself. His eyes wandered restlessly from candle to candle as he spoke, as if only their dancing flames interested him. 'Her father really didn't know he had the wrong book. This woman who says she's a friend of his,' added Dustfinger, pointing to Elinor, 'changed the books round without telling him. She's a real bookworm. I think she lives on print. Her whole house is full of books – looks as if she likes them better than human company.' The words came spilling out of Dustfinger's mouth as if he wanted to be rid of them. 'I didn't like her from the first, but you know our friend Silvertongue. He always thinks the best of everyone. He'd trust the Devil himself if Old Nick gave him a friendly smile.'

Meggie looked at Elinor. She was standing there as if tongue-tied. Anyone could see she had a guilty conscience.

Capricorn merely nodded at Dustfinger's explanations. He tightened the belt of his dressing gown, clasped his hands behind his back, and came slowly over to Meggie. She did her best not to flinch, to look firmly and undaunted into those colourless eyes, but fear constricted her throat. What a coward she was after all! She tried to think of some hero out of one of her books, someone whose skin she could slip into, to make her feel stronger, bigger, braver. Why could she remember nothing but stories of frightened people when Capricorn looked at her? She usually found it so easy to escape somewhere else, to get right inside the minds of people and animals who existed only on paper, so why not now? Because she was afraid. 'Because fear kills everything,' Mo had once told her. 'Your mind, your heart, your imagination.'

Mo . . . where was he? Meggie bit her lip to stop herself shaking, but she knew the fear showed in her eyes, and she knew that Capricorn saw it. She wished she had a heart of ice and a clever smile, not the trembling lips of a child whose father had been stolen away.

Now Capricorn was very close to her. He scrutinised her. No one had ever looked at her like that. She felt like a fly stuck to a flypaper just waiting to die.

'How old is she?' Capricorn looked at Dustfinger as if he didn't trust Meggie to know the answer herself.

'Twelve!' she said in a loud voice. It wasn't easy to speak with her lips quivering so hard. 'I'm twelve. And I want to know where my father is.'

Capricorn acted as if he hadn't heard the last sentence. 'Twelve?' he repeated in the dark voice that weighed so heavily on Meggie's ears, 'Three or four more years and she'll be a pretty little thing, useful to have around the place. We'll have to feed her up a bit, though.' He felt her arm with his long fingers. He wore gold rings on them, three on each hand. Meggie tried to pull away, but Capricorn was gripping her tightly as his pale eyes examined her. Just as he might have looked at a fish. A poor little fish wriggling on a hook.

'Let the girl go!' For the first time Meggie was glad Elinor's voice could sound so sharp. And Capricorn actually did let go of her arm.

Elinor stepped up behind Meggie and put her hands protectively on her shoulders. 'I don't know what's going on here,' she snapped at Capricorn. 'I don't know who you are, or what you and all these men with guns are doing in this God-forsaken village, and I don't want to know either. I'm here to see that this girl gets her father back. We'll leave you the book you're so keen to have – although that's enough to give me heart-ache, but you'll get it as soon as Meggie's father is safe in my car. And if for any reason he wants to stay here we'd like to hear it from his own lips.'

Capricorn turned his back to her without a word. 'Why did you bring this woman?' he asked Dustfinger. 'Bring the girl and the book, I said. Why would I want the woman?'

Meggie looked at Dustfinger.

The girl and the book. The words kept repeating inside her head, like an echo. *The girl and the book, I said.* Meggie tried to look Dustfinger in the eye, but he avoided her gaze as if it would burn him. It hurt to feel so stupid. So terribly, terribly stupid.

Dustfinger perched on the edge of the table and pinched out one of the candles, gently and slowly as if waiting for the pain, the sharp little stab of the candle flame. 'I've told Basta already: our dear friend Elinor couldn't be persuaded to stay behind,' he said. 'She didn't want to let the girl go with me alone, and she was very reluctant to give up the book.'

'And wasn't I right?' Elinor's voice rose to such a pitch that

Meggie jumped. 'Listen to him, Meggie, listen to that fork-tongued matchstick-eater! I ought to have called the police when he turned up again. He came back for the book; that was the only reason.'

And for me, thought Meggie. The girl and the book.

Dustfinger pretended to be preoccupied with pulling a loose thread from his coat-sleeve. But his hands, usually so skilful, were shaking.

'And as for you!' said Elinor, jabbing Capricorn in the chest with her forefinger. Basta took a step forward, but Capricorn waved him away. 'I've had a lot of experience with books. I myself have had a number of books stolen from me, and I can't claim that all the books on my shelves got there exactly as they should have done – perhaps you know the saying that all book collectors are vultures and hunters? But you really seem to be the craziest of us all. I'm surprised I've never heard of you before. Where's your collection?' She looked enquiringly round the big room. 'I don't see a single book.'

Capricorn put his hands in his dressing-gown pockets and signed to Basta. Before Meggie knew what was happening, Basta had snatched the plastic bag from her hands. He opened it, peered inside suspiciously as if he thought it could contain a snake or something else that might bite, then reached in and brought out the book.

Capricorn took it from him. Meggie couldn't see on his face any of the tenderness with which Elinor and Mo looked at books. No, there was nothing but dislike on Capricorn's face – dislike and relief. That was all.

'These two know nothing?' Capricorn opened the book, leafed through it, then closed it again. It was the right book. Meggie could tell from his face. It was exactly the book he had been looking for.

'No, they know nothing. Even the girl doesn't know.' Dustfinger was looking out of the window very intently, as if there were more to be seen there than the pitch dark. 'Her father hasn't told her, so why should I?'

Capricorn nodded. 'Take these two round behind the house,' he told Basta, who was still standing there holding the empty bag.

'What do you mean?' Elinor began, but Basta was already hauling her and Meggie away.

'It means we're going to shut you two pretty birds in one of our cages overnight,' said Basta, prodding them roughly in the back with his shotgun.

'Where's my father?' shouted Meggie. Her own voice was shrill in her ears. 'You've got the book now! What more do you want of him?'

Capricorn strolled over to the candle that Dustfinger had pinched out, passed his forefinger over the wick and looked at the soot on his fingertip. 'What do I want of your father?' he said, without turning to look at Meggie. 'I want to keep him here, what else? You don't seem to know about his extraordinary talent. Up to now he's been unwilling to use it in my service, hard as Basta has tried to persuade him. But now Dustfinger has brought you here he'll do anything I want. I'm confident of that.'

Meggie tried to push Basta's hands away when he reached for her, but he took her by the back of the head like a chicken whose neck he was going to wring. Elinor tried coming to her aid, but he casually pointed the shotgun at her chest and forced Meggie over to the door.

When Meggie turned round again she saw Dustfinger still

leaning against the big table. He was watching her, but this time he wasn't smiling. Forgive me, his eyes seemed to say. I had to do it. I can explain everything! But Meggie didn't want to know, and she certainly wasn't about to forgive him. 'I hope you drop dead!' she screamed as Basta hauled her out of the room. 'I hope you burn to death! I hope you suffocate in your own smoke!'

Basta laughed as he closed the door. 'Just listen to this little wildcat!' he said. 'I think I'll have to watch my step with you around!'

137

15

Good Luck and Bad Luck

It was the middle of the night, and Bingo couldn't sleep. The ground was hard, but he was used to that . . . His blanket was dirty and smelled disgusting, but he was used to that too. A tune kept going through his head, and he couldn't get it out of his mind. It was the Wendels' victory song.
Michael de Larrabeiti, *The Borribles Go for Broke*

The cages, as Basta had called them, kept ready by Capricorn for unwelcome guests were behind the church, in a paved area where rubbish containers stood next to mountains of building rubble. There was a slight smell of petrol in the air, and even the glow-worms whirling aimlessly through the night didn't seem to know what had brought them to this place. A row of tumbledown houses stood behind the bins and the rubble. The windows were just holes in the grey walls, and a couple of rotten shutters hung from their hinges at such an angle they looked as if a sudden gust of wind would blow them right off. Only the doors on the ground floor had obviously been given a fresh coat of paint fairly recently, in a dull brown shade with numbers painted on them clumsily, as if by a child, one for each door. As far as Meggie could see in the dark the last door had a number 7 on it. Basta propelled her and Elinor towards number 4. For a moment Meggie was relieved that he hadn't really meant a cage, although the door in the blank wall looked anything but inviting.

'This is ridiculous!' said Elinor furiously, as Basta unlocked and unbolted the door. He had brought reinforcements with him from the house in the form of a skinny lad who wore the same black uniform as the grown men in Capricorn's village, and who obviously liked to menace Elinor by pointing his gun at her whenever she opened her mouth. But that didn't keep her quiet for long.

'What do you think you're playing at?' she said angrily, without taking her eyes off the muzzle of the gun. 'I've heard that these mountains were always a paradise for robbers, but for heaven's sake, we're living in the twenty-first century! These days people don't go pushing visitors around at gunpoint – certainly not a youngster like him.'

'As far as I'm aware people in this fine century of yours still do exactly as they always did,' replied Basta. 'And that youngster is just the right age to be apprenticed to us. I was even younger when I joined.' He pushed the door open. The darkness inside was blacker than night itself. Basta shoved first Meggie, then Elinor in, and slammed the door behind them.

Meggie heard the key turn in the lock, then Basta saying something which made the boy laugh, and the sound of their footsteps retreating. She reached her hands out until her fingertips touched a wall. Her eyes were useless; she might as well have been blind, she couldn't even see where Elinor was. But she heard her muttering, letting off steam somewhere over to her left.

'Isn't there at least a bloody light switch somewhere in this hole? Oh, to hell with it, I feel as if I've fallen into some far-fetched adventure story where the villains wear black eye-patches and throw knives. Damn, damn, damn!' Meggie had already noticed that Elinor swore a lot, and the more upset she was the worse her language became.

'Elinor?' The voice came from somewhere in the darkness, and that one word expressed delight, horror and surprise.

Meggie spun round so suddenly she almost fell over her own feet. 'Mo?'

'Oh no! Meggie, not you too! How did you get here?'

'Mo!' Meggie stumbled through the darkness towards Mo's voice. A hand took her arm and fingers felt her face.

'Ah, at last!' A naked electric light bulb hanging from the ceiling came on, and Elinor, looking pleased with herself, took her finger off a dusty switch. 'Electric light is a wonderful invention!' she said. 'That at least is an improvement on past centuries, don't you agree?'

'What are you two doing here, Elinor?' demanded Mo, holding Meggie very close. 'I trusted you to look after her at least as well as your books! How could you let them bring her here?'

'How could I *let* them?' Elinor's indignant voice almost cracked. 'I never asked to baby-sit your daughter! I know how to look after books, but children are something else, dammit! And she was worried about you – wanted to go looking for you. So what does stupid Elinor do instead of staying comfortably at home? I mean, I couldn't let the child go off on her own, I told myself. And what do I get for my noble conduct? Insults, a gun held to my chest, and now I'm here in this hole with you carrying on at me too!'

'All right, all right!' Mo held Meggie at arm's length and

looked her up and down.

'I'm fine, Mo!' said Meggie, although her voice shook just a little. 'Honestly.'

Mo nodded and glanced at Elinor. 'You brought Capricorn the book?'

'Of course! You'd have given it to him yourself if I hadn't . . .' said Elinor, going red and looking down at her dusty shoes.

'If you hadn't swapped them round,' Meggie ended her sentence for her. She reached for Mo's hand and held it very tightly. She couldn't believe he was back with her, apparently perfectly all right except for the scratch on his forehead, almost hidden by his dark hair. 'Did they hit you?' She felt the dried blood anxiously with her forefinger.

Mo had to smile, although he couldn't have been feeling much like it. 'That's nothing. I'm fine too. Don't worry.'

Meggie didn't think that was really much of an answer, but she asked no more questions.

'So how did you come here?' asked Mo. 'Did Capricorn send his men back again?'

Elinor shook her head. 'No need for that,' she said bitterly. 'Your slimy-tongued friend fixed it. A nice kind of snake you brought to my house, I must say. First he gives you away, then he serves up the book and your daughter to this man Capricorn. "Bring the girl and the book." We heard Capricorn say so himself. That was our little matchstick-eater's mission, and he carried it out to his master's complete satisfaction.'

Meggie put Mo's arm round her shoulders and buried her face against him.

'The girl and the book?' Mo held Meggie close again. 'Of course. Now Capricorn can be sure I'll do what he wants.' He turned round and went over to the pile of straw lying on the floor in a corner of the room. Sighing, he sat down on it, leaned his back against the wall, and closed his eyes for a moment. 'Well, now we're quits, Dustfinger and I,' he said. 'Although I wonder how Capricorn is going to pay him for his treachery. Because what Dustfinger wants is something Capricorn can't give him.'

'Quits? What do you mean?' Meggie sat down beside him. 'And what are *you* supposed to do for Capricorn? What does he want you for, Mo?' The straw was damp, not a good place to sleep, but still better than the bare stone floor.

Mo said nothing for what seemed an eternity. He stared at the bare walls, the locked door, the dirty floor.

'I think it's time I told you the whole story,' he said at last. 'Although I would rather not have had to tell you in a grim place like this, and not until you're a little older.'

'Mo, I'm twelve!' Why do grown-ups think it's easier for children to bear secrets than the truth? Don't they know about the horror stories we imagine to explain the secrets?

'Sit down, Elinor,' said Mo, making space. 'It's quite a long story.'

Elinor sighed, and sat down unceremoniously on the damp straw. 'This can't be happening!' she murmured. 'This really *can't* be happening!'

'That's what I thought for nine years, Elinor,' said Mo. And then he began his story.

16

Once Upon a Time

He held up the book then. 'I'm reading it to you for relax.'

'Has it got any sports in it?'

'Fencing. Fighting. Torture. Poison. True love. Hate. Revenge. Giants. Hunters. Bad men. Good men. Beautifulest ladies. Snakes. Spiders . . . Pain. Death. Brave men. Cowardly men. Strongest men. Chases. Escapes. Lies. Truths. Passion. Miracles.'

'Sounds okay,' I said, and I kind of closed my eyes.

William Goldman, *The Princess Bride*

'You were just three years old, Meggie,' Mo began. 'I remember how we celebrated your birthday. We gave you a picture book – you know, the one about the sea-serpent with toothache winding itself round the lighthouse . . .'

Meggie nodded. It was still in her book-box – Mo had twice given it a new dress. '*We?*' she asked.

'Your mother and I . . .' Mo picked some straw off his trousers. 'I could never pass by a bookshop. The house where we lived was very small – we called it our shoebox, our mousehole, we had all sorts of names for it – and that very day I'd bought yet another crate full of books from a second-hand bookseller. Elinor would have liked some of them,' he added, glancing at her and smiling. 'Capricorn's book was there too.'

'You mean it belonged to him?' Meggie looked at Mo in surprise, but he shook his head.

'No, but . . . well, let's take it all in order. Your mother sighed when she saw all those new books and asked where we were going to put them, but then of course she helped me to unpack the crate. I always used to read aloud to her in the evenings—'

'You? *You* read aloud?'

'Yes, every evening. Your mother enjoyed it. That evening she chose *Inkheart*. She always did like tales of adventure – stories full of brightness and darkness. She could tell you the names of all King Arthur's knights, and she knew everything about Beowulf and Grendel, the ancient gods and the not-quite-so ancient heroes. She liked pirate stories too, but most of all she loved books which had at least a knight or a dragon or a fairy in them. She was always on the dragon's side, by the way. There didn't seem to be any of them in *Inkheart*, but there was any amount of brightness and darkness, fairies and brownies. Your mother liked brownies as well: hobgoblins, bugaboos, the Fenoderee, the *folletti* with their butterfly wings, she knew them all. So we gave you a pile of picture books, sat down on the rug beside you, and I began to read.'

Meggie leaned her head against Mo's shoulder and stared at the blank wall. She saw herself against its dirty white background as she had looked in old photos: small, with plump legs, very fair hair (it had darkened a little since then), her little fingers turning the pages of big picture books.

'We enjoyed the story,' her father went on. 'It was exciting, well written, and full of all sorts of amazing creatures. Your mother loved a book to lead her into an unknown land, and the world into which *Inkheart* led her was exactly what she liked. Sometimes the story took a very dark turn, and whenever the suspense got too much, your mother put a finger to her lips, and I read more quietly, although we were sure you were too busy with your own books to listen to a sinister story which you wouldn't have understood anyway. I remember it as if it were yesterday; night had fallen long ago. It was autumn, with draughts coming in through the windows. We had lit a fire – there was no central heating in our shoebox of a house, but it had a stove in every room – and I began reading the seventh chapter. That's when it happened—'

Mo stopped. He stared ahead of him as if lost in his own thoughts.

'What?' whispered Meggie. 'What happened, Mo?'

Her father looked at her. 'They came out,' he said. 'There they were, all of a sudden, standing in the doorway to the corridor outside the room, as if they'd just come in from out of doors. There was a crackling noise when they turned to us – like someone slowly unfolding a piece of paper. I still had their names on my lips: Basta, Dustfinger, Capricorn. Basta was holding Dustfinger by the collar, as if he were shaking a puppy for doing something forbidden. Capricorn liked to wear red even then, but he was nine years younger and not quite as gaunt as he is today. He wore a sword, something I'd never seen at close quarters before. Basta had one hanging from his belt too, while Dustfinger . . .' Here Mo shook his head. 'Well, of course the poor fellow had nothing but the horned marten whose tricks earned him a living. I don't think any of the three of them realised what had happened. Indeed, I didn't understand it myself until much later. My voice had brought them slipping out of their story like a bookmark forgotten by some reader between the pages. How could they understand what had happened? Basta pushed Dustfinger away so roughly that he fell down, then he tried to draw his sword, but his hands were white as paper and they obviously didn't yet have the strength for it. The sword slipped from his fingers and fell on the rug. Its blade looked as if there were dried blood on it, but perhaps it was only the reflection of the fire. Capricorn stood there, looking round. He seemed dizzy; he was staggering on the spot like a dancing bear that has been made to turn round too often. And that may well have saved us, or so Dustfinger has always claimed. If Basta and his master had been in full command of their powers, they'd probably have killed us outright, but they hadn't fully arrived in this world yet, and I picked up the terrible sword lying on the rug among my books. It was heavy, much heavier than I'd expected. I must have looked absolutely ridiculous holding the thing. I probably clutched it like a vacuum cleaner or a walking stick, but when Capricorn staggered towards me and I held the blade between us he stopped. I stammered something, tried to explain what had happened, not that I understood it myself, but Capricorn just stared at me with those pale eyes, the colour of water; while Basta stood beside him with a hand on the hilt of his dagger. He seemed to be waiting for his master to tell him to cut all our throats.'

'And what about Dustfinger?' Elinor's voice sounded hoarse too.

'He was still where he'd fallen on the rug, sitting there as if paralysed, not making a sound. I didn't stop to think about

Dustfinger. If you open a basket and see two snakes and a lizard crawl out, you're going to deal with the snakes first, right?'

'What about my mother?' Meggie could only whisper. She wasn't used to saying that word.

Mo looked at her. 'I couldn't see her anywhere. You were still kneeling among your books, staring wide-eyed at the strange men standing there with their heavy boots and their weapons. I was terrified for you, but to my relief both Basta and Capricorn ignored you. "That's enough talk," Capricorn said finally, as I became more and more entangled in my own words. "Never mind how we arrived in this miserable place, just send us back at once, you accursed magician, or Basta here will cut the talkative tongue out of your mouth." Which didn't sound exactly reassuring, and I'd read enough about those two in the first chapters of the book to know that Capricorn meant what he said. I was wondering so desperately how to end the nightmare that I felt quite dizzy. I picked up the book. Perhaps if I read the same passage again, I thought . . . I tried. I stumbled over the words while Capricorn glared at me and Basta drew the knife from his belt. Nothing happened. The two of them just stood there in my house, showing no sign of going back into their story. And suddenly I knew for certain that they meant to kill us. I put down the fatal book and picked up the sword I'd dropped on the rug. Basta tried to get to it before me, but I moved faster. I had to hold the wretched thing with both hands; I still remember how cold the hilt felt. Don't ask me how I did it, but I managed to drive Basta and Capricorn out into the passage. There were several breakages because I was brandishing the sword so clumsily. You began to cry, and I wanted to turn

round and tell you it was all just a bad dream, but I was fully
occupied keeping Basta's knife away from me with Capricorn's
sword. So it's happened, I kept thinking, you're in the middle
of a story exactly as you've always wanted, and it's horrible.
Fear tastes quite different when you're not just reading about
it, Meggie, and playing hero wasn't half as much fun as I'd
expected. The two of them would certainly have killed me if
they hadn't still been rather weak at the knees. Capricorn
cursed me, his eyes almost bursting out of his head with fury.
Basta swore and threatened, giving me a nasty cut on my
upper arm, but then, suddenly, the front door was thrown
open and they both disappeared into the night, still reeling like
drunks. My hands were trembling so much I could scarcely
manage to bolt the door. I leaned against it and listened for
sounds outside, but all I heard was my own racing heart. Then
I heard you crying in the living room, and remembered that
there had been a third man. I staggered back, still holding the
sword, and there stood Dustfinger in the middle of the room.
He had no weapon, just the marten sitting on his shoulders.
He flinched, face white as a sheet, when I came towards him.
I must have been a terrible sight with the blood running down
my arm, and I was shaking all over, whether from fear or
anger I couldn't have said. "Please," he kept whispering,
"don't kill me! I'm nothing to do with those two. I'm only a
juggler, just a harmless fire-eater. I can show you." And I
said, "Yes, yes, all right, I know who you are, you're
Dustfinger – I even know your name, you see." At which he
cowered in awe before me – a magician, he thought, who
seemed to know all about him and who had plucked him out
of his world as easily as picking an apple off a tree. The
marten scampered along his arm, jumped down on the carpet

and ran towards you. You stopped crying and put out your hand. "Careful, he bites," said Dustfinger, shooing him away from you. I took no notice. I suddenly realised how quiet the room was, that was all. How quiet and how empty. I saw the book lying open on the carpet where I had dropped it, and I saw the cushion where your mother had been sitting. And she wasn't there. Where was she? I called her name again and again, I ran from room to room. But she had gone.'

Elinor was sitting bolt upright, staring at him in horror. 'For heaven's sake, Mortimer, what are you saying?' she cried. 'You told me she went away on some stupid adventure holiday and never came back!'

Mo leaned his head against the wall. 'I had to think up something, Elinor,' he said. 'I mean, I could hardly tell the truth, could I?'

Meggie stroked his arm where his shirt hid the long, pale scar. 'You always told me you'd cut your arm climbing through a broken window.'

'Yes, I know. The truth would have sounded too crazy, don't you think?'

Meggie nodded. He was right; she would just have thought it was another of his stories. 'So she never came back?' she whispered, although she knew the answer already.

'No,' replied Mo softly. 'Basta, Capricorn and Dustfinger came out of the book and she went into it, along with our two cats who were curled up on her lap as usual while I read aloud. I expect some creature from here changed places with Gwin too, maybe a spider or a fly or a bird that happened to be flying round the house. Oh, I don't know . . .' Mo fell silent.

Sometimes, when he had made up such a good story that Meggie thought it was true, he would suddenly smile and say,

'You fell for that one, Meggie!' Like the time on her seventh birthday when he told her he'd seen fairies among the crocuses in the garden. But the smile didn't come this time.

'I searched the whole house for your mother. No sign of her,' he went on, 'and when I came back to the living room, Dustfinger had vanished and so had his friend with the horns. But the sword was still there, and it felt so real that I decided not to doubt my sanity. I put you to bed – I think I told you your mother had already gone to sleep – and then I began reading *Inkheart* out loud again. I read the whole damn book until I was hoarse and the sun was rising, but nothing came out of it except a bat and a silken cloak, which I used later to line your book-box. I tried again and again during the days and nights that followed, until my eyes were burning and the letters danced drunkenly on the page. I didn't eat, I didn't sleep, I kept making up different stories for you to explain where your mother was, and I took good care you were never in the room with me when I was reading aloud, in case you disappeared too. I wasn't worried about myself. Oddly enough, I had a feeling that the person reading the book ran no risk of slipping into its pages. I still don't know whether I was right.' Mo flicked a midge off his hand. 'I read until I couldn't hear my own voice any more,' he went on, 'but your mother didn't come back, Meggie. Instead, a strange little man as transparent as if he were made of glass appeared in my living room on the fifth day, and the postman disappeared just as he was putting the mail into our letterbox. I found his bike out in the yard. After that I knew that neither walls nor locked doors would keep you safe – you or anybody else. So I decided never to read aloud from a book again. Not from *Inkheart* or from any other book.'

'What happened to the little glass man?' asked Meggie.

Mo sighed. 'He broke into pieces only a few days later when a heavy truck drove past the house. Obviously, very few creatures move easily from one world to another. We both know what fun it can be to get right into a book and live there for a while, but falling out of a story and suddenly finding yourself in this world doesn't seem to be much fun at all. It broke Dustfinger's heart.'

'Oh, he has a heart, does he?' enquired Elinor bitterly.

'It would be better for him if he didn't,' replied Mo. 'More than a week passed before he was back at my door again. It was night, of course. He prefers night to day. I was just packing. I'd decided it was safer to leave, since I didn't want to be driving Basta and Capricorn out of my house at sword-point again. Dustfinger's reappearance showed that I was right to feel anxious. It was well after midnight when he turned up, but I couldn't sleep anyway.' Mo stroked Meggie's hair. 'You weren't sleeping well then either. You had bad dreams, however much I tried to keep them away with my stories. I was just packing the tools in my workshop when there was a knock on the front door, a very soft, almost furtive knock. Dustfinger emerged from the dark as suddenly as he did when he came to our house four days ago – heavens, was it really only four days? Well, when he came back that first time he looked as if it had been too long since he'd eaten. He was thin as a stray cat and his eyes were dull. "Send me back," he begged, "send me back! This world will be the death of me. It's too fast, too crowded, too noisy. If I don't die of homesickness I shall starve to death. I don't know how to make a living. I don't know anything. I'm like a fish out of water," he said. And he refused to believe that I couldn't do it. He wanted to see the book and try for himself, even though he could scarcely read, but there was no way I could let him have it. It would have been like giving away the very last part I still had of your mother. Luckily, I'd hidden it well. I let Dustfinger sleep on the sofa, and came down next morning to find him still searching the bookshelves. Over the next few years he kept on turning up, following us wherever we went, until I got sick and tired of it and made off with you in secret like a thief in the night. After that I saw no more of him for five years. Until four days ago.'

Meggie looked at him. 'You still feel sorry for him,' she said.

Mo was silent. At last, he said, 'Sometimes.'

Elinor's comment on that was a snort of contempt. 'You're even crazier than I thought,' she said. 'It's that idiot's fault we're in this hole, it's his fault if they cut our throats, and you still feel sorry for *him*?'

Mo shrugged his shoulders and looked up at the ceiling, where a few moths were fluttering around the naked light bulb. 'No doubt Capricorn has promised to take him back,' he said. 'Unlike me, he realised that Dustfinger would do anything in return for such a promise. All he wants is to go back to his own world. He doesn't even stop to ask if his story there has a happy ending!'

'Well, that's no different from real life,' remarked Elinor gloomily. 'You never know if things will turn out well. Just now our own story looks like coming to a bad end.'

Meggie sat with her arms clasped round her legs, her chin on her knees, staring at the dirty white walls. In her mind's eye she saw the 'N' in front of her, the 'N' with the horned marten sitting on it, and felt as if her mother were looking out from beyond the big capital letter, her mother as she was in the faded photograph under Mo's pillow. So she hadn't run away after all. Did she like it in that other world? Did she still remember her daughter? Or were Meggie and Mo just a fading picture for her too? Did she long to be back in her own world, just as Dustfinger did?

And did Capricorn long to be back in his own world as well? Was that what he wanted – for Mo to read him back again? What would happen when Capricorn realised that Mo simply couldn't do it? Meggie shuddered.

'It seems Capricorn has someone else to read aloud to him now,' Mo went on, as if he had guessed her thoughts. 'Basta told me about the man, probably to show me I'm not by any means indispensable. Apparently he's read several useful assistants for Capricorn out of a book already.'

'Oh yes? Then why does he want you?' Elinor sat up, rubbing her behind and groaning. 'I don't understand any of this. I just hope it's all a bad dream, the kind you wake up from with a stiff neck and a bad taste in your mouth.'

Meggie doubted whether Elinor really had any such hope. The damp straw felt too real, and so did the cold wall behind them. She leaned against Mo's shoulder again and closed her eyes. She was very sorry she had scarcely read a line of *Inkheart*. She knew nothing at all about the story into which her mother had disappeared. All she knew was Mo's *other* stories, about the fabulous exploits that had kept her mother away, tales of the adventures she was having in distant lands, of fearsome enemies who kept preventing her from coming home, and of a box she was filling for Meggie, putting something new and wonderful in it at every enchanted place she visited.

'Mo,' she asked, 'do you think she likes being in that story?'

It took Mo quite a long time to answer. 'She'd certainly like the fairies,' he said at last, 'although they're deceitful little things. And if I know her she'll be putting out bowls of milk for the brownies. Yes, I think she'd like that part of it . . .'

'So . . . so what wouldn't she like?' Meggie looked at him anxiously.

Mo hesitated. 'The evil in it,' he finally said. 'So many bad things happen in that book, and she never found out that it all ends reasonably well – after all, I never finished reading her the whole story. That's what she wouldn't like.'

'No, of course not,' said Elinor. 'But how do you know the story hasn't changed anyway? After you read Capricorn and his friend out of it. And now we're lumbered with them here.'

'Yes,' said Mo, 'but they're still in the book too. Believe me, I've read it often enough since they came out of it, and the story's still about them: Dustfinger, Basta and Capricorn. Doesn't that mean everything is still the way it was? Capricorn is still there, and we're only up against a shadow of him in this world.'

'He's pretty frightening for a shadow,' said Elinor.

'Yes, you're right,' agreed Mo. 'Perhaps things have changed there after all. Perhaps there's another, much larger story behind the printed one, a story that changes just as our own world does. And the letters on the page tell us only as much as we'd see peering through a keyhole. Perhaps the story in the book is just the lid on a pan; it always stays the same, but underneath there's a whole world that goes on developing and changing like our own.'

Elinor groaned. 'For heaven's sake, Mortimer!' she said.

'Stop it, do. You're giving me a headache.'

'It made my own head feel like bursting when I tried to make sense of it all,' replied Mo gloomily.

After that they said nothing for quite a long time, all three of them absorbed in their own thoughts. Elinor was the first to speak again, although it sounded almost as if she were talking to herself. 'Heavens above,' she murmured, taking off her shoes. 'To think of all the times I've wished I could slip right into one of my favourite books. But that's the advantage of reading – you can shut the book whenever you want.'

Groaning, she wriggled her toes and began walking up and down. Meggie had to suppress a giggle. Elinor looked so funny hobbling from the wall to the door and back again with her aching feet, back and forth like a clockwork toy.

'Elinor, you're driving me bonkers! Do sit down again,' said Mo.

'No, I won't!' she snapped back. 'I'll go mad myself if I stay sitting down.'

Mo made a face and put his arm round Meggie's shoulders. 'All right, let's leave her to it!' he whispered. 'By the time she's covered ten kilometres she'll fall down exhausted. But you ought to get some sleep now. You can have my bed. It's not as bad as it looks. If you close your eyes very tight you can imagine you're Wilbur the pig sleeping comfortably in his sty . . .'

'Or Wart sleeping in the grass with the wild geese.' Meggie couldn't help yawning. How often she and Mo had played this game! 'Which book can you think of? Which part have we forgotten? Oh yes, that one! It's ages since I thought about that story . . . !' Wearily, she lay down on the prickly straw.

Mo pulled his sweater off over his head and covered her up

with it. 'You need a blanket all the same,' he said. 'Even if you're a pig or a goose.'

'But you'll freeze.'

'Nonsense.'

'And where will you and Elinor sleep?' Meggie yawned again. She hadn't realised how tired she was.

Elinor was still pacing from wall to wall. 'What's all this about sleeping?' she said. 'We're going to keep watch, of course.'

'All right,' murmured Meggie, burying her nose in Mo's sweater. He's back with me, she thought, as drowsiness weighed down her eyelids. Nothing else matters. And then she thought: Oh, if only I could read some more of that book! But *Inkheart* was in Capricorn's hands – and she didn't want to think of him now, or she would never get to sleep. Never . . .

Later, she didn't know how long she had slept. Perhaps her cold feet woke her, or the itchy straw under her head. Her watch said four o'clock. There was nothing in the windowless room to tell her whether it was night or day, but Meggie couldn't imagine that the night was over yet. Mo was sitting near the door with Elinor. They both looked tired and anxious, and they were talking in low voices.

'Yes, they still think I'm a magician,' Mo was saying. 'They gave me that ridiculous name – Silvertongue. And Capricorn is firmly convinced I can repeat the trick any time, with any book at all.'

'And . . . and can you?' asked Elinor. 'You weren't telling us the whole story earlier, were you?'

Mo didn't answer for a long time. 'No,' he said at last. 'Because I don't want Meggie thinking I'm some kind of a magician too.'

'So you've – well, read things out of a book quite often?'

Mo nodded. 'I always liked reading aloud, even as a boy, and one day, when I was reading *Tom Sawyer* to a friend, a dead cat suddenly appeared on the carpet, lying there stiff as a board. I only noticed later that one of my soft toys had vanished. I think both our hearts missed a beat, and my friend and I swore to each other, sealing the oath with blood like Tom and Huck, that we'd never tell anyone about the cat. After that, of course, I kept trying again in secret, without any witnesses, but it never seemed to happen when I wanted. In fact, there didn't seem to be any rules at all, except that it only happened with stories I liked. Of course I kept everything that came out of books, except for the snozzcumber I got out of the book about the friendly giant. It stank too much. When Meggie was still very small, things sometimes came out of her picture books: a feather, a tiny shoe. We put them in her book-box, without telling her where they came from, otherwise she'd never have picked up a book again for fear the giant serpent with toothache or some other alarming creature might appear! But I'd never, never managed to bring anything living out of a book, Elinor. Until that night.' Mo looked at the palms of his hands, as if seeing there all the things his voice had lured out of books. 'Why couldn't it have been some nice creature if it had to happen? Something like – oh, Babar the elephant. Meggie would have been enchanted.'

Yes, I certainly would, thought Meggie. She remembered the little shoe, and the feather as well. It had been emerald green, like the plumage of Dr Dolittle's parrot Polynesia.

'Well, it could have been worse.' Typical Elinor! As if it wasn't bad enough to be locked up in a tumbledown house far away from ordinary life, surrounded by black-clad men with faces like birds of prey and knives in their belts. But obviously Elinor really could imagine something worse. 'Suppose Long John Silver had suddenly appeared in your living room, striking out with his wooden crutch?' she whispered. 'I think I prefer this Capricorn after all. You know what? When we're home again – in my house, I mean – I'll give you a really nice book. *Winnie the Pooh*, for instance, or maybe *Where the Wild Things Are*. I really wouldn't mind one of those monsters. I'll sit you down in my most comfortable armchair, make you a coffee, and then you can read aloud. How about it?'

Mo laughed quietly, and for a moment his face didn't look quite so careworn. 'No, Elinor, I shall do no such thing. Although it sounds very tempting. But I swore never to read aloud again. Who knows who might disappear next time? And perhaps there's some unpleasant character we never noticed even in the Pooh books. Or suppose I read Pooh himself out of his book? What would he do here without his friends and the Hundred Acre Wood? His poor little heart would break, like Dustfinger's.'

'Oh, for goodness' sake!' Elinor impatiently dismissed this idea. 'How often do I have to tell you that fool *has* no heart? Very well, then. Let me ask you another question, because I'd very much like to know the answer.' Elinor lowered her voice, and Meggie had to strain her ears to make out what she was saying. 'Who was this Capricorn in his own story? The villain of the piece, I suppose, but can you tell me any more about him?'

Meggie would have liked to know more about Capricorn too, but Mo was suddenly not very forthcoming. All he would say was, 'The less you know about him, the better.' Then he fell silent. Elinor kept on at him for a while, but Mo evaded all her questions. He simply did not seem to want to talk about Capricorn. Meggie could see from his face that his thoughts were somewhere else entirely. At some point Elinor nodded off, curled up on the cold floor as if trying to keep herself warm with her own body. But Mo went on sitting there with his back against the wall.

As Meggie felt herself drift off to sleep again, Mo's face stayed with her in her slumbers. It emerged in her dreams like a dark moon with figures leaping from its mouth, living creatures – fat, thin, large, small, they hopped out and ran away in a long line. A woman, scarcely more than a shadow, was dancing on the moon's nose – and suddenly the moon smiled.

17

The Betrayer Betrayed

It was a special pleasure to see things eaten, to see things blackened and changed . . . He wanted . . . to shove a marshmallow on a stick in the furnace, while the flapping pigeon-winged books died on the porch and lawn of the house. While the books went up in sparkling whirls, and blew away on a wind turned dark with burning.

Ray Bradbury, *Fahrenheit 451*

Some time near daybreak the feeble light from the electric bulb that had helped them through the night flickered out. Mo and Elinor were asleep near the locked door, but Meggie lay in the dark with her eyes open, feeling fear ooze out of the cold walls. She listened to Elinor's breathing, and her father's, and more than anything wished for a candle – and a book to keep the fear away. It seemed to be everywhere, a malicious, disembodied creature that had just been waiting for the light to go out so that it could steal close to her in the darkness and take her in its cold arms. Meggie sat up, fought for breath, and crawled over to Mo on all fours. She curled up in a ball beside him the way she used to when she was little, and waited for the light of dawn to come in under the door.

With the light came two of Capricorn's men. Mo had only just sat up, wearily, and Elinor was rubbing her aching back and muttering crossly when they heard the footsteps.

They weren't Basta's footsteps. One of the two men, a great tall beanpole, looked as if a giant had pressed his face flat with his thumb. The other was small and thin, with a goatee beard on his receding chin. He kept fiddling with his shotgun, and glowered unpleasantly at the three of them, as if he felt like shooting them on the spot.

'Come on, then. Get a move on!' he snapped as they stumbled out into the bright light of day, blinking. Meggie tried to remember whether his voice was one of those she had heard in Elinor's library, but she wasn't sure. Capricorn had many men.

It was a fine, warm morning. The sky arched blue and cloudless above Capricorn's village, and a couple of finches were twittering in a rose bush growing wild among the old houses, as if there were no danger in the world but a hungry cat or two. Mo took Meggie's arm as they stepped outside. Elinor had to get her shoes on first, and when the man with the goatee tried hauling her roughly out because she didn't move fast enough for him, she pushed his hands away and fired a volley of bad language at him. That simply made the two men laugh, whereupon Elinor tightened her lips and confined herself to hostile glances.

Capricorn's men were in a hurry. They led Mo, Meggie and Elinor back the way Basta had brought them the night before. The flat-faced man went ahead of them and the man with the goatee brought up the rear, shotgun at the ready. He dragged one leg as he walked, but nonetheless he kept urging them on, as if to prove that he could move faster than they could even though he limped.

Even by day Capricorn's village appeared curiously deserted, and not just because of the many empty houses, which looked even more dismal in the sunlight. There was hardly anyone to be seen in the narrow alleys, only a few of the Black Jackets, as Meggie had secretly baptised them, with skinny boys following them like puppies. Meggie only twice saw a woman passing in a hurry. She could see no children playing or running after their mothers, only cats: black, white, ginger, tortoiseshell, tabby cats, lying in the warm sun on top of walls, in doorways, on lintels. It was deathly quiet among the houses of Capricorn's village, and everything that went on seemed to be done in secret. Only the men with the guns didn't hide. They hung around together in gateways and at the corners of buildings, leaning lovingly on their weapons as they talked. There were no flowers outside the houses, like the flowers Meggie had seen in the towns and villages all along the coast, instead roofs had fallen in and wild bushes were in bloom, growing out through glassless windows. Some were so heavy with scent that they made Meggie feel dizzy.

When they reached the square outside the church, Meggie thought the two men were taking them to Capricorn's house again, but they passed it on their left and went straight to the big church door. The tower of the church looked as if wind and weather had been wearing the masonry down for a dangerously long time. A rusty bell hung under the pointed roof, and scarcely a metre lower down a seed carried by the wind had grown into a stunted tree that now clung to the sand-coloured stone.

There were eyes painted on the church door, narrow red eyes, and ugly stone demons the height of a man stood on either side of the entrance, their teeth bared like savage dogs.

'Welcome to the Devil's house!' said the bearded man with a mocking bow before opening the heavy door.

'Don't do that, Cockerell!' the flat-faced man snapped at him, spitting three times on the dusty paving stones at his feet. 'It's bad luck.'

The man with the goatee just laughed and patted the fat belly of one of the stone figures. 'Oh, come on, Flatnose. You're almost as bad as Basta. Carry on like this and you'll be hanging a stinking rabbit's foot round your own neck too.'

'I like to be on the safe side,' growled Flatnose. 'You hear strange tales.'

'Yes, and who made them up? We did, you fool.'

'Some of them date from before our time.'

'Whatever happens,' Mo whispered to Elinor and Meggie as the two men argued, 'leave the talking to me. A sharp tongue can be dangerous here, believe me. Basta is quick to draw his knife, and he'll use it too.'

'Basta's not the only one here with a knife, Silvertongue!' said Cockerell, pushing Mo into the dark church. Meggie hurried after him.

It was dim and chilly inside the church. The morning light made its way in only through a few windows, painting pale patches high up on the walls and columns. No doubt these had once been grey like the flagstone floor, but now there was only one colour in Capricorn's church. Everything was red. The walls, the columns, even the ceiling, were vermilion, the colour of raw meat or dried blood. For a moment, Meggie felt as if she had stepped into the belly of some monster.

In a corner near the entrance stood the statue of an angel. A wing was broken off, and the black jacket of one of Capricorn's men had been hung over the other wing while someone had stuck a pair of fancy dress horns on its head, the kind children wear to parties. Its halo was still there between them. The angel had probably once stood on the stone plinth in front of the first column, now it had had to give way to another statue, whose gaunt, waxen face seemed to look down at Meggie with a supercilious expression. Whoever had carved it wasn't very good at his trade; its features were painted like the face of a plastic doll, with oddly red lips and blue eyes that held none of the cold detachment the colourless eyes of the real Capricorn turned on the world. But, to make up for that, the statue was at least twice the height of its living model, and all who passed it had to tilt their head back to look up at its pale face.

'Is that allowed, Mo?' asked Meggie quietly. 'Putting up a statue of yourself in a church?'

'Oh, it's a very old custom!' Elinor whispered back. 'Statues in churches aren't often the statues of saints. Most saints couldn't have paid the sculptor. In the cathedral of—'

Cockerell prodded her in the back so roughly that she stumbled forward. 'Get a move on!' he growled. 'And bow next time you pass him, understand?'

'Bow!' Elinor was going to stand her ground, but Mo quickly made her go on. 'Who on earth can take this circus seriously?' she said crossly.

'If you don't keep your mouth shut,' Mo told her in a whisper, 'you'll soon find out how seriously they take everything here.'

Elinor looked at the scratch on his forehead, and said no more.

Capricorn's church contained no pews of the kind Meggie had seen in other churches, just two long wooden tables with benches, one on each side of the nave. There were dirty plates on them, coffee-stained mugs, wooden boards where cheese rinds lay, knives, sausages, empty bread baskets. Several women were busy clearing all this away. Without pausing in their work, they glanced up as Cockerell and Flatnose passed with their three captives. Meggie thought they looked like birds hunching their heads down beneath their wings in case someone might strike them off.

Not only were the pews missing from Capricorn's church, but the altar had gone too. In its place there now stood a massive chair, upholstered in red and with designs carved thickly into its legs and arms. Leading up to it were four shallow steps, carpeted in black. Meggie wasn't sure why she counted them. And crouching on the top step just a few paces away from the chair, his sandy hair ruffled as usual, was Dustfinger, apparently lost in thought as he let Gwin run up and down his outstretched arm.

As Meggie came down the nave with Mo and Elinor, Dustfinger raised his head briefly. Gwin climbed up to his shoulder, baring his tiny teeth, sharp as splinters of glass, as if he had recognised the hatred in Meggie's eyes as they rested on his master. Now she knew why the marten had horns, and why his twin was shown on the page of a book. She understood it all: why Dustfinger thought the world too fast and too noisy, why he didn't understand cars and often looked as if he were somewhere else entirely. But she felt none of the sympathy Mo had shown for him. His scarred face only reminded her of the lies he had told to lure her out to him, like the Pied Piper in the story. He had played with her as he played with fire, with his brightly coloured juggler's balls: come along, Meggie; this way, Meggie; trust me, Meggie. She felt like running up the steps and striking his lying mouth.

Dustfinger must have guessed her thoughts, and was avoiding her eyes. Not looking at Mo and Elinor either, he put a hand in his trouser pocket and brought out a matchbox. As if unconscious of what he was doing, he took out a match, lit it, and gazed at the flame, lost in thought as he passed a finger through it almost caressingly until it singed his fingertip.

Meggie looked away. She didn't want to see him; she wanted to forget he was there. To her left, at the foot of the steps, stood two drum-shaped iron braziers, rusty brown, with wood heaped up in them: pale, freshly cut firewood, log upon log. Meggie was just wondering what the wood was for when more steps echoed through the church. Basta was walking down the nave with a petrol can in his hand. Reluctantly, Cockerell and Flatnose gave way as he pushed past them.

'Ah, so Dustfinger's playing with his best friend again,' he sneered as he climbed the shallow steps. Dustfinger lowered the matchstick and straightened up. 'Here you are,' said Basta, putting the petrol can down at his feet. 'Another toy for you. Light us a fire; that's what you like best.'

Dustfinger threw away the spent match and lit another. 'So how about you?' he asked quietly, raising the burning match to Basta's face. 'Still afraid of fire, are you?'

Basta knocked the match out of his hand.

'Oh, you shouldn't do that!' said Dustfinger. 'It means bad luck. You know how quickly fire takes offence.'

For a moment Meggie thought Basta was going to hit him, and she wasn't the only one. All eyes were turned on the two men. But something seemed to protect Dustfinger. Perhaps it really was the fire.

'You're lucky I've only just cleaned my knife!' spat Basta. 'One more trick like that, though, and I'll carve a few nice new patterns on your ugly face. And make myself a fur collar out of your marten.'

Gwin uttered a soft, threatening snarl, and wrapped himself around Dustfinger's neck. Dustfinger bent, picked up the spent matches, and put them back in the matchbox. 'Yes, I'm sure you'd enjoy that,' he said, still without looking at Basta. 'But why would I want to light a fire just now, I wonder?'

'Never you mind that, just do it. Then the rest of us can keep it fed. But make sure it's a large, hungry blaze, not one of the tame little fires you like to play with.'

Dustfinger picked up the petrol can and slowly climbed down the steps. He was standing beside the rusty braziers when the church door opened for the second time.

Meggie turned at the sound of the heavy wooden door creaking, and saw Capricorn appear between the red columns. He glanced at his statue, as if to make sure it still gave a flattering enough image of him, then strode quickly down the nave. He was wearing a suit as red as the church walls. Only the shirt beneath it was black, and he had a black feather in his buttonhole. A good half-dozen of his men were following him, like crows following a peacock. Their steps seemed to echo all the way up to the ceiling. Meggie reached for Mo's hand.

'Ah, so our guests are here already,' said Capricorn, stopping in front of them. 'Did you sleep well, Silvertongue?' He had curiously soft, curving, almost feminine lips, and as he spoke he kept running his little finger along them as if to retrace them. They were as bloodless as the rest of his face.

'Wasn't it kind of me to reunite you with your little girl last night? At first I meant it to be a surprise present for you today, but then I thought: Capricorn, you really owe that child something for bringing you what you've wanted so long, and of her own free will too.'

He was holding *Inkheart*. Meggie saw Mo's gaze linger on the book. Capricorn was a tall man, but Mo stood a few centimetres taller, which obviously displeased Capricorn. He stood very upright, as if that would make up for the difference.

'Let Elinor take my daughter home with her,' said Mo. 'Let them go and I'll try to read you back again. I'll read you anything you like, but let the two of them go first.'

What was he talking about? Meggie looked at him in horror. 'No!' she said. 'No, Mo, I don't want to go away.' But no one was paying any attention to her.

'Let them go?' Capricorn turned to his men. 'Hear that? Why would I do such a crazy thing now they're here?' The men laughed. But Capricorn turned to Mo again. 'You know as well as I do that from now on you'll do whatever I want,' he said. 'Now that she's here, I'm sure you won't go on denying us a demonstration of your skill.'

Mo squeezed Meggie's hand so hard her fingers hurt.

'And as for this book,' said Capricorn, looking at *Inkheart* with as much dislike as if it had bitten his pale fingers, 'this extremely tedious, stupid and extraordinarily long-winded book, I can assure you I have no intention of ever again letting myself be spellbound by its story. All those troublesome creatures, those fluttering fairies with their twittering voices, the swarming, scrabbling stupid beasts everywhere, the smell of fur and dung. All through this book you kept falling over bandy-legged brownies in the market-place, and when you went hunting the giants scared the game away with their huge feet. Talking trees, whispering pools – was there anything in that world that didn't have the power of speech? And then those endless muddy roads to the nearest town, if town it could be called – that pack of well-born, finely dressed princes in their castles, those stinking peasants, so poor there was nothing to be got out of them, and the vagabonds and beggars with vermin dropping from their hair – oh, how sick I was of them all.'

Capricorn made a sign, and one of his men brought in a large cardboard box. You could see from the way he carried it that it was very heavy. The man put it down on the grey flag-stones in front of Capricorn with a sigh of relief. Capricorn handed Cockerell, who was standing beside him, the book that Mo had kept from him so long, and bent to open the box. It was full to the brim with books.

'It's been a great deal of trouble finding them all,' said Capricorn as he reached into the box and took out two books. 'They may look different, but the contents are the same. The fact that the story has been printed in several languages made the search even more difficult – a particularly useless feature of this world, all those different languages. It was simpler in our own world, wasn't it, Dustfinger?'

Dustfinger made no answer. He stood there holding the petrol can and staring at the box. Capricorn strolled over to him and threw the two books into one of the braziers.

'What are you doing?' Dustfinger tried to snatch them out, but Basta pushed him away.

'Those stay where they are,' he growled.

Dustfinger stepped back, holding the can behind his back,

but Basta grabbed it from his hands. 'Why, it looks as if our fire-eater would rather let someone else light the fire today,' he mocked.

Dustfinger cast him a glance full of hatred. Face rigid, he watched Capricorn's men throw more and more books into the braziers. In the end there were over two dozen copies of *Inkheart* on the piles of firewood, their pages crumpled, their bindings wrenched apart like broken wings.

'You know what always got me down back in our old world, Dustfinger?' asked Capricorn as he took the petrol can from Basta's hand. 'The difficulty of lighting a fire. It wasn't any problem to you, of course – you could even talk to fire, very likely one of those grunting brownies taught you how – but it was a tedious business for the rest of us. The wood was always damp, or the wind blew down the chimney. I know you long for the good old days, you miss all your chirping, fluttering friends, but I don't shed a tear for any of that. This world is far better equipped than the one we had to be content with for so many long years.'

Dustfinger did not seem to hear a word of what Capricorn was saying. He just stared at the petrol and smelled its fumes as it was poured over the books. The pages sucked it up as greedily as if they were welcoming their own end.

'Where did they all come from?' he stammered. 'You always told me there was just one copy left – Silvertongue's.'

'Yes, yes, I told you all kinds of things.' Capricorn put his hand in his trouser pocket. 'You're such a gullible fellow, Dustfinger. It's fun to tell you lies. Your innocence always amazed me – after all, you lie very cleverly yourself. But you're too ready to believe what you want to believe, that's your trouble. Well, you can safely believe me now. These,' he said, tapping the petrol-soaked pile of books, 'these really are the last copies of our ink-black home. It's taken Basta and the others years to track them all down in shabby lending libraries and second-hand bookshops.'

Dustfinger looked longingly at the books, as a man dying of thirst might look at the last glass of water in existence. 'But you can't burn them!' he stammered. 'You promised to send me back if I found you Silvertongue's book. That's why I told you where he was. That's why I brought you his daughter.'

Capricorn merely shrugged his shoulders and took the book from Cockerell's hands – the book with the green binding that Meggie and Elinor had been so eager to give him, the book for which he had made his men bring Mo all this way, the book for which Dustfinger had betrayed them all.

'I'd have promised to fetch you down the moon from the sky if that would have done me any good,' said Capricorn, looking bored as he flung the last copy of *Inkheart* on to the pile with its companions. 'I'm happy to make promises, especially promises I can't keep.' Then he took a lighter from his trouser pocket. Dustfinger was about to leap at him to strike it out of his hand, but Capricorn made a sign to Flatnose.

Flatnose was so tall and broad that beside him Dustfinger looked almost like a child, and indeed the man took hold of him as if he were a badly behaved little boy. Fur bristling, Gwin leaped off Dustfinger's shoulder. One of Capricorn's men kicked out as the marten shot past his legs, but Gwin got away and disappeared behind one of the red columns. The other men stood there laughing at Dustfinger's desperate attempts to free himself from Flatnose's iron grasp. Flatnose thought it greatly amusing to let Dustfinger get just close enough to the petrol-soaked books to touch the top volumes with his fingers.

Such cruelty made Meggie feel quite ill. Mo took a step forward as if to go to Dustfinger's aid, but Basta barred his way, a knife in his hand. Its blade, narrow and shiny, looked terribly sharp held against Mo's throat.

Elinor screamed, and directed a torrent of curses at Basta that Meggie had never even heard before, but she herself could not move. She just stood there, in numb and silent terror, staring at the blade against Mo's bare throat.

'Let me have one of them, Capricorn, just one!' Mo cried, and only then did Meggie realize that he had not been going to help Dustfinger but was thinking of the book. 'I promise never to read aloud a line of it that mentions your name.'

'You! Are you mad? You're the last man I'd give one to,' replied Capricorn. 'One day you might be unable to control your tongue after all, and I'd land back in that ridiculous story again. No thank you very much!'

'Nonsense!' cried Mo. 'I couldn't read you back into it even if I wanted to – how often do I have to tell you that? Ask Dustfinger. I've explained it to him a thousand times. I myself don't understand how or when these things happen. For heaven's sake, believe me!'

With a chilling smirk, Capricorn answered merely with a smile, 'I'm sorry, Silvertongue, but the fact is I don't believe anyone. You ought to know that by now. We're all liars when it serves our purpose.' And with those words he flicked the lighter and held its flame to one of the books. The petrol had made the pages almost transparent, like parchment, and they flared up at once. Even the stout cloth bindings caught light immediately, the linen turning black as the flames licked round it.

When the third book caught fire, Dustfinger kicked Flatnose's kneecap so hard that the man screamed with pain and let go of him. Nimble as his marten, Dustfinger wriggled out of those powerful arms and stumbled towards the braziers. Without hesitating, he reached into the flames, but the book he plucked out was already burning like a torch. Dustfinger dropped it on the flagstone floor and reached into the fire again, with his other hand this time, but by now Flatnose had already grasped him by the collar and was shaking him so roughly that Dustfinger was gasping for air.

'Look at the lunatic!' sneered Basta as Dustfinger stared at his hands, his face distorted with pain. 'Can anyone explain what he wants so much? Maybe those ugly brownie girls who thought him so wonderful when he juggled in the market-place? Or the filthy hovels where he lived with other vagabonds? They smelled even worse than the rucksack he carries that stinking marten around in.'

Capricorn's men laughed as the books slowly crumpled into ashes. There was still a smell of petrol in the church, such an acrid smell that it made Meggie cough. Mo put a protective arm around her shoulders, as if Basta had threatened her rather than him. But who, thought Meggie, who could protect Mo?

Elinor was looking at his neck as anxiously as if she feared Basta's knife might have left its mark there after all. 'These fellows are out of their minds!' she whispered. 'You know what they say: when people start burning books they'll soon burn human beings. Suppose we're the next to find ourselves on a pyre?'

Basta seemed to hear what she was saying. He caught her eye, and with a twisted smile kissed the blade of his knife.

Elinor fell silent, as if she had swallowed her tongue.

Capricorn had taken a snow-white handkerchief from his pocket. He cleaned his fingers with it carefully, as if to wipe even the memory of *Inkheart* off his hands. 'Well, that's done at last,' he remarked with a final nod at the smoking embers. Then, with a satisfied expression on his face, he climbed up to the chair that had replaced the altar. Capricorn sank into its red upholstery with a deep sigh.

'Dustfinger, go to the kitchen and get Mortola to put something on your burns,' he ordered in a commanding voice. 'You'll be no use for anything without the use of your hands.'

Dustfinger looked at Mo for a long time before obeying this order. Head bent, with unsteady steps, he walked past Capricorn's men. The way to the church porch seemed endless. For a moment, as Dustfinger opened the door, bright sunlight shone into the building. As it closed behind him, Meggie, Mo and Elinor were left with Capricorn and his men – and the reek of petrol and burnt paper.

'And now let's come to you, Silvertongue!' said Capricorn, stretching his legs. He was wearing black boots. He examined the gleaming leather with satisfaction, removing a scrap of charred paper from the toe of one boot. 'Until now I, Basta and the unfortunate Dustfinger are the only evidence that you can conjure up extraordinary magic out of little black letters. You yourself don't seem to trust your gift, if we're to believe you – which, as I was saying just now, I don't. On the contrary, I think you are a master of your craft, and I can scarcely wait for you to give us another taste of your skill at long last. Cockerell!' His voice sounded irritated. 'Where's the reader? Didn't I tell you to bring him?'

Cockerell stroked his beard nervously. 'He was still busy

choosing books,' he stammered. 'I'll fetch him right away.' And with a hasty bow, he limped off.

Capricorn began drumming his fingers on the arms of his chair. 'No doubt you've already heard that I had to resort to the services of another reader while you were hiding from me so successfully,' he said to Mo. 'I found him by chance five years ago, but he's useless. You only have to look at Flatnose's face.' Flatnose lowered his head, embarrassed, when all eyes turned on him. 'And Cockerell owes him his limp too. As for the girls he read out of his books for me, you should have seen them. It'd give a man nightmares just to see their faces. Finally, I had him read to me only when I felt like amusing myself with his monsters, and I actually found my men in this world of yours, just by recruiting them when they were still young. There's a lonely boy who likes to play with fire in almost every village.' Smiling, he inspected his fingernails like a satisfied cat examining its claws. 'I've told the reader to find the right books for you. At least the poor fool does know his way around books – he lives in them like one of those pale worms that feed on paper.'

'And just what am I supposed to read out of his books for you?' Mo's voice sounded bitter. 'A few monsters, a couple of human horrors to suit the present company?' He nodded in Basta's direction.

'For heaven's sake, Mortimer, don't put ideas into his head!' whispered Elinor, with a nervous glance at Capricorn.

But Capricorn merely flicked some ash off his trousers and smiled. 'No, thank you, Silvertongue,' he said. 'I have enough men, and as for the monsters, well, perhaps we'll get around to them later. For the time being we're doing very well with Basta's trained dogs and the local snakes. They make excellent and deadly presents. No, Silvertongue, all I want today as a test of your skill is gold. I have such an appetite for money! My men do their best to squeeze all that can be squeezed out of this part of the country.' At these words from Capricorn, Basta lovingly stroked his knife. 'But it's never enough for all the wonderful things that can be bought in this infinitely wide world of yours. A world of so many pages, Silvertongue, so very many pages, and I want to write my name on every one of them.'

'In what kind of letters?' enquired Mo. 'Is Basta going to scratch them into the paper with his knife?'

'Oh, Basta can't write,' replied Capricorn calmly. 'None of my men can either read or write. I've forbidden them to learn. But I got one of my maidservants to teach *me* how to read. And when there's something to be written the reader does it. So you see, my dear Silvertongue, I can make my mark on your world.'

The church door opened as if Cockerell had just been waiting for this cue. The man he ushered in had his head hunched between his shoulders and looked neither right nor left as he followed Cockerell. He was small and thin, and couldn't be any older than Mo, but his back was bent like an old man's, and his arms and legs moved awkwardly, as if he didn't quite know what to do with them. He kept nervously adjusting his glasses. The frame was held together over the bridge of his nose with sticky tape, as if it had often been broken. He was clutching a number of books to his chest with his left arm, as if they offered some protection from the stares turned on him from all sides and the sinister place to which he had been brought.

When the two men eventually reached the foot of the steps

Cockerell dug an elbow into his companion's ribs, and the man bowed so hurriedly that two of the books fell to the floor. He was quick to snatch them up, and bowed to Capricorn a second time.

'We've been waiting for you, Darius!' said Capricorn. 'I trust you've found what I wanted.'

'Oh yes, yes!' stammered Darius, casting an almost reverent glance at Mo. 'Is that him?'

'Yes. Show him the books you've chosen.'

Darius nodded and bowed again, this time to Mo. 'These – these are all stories with treasure in them,' he stammered. 'Finding them wasn't as easy as I had expected,' he added, with the faintest note of reproach in his voice. 'After all, there aren't so many books in this village. And however often I ask no one brings me any more, or if they do the books are useless. But never mind that – here they are. I think you'll be happy with my choice, anyway.' He knelt down on the floor in front of Mo and began setting out the books side by side, so that Mo could read the titles.

The very first one alarmed Meggie. *Treasure Island*. She looked uneasily at Mo. Not that one, she thought. Not that book, Mo. But Mo had already picked up another book: *Tales From the Thousand and One Nights*.

'I think this will do,' he said. 'There's sure to be plenty of gold in those stories. But I'm warning you again, I don't know what will happen. Because it never does happen when I want it to. I know you all think I'm a magician, but I'm not. The magic comes out of the books themselves, and I have no more idea than you or any of your men how it works.'

Capricorn leaned back in his chair looking expressionlessly at Mo. 'How many more times are you going to tell me that,

Silvertongue?' he asked in bored tones. 'You can say so as often as you like, but I don't believe it. In the world on which we finally slammed the door today I frequently mingled with magicians, wizards and witches, and I very often had to deal with their obstinacy. I know that Basta has given you a graphic account of the way we used to break their will. But in your case, and now that your daughter is here as our guest, I'm sure such painful methods will not be necessary.' With these words, Capricorn looked pointedly at Basta.

Mo tried to hold on to Meggie, but Basta moved faster. Pulling her towards him, he quickly put an arm around her neck and held her in a headlock.

'From now on, Silvertongue,' continued Capricorn, his voice still sounding as indifferent as if he was talking about the weather, 'from now on, Basta will be your daughter's personal shadow. This will provide her with reliable protection from snakes and fierce dogs but not, of course, from Basta himself, who will be kind to her only as long as I say so. And that in turn will depend on whether I am pleased with your services. Have I made myself clear?'

Mo looked first at him and then at Meggie. She did her best to look unafraid, so that he would think there was no need to worry about her – after all, she had always been a better liar than he was. But this time he saw through the lie. He knew that her fear was as great as the fear she saw in his own eyes.

Perhaps all this is just a story too, thought Meggie desperately. And any moment someone will close the book because it's so horrible and scary, and Mo and I will be back at home and I'll make him a coffee. She closed her eyes very tight, as if that would make her thoughts come true, but when she peered through her lashes Basta was still standing behind her, and Flatnose was rubbing his squashed nostrils and turning his dog-like gaze on Capricorn.

'Very well,' said Mo wearily into the silence. 'I'll read aloud to you. But Meggie and Elinor can't stay in here.'

Meggie knew exactly what he was thinking. He was thinking of her mother, and wondering who might disappear this time.

'Nonsense. Of course they stay here.' Capricorn's voice was no longer careless. 'And you'd better get started before the book there in your hand falls to dust.'

Mo closed his eyes for a moment. 'Very well, but tell Basta to put his knife away,' he said hoarsely. 'If he hurts a hair of Meggie or Elinor's heads I promise you I'll read the Plague out of a book to infect you and your men.'

Cockerell looked at Mo in alarm, and a shadow passed over even Basta's face, but Capricorn just laughed.

'Let me remind you, Silvertongue, that you're speaking of a contagious disease,' he said. 'And it doesn't stop short at little girls. So never mind the empty threats, just start reading. Now. At once. And I want to hear something out of *that* book first!'

He pointed to the book that Mo had just laid aside.

Treasure Island.

18

Treasure Island

Squire Trelawney, Dr Livesey, and the rest of these gentlemen having asked me to write down the whole particulars about Treasure Island, from the beginning to the end, keeping nothing back but the bearings of the island . . . I take up my pen in the year of grace 17—, and go back to the time when my father kept the Admiral Benbow inn, and the brown old seaman, with the sabre cut, first took up his lodging under our roof.

Robert Louis Stevenson, *Treasure Island*

And so Meggie heard her father read aloud, for the first time in nine years, in a draughty old church. Even many, many years later the smell of burnt paper would come back to her as soon as she opened one of the books from which he had read that awful morning.

It was chilly in Capricorn's church – Meggie was to remember that later, too – although the sun must have been hot outside and high in the sky by the time Mo began to read. He simply sat down on the floor where he was, legs crossed,

one book on his lap and the others beside him. Meggie quickly knelt down close to him before Basta could catch hold of
her.

'Here, get up these steps, all of you,' Capricorn told his
men. 'And take the woman with you, Flatnose. Only Basta
stays where he is.'

Elinor resisted, but Flatnose merely seized a handful of her
hair and hauled her along after him. Capricorn's men climbed
the steps and sat at their master's feet, Elinor among them like
a pigeon with ruffled feathers in the middle of a mob of
marauding crows. The only person who looked equally out of
place was the thin reader, Darius, who was sitting at the very
end of the row of black-clad men and kept fiddling with his
glasses.

Mo opened the book on his lap and began leafing through
it, frowning, as if searching the pages for the gold he was to
read out of it for Capricorn.

'Cockerell, you will cut out the tongue of anyone who
utters the slightest sound while Silvertongue is reading,' said
Capricorn, and Cockerell drew a knife from his belt and
looked along the row of men as if already selecting his first
victim. All was so deathly quiet inside the red church that
Meggie thought she could hear Basta breathing behind her.
But perhaps it was only the sound of her own fear.

Judging by their faces, Capricorn's men seemed to be feeling far from happy. They were looking at Mo with expressions
of apprehension mingled with dislike. Meggie understood that
only too well. Perhaps one of them would soon vanish into the
book through which Mo was leafing so undecidedly. Had
Capricorn told them that such a thing might happen? Did
even *he* know it? What if she herself vanished, as Mo

181

obviously feared? Or Elinor?

'Meggie!' Mo whispered to her, as if he had heard her thoughts. 'Hold on to me tight any way you can.' Meggie nodded, and clutched his sweater. As if that would be any use!

'Yes, I think I've found the right place,' said Mo into the silence. He cast a last glance at Capricorn, looked at Elinor, cleared his throat – and began to read.

Everything disappeared: the red walls of the church, the faces of Capricorn's men, Capricorn himself sitting in his chair. There was nothing but Mo's voice and the pictures forming in their minds from the letters on the page, like the pattern of a carpet taking shape on a loom. If Meggie could have hated Capricorn any more, she would have done so now. It was his fault that Mo had never once read aloud to her in all these years. To think of the magic he could have worked in her room with his voice, a voice that gave a different flavour to every word, made every sentence a melody! Even Cockerell had forgotten his knife and the tongues he was supposed to cut out, and was listening with a faraway expression on his face. Flatnose was staring into space, enraptured, as if a pirate ship with all sails set were truly cruising in through one of the church windows. The other men were equally entranced.

There was not a sound to be heard but Mo's voice bringing the letters and words on the page to life.

Only one of his audience seemed immune to the magic of it. Face expressionless, pale eyes fixed on Mo, Capricorn sat there waiting: waiting for the clink of coins amidst the harmony of the words, for chests of damp wood heavy with gold and silver.

Mo did not keep him waiting long. It happened as he was

reading what Jim Hawkins – a boy not much older than Meggie when he embarked on his terrifying adventure – saw in a dark cave:

. . . Georges, and Louises, doubloons and double guineas and moidores and sequins, the pictures of all the kings of Europe for the last hundred years, strange Oriental pieces stamped with what looked like wisps of string or bits of spider's web, round pieces and square pieces, and pieces bored through the middle, as if to wear them round your neck – nearly every variety of money in the world must, I think, have found a place in that collection; and for number, I am sure they were like autumn leaves, so that my back ached with stooping and my fingers with sorting them out.

The maidservants were cleaning the last crumbs off the tables when coins suddenly came rolling over the bare wood. The women stumbled back, dropping their dish-cloths, and pressing their hands to their mouths as the coins tumbled and leaped about their feet. Gold, silver and copper coins jingled over the flagstone floor, clinking as they gathered in heaps under the benches – more and more and more of them. Some rolled as far as the steps. Capricorn's men came to life, bent to pick up the glittering little things bouncing off their boots – but then snatched back their hands. None of them dared touch the magic money. For what else could it be? Gold made of paper and printer's ink – and the sound of a human voice.

As the shower of gold stopped, at the very moment when Mo closed the book, Meggie saw there was a little sand among all the gleaming, glittering money. A few iridescent blue beetles scuttled away, and the head of an emerald-green lizard emerged from a heap of tiny coins. It stared around with fixed eyes, tongue flicking out of its sharp little mouth. Basta threw his knife at it, as if he could skewer not just the lizard but the cowardice that had seized them all. However, Meggie gave a warning cry, and the lizard darted away so fast that the tip of the blade struck the stones. Basta ran over to his knife, picked it up, and pointed it threateningly in Meggie's direction.

Capricorn rose from his chair, his face still as cold and blank as if nothing worth getting excited about had happened, and clapped his ringed hands graciously. 'Not bad for a start, Silvertongue!' he said. 'See that, Darius? That's what gold looks like – not the rusty, dented metal you've read out of books for me. But now you've heard how the thing is done I hope you'll have learnt from it. Just in case I ever require your services again.'

Darius did not reply. His eyes were fixed on Mo with such admiration in them that it wouldn't have surprised Meggie had he flung himself at her father's feet. When Mo straightened up, Darius approached him hesitantly.

Capricorn's men were still gazing at the gold as if they didn't know what to do next.

'What are you standing there for, gaping like a lot of sheep?' cried Capricorn. 'Pick it up. Go on.'

'That was wonderful!' Darius whispered to Mo, while Capricorn's men cautiously began shovelling the coins into bags and boxes. His eyes were gleaming behind his glasses like the eyes of a child who has just been given a much-wanted present. 'I've read that book many times,' he said, in a voice that shook, 'but I never saw it all as vividly as I did today. And I didn't just see it . . . I smelled it, the salt and the tar and the musty odour of the whole accursed island . . .'

'*Treasure Island!* Heavens above, I was petrified!' Elinor appeared behind Darius, pushing him impatiently aside. Flatnose had obviously forgotten her for the moment. 'He'll be here any minute, that's what I kept thinking. *Long John Silver* will be here, lashing out at us with his crutch.'

Mo just nodded, but Meggie could see the relief on his face. 'Here, take it!' he told Darius, handing him the book. 'I hope I never have to read out of it again. One shouldn't push one's luck.'

'You said his name not quite right every time,' Meggie whispered.

Mo tenderly stroked the bridge of her nose. 'Ah, so you noticed,' he whispered back. 'Yes, I thought that might help. Perhaps the savage old pirate won't feel we're calling to him then, I told myself, and he'll stay where he belongs. Why are you looking at me like that?'

'Why do you think?' said Elinor, answering instead of Meggie. 'Why is she looking so admiringly at her father? Because no one ever read aloud like that – even apart from the money. I saw it all, the sea and the island, as clear as if I could touch it, and I don't expect it was any different for your daughter.'

Mo had to smile. He kicked aside a few of the coins on the floor in front of him. One of Capricorn's men picked them up and surreptitiously pocketed them. As he did so, he looked at Mo as uneasily as if he feared a word from him might turn him into a frog, or one of the beetles still crawling around among the coins.

'They're afraid of you, Mo!' whispered Meggie. She could see the trepidation even on Basta's face, although he was doing his best to hide it by assuming a particularly bored expression.

Only Capricorn seemed to be left cold by what had happened. Arms folded, he stood there watching his men pick up the last of the coins. 'How much longer is this going to take?' he asked finally. 'Leave the small change where it is and sit down again. And you, Silvertongue, open the next book!'

'The *next* book!' Elinor's voice almost cracked with indignation. 'What on earth's the idea of that? The gold your men are shovelling up there is enough to last you at least two lifetimes. We're going home now!'

She was about to turn round, but Flatnose, who had finally remembered he was meant to be guarding Elinor, seized her arm roughly. Mo looked up at Capricorn.

Basta, smiling unpleasantly, laid his hand on Meggie's shoulder. 'Get on with it, Silvertongue!' he said. 'You heard. There are still plenty of books here.'

Mo looked at Meggie for a long time before bending to pick up the book he had chosen first: *Tales From the Thousand and One Nights*.

'The book that goes on and on forever,' he murmured, opening it. 'Did you know the Arabs say no one can read it right through to the end, Meggie?'

She shook her head as she sat down beside him on the cold flagstones. Basta let her, but he planted himself right behind her. Meggie didn't know much about *The Thousand and One Nights*, except that it was really a book in many volumes. The copy that Darius had given Mo could only be a small selection. Were *Ali Baba and the Forty Thieves* in it, and *Aladdin and the Wonderful Lamp*? Which story would Mo read?

Meggie thought she saw contradictory feelings on the faces of Capricorn's men: fear of what Mo might bring to life and, at the same time, a wish, a yearning almost, to be carried away by his voice once more, transported far away to a place where they could forget everything, even themselves.

There was no smell of salt and rum when Mo began reading this time. The air in Capricorn's church grew hot. Meggie's eyes began to burn, and when she rubbed them she found sand sticking to her knuckles. Once again, Capricorn's men listened to Mo's voice with bated breath, as if they were turned to stone. Capricorn alone seemed to feel nothing of the magic. But his eyes showed that even he was spellbound. They were fixed on Mo's face, as unmoving as the eyes of a snake. His red suit made his pupils look even more washed out, and his body seemed tense, like a dog scenting its prey. But this time Mo disappointed him.

The words offered up no riches, none of the treasure chests, pearls and swords set with precious stones that Mo's voice conjured up, shining and sparkling, until Capricorn's men felt as if they could pluck them from the air. Something else slipped out of the pages, though, something breathing, a creature made of flesh and blood.

A boy was suddenly standing between the still smouldering braziers where Capricorn had burned the books. Meggie was the only one to notice him. All the others were too absorbed in the story. Even Mo didn't see him, far away as he was, somewhere in the sand and the wind as his eyes made their way through the labyrinth of letters.

The boy was some three or four years older than Meggie. The turban round his head was dirty, his eyes dark with fear in his brown face. He blinked and rubbed them as if he could wipe it all away – the wrong picture, the wrong place. He looked round the church as if he had never seen such a building before, and how could he? There wouldn't be any churches with spires in his story, or green hills like those he would see outside. The robe he wore went down to his brown feet, and in the dim light of the church it shone blue as a patch of the sky.

Meggie wondered: what will happen when they see him? He's certainly not what Capricorn was hoping for.

But Capricorn had already noticed the boy.

'Stop!' he commanded, so sharply that Mo broke off in mid-sentence and raised his head.

Abruptly, and rather unwillingly, Capricorn's men returned to reality. Cockerell was the first on his feet. 'Hey, where did *he* come from?' he growled.

The boy ducked, looked round with a terrified expression, and ran for it, doubling back and forth like a rabbit. But he didn't get far. Three men immediately sprang forward and caught him at the feet of Capricorn's statue.

Mo put the book down on the flagstones beside him and buried his face in his hands.

'Hey, Fulvio's gone!' cried one of Capricorn's men. 'Vanished into thin air!' They all stared at Mo. There it was again, the nervousness in their faces, but this time mingled not with admiration but with anger.

'Get rid of that boy, Silvertongue!' ordered Capricorn angrily. 'I have more than enough of his kind. And bring Fulvio back.'

Mo took his hands away from his face and stood up.

'For the millionth time, I *can't* bring anyone back,' he said. 'The fact that you don't believe me doesn't make that a lie. I can't do it. I can't decide who or what comes out of a book, nor who goes into it.'

Meggie reached for Mo's hand. Some of Capricorn's men came closer, two of them holding the boy. They were pulling on his arms as if to tear him in half. Eyes wide with terror, the boy stared into their unfamiliar faces.

'Back to your places!' Capricorn ordered the angry men. A couple of them were already dangerously close to Mo. 'Why all this fuss? Have you forgotten how stupidly Fulvio acted on the last job? We almost had the police down on us. So it's the right man to have gone. And who knows, perhaps this lad will turn out to have a talent for arson. All the same, I want to see pearls now. And gold and jewels. After all, they're what this story is all about, so let's have some!'

An uneasy murmuring rose among the men. Nonetheless, most of them returned to the steps and perched once more on the worn treads. Only three still stood in front of Mo, staring at him with intense hostility. One of them was Basta. 'Very well, so we can dispense with Fulvio,' he said, never taking his eyes off Mo. 'But who is this wretched wizard going to magic into thin air next time? I don't want to end up in some thrice-accursed desert story!' The men standing near him nodded in agreement, and looked at Mo so darkly that Meggie almost stopped breathing.

'Basta, I won't tell you again.' Capricorn's voice sounded menacingly calm. 'Let him go on reading, all of you. And anyone whose teeth start chattering with fear had better go outside and help the women with the laundry.'

Some of the men looked longingly at the church door, but none ventured to leave. Finally, even the two who had been standing beside Basta turned without a word and sat down with the others.

'You'll pay for Fulvio yet!' Basta whispered to Mo before he stationed himself behind Meggie again. Why couldn't *he* have disappeared? she thought.

The boy still hadn't uttered a sound.

'Lock him up. We'll see if he can be of any use to us later,' ordered Capricorn.

The boy did not resist as Flatnose led him away. Apparently numb, he stumbled along as if he were still expecting to wake up. When would he realise this dream was never going to end?

When the door closed behind the two of them Capricorn returned to his chair. 'Go on reading, Silvertongue,' he said. 'We still have a long day ahead of us.'

But Mo looked at the books lying at his feet, and shook his head. 'No,' he said. 'You saw. It happened again. I'm tired. Be content with what I've brought you from *Treasure Island*. Those coins are worth a fortune. I want to go home, and I never want to set eyes on you again.' His voice sounded rougher than usual, as if it had read too many words aloud.

Capricorn looked at Mo appraisingly before turning his eyes to the bags and chests his men had filled with coins. He seemed to be working out how long their contents would keep him in comfort.

'Yes, you're right,' he said at last. 'We'll go on tomorrow. Otherwise we might find a stinking camel turning up here next, or another half-starved boy.'

'Tomorrow?' Mo took a step towards him. 'What do you mean? Aren't you satisfied yet? One of your men has disappeared already. Do you want to be the next?'

'I can live with the risk,' replied Capricorn, unimpressed. His men leaped to their feet as he rose from his chair and walked slowly down the altar steps. They stood there like schoolboys, although some of them were taller than Capricorn, hands clasped behind their backs as if at any moment he would inspect their fingernails for cleanliness. Meggie couldn't help remembering what Basta had said – how young he himself had been when he had joined Capricorn – and she wondered whether it was out of fear or admiration that the men bowed their heads.

Capricorn had stopped beside one of the bulging money-bags. 'Oh, I have a great many plans for you, Silvertongue, believe me,' he said, putting his hand into the sack and running the coins through his fingers. 'Today was just a test. After all, I had to convince myself of your talents with my own eyes and ears, right? I can certainly use all this gold, but tomorrow you're going to read something else out of a book for me.'

He strolled over to the boxes which had contained the books that were now burnt to ashes, and reached into one. 'Surprise!' he announced, smiling as he held up a single book. It didn't look at all like the copy Meggie and Elinor had brought him. It still had a brightly coloured paper dust-jacket with a picture that Meggie couldn't make out from a distance. 'Oh yes, I still have one!' remarked Capricorn, scanning the uncomprehending faces with pleasure. 'My own personal copy, you might say, and tomorrow, Silvertongue, you're going to read to me from it. As I was saying, I like this world of yours very much indeed, but there's a friend from the old days that I miss. I never let your substitute try his skill with my friend – I was afraid he might fetch him here without a head, or with only one leg. But now I have you, and you're a master of your art.'

Mo was staring incredulously at the book in Capricorn's hand as if he expected it to dissolve into thin air at any moment.

'Have a rest, Silvertongue,' said Capricorn. 'Spare your precious voice. You'll have plenty of time for that, because I have to go away, and I won't be back till noon tomorrow. Take these three back to their quarters,' he told his men. 'Give them enough to eat, and some blankets for the night. Oh yes, and get Mortola to bring him tea. That kind of thing works wonders on a hoarse, tired voice. Didn't you always swear by tea sweetened with honey, Darius?' He turned enquiringly to his old reader, who simply nodded, and looked sympathetically at Mo.

'Back to our quarters? Do you mean that hole where your man with the knife put us last night?' Elinor's cheeks were flushed red, whether in horror or indignation Meggie couldn't guess. 'This is wrongful detention! No, worse – abduction! That's it, abduction. Are you aware how many years in jail you'd get for it?'

'Abduction!' Basta savoured the word. 'Sounds good to me. Really good.'

Capricorn gave him a smile. Then he looked Elinor up and down as if he were seeing her for the first time. 'Basta,' he said. 'Is this lady any use to us?'

'Not that I know of,' replied Basta, smiling like a child who has just been given permission to smash a toy. Elinor went pale, and tried to step backwards, but Cockerell barred her way and held her firmly.

'What do we generally do with useless things, Basta?' asked Capricorn quietly.

Basta went on smiling.

'Stop that!' Mo said angrily to Capricorn. 'Stop frightening her at once, or I'm not reading you another word.'

With every appearance of indifference, Capricorn turned

his back to him. And Basta kept smiling.

Meggie saw Elinor press a hand to her trembling lips, and quickly went over to stand beside her. 'She's not useless. She knows more about books than anyone else in the world!' she said, holding Elinor's other hand very tight.

Capricorn turned round. The look in his eyes made Meggie shudder, as if someone were running cold fingers down her spine. His eyelashes were pale as cobwebs.

'Elinor definitely knows more stories with treasure in them than that spineless reader of yours!' Meggie stammered. 'Definitely!'

Elinor squeezed Meggie's fingers hard. Her own hand was damp with sweat. 'Yes. Absolutely, that's true,' she said huskily. 'I'm sure I can think of several more.'

'Well, well,' was all Capricorn said, his curved lips tracing a smile. 'We'll see.' Then he gave his men a signal, and they made Elinor, Meggie and Mo file past the tables, past Capricorn's statue and the red columns, and out through the heavy door that groaned as they pushed it open.

Outside, beyond the shadow of the church on the village square, the sun shone down from a cloudless blue sky, and the air was filled with scents of summer. It was as if nothing unusual had happened.

19

Gloomy Prospects

The python dropped his head lightly for a moment on
Mowgli's shoulders. 'A brave heart and a courteous
tongue,' said he. 'They shall carry thee far through the jungle, manling. But now go hence quickly with thy friends.
Go and sleep, for the moon sets, and what follows it is not
well that thou shouldst see.'

Rudyard Kipling, *The Jungle Book*

They did indeed get enough to eat. Around noon a woman
brought them bread and olives, and towards evening
there was pasta smelling of fresh rosemary. But the food
couldn't cut short the endless hours, any more than full stom-
achs dispelled their fear of what the next day might bring.
Perhaps not even a book would have done it, but there was no
point thinking of that, since they had no books, only the blank
walls and the locked door. At least a new light bulb was hanging from the ceiling, so they didn't have to sit in the dark the
whole time. Meggie kept looking at the crack under the door
to see if night was falling yet. She imagined lizards sitting out-

side in the sun. She'd seen some in the square outside the church. Had the emerald-green lizard that scurried out of the heaps of coins found its way outside? And what had happened to the boy? Meggie saw his frightened expression whenever she closed her eyes.

She wondered whether the same thoughts were going through Mo's head. He had hardly said a word since they were locked up again, but had flopped down on the pile of straw and turned his face to the wall. Elinor was no more talkative. 'How generous!' was all she had muttered when Cockerell had bolted the door after them. 'Our host has graciously provided two more heaps of mouldy straw.' Then she had sat down in a corner, legs outstretched, and begun staring gloomily at her knees, then at the grubby wall.

'Mo,' asked Meggie at last, when she could no longer stand the silence, 'what do you think they're doing to the boy? And what kind of a friend are you supposed to read out of the book for Capricorn?'

'I don't know, Meggie,' was all he replied, without turning round.

So she left him alone, made herself a bed of straw beside his, then paced up and down between the bare walls. Perhaps the strange boy was the other side of one of them? She put her ear to the wall. Not a sound came through. Someone had scratched a name in the plaster: Ricardo Bentone, 19.5.96. Meggie ran her finger over the letters. A little further on there was another name, and then another. Meggie wondered what had become of them, Ricardo, Ugo and Bernardo. Perhaps I ought to scratch my name here too, she thought, just in case . . . but she was careful not to think her way to the end of that sentence.

Behind her, Elinor lay down on her straw bed, sighing. When Meggie turned to her, she forced a smile. 'What would-n't I give for a comb!' she said, pushing the hair back from her forehead. 'I'd never have thought that in a situation like this I'd miss a comb so much, of all things, but I do. Heavens, I don't even have a hairpin left. I must look like a witch, or a washing-up brush that's seen better days.'

'No, really, you look fine. Your hairpins were always falling out anyway,' said Meggie. 'Actually, I think you look younger.'

'Younger? Hmm. Well, if you say so.' Elinor glanced down at herself. Her mouse-grey sweater was filthy, and there were three ladders in her tights. 'Meggie, it was very kind of you to help me back there in the church,' she said, pulling her skirt down over her knees. 'My knees were like jelly, I was so scared. I don't know what's come over me. I feel like someone else, as if the old Elinor has driven home and left me here by myself.' Her lips began to tremble, and Meggie thought she was going to cry, but next moment the familiar Elinor was back again. 'Well, there we are!' she said. 'It's only in an emergency that you find out what you're truly made of. Personally, I always thought if I was a wooden statue I'd be carved out of oak, but it seems I'm more like pearwood or something else very soft. It only takes a villain like that to play with his knife in front of my nose and the wood shavings start flaking away.'

And now the tears did come, hard as Elinor tried to keep them back. Angrily, she rubbed her eyes with the back of her hand.

'I think you're doing splendidly, Elinor.' Mo was still lying with his face to the wall. 'You're both doing splendidly. And I could wring my own neck for dragging you two into all this.'

'Nonsense. If anyone around here needs his neck wrung it's Capricorn,' said Elinor. 'And that man Basta. My God, I'd never have thought the idea of strangling another human being would give me such enormous satisfaction. But I'm sure if I could just get my hands round that Basta's neck, I—'

On seeing the shock in Meggie's eyes she fell guiltily silent, but Meggie just shrugged her shoulders.

'I feel the same,' she murmured, and began scratching an 'M' on the wall with the key of her bicycle lock. Weird to think she still had that key in her trouser pocket – like a souvenir of another life.

Elinor ran her finger down one of the ladders in her tights, and Mo turned on his back and stared up at the ceiling. 'I'm so sorry, Meggie,' he said suddenly. 'I'm so sorry I let them take the book away from me.'

Meggie scratched an 'E' in the wall. 'It doesn't make any difference,' she said, stepping back. The Gs in her name looked like nibbled Os. 'You probably couldn't have read her back out of it again anyway.'

'No, probably not,' murmured Mo, and went on staring at the ceiling.

'It's not your fault,' said Meggie. She wanted to add: the main thing is you're with me. The main thing is for Basta never to put his knife to your throat again. I mean, I hardly remember my mother. I only know her from a couple of photographs. But Meggie said none of that, for she knew it wouldn't comfort Mo, it would probably just make him sadder than ever. For the first time, Meggie had some idea of how much he missed her mother. And for one crazy moment she felt jealous.

She scratched an 'I' in the plaster – that was an easy letter

– then she lowered the key.

Footsteps were approaching outside. Elinor put her hand to her mouth when they stopped.

Basta pushed open the door, and there was someone behind him. Meggie recognised the old woman she had seen in Capricorn's house. With a dour expression on her face, she pushed past Basta and put a mug and a thermos jug on the floor. 'As if I didn't have enough to do!' she muttered, before going out again. 'So now we have to feed up our fine guests too! They might at least be put to work if you have to keep them here.'

'Tell that to Capricorn,' was all Basta replied. Then he drew his knife, smiled at Elinor, and wiped the blade on his jacket. It was getting dark outside, and his snow-white shirt shone in the gathering twilight.

'Enjoy your tea, Silvertongue,' he said, relishing the discomfort on Elinor's face. 'Mortola's put so much honey in the jug your mouth will probably stick up with the first sip you take, but your throat will be as good as new tomorrow.'

'What have you done with the boy?' asked Mo.

'Oh, I think he's next door to you. Capricorn hasn't decided what's to become of him yet. Cockerell will try him out with a little ordeal by fire tomorrow, then we'll know if he's any use to us.'

Mo sat up. 'Ordeal by fire?' he asked, his voice both bitter and mocking. 'Well, you can't have passed that one yourself. You're even afraid of Dustfinger's matches.'

'Watch your tongue!' Basta hissed at him. 'One more word and I'll cut it out, however precious it may be.'

'Oh no, you won't,' said Mo, standing up. He took his time over filling the mug with steaming tea.

'Maybe not.' Basta lowered his voice, as if afraid of being overheard. 'But your little daughter has a tongue too, and hers isn't as valuable as yours.'

Mo flung the mug of hot tea at him, but Basta closed the door so quickly that the mug smashed into the wood. 'Sweet dreams!' he called from outside as he shot the bolts. 'See you in the morning.'

None of them said a word when he was gone, not for a long, long time. 'Mo, tell me a story,' Meggie whispered at last.

'What story do you want to hear?' he asked, putting his arm round her shoulders.

'Tell me the one about us being in Egypt,' she whispered, 'and we're looking for treasure and surviving sandstorms and scorpions and all the scary ghosts rising from their tombs to watch over their precious grave goods.'

'Oh, that story,' said Mo. 'Didn't I make it up for your eighth birthday? It's rather a gloomy tale, as far as I remember.'

'Yes, very!' said Meggie. 'But it has a happy ending. Everything turns out all right, and we come home laden with treasure.'

'I wouldn't mind hearing that one myself,' said Elinor, her voice unsteady. She was probably still thinking of Basta's knife.

So Mo began to tell his story, without the rustle of pages, without the endless labyrinth of letters.

'Mo, nothing ever came out of a story you were just *telling*, did it?' asked Meggie at one point, suddenly feeling anxious.

'No,' he said. 'For that to happen, it seems that printer's ink is necessary and someone else needs to have made up the story.' Then he continued, and Meggie and Elinor listened until his voice had carried them far, far away. Finally, they went to sleep.

A sound woke them all. Someone was fiddling with the lock of the door. Meggie thought she heard a muffled curse.

'Oh no!' breathed Elinor. She was the first on her feet. 'They're coming to take me away! That old woman's persuaded them! Why feed us up? You, maybe,' she said, looking frantically at Mo, 'but why me?'

'Go over to the wall, Elinor,' said Mo as he moved Meggie behind him. 'Both of you keep well back from the door.'

The lock sprang open with a muffled little click, and the door was pushed just far enough open for someone to squeeze through it. Dustfinger. He cast a last anxious glance outside, then pulled the door shut behind him and leaned against it.

'So I hear you've done it again, Silvertongue!' he said, lowering his voice. 'They say the poor boy still hasn't uttered a sound. I don't blame him. I can tell you, it's a horrible feeling suddenly landing in someone else's story.'

'What are you doing here?' snapped Elinor. But the sight of Dustfinger had actually filled her with relief.

'Leave him alone, Elinor,' said Mo, moving her aside and going over to Dustfinger. 'How are your hands?' he asked.

Dustfinger shrugged. 'They put cold water on them in the kitchen, but the skin's still almost as red as the flames that licked at it.'

'Ask him what he wants!' hissed Elinor. 'And if he's just come to tell us he can't do anything about the mess we're in, then you might as well wring his lying neck!'

By way of answer, Dustfinger tossed her a bunch of keys.

'Why do you think I'm here?' he grumbled back, switching off the light. 'Stealing the car keys from Basta wasn't easy, and a word of thanks might not be out of place, but we can think about that later. We don't want to hang about any longer – let's get out of here.' Cautiously, he opened the door and listened. 'There's a sentry posted up on the church tower,' he whispered, 'but the guards are keeping watch on the hills, not the village. The dogs are in their kennels, and even if we do have to deal with them, luckily they like me better than Basta.'

'Why should we suddenly trust him?' whispered Elinor to Mo. 'Suppose there's some other devilry behind this?'

'I want you to take me with you. That's my only motive!' snapped Dustfinger. 'There's nothing here for me any more. Capricorn's let me down. He's sent the only scrap of hope I still had up in smoke! He thinks he can do what he likes with me. Dustfinger's only a dog you can kick without fearing he may bite back, but he's wrong there. He burned the book, so I'm taking away the reader I brought him. And as for you,' he said, jabbing his burnt finger into Elinor's chest, 'you can come because you have a car. No one gets out of this village on foot, not even Capricorn's men, not with the snakes that infest these hills. But I can't drive, and so . . .'

'I knew it!' Elinor almost forgot to keep her voice down. 'He just wants to save his own skin. That's why he's helping us! He doesn't have a guilty conscience, oh no. Why should he?'

'I don't care why he's helping us, Elinor,' Mo interrupted her impatiently. 'We have to get away from here, that's what matters. But we're going to take someone else with us too.'

'Someone else? Who?' Dustfinger looked at him uneasily.

'The boy. The one I condemned yesterday to the same fate

as you,' replied Mo, making his way past Dustfinger and out of the door. 'Basta said he's next door to us, and a lock is no obstacle to your clever fingers.'

'I burned those clever fingers today!' muttered Dustfinger angrily. 'Still, just as you please. Your soft heart will be the ruin of us yet.'

When Dustfinger knocked on the door bearing the number 5 a faint rustling could be heard on the other side of it. 'Seems like they were going to let him live,' he whispered as he got to work on the lock. 'They put people condemned to death in the crypt under the church. Ever since I told Basta for a joke that a White Lady haunts the stone coffins down there, he turns white as a sheet whenever Capricorn sends him into the crypt.' He chuckled quietly at the memory, like a schoolboy who's just played a particularly good practical joke.

Meggie looked across at the church. 'Do they often condemn people to death?' she asked quietly.

Dustfinger shrugged. 'Not as often as they used to. But it does happen.'

'Stop telling her such stories!' whispered Mo. He and Elinor never took their eyes off the church tower. The sentry was posted high up on the wall beside the belfry. It made Meggie dizzy just to look up there.

'Those are no stories, Silvertongue, it's the truth! Don't you recognise the truth when you meet it any more? The truth's not pretty, of course. No one likes to look it in the face.' Dustfinger stepped back from the door and bowed. 'After you. I've picked the lock, you can fetch him out.' Even with his burnt fingers it hadn't taken him long.

'You go in,' Mo whispered to Meggie. 'He'll be less afraid of you.'

It was pitch dark on the other side of the door, but Meggie heard a rustle as she stepped into the room, as if an animal were moving somewhere in the straw. Dustfinger put his arm through the doorway and handed her a torch. When Meggie switched it on, the beam of light fell on the boy's dark face. The straw they had given him seemed even mouldier than the pile on which Meggie had slept, but the boy looked as if he hadn't closed his eyes since Flatnose had locked him in anyway. His arms were tightly clasped round his legs, as if they were all he could rely on. Perhaps he was still waiting for his nightmare to end.

'Come with us!' whispered Meggie, reaching out a hand to him. 'We want to help you! We'll take you away from here!'

He didn't move, just stared at her, his eyes narrow with distrust.

'Hurry up, Meggie!' breathed Mo through the door.

The boy glanced at him and retreated until his back was right up against the wall.

'Please!' whispered Meggie. 'You must come! The people here will do bad things to you.'

He was still looking at her. Then he stood up, cautiously, never taking his eyes off her. He was taller than she was by almost a hand's breadth. Suddenly, he leaped forward, making for the open door. He pushed Meggie aside so roughly that she fell over, but he couldn't get past Mo.

'Here, take it easy!' Mo said under his breath. 'We really do want to help you, but you must do as we say, understand?'

The boy glared at him with dislike. 'You're all devils!' he whispered. 'Devils or demons!' So he did understand their language, and why not? His own story was told in every language in the world.

Meggie got up and rubbed her knee. She must have grazed it on the stone floor. 'If you want to see some real devils then all you have to do is stay here!' she hissed at the boy as she pushed her way past him. He flinched as if she were a witch.

Mo drew the boy to his side. 'See that man on watch up there?' he whispered, pointing to the church tower. 'If he sees us they'll kill us.'

The boy looked up at the man on guard.

Dustfinger went over to him. 'Hurry up, will you?' he said quietly. 'If the lad doesn't want to go with us then he can just stay here. And the rest of you take your shoes off,' he added, glancing at the boy's bare feet, 'or you'll make more noise than a flock of goats.'

Elinor grumbled something in a cross voice, but she obeyed, and the boy did follow them, if hesitantly. Dustfinger hurried on ahead as if trying to outstrip his own shadow. The alley down which he led them sloped so steeply that Meggie kept stumbling, and every time Elinor stubbed her toes on the bumpy cobblestones she uttered a quiet curse. It was dark between the close-set houses. Masonry arches stretched from one side of the street to the other, as if to prevent the walls from collapsing. The rusty street lights cast ghostly shadows. Every noise sounded threatening, every cat scurrying out of a doorway made Meggie jump. But Capricorn's village was asleep. They passed only one guard, leaning on the wall in a side street and smoking. Two tom cats were fighting some- where on the rooftops, and the guard bent to pick up a stone to throw at them. Dustfinger took advantage of the moment. Meggie was very glad he had made them take off their shoes. They slipped soundlessly past the guard whose back was still turned, but Meggie dared not breathe again until they were round the next corner. Once again, she noticed the many empty houses, the blank windows, the dilapidated doors. What had wrecked these homes? Just the course of time? Had the people who once lived here run away from Capricorn, or was the village already abandoned before he and his men took up residence? Hadn't Dustfinger said something like that?

He had stopped. He raised his hand in a warning gesture, and put a finger to his lips. They had reached the outskirts of the village. Only the car park still lay ahead. Two street lights illuminated the surface of the cracked asphalt, and a tall wire-netting fence rose to their left. 'The arena for Capricorn's ceremonies and festivities is on the other side of that fence,' whispered Dustfinger. 'I suppose the village children once played football there, but these days it's the scene of Capricorn's diabolical celebrations: bonfires, brandy, a few shots fired into the air, fireworks – that's their idea of fun.'

They put their shoes on before following Dustfinger into the car park. Meggie kept looking at the wire fence. Diabolical celebrations. She could almost see the bonfires . . . 'Come on, Meggie!' urged Mo, leading her on. The sound of rushing water could be heard somewhere in the darkness, and Meggie remembered the bridge they had crossed on the way here. Suppose a guard was stationed there this time?

There were several cars in the car park, including Elinor's, which was parked a little way from the others. They all kept looking around anxiously as they ran towards it. Behind them the church tower rose high above the rooftops, and there was nothing now to shield them from the sentry's eyes. Meggie couldn't see him at this distance, but she was sure he was still there. From such a height they must look like black beetles crawling over a table. Did he have a pair of binoculars?

'Come on, Elinor!' whispered Mo. It seemed to be taking her forever to unlock the car door.

'All right, all right!' she growled back. 'I just don't have such nimble hands as our light-fingered friend.'

Mo put his arm round Meggie's shoulders as he looked around, but apart from a few stray cats he could see nothing moving in the car park or among the houses. Reassured, he made Meggie get into the back seat. The boy hesitated for a moment, examining the car as if it were some strange animal and he couldn't be sure whether it was kindly disposed or would swallow him alive, but finally he got in too. Meggie scowled at him and moved as far away from him as possible. Her knee still hurt.

'Where's the matchstick-eater?' whispered Elinor. 'Dammit, don't tell me the man's disappeared again.'

Meggie was the first to spot him. He was stealing over to the other cars. Elinor clutched the steering-wheel as if resisting only with difficulty the temptation to drive off without him. 'What's he up to this time?' she hissed.

None of them knew the answer. Dustfinger was gone for an excruciatingly long time, and when he came back he was closing a flick-knife.

'What was the idea of that?' Elinor snapped, when he squeezed into the back seat next to the boy. 'Didn't you say we must hurry? And what were you doing with that knife? Not cutting someone open, I hope!'

'Is my name Basta?' enquired Dustfinger, annoyed, as he forced his legs in behind the driver's seat. 'I was slitting their tyres, that's all. Just to be on the safe side.' He was still holding the knife.

Meggie looked at it uneasily. 'That's Basta's knife,' she said.

Dustfinger smiled as he put it in his trouser pocket. 'Not any more. I'd like to have stolen his silly amulet too, but he wears it round his neck even at night, and that *would* have been too dangerous.'

Somewhere a dog began to bark. Mo wound down his window and put his head out, looking concerned.

'Believe it or not, it's only toads making all that racket,' said Elinor. But what Meggie suddenly heard echoing through the night was nothing like the croaking of toads, and when she looked in alarm through the back window a man was climbing out of one of the parked vehicles, a dusty, dirty white delivery van. It was one of Capricorn's men. Meggie had seen him in the church. He looked around him with a face still dazed by sleep.

Before Meggie could stop her, Elinor started the engine, and the man snatched a shotgun from his back and stumbled towards the car. For a moment Meggie almost felt sorry for him – he looked so sleepy and baffled. What would Capricorn do to a guard who fell asleep on duty? But then he aimed the gun and fired it. Meggie ducked her head well below the back of the seat, and Elinor pressed her foot down hard on the accelerator.

'Damn it all!' she shouted at Dustfinger. 'Didn't you see that man when you were slinking about among the cars?'

'No, I didn't!' Dustfinger shouted back. 'Now, drive! Not *that* way! It's over there. We must get to the road!'

Elinor wrenched the steering-wheel around. The boy was huddled down beside Meggie. At every shot he had closed his eyes tight and put his hands over his ears. Were there any guns in his story? Probably not, any more than there were cars. His and Meggie's heads knocked together as Elinor's car bumped over the stony track. When it finally reached the road things weren't much better.

'This isn't the road we came along!' cried Elinor. Capricorn's village loomed over them like a fortress. The houses simply refused to get any smaller.

'Oh yes, it is! But Basta met us further down when we arrived.' Dustfinger was clinging to the seat with one hand and to his rucksack with the other. A furious chattering came from the bag, and the boy cast it a terrified glance.

Meggie thought she recognised the place where Basta had met them when they drove past it – it was the hill from which she had seen the village for the first time. Then the houses suddenly disappeared, engulfed by the night, as if Capricorn's village had never existed.

There was no guard posted on the bridge, nor at the rusty barrier across the road cutting off the way to the village. Meggie looked back at it until the darkness had swallowed it up. It's over, she thought. It really is all over.

The night was clear. Meggie had never seen so many stars. The sky stretched above the black hills like a cloth embroidered with tiny beads. The whole world seemed to consist of hills, like a cat arching its back at the face of the night – no human beings, no houses. No fear.

Mo turned round and stroked the hair back from Meggie's forehead. 'Everything all right?' he asked.

She nodded and closed her eyes. Suddenly, all Meggie wanted to do was sleep – if only the pounding of her heart would let her.

'It's a dream,' murmured a toneless voice beside her. 'Only a dream. It's just a dream. What else can it be?'

Meggie turned to the boy, who wasn't looking at her. 'It has to be a dream!' he repeated, nodding vigorously as if to encourage himself. 'Everything looks wrong, false, weird, like in dreams, and now,' he murmured, turning his head to indicate the surroundings outside, 'now we're flying. Or the night is flying past us. Or something.'

Meggie could almost have smiled. She wanted to tell him it wasn't a dream, but she was just too tired to explain the whole complicated story. She looked at Dustfinger. He was patting the fabric of his rucksack, probably trying to soothe his angry marten.

'Don't look at me like that!' he said when he saw Meggie watching him. 'You can't expect *me* to explain. Your father will have to do that. After all, the poor lad's nightmare is his fault.'

Mo's guilty conscience showed clearly on his face when he turned to the boy. 'What's your name?' he asked. 'It wasn't in the—' But there he broke off.

The boy looked at him suspiciously, then bowed his head. 'Farid,' he said dully. 'My name is Farid, but I believe it's unlucky to speak in a dream. You never find your way back if you do.' He shut his mouth tightly and stared straight ahead, as if to avoid looking at anyone, and said no more. Did he have a mother and father in his story? Meggie couldn't remember. It had just mentioned a boy, a boy without a name who served a band of thieves.

'It's a dream,' he whispered again. 'Only a dream. The sun will rise and it will all disappear. That's what it'll do.'

Mo looked at him, unhappy and at a loss, like someone

who has handled a young bird, knowing it can never return to the nest. Poor Mo, thought Meggie. Poor Farid. But she was thinking of something else too, and she was ashamed of herself for it. Ever since she had seen the lizard crawl out of the golden coins in Capricorn's church she couldn't help thinking about it. I wish I could do that, her thoughts had kept saying to her, very quietly. The wish had settled like a cuckoo in the nest of her heart, where it kept fluffing up its plumage and making itself at home, no matter how hard she tried to throw it out. I wish I could do that, it whispered. I'd like to bring them out of books, touch them, all those characters, all those wonderful characters. I want them to come out of the pages and sit beside me, I want them to smile at me, I want, I want, I want . . .

Outside, it was still as dark as if morning would never come.

'I'm going to drive straight on,' said Elinor, 'until we reach my house.'

Far behind them, headlights showed, like fingers probing the night.

20

Snakes and Thorns

'None of that matters now,' said Twilight. 'Look behind you.'

The Borribles did and there, just a little beyond the rim of the bridge, they saw a halo of harsh whiteness reflected on the underneath of the dark sky. It was the beam of a car's headlights as it got into position on the north side of the bridge, the side the runaways had left only moments before.

Michael de Larrabeiti, *The Borribles Go For Broke*

Behind them the headlights were getting closer, no matter how fast Elinor drove.

'It could be just any old car,' said Meggie, but she knew that was unlikely. There was only one village on the bumpy, potholed road they had been following for almost an hour, and that was Capricorn's. Their pursuers could only have come from there.

'Now what?' asked Elinor. She was in such a state the car was weaving all over the road. 'I'm not letting them lock me up in that hole again. No. No. No.' At each 'No' she struck the steering-wheel with the palm of her hand. 'Didn't you say you'd slit their tyres?' she snapped at Dustfinger.

'Yes, and so I did!' he replied angrily. 'Obviously they've thought of that kind of thing. Ever heard of spare tyres? Go on, step on it! There ought to be a village quite soon. It can't be far away now. If we can make it that far . . .'

'*If*, yes. *If* is the question,' said Elinor, tapping the fuel gauge. 'I've got enough petrol for about another ten kilometres, twenty at the most.'

But they never got that far. As they swerved round a sharp bend one of the front tyres blew out. Elinor only just managed to wrench the steering-wheel round before the car skidded off the road. Meggie screamed, burying her face in her hands. For a terrible moment she thought they were going to plunge down the steep slope to their left, the bottom of which disappeared in the darkness, but the car skidded to the right, scraped its wing against the low stone wall on the other side of the road, gave a last gasp and came to a halt under the low branches of a chestnut oak that leaned over the road.

'Oh hell, hell, bloody hell!' swore Elinor, undoing her seat-belt. 'Everyone all right?'

'Now I know why I've never trusted cars,' muttered Dustfinger, opening his door.

Meggie sat there trembling all over. Mo pulled her out of the car and looked anxiously at her face. 'Are you all right?'

Meggie nodded.

Farid climbed out on Dustfinger's side. Did he still think he was dreaming?

Dustfinger stood in the road, rucksack over his shoulder, listening. The umistakable sound of an engine came purring through the night from far away.

'We must get the car off the road!' he said.

'What?' Elinor looked at him in horror.

'We'll have to push it down the slope.'

'My car!' Elinor was almost screaming.

'He's right, Elinor,' said Mo. 'Perhaps we can shake them off that way. We'll push the car down the slope – they may not notice it in the dark, and even if they do, they'll think we came off the road. Then we can climb up the hill on the other side and hide among the trees.'

Elinor cast a doubtful glance at the hill on their right. 'But it's much too steep! And what about the snakes?'

'I'm sure Basta has a new knife by now,' Dustfinger reminded her.

Elinor gave him her darkest look and, without another word, went round to the back of her car to check inside the boot. 'Where's our luggage?' she asked.

Dustfinger looked at her with amusement. 'I expect Basta's divided it out among Capricorn's maids. He likes to ingratiate himself with them.'

Elinor looked at him as if she didn't believe a word of it, but then quickly closed the boot, braced her arms against the car, and began to push.

They couldn't do it.

Hard as they pushed and shoved, Elinor's car only rolled off the road but would not slide more than a few metres down the slope. Then it stopped with its bonnet stuck in the under-growth and refused to go any further. Meanwhile, the sound of the engine, so curiously out of place in this desolate wilderness, was getting alarmingly loud. Dustfinger gave the obsti-nate car a final kick, and they all clambered back up to the road, sweating. After climbing over an ancient wall on the other side they struggled on up the slope. Anything to get away from the road itself. Mo hauled Meggie along behind him whenever she got stuck, and Dustfinger helped Farid. Elinor had her work cut out getting herself up the hillside, which was criss-crossed with low walls that had been built in a laborious attempt to wrest narrow fields and orchards from the poor soil, somewhere to grow a few olive trees and grape vines, anything that would bear fruit here. But the trees had run wild, and the ground was covered with fruit that was no longer harvested, for the people who once lived here had long since left to find an easier life elsewhere.

'Keep your heads down!' gasped Dustfinger, ducking behind one of the ruined walls. 'They're coming!' Mo pulled Meggie down under the nearest tree. The tangled thorn bushes growing among its gnarled roots were just tall enough to hide them.

'What about the snakes?' Elinor whispered as she stumbled after them.

'Too cold for snakes at the moment!' whispered Dustfinger from his hiding-place. 'Haven't you learnt anything from all those clever books of yours?'

Elinor was about to snap back an answer, but Mo quickly put a hand over her mouth to keep her quiet. The vehicle appeared on the road below them. It was the white delivery van in which the guard had been sleeping. Without slowing down, it drove past the place where they had pushed Elinor's estate car over the slope, and disappeared round the next bend. Relieved, Meggie was about to raise her head above the thorn bushes when Mo pushed her down again. 'Not yet!' he muttered, straining his ears.

The night was perfectly still. Meggie had never known one like it. It was as if she could hear the trees breathing – the trees, the grass, the night itself.

They watched the van headlights emerge on the slope of the next hill: two fingers of light groping their way along an invisible road in the dark. But suddenly they stopped moving.

'They're turning!' whispered Elinor. 'Oh God! Now what?'

She tried to stand up, but Mo held her back. 'Are you mad?' he hissed. 'It's too late to climb any further. They'd see us.'

Mo was right. The delivery van was speeding back up the road. Meggie saw it stop just a few metres from where they had pushed Elinor's car off the road. She heard the van doors open and saw two men get out. Both had their backs to the fugitives, but when one of them turned and looked suspiciously up the slope Meggie thought she recognised Basta's face, though it was little more than a patch of paler colour in the night.

'There's the car,' said the other man.

Was that Flatnose? He was certainly tall and broad enough. 'See if they're in it.'

Yes, that *was* Basta. Meggie would have known his voice among a thousand others.

Flatnose made his way down the slope, clumsy as a bear. Meggie heard him cursing the thorns, the prickles, the darkness and the wretched riff-raff he was having to stumble after in the middle of the night. Basta was still standing in the road. His face was sharply outlined when he lit a cigarette with a lighter. The white smoke drifted up to them until Meggie thought she could almost smell it.

'They're not here,' called Flatnose. 'They must have got

away on foot. Hell, do you think we have to follow them?'

Basta went over to the roadside and looked down. Then he turned and looked up at the slope where Meggie was crouching beside Mo, her heart thudding wildly. 'They can't have got far,' he said. 'But it'll be difficult to find their trail in the dark.'

'Exactly!' Flatnose was panting as he appeared back on the road. 'We're not bloody trackers, are we?'

Basta did not reply. He just stood there, listening and inhaling his cigarette smoke. Then he whispered something to Flatnose. Meggie's heart almost stopped.

Flatnose looked round anxiously. 'Nah, let's get the dogs instead!' Meggie heard him say. 'Even if they're hiding somewhere around here, how do we know whether they climbed up or down?'

Basta glanced at the trees, looked down the road, and trod out his cigarette. Then he went back to the van and took out two shotguns. 'We'll try going down first,' he said, tossing Flatnose one of the guns. 'I'm sure that fat woman would rather climb downhill.' And without another word, he vanished into the darkness. Flatnose cast the van a longing glance, then trudged after him, grumbling.

The two were barely out of sight before Dustfinger rose to his feet, soundless as a shadow, and pointed up the slope. Meggie's heart was beating in her throat as they followed him. They darted from tree to tree, from bush to bush, constantly looking behind them. Every time a twig cracked underfoot Meggie jumped, but luckily Basta and Flatnose were making a fair amount of noise themselves as they worked their way downhill through the undergrowth.

A time came when they couldn't see the road any more. But their fear did not leave them, the fear that Basta might have turned back already and was now following them uphill. Yet, however often they stopped and listened, all they could hear was their own breathing.

'They'll soon realise they've gone the wrong way,' Dustfinger whispered after a while. 'Then they'll go back for the dogs. We're lucky they didn't bring them in the first place. Basta doesn't think much of those dogs, and he's right. I've fed them cheese often enough, and cheese dulls a dog's nose. All the same, he'll fetch them sooner or later, because even Basta doesn't like taking bad news back to Capricorn.'

'Then we must just go faster,' said Mo.

'Go faster where?' Elinor was still fighting for breath.

Dustfinger looked round. Meggie wondered why. She could hardly make anything out, it was so dark. 'We must keep going south,' said Dustfinger. 'Towards the coast. We must hide among other people. That's the only thing that can save us. Down there the nights are bright and nobody believes in the Devil.'

Farid was standing beside Meggie, gazing at the night sky as if he could make morning come, or find the people Dustfinger had mentioned somewhere, but there wasn't a light to be seen in the darkness except for the tangle of stars sparkling cold and distant in the heavens. For a moment, Meggie felt as if those stars were eyes giving their presence away, and imagined she could hear them whispering, 'Look, Basta, there they go, down there! Quick, catch them!'

They stumbled on, keeping close together so that no one would get lost. Dustfinger had taken Gwin out of his rucksack and put him on his chain before letting him run with them.

The marten didn't seem to like it. Dustfinger had to keep hauling him out of the undergrowth, away from all the promising scents that their human noses couldn't pick up. The marten spat and snarled with annoyance, biting and tearing at the chain.

'Curse the little brute, I'm sure to fall over it,' said Elinor crossly. 'Can't you keep it away from my sore feet? I tell you one thing, the moment we're in decent human company again I'm going to take the best hotel room money can buy and put my poor feet up on a big soft cushion.'

'You've still got money on you?' Mo sounded incredulous. 'They took all mine first thing.'

'Yes, Basta took my wallet too,' said Elinor. 'But I think ahead. I have my credit card somewhere safe.'

'Is anywhere safe from Basta?' Dustfinger dragged Gwin away from a tree trunk.

'Oh yes,' replied Elinor. 'Men are never particularly keen to search fat old ladies. Which can be useful. That was how some of my most valuable books came into my—' She interrupted herself abruptly, clearing her throat when her eyes fell on Meggie. But Meggie acted as if she hadn't heard Elinor's last remark, or at least hadn't understood what she meant.

'You're not all that fat!' Meggie said. 'And *old* is a bit of an exaggeration!' Oh, how her own feet hurt.

'Well, thank you very much, darling!' said Elinor. 'I think I'll buy you from your father so you can say nice things like that to me three times a day. How much do you want for her, Mo?'

'I'll have to think about it,' replied Mo. 'Suppose I lend her to you for a few days now and then?'

They chatted like this, voices scarcely raised above a

whisper, as they struggled through the thorny growth on the hillside. It didn't matter what they talked about, for their hushed conversation had only one purpose: to fend off the fear and exhaustion weighing down all their limbs. On and on they walked, hoping that Dustfinger knew where he was taking them. Meggie kept close behind Mo all the time. At least his back offered some protection from the thorny branches which kept catching at her clothes and scratching her face, like vicious animals with needle-sharp claws lying in wait in the dark.

At last, they came upon a footpath they could follow. It was littered with empty cartridge cases dropped by hunters who had dealt out death in this silent place. Walking was easier on the trodden earth, although Meggie was so tired she could hardly pick her feet up. When she stumbled against the back of Mo's legs for the second time, he put her on his back and carried her as he used to do before she could keep up with his long legs. He had called her 'Little Flea' in those days, or 'Feather Girl', or 'Tinker Bell' after the fairy in *Peter Pan*. Sometimes he still called her Tinker Bell.

Wearily, Meggie rested her face against his shoulders and tried to think of *Peter Pan* instead of snakes, or men with knives. But this time her own story was too strong to give way to an invented one. Mo was right: fear, unfortunately, devours everything.

It was a long time since Farid had said anything. Most of the time he stumbled along after Dustfinger. He seemed to have taken a fancy to Gwin. Whenever the marten's chain got caught up somewhere Farid would rush to free him, even if Gwin only hissed at him in return and snapped at his fingers. Once he sank his teeth into the boy's thumb and made it bleed.

'Well, do you still think this is a dream?' asked Dustfinger ironically as Farid wiped the blood away.

The boy didn't answer, just examined his sore thumb. Then he sucked it and spat. 'What else could it be?' he asked.

Dustfinger looked at Mo, but he seemed so deep in thought that he didn't notice the glance. 'How about another story?' said Dustfinger.

Farid laughed. 'Another story. I like that idea. I've always been fond of stories.'

'Oh yes? And how do you like this one?'

'Too many thorns, and I wish it would get light, but at least I haven't had to work yet. That's something.'

Meggie couldn't help smiling.

A bird called in the distance. Gwin stopped and raised his round muzzle, sniffing the air. The night belongs to beasts of prey, and always has. It's easy to forget that when you're indoors, protected by light and solid walls. Night provides cover for hunters, making it easy for them to creep up and strike their prey blind. Words about the night from one of her favourite books slipped into Meggie's mind: *'This is the hour of pride and power, talon and tush and claw.'*

She snuggled her face against Mo's shoulder once more. Perhaps I ought to walk again, she thought. He's been carrying me for so long. But then she nodded off to sleep still perched on his back.

21

Basta

This grove, that was now so peaceful, must then have rung with cries, I thought; and even with the thought I could believe I heard it ringing still.

Robert Louis Stevenson, *Treasure Island*

Meggie woke up when Mo stopped. The path had brought them almost to the crest of the hill. It was still dark, but the night was growing paler as if lifting her skirts a little way off to let the new morning appear.

'We must take a breather, Dustfinger,' Meggie heard Mo saying. 'The boy can hardly keep up, Elinor's feet must need a rest, and if you ask me this wouldn't be a bad place for one.'

'What feet?' asked Elinor, sinking to the ground with a groan. 'You mean those poor sore objects attached to my legs?'

'That's what I mean,' said Mo, as he pulled her up again. 'But they must go just a little further. We'll rest up there.'

A good fifty metres to their left, at the very top of the hill, there was a house, if you could call it that, huddled among the olive trees. Meggie slipped off Mo's back before they climbed up to it. The walls looked as if someone had piled up a number of stones in a hurry, the roof had collapsed, and where there must once have been a door only a black hole now gaped.

Mo had to bend low to make his way in. Broken shingles from the roof covered the floor, there was an empty sack in a corner, some broken earthenware shards, perhaps from a dish or a plate, and a few bones gnawed clean. Mo sighed.

'Not a very comfortable place, Meggie,' he said. 'But try imagining you're hiding out with the Lost Boys, or . . .'

'Or in Huckleberry Finn's tub.' Meggie looked round. 'I think I'd rather sleep outside, all the same.'

Elinor came in. The accommodation didn't seem to appeal much to her either.

Mo gave Meggie a kiss and went back to the door. 'Believe me, it'll be safer in here,' he said.

Meggie looked at him in concern. 'Where are you going? You have to get some sleep too.'

'Oh, I'm not tired.' His face gave away his lie. 'Go to sleep now, all right?' Then he went out again.

Elinor pushed the broken shingles aside with her foot. 'Come on,' she said, taking off her jacket and spreading it on the floor. 'Let's try to make ourselves comfortable together. Your father's right, we must just imagine we're somewhere else. Why are adventures so much more fun when you read about them?' she murmured, stretching out on the floor.

Cautiously, Meggie lay down beside her. 'At least it isn't raining,' remarked Elinor, looking at the collapsed roof. 'And we have the stars above us, even if they're fading. Perhaps I ought to have a few holes knocked in my own roof at home.' With an impatient nod, she told Meggie to lay her head on her arm. 'In case any spiders try crawling into your ears while you're asleep,' she said, closing her eyes. 'Oh Lord,' Meggie heard her add in a murmur, 'I'll have to buy a new pair of feet, I really will. There's no hope for these.' With that she was asleep.

But Meggie lay with her eyes wide open, listening to the sounds outside. She heard Mo talking quietly to Dustfinger, but she couldn't make out the words. Once she thought she heard Basta's name. The boy Farid had stayed outside too, but he made no sound.

Elinor began snoring after only a few minutes, but hard as Meggie tried she couldn't get to sleep, so she got up quietly and slipped outside. Mo was awake, sitting with his back against a tree, watching the morning light drive the night from the sky above the surrounding hills. Dustfinger was sitting a little further off. He raised his head only briefly when Meggie came out of the hut. Was he thinking of the fairies and the brownies? Farid lay beside him, curled up like a dog, and Gwin was sitting at his feet eating something – Meggie quickly turned her head away.

Dawn was breaking over the hills, casting light on summit after summit. Meggie saw houses in the distance, scattered like toys on the green slopes. The sea must lie somewhere beyond them. She put her head on Mo's lap and looked up at his face.

'They won't find us here, will they?' she asked.

'No, of course not!' he said, but his face wasn't half as carefree as his voice. 'Why aren't you asleep in there with Elinor?'

'She snores,' murmured Meggie.

Mo smiled. Then, frowning, he looked down the hillside to the place where the path lay, hidden by rockroses, gorse and thorns.

Dustfinger never took his eyes off the path either. The sight of the two men on watch made Meggie feel better, and soon she was sleeping as deeply as Farid – as if the ground outside the tumbledown house were covered with downy feathers instead of thorns.

When Mo shook her awake, she thought at first it had all been just a bad dream – but his hand was over her mouth. He was holding a finger to his lips in warning. Meggie heard the rustle of grass and the barking of a dog. Mo pulled her to her feet and pushed her and Farid into the shelter of the dark hovel. Elinor was still snoring. She looked like a young girl with the light of dawn on her face, but as soon as Mo had woken her all her weariness, anxiety and fear came rushing back.

Mo and Dustfinger stationed themselves by the doorway, one to the left and the other to the right, their backs pressed to the wall. Men's voices broke the quiet of the morning. Meggie thought she could hear the dogs sniffing, and wished she could dissolve into thin air, odourless and invisible air. Farid stood beside her, his eyes wide. Meggie noticed for the first time that they were almost black. She had never seen such dark eyes, and his lashes were as long as a girl's.

Elinor was leaning against the wall opposite, biting her lips nervously. Dustfinger made a sign to Mo, and before Meggie realised what their plan was they made their way out. The olive trees where they took cover were stunted, with matted branches hanging almost to the ground, as if the weight of their leaves was too much for them. A child could easily have hidden behind them, but did they provide enough shelter for two grown men?

Meggie peered out of the doorway. Her heart was beating so fast that it almost suffocated her. Outside, the sun was rising higher and higher. Daylight crept into every valley, beneath every tree, and suddenly Meggie wished for the night again. Mo was kneeling down so that his head couldn't be seen above the tangled branches. Dustfinger was pressed close to a crooked tree trunk, and there, terrifyingly close, twenty paces at most away from the two of them, was Basta. He was making his way up the slope through thistles and knee-high grass.

'They'll have reached the valley by now!' Meggie heard a rough voice call, and next moment Flatnose appeared beside Basta. They had brought two vicious-looking dogs with them. Meggie saw the dogs' broad skulls pushing through the grass, and heard them snuffling.

'What, with two children and that fat woman?' Basta shook his head and looked round. Farid peered past Meggie – and flinched back as if something had bitten him when he saw the two men.

'Basta?' Soundlessly, Elinor's lips formed his name. Meggie nodded, and Elinor went even paler than she was already.

'Damn it, Basta, how much longer are you going to trudge around here?' Flatnose's voice echoed a long way in the silence that lay over the hills. 'The snakes will soon be waking up, and I'm hungry. Let's just say they fell into the valley with the car. We'll give it another push and no one will find out! The snakes will probably get them anyway. And if not, then they'll lose their way, starve, get sunstroke – oh, who cares what happens? But anyway we'll never see them again.'

'He's been feeding them cheese!' Basta furiously hauled the dogs to his side. 'That bloody little fire-eater has been feeding them cheese to ruin their noses. But nobody would believe me. No wonder they whine with joy every time they see his ugly mug.'

'You beat them too much,' grunted Flatnose. 'That's why they won't go to any trouble for you. Dogs don't like being beaten.'

'Nonsense. You have to beat them or they'll bite you! They like the fire-eater because he's like them – he whines, he's sly and he bites.' One of the dogs lay down in the grass and licked its paws. Angrily, Basta kicked it in the ribs and hauled it to its feet. 'You can go back to the village if you like!' he spat at Flatnose. 'But I'm going to get that fire-eater and cut off all his fingers one by one. Then we'll see how cleverly he can juggle. I always said he couldn't be trusted, but the boss thought his little tricks with fire were *so* entertaining.'

'OK, OK. Everyone knows you can't stand him.' Flatnose sounded bored. 'But he may have nothing to do with the disappearance of that lot. You know he's always come and gone as he pleased. Maybe he'll turn up again tomorrow knowing nothing about it.'

'Yeah, right,' growled Basta. He walked on. Every step brought him closer to the trees behind which Mo and Dustfinger were hiding. 'And Silvertongue pinched the fat woman's car key from under my pillow, did he? No. This time no excuses will do Dustfinger any good. Because he took something else too – something of mine.'

Involuntarily, Dustfinger put his hand to his belt, as if he were afraid that Basta's knife could call out to its master. One of the dogs raised its head and tugged Basta on towards the trees.

'He's found something!' Basta lowered his voice. 'The stupid creature's picked up a scent!'

Ten more paces, perhaps fewer, and he would be among the trees. What were they going to do? What on earth were they going to do?

Flatnose was trudging along after Basta with a sceptical expression on his face. 'They've probably scented a wild boar,' Meggie heard him say. 'You want to be careful, they can run you right down. Oh no, I think there's a snake there. One of those black snakes. You've got the antidote in the car, right?'

He stood there perfectly still, rooted to the spot and staring down at the ground in front of his feet. Basta took no notice of him. He followed the snuffling dog. A few more steps and Mo would only have to reach out a hand to touch him. Basta unslung the shotgun from his shoulder, stopped and listened. The dogs pulled to the left and jumped up at one of the tree trunks, barking.

Gwin was up there in the branches.

'What did I say?' called Flatnose. 'They've scented a marten, that's all. Those brutes stink so strong even I could pick up their smell!'

'That's no ordinary marten!' hissed Basta. 'Don't you recognise him?' His eyes were fixed on the ruined hovel.

Mo seized his opportunity. He sprang out from behind the tree, seized Basta and tried to wrench the gun from his hands.

'Get him! Get him, you brutes!' bellowed Basta, and obviously the dogs were willing to obey him this time. They leaped up at Mo, baring their yellow teeth. Before Meggie could run to his aid Elinor seized her, and held her tight no matter how hard she struggled, just as she had done before back in her own house. But this time there was someone else to help Mo. Before the dogs could get their teeth into him, Dustfinger had grabbed their collars. Meggie thought they would tear him apart when he dragged them off Mo, but instead they licked his hands, jumping up at him like an old friend and almost knocking him down.

But there was still Flatnose. Luckily, he wasn't too quick on the uptake. That saved them – for a brief moment he simply stood there staring at Basta, who was still struggling in Mo's grip.

Meanwhile, Dustfinger had hauled the dogs over to the nearest tree, and he was just winding their leashes round the cracked bark when Flatnose came out of his daze.

'Let them go!' he bellowed, pointing his shotgun at Mo.

With a suppressed curse, Dustfinger let the dogs loose, but the stone Farid threw moved faster than he did. It hit Flatnose in the middle of the forehead – an insignificant little stone, but the huge man collapsed in the grass at Dustfinger's feet like a felled tree.

'Keep the dogs off me!' called Mo as Basta fought to get control of his gun. One of the dogs had bitten Mo's sleeve. At least, Meggie hoped it was just his sleeve. Before Elinor could restrain her again she ran to the big dog and seized its studded collar. The dog wouldn't let go, however hard she pulled. She saw blood on Mo's arm, and she almost got hit on the head with the barrel of Basta's shotgun. Dustfinger tried to call the dogs off, and at first they obeyed him, or at least they let go of Mo, but then Basta succeeded in freeing himself. 'Get him!' he shouted, and the dogs stood there growling, not sure whether to obey Basta or Dustfinger.

'Bloody brutes' shouted Basta, pointing his shotgun at Mo's chest, but at that very moment Elinor pressed the muzzle of Flatnose's gun against his head. Her hands were shaking, and her face was covered with red blotches as it always was when she was worked up, but she looked more than determined to use the gun.

'Drop it, Basta,' she said, her voice unsteady. 'And not another word to those dogs! I may never have used a gun before but I'm sure I can manage to pull the trigger.'

'Sit!' Dustfinger ordered the dogs. They looked uncertainly at Basta, but when he said nothing they lay down in the grass and let Dustfinger tie them to the tree.

Blood was trickling from Mo's sleeve. Meggie felt herself turn faint at the sight of it. Dustfinger bound up the wound with a red silk scarf that soaked up the blood. 'It's not as bad as it looks,' he assured Meggie, as she came closer, feeling weak at the knees.

'Got anything else in your rucksack that we can use to tie him up?' asked Mo, nodding at the still unconscious Flatnose.

'Our friend with the knife here will need some packaging too,' said Elinor. Basta glared at her viciously. 'Don't stare at me like that,' she said, jamming the barrel of the gun into his chest. 'I'm sure a gun like this can do as much damage as a knife, and believe you me, that gives me some very unpleasant ideas.'

Basta twisted his mouth scornfully, but he never took his eyes off Elinor's forefinger, which was still on the trigger.

There was a length of cord in Dustfinger's rucksack, strong if not particularly thick. 'It won't be enough for both of them,' Dustfinger said.

'Why do you want to tie them up?' enquired Farid. 'Why not kill them? That's what they were going to do to us!'

Meggie looked at him in horror, but Basta laughed. 'Well, fancy that!' he mocked. 'We could have used that boy after all! But who says we were going to kill you? Capricorn wants you alive. Dead men can't read aloud.'

'Oh, really? And weren't you planning to cut off some of

my fingers?' asked Dustfinger, tying the cord round Flatnose's legs.

Basta shrugged. 'Since when does a man die of that?'

Elinor jabbed the barrel of the gun into his ribs so hard that he stumbled back. 'Hear that? I think the boy's right. Maybe we really ought to shoot these thugs.'

But of course they didn't. They found a rope in the rucksack that Flatnose had brought with him, and it gave Dustfinger obvious pleasure to tie Basta up. Farid helped him. He clearly knew something about tying up prisoners.

Then they put Basta and Flatnose in the ruined house. 'Nice of us, right? The snakes won't find you quite so soon,' said Dustfinger as they carried Basta through the narrow doorway. 'Of course it'll get pretty hot in here around midday, but maybe someone will have found you by then. We'll let the dogs go. If they have any sense they won't return to the village, but dogs don't often have much sense – so the whole gang will probably be out searching for you by this afternoon at the latest.'

Flatnose did not come round until he was lying beside Basta under the ruined roof. He rolled his eyes furiously and went purple in the face, but neither he nor Basta could utter a sound because Farid had gagged them both, again very expertly.

'Wait a minute,' said Dustfinger, before they left the two men to their fate. 'There's something else – something I've always wanted to do.' And to Meggie's horror he drew Basta's knife from his belt and went over to the prisoners.

'What's the idea?' asked Mo, barring his way. Obviously the same thought had occurred to him as to Meggie, but Dustfinger only laughed.

'Don't worry, I'm not going to cut a pattern in his face the way he decorated mine,' he said. 'I only want to scare him a little.'

And he bent down to cut through the leather thong that Basta wore round his neck. It had a little bag tied with a red drawstring hanging from it. Dustfinger leaned over Basta and swung the bag back and forth in front of his face. 'I'm taking your luck, Basta!' he said softly straightening up. 'Now there's nothing to protect you from the Evil Eye and the ghosts and demons, black cats and all the other things you're afraid of.'

Basta tried to kick out with his bound legs, but Dustfinger avoided him easily. 'This is goodbye for ever, I hope, Basta!' he said. 'And if our paths should ever cross again, then I'll have this.' He tied the leather thong around his own neck. 'I expect there's a lock of your hair in it, right? No? Well, then perhaps I'll take one. Doesn't burning someone's hair have a terrible effect on him?'

'That's enough!' said Mo, urging him away. 'Let's get out of here. Who knows when Capricorn will realise these two are missing? By the way, did I tell you that he didn't burn quite all the books? There's one copy of *Inkheart* left.'

Dustfinger stopped as suddenly as if a snake had bitten him.

'I thought I ought to tell you,' said Mo. 'Even if it does put stupid ideas in your head.'

Dustfinger just nodded. Then without a word he walked on.

'Why don't we take their van?' suggested Elinor when Mo headed back to the path. 'They must have left it on the road?'

'Too dangerous,' said Dustfinger. 'How do we know who

might be waiting for us down there? And going back to it would take us longer than going on to the nearest village. A van like that is easily spotted, too. Do you want to set Capricorn on our trail?'

Elinor sighed. 'It was just a thought,' she murmured, massaging her aching ankles. Then she followed Mo.

They kept to the path, because the snakes were already moving through the tall grass. Once a thin black snake wriggled over the yellow soil in front of them. Dustfinger pushed a stick under its scaly body and threw it back into the thorn bushes. Meggie had expected the snakes to be bigger, but Elinor assured her that the smallest were the most dangerous. Elinor was limping, but she did her best not to hold the others up. Mo too was walking more slowly than usual. He tried to hide it, but the dog-bite obviously hurt.

Meggie walked close to him, and kept looking anxiously at the red scarf Dustfinger had used to bandage the wound. At last they came to a paved road. A truck with a load of rusty gas cylinders was coming towards them. They were too tired to hide, and anyway it wasn't coming from the direction of Capricorn's village. Meggie saw the surprised expression of the man at the wheel as he passed them. They must look very disreputable in their dirty clothes, which were drenched with sweat and torn by all the thorn bushes.

Soon afterwards they passed the first houses. There were more and more of them on the slopes now, brightly colour-washed, with flowers growing outside their doors. Trudging on, they came to the outskirts of a fairly large town. Meggie saw multi-storey buildings, palm trees with dusty leaves and suddenly, still far away but shining silver in the sun, a glimpse of the sea.

'Heavens, I hope they'll let us into a bank,' said Elinor. 'We look as if we'd fallen among thieves.'

'Well, so we have,' said Mo.

22

In Safety

The slow days drifted on, and each left behind a slightly
lightened weight of apprehension.
Mark Twain, *The Adventures of Tom Sawyer*

They did let Elinor into the bank, despite her torn tights.
Before that, however, she had disappeared into the ladies'
room of the first café they came to. Meggie never did find out
exactly where Elinor hid her valuables, but when she returned
her face was washed, her hair not quite as tangled, and she was
triumphantly waving a gold credit card in the air. Then she
ordered breakfast for everyone.

It was an odd feeling to be suddenly sitting in a café having
breakfast, watching perfectly ordinary people outside in the
street, going to work, shopping, or just standing about chat-
ting. Meggie could hardly believe they had spent just two
nights and a day in Capricorn's village, and that all this – the
bustle of ordinary life going on outside the window – hadn't
stood still the whole time.

Nonetheless, something had changed. Ever since Meggie had seen Basta hold his knife to Mo's throat it had seemed as if there was a stain on the world, an ugly, dark burn mark still eating its way towards them, stinking and crackling.

Even the most harmless things seemed to be casting suspicious shadows. A woman smiled at Meggie, then stood looking at the bloody display in a butcher's window. A man pulled a child along after him so impatiently that the little boy stumbled, and cried as he rubbed his grazed knee. And why was that man's jacket bulging over his belt? Was he carrying a knife, like Basta?

Normal life now seemed improbable, unreal. Their flight through the night and the terror she had felt in the ruined house seemed more real to Meggie than the lemonade that Elinor passed over to her.

Farid hardly touched his own glass. He sniffed its yellow contents, took a sip, and went back to looking out of the window. His eyes could hardly decide what to follow first. His head moved back and forth as if he were watching an invisible game and desperately trying to understand it rules.

After breakfast, Elinor asked at the cash desk which was the best hotel in town. While she paid the bill with her credit card, Meggie and Mo examined all the delicacies behind the glass counter. Then, to their surprise, they turned round and found that Dustfinger and Farid had disappeared. Elinor was very worried, but Mo calmed her fears. 'You can't tempt him with a hotel bed. He doesn't like to sleep under any roof,' he said, 'and he's always gone his own way. Perhaps he just wants to get away from here, or perhaps he's round the next corner putting on a performance for tourists. I can assure you he won't go back to Capricorn.'

'What about Farid?' Meggie couldn't believe he had simply run off with Dustfinger.

But Mo only shrugged his shoulders. 'He was sticking close to Dustfinger all the time,' he pointed out. 'Though I don't know whether he or Gwin was the real attraction.'

The hotel recommended to Elinor by the staff in the café was on a square just off the main street that passed right through the town and was lined with palm trees and shops. Elinor took two rooms on the top floor, with balconies that had a view of the sea. It was a big hotel. A doorman in an elaborate costume stood at the entrance, and although he seemed surprised by their lack of luggage he overlooked their dirty clothes with a friendly smile. The pillows were so soft and white that Meggie had to bury her face in them at once. All the same, the sense of unreality didn't leave her. A part of her was still in Capricorn's village, or trudging through thorns, or cowering in the ruined hovel and trembling as Basta came closer. Mo seemed to feel the same. Whenever she glanced at him there was a distant expression on his face, and instead of the relief she might have expected after all they'd been through, she saw sadness in it – and a thoughtfulness that frightened her.

'You're not thinking of going back, are you?' she asked at last. She knew him very well.

'No, don't worry!' he replied, stroking her hair. But she didn't believe him.

Elinor seemed to share Meggie's fears, for she was to be seen several times talking earnestly to Mo – in the hotel corridor outside her room, at breakfast, at dinner. But she fell silent abruptly as soon as Meggie joined them. Elinor called a doctor to treat Mo's arm, although he didn't think it necessary, and she bought them all new clothes, taking Meggie with her because, as she said, 'If I choose you something myself you won't wear it.' She also did a great deal of telephoning, and visited every bookshop in the town. At breakfast on the third day she suddenly announced that she was going home.

'I've already hired another car,' she said. 'My feet are better now, I'm dying to see my books again, and if I see one more tourist in swimming trunks I shall scream. But before I leave, let me give you this!'

With these words she passed Mo a piece of paper across the table. It had a name and address on it in Elinor's large, bold handwriting. 'I know you, Mortimer!' she said. 'I know you can't get *Inkheart* out of your head. So I've found you Fenoglio's address. It wasn't easy, I can tell you, but after all there's a fair chance that he still has a few copies. Promise me you'll go to see him – he lives not far from here – and put the copy of the book still in that wretched village out of your mind once and for all.'

Mo stared at the address as if he were learning it off by heart, and then put the piece of paper in his new wallet. 'You're right, it really is worth a try!' he said. 'Thank you very much, Elinor!' He looked almost happy.

Meggie didn't understand any of this. But she knew one thing: she'd been right. Mo was still thinking of *Inkheart*; he couldn't come to terms with losing it.

'Who's Fenoglio?' she asked uncertainly. 'A bookseller or something?' The name seemed familiar, though she couldn't remember where she had heard it. Mo did not reply, but gazed out of the window.

'Let's go back with Elinor, Mo!' said Meggie. 'Please!'

It was nice going down to the sea in the morning, and she

liked the brightly coloured houses, but all the same she wanted to leave. Every time she saw the hills rising behind the
town her heart beat faster, and she kept thinking she saw
Basta's face, or Flatnose's, among the crowds in the streets.
She wanted to go home, or at least to Elinor's house. She
wanted to watch Mo giving Elinor's books new clothes, pressing fragile gold leaf into the leather with his stamps, choosing
endpapers, stirring glue, fastening the press. She wanted
everything to be as it had been before the night when
Dustfinger turned up.

But Mo shook his head. 'I have to pay this visit first,
Meggie,' he said. 'After that we'll go to Elinor's. The day after
tomorrow at the latest.'

Meggie stared at her plate. What amazing things you could
have for breakfast in an expensive hotel . . . but she didn't feel
like waffles with fresh strawberries any more.

'Right, then I'll see you in a couple of days' time. Give me
your word of honour, Mortimer!' There was no missing the
concern in Elinor's voice. 'You'll come even if you don't have
any luck with Fenoglio. Promise!'

Mo had to smile. 'My solemn word of honour, Elinor,' he
said.

Elinor heaved a deep sigh of relief and bit into the crois-
sant that had been waiting on her plate all this time. 'Don't
ask me what I had to do to get hold of that address!' she said
with her mouth full. 'And in the end the man doesn't live far
from here at all – about an hour's car journey. Odd that he
and Capricorn live so close to one another, isn't it?'

'Yes, odd,' murmured Mo, looking out of the window. The
wind blew through the leaves of the palms in the hotel garden.

'His stories are nearly always set in this region,' Elinor

went on, 'but I believe he lived abroad for a long time and moved back here only a few years ago.' She beckoned to a waitress and asked for more coffee.

Meggie shook her head when the waitress asked if she would like anything else.

'Mo, I don't want to stay here,' she said quietly. 'I don't want to visit anyone either. I want to go home, or at least back to Elinor's.'

Mo picked up his coffee cup. It still hurt when he moved his left arm. 'We'll get it over with tomorrow, Meggie,' he said. 'You heard Elinor – it's not far away. And by the end of the day after that you'll be back in Elinor's huge bed, the one that a whole school class could sleep in.' He was trying to make her laugh, but Meggie couldn't. She looked at the strawberries on her plate. How red they were.

'I'll have to hire a car too, Elinor,' said Mo. 'Can you lend me the money? I'll pay you back as soon as we meet again.'

Elinor nodded, her gaze lingering on Meggie. 'You know something, Mortimer?' she said. 'I don't think your daughter is very keen on books just now. I remember the feeling. Whenever my father got so absorbed in a book that we might have been invisible I felt like taking a pair of scissors and cutting it up. And now I'm as mad about them as he was. Oh well, that's something to think about, eh?' She folded her napkin and pushed her chair back. 'I'm going upstairs to pack, and you can tell your daughter who Fenoglio is.'

Then she was gone, leaving Meggie at the table with Mo. He ordered another coffee, even though he usually drank no more than one cup.

'What about your strawberries?' he asked. 'Don't you want them?'

Meggie shook her head.

Mo sighed, and took one. 'Fenoglio is the man who wrote *Inkheart*,' he said. 'It's possible that as the author he will still have some copies. Indeed, it's more than possible, it's very probable.'

'Oh, come on!' said Meggie scornfully. 'Capricorn's sure to have stolen them long ago! He stole all the copies – you saw that!'

But Mo shook his head. 'I don't believe he will have thought of Fenoglio. You know, it's a funny thing about writers. Most people don't stop to think of books being written by people much like themselves. They think that writers are all dead long ago – they don't expect to meet them in the street, or out shopping. They know their stories but not their names, and certainly not their faces. And most writers like it that way – you heard Elinor say it was quite hard for her to get hold of Fenoglio's address. Believe me, it's more than likely that Capricorn has no idea the man who wrote his story lives scarcely two hours' drive away from him.'

Meggie wasn't so sure. She thoughtfully pleated the table-cloth, then smoothed out the pale yellow fabric again. 'All the same, I'd rather we went to Elinor's house,' she said. 'I don't see why . . .' She hesitated, but then finished what she had been going to say. 'I don't see why you want the book so much. It's no use anyway.' My mother's gone, she added in her thoughts. You tried to bring her back but it doesn't work. Let's go home.

Mo helped himself to another of her strawberries, the smallest of all. 'The little ones are always the sweetest,' he said, and put it in his mouth 'Your mother loved strawberries. She couldn't get enough of them, and was always terribly cross if it rained so much in spring that they rotted in her strawberry bed.'

A smile lit up his face as he looked out of the window again. 'Just this one last shot, Meggie,' he said. 'Just this one. And the day after tomorrow we'll go back to Elinor's. I promise.'

23

A Night Full of Words

What child unable to sleep on a warm summer night hasn't thought he saw Peter Pan's sailing ship in the sky? I will teach you to see that ship.

   Roberto Cotroneo, *When a Child on a Summer Morning*

Meggie stayed in the hotel while Mo went to the hire-car firm to collect the car he had booked. She took a chair out on to the balcony, looked out over its white-painted railing to the sea shining like blue glass beyond the buildings, and tried to think of nothing, nothing at all. The sound of the traffic drifting up to her was so loud that she almost didn't hear Elinor's knock.

Elinor was already on her way down the corridor when Meggie opened the door. 'Oh, you are there,' Elinor said, coming back and looking rather embarrassed. She was hiding something behind her back.

'Yes, Mo's gone to fetch the hire car.'

'I've got something for you – a goodbye present.' Elinor produced a flat parcel from behind her back. 'It wasn't easy to find a book without any unpleasant characters in it, but I absolutely had to find one your father could read aloud to you without doing any damage. I don't think anything can happen with this one.'

Meggie undid the flower-patterned gift wrapping. The cover of the book showed two children and a dog. The children were kneeling on a narrow piece of rock or stone, looking anxiously down at the abyss yawning beneath them.

'They're poems,' explained Elinor. 'I don't know if you like that kind of thing, but I thought that if your father read them aloud they'd sound wonderful.'

Meggie opened the book. She read:

> Oh, if you're a bird be an early bird
> And catch the worm for your breakfast plate.
> If you're a bird, be an early bird
> But if you're a worm, sleep late.

The words were like a little melody singing to her off the pages. She carefully closed the book. 'Thank you, Elinor,' she said. 'I— I'm sorry I don't have anything for you.'

'Oh, and here's something else you might like,' said Elinor, taking another little parcel out of her new handbag. 'Someone who devours books like you should have this one,' she said. 'But I think you'd better read it on your own. There are any number of villains in it. All the same, I think you'll enjoy it. After all, there's nothing like a few comforting pages of a book when you're away from home, right?'

Meggie nodded. 'Mo's promised we'll join you the day after tomorrow,' she said. 'But you'll say goodbye to him too before you leave, won't you?' She put Elinor's first present on the chest of drawers near the door and unwrapped the second. Meggie was pleased to see that it was a thick book.

'Oh, never mind that. You do it for me!' said Elinor. 'I'm not good at saying goodbye. Anyway, we'll be seeing each other again soon – and I've already told him to look after you. Oh, and never leave books lying about open,' she added, before turning round. 'It breaks their spines. But I expect your father's told you that a thousand times already.'

'More often than that,' said Meggie, but Elinor had already gone. A little later Meggie heard someone dragging a case to the lift, but she didn't go out into the corridor to see if it was Elinor. She didn't like goodbyes either.

Meggie was very quiet for the rest of the day. Late in the afternoon Mo took her out for a meal in a little restaurant nearby. Dusk was falling when they came out again, and there were a great many people in the darkening streets. In one square the crowds were particularly dense, and as Meggie pushed her way through them with Mo she saw that they were standing round a fire-eater.

It was very quiet as Dustfinger let the burning torch lick his bare arms. But as soon as he bowed and the audience clapped Farid went round with a little silver dish, which was the only thing that didn't quite seem to belong in these sur-roundings. Farid, however, looked much the same as the boys who lounged around on the beach nudging each other when girls passed by. His skin was a little darker, perhaps, and his hair a little blacker, but it would never have occurred to any-one looking at him that he had just slipped out of a story-book in which carpets could fly, mountains could open, and lamps granted wishes. He wore trousers and a T-shirt instead of his blue, full-length robe. He looked older in them. Dustfinger must have bought the clothes for him, as well as the shoes in which he walked very carefully, as if his feet weren't quite used to them yet. When he saw Meggie in the crowd he gave her a shy nod and passed on quickly.

Dustfinger spat out one last fireball into the air – its size made even the bravest in the audience step back – then he put down the torches and picked up his juggling balls. He threw them so high in the air that the spectators had to tilt their heads right back to watch, then caught them and knocked them up in the air again with his knee. They rolled along his arms as if pulled by invisible threads, emerged from behind his back as if he had plucked them out of empty air, bounced off his forehead, his chin, such light, weightless, dancing little things . . . it would all have seemed easy, cheerful, just a pretty game, if it hadn't been for Dustfinger's face. That remained deadly serious behind the whirling balls, as if it had nothing to do with his dancing hands, nothing to do with their skill, nothing to do with their carefree lightness. Meggie wondered whether his fingers still hurt. They looked red, but perhaps that was just the firelight.

When Dustfinger bowed and put his balls back in the rucksack the spectators were slow to disperse, but finally only Mo and Meggie were left. Farid was sitting on the paving stones counting the money he had collected. He looked happy – as if he had never done anything else in his life.

'So you're still here,' said Mo.

'Why not?' Dustfinger was collecting his props: the two bottles he had used in Elinor's garden, the burnt-out torches, the bowl into which he spat and whose contents he now tipped carelessly out on the pavement. He had got himself a new bag; the old one was probably still in Capricorn's village. Meggie went over to the rucksack, but Gwin wasn't in it.

'I'd hoped you'd be well away by now, going back north or somewhere else. Somewhere Basta can't find you.'

Dustfinger shrugged his shoulders. 'I have to earn some money first. Anyway, I like the weather here better, and the people are more likely to stop and watch. They're generous too. Right, Farid? How much did we make this time?'

The boy jumped when Dustfinger turned to him. Farid had put aside the dish with the money in it and was just about to place a burning matchstick in his mouth. He quickly pinched it out with his fingers. Dustfinger suppressed a smile. 'He's dead set on learning to play with fire. I've shown him how to make little practice torches, but he's in too much of a hurry. He has blisters on his lips all the time.'

Meggie looked sideways at Farid. He seemed to be ignoring them as he packed Dustfinger's things back in the bag, but she felt sure he was listening to every word they said. She met his eyes twice, those dark eyes, and the second time he turned away so abruptly that he almost dropped one of Dustfinger's bottles.

'Hey, go carefully with that, will you?' snapped Dustfinger impatiently.

'I hope there's no other reason why you're still here?' asked Mo as Dustfinger turned back to him.

'What do you mean?' Dustfinger avoided his gaze. 'Oh, that. You think I might go back for the book. You overestimate me. I'm a coward.'

'Nonsense!' Mo sounded irritated. 'Elinor will be home tomorrow,' he said.

'Nice for her.' Dustfinger looked impassively at Mo's face. 'So why aren't you with her?'

Mo looked at the buildings around them and shook his

head. 'There's someone I have to visit first.'

'Here? Who is it?' Dustfinger put on a short-sleeved shirt, a bright garment with a pattern of large flowers. It didn't suit his scarred face.

'There's someone who might still have a copy.'

Dustfinger's face remained unmoved, but his fingers gave him away. They were suddenly having difficulty getting the buttons of his shirt through the buttonholes. 'That's impossible!' he said hoarsely. 'Capricorn would never have overlooked one.'

Mo shrugged. 'Maybe not, but I'm going to try all the same. The man I'm talking about doesn't sell books either new or second-hand. Capricorn probably doesn't even know he exists.'

Dustfinger looked round. Someone was closing the shutters in one of the surrounding houses, and on the other side of the square a few children were playing about among the chairs of a restaurant until a waiter shooed them away. There was a smell of warm food and the liquid spirits Dustfinger used in his fiery games, but no black-clad man could be seen anywhere, except for the bored-looking waiter who was straightening the chairs.

'So, who is this mysterious stranger?' Dustfinger lowered his voice to little more than a whisper.

'The man who wrote *Inkheart*. He lives not far from here.'

Farid came over to them, holding the silver dish with the money in it. 'Gwin hasn't come back,' he told Dustfinger. 'And we don't have anything to tempt him. Shall I buy a couple of eggs?'

'No, he can look after himself.' Dustfinger ran a finger over one of his scars. 'Put the money we've taken into the leather bag – you know, the one in my rucksack!' he told Farid. His voice sounded impatient. Meggie would have given Mo a hurt look if he had spoken to her like that, but Farid didn't seem to mind. He just hurried off purposefully.

'I really thought it was all over, no way to get back ever again . . .' Dustfinger broke off and looked up at the sky. A plane crossed the horizon, coloured lights blinking. Farid looked up at it too. He had put the money away and was standing expectantly beside the rucksack. Something furry scuttled across the square, dug its claws into his trouser legs and clambered up to his shoulder. With a smile, Farid dug his hand into his trouser pocket and offered Gwin a piece of bread.

'Suppose there really is still a copy?' Dustfinger pushed his long hair back from his forehead. 'Will you give me another chance? Will you try to read me back into it? Just once?' There was such longing in his voice that it went to Meggie's heart.

But Mo's face was not forthcoming. 'You can't go back, not into *that* book!' he said. 'I know you don't want to hear me say so, but it's the truth, and you'd better resign yourself to it. Perhaps I can help you some other way. I've got an idea – rather crazy, but still . . .' He said no more, just shook his head and kicked an empty matchbox that was lying on the paving stones.

Meggie looked at Mo in surprise. What kind of idea? Did he really have one, or was he just trying to comfort Dustfinger? If so, it hadn't worked. Dustfinger was looking at him with all his old hostility. 'I'm coming,' he said. His fingers had left a little soot on his face when he stroked his scar. 'I'm coming when you go to visit this man. Then we'll see.'

There was loud laughter behind them. Dustfinger looked

round. Gwin was trying to climb on to Farid's head, and the boy was laughing as if there were nothing better than to have a marten's sharp claws digging into his scalp.

'Well, *he's* not homesick, anyway,' muttered Dustfinger. 'I asked him. Not homesick in the least! All this,' he added, waving a hand at his surroundings, 'all this appeals to him. Even the noisy, stinking cars. He's glad to be here. You've obviously done him a favour.' The look he gave her father as he said these words was so reproachful that Meggie instinctively reached for Mo's hand.

Gwin had jumped down from Farid's shoulder and was sniffing curiously at the road surface. One of the children who had been romping among the tables bent down and looked incredulously at the little horns. But before the child could put a hand out to touch, Farid quickly intervened, picked Gwin up and put the marten back on his shoulders.

'So where does he live, this—?' Dustfinger did not finish his sentence.

'About an hour's drive from here.'

Dustfinger said nothing. The lights of another plane were blinking up in the sky. 'Sometimes, when I went to the spring to wash early in the morning,' he murmured, 'there'd be tiny fairies flitting about above the water, not much bigger than the butterflies you have here, and blue as violet petals. They liked to fly into my hair. Sometimes they spat in my face. They weren't very friendly, but they shone like glow-worms by night. I sometimes caught one and put it in a jar. If I let it out at night before going to sleep I had wonderful dreams.'

'Capricorn said there were trolls and giants too,' said Meggie quietly.

Dustfinger gave her a thoughtful look. 'Yes, there were,' he said. 'But Capricorn wasn't particularly fond of them. He'd have liked to do away with them all. He had them hunted. He hunted anything that could run.'

'It must be a dangerous world.' Meggie was trying to imagine it all: the giants, the trolls, and the fairies. Mo had once given her a book about fairies.

Dustfinger shrugged. 'Yes, it's dangerous, so what? This world's dangerous too, isn't it?' Abruptly, he turned his back on Meggie, picked up his rucksack, threw it over his shoulder, then waved to the boy. Farid picked up the bag with the balls and torches, and followed him eagerly. Dustfinger went over to Mo once more.

'Don't you dare tell that man about me!' he said. 'I don't want to see him. I'll wait in the car. I only want to know if he still has a copy of the book, understand?'

Mo shrugged his shoulders. 'As you like.'

Dustfinger inspected his reddened fingers and felt the taut skin. 'He might tell me how my story ends,' he murmured.

Meggie looked at him in astonishment. 'You mean you don't know?'

Dustfinger smiled. Meggie still didn't particularly like his smile. It seemed to appear only to hide something else. 'What's so unusual about that, princess?' he asked quietly. 'Do *you* know how *your* story ends?'

Meggie had no answer to that.

Dustfinger winked at her and turned. 'I'll be at the hotel tomorrow morning,' he said. Then he walked off without turning back. Farid followed him, carrying the heavy bag, happy as a stray dog who has found a master at last.

That night the full moon hung round and orange in the sky. Before they went to bed, Mo pulled back the curtains so that they could see it – a brightly coloured Chinese lantern among all the white stars.

Neither of them could sleep. Mo had bought a couple of well-worn paperbacks that looked as if they had already passed through the hands of several people. Meggie was reading the book full of unpleasant characters that Elinor had given her. She liked it, but at last her eyes closed with weariness and she fell asleep. Beside her, Mo read on and on while the orange moon shone in the foreign sky outside.

When a confused dream woke her with a start some time in the night, Mo was still sitting up in bed, an open book in his hand. The moon had disappeared long ago, and there was nothing but darkness to be seen through the window.

'Can't you sleep?' asked Meggie, sitting up.

'It was my left arm that stupid dog bit – and you know I sleep best on my left side. Anyway, there's too much going around in my head.'

'There's a lot going around in my head too.' Meggie turned to the bedside table and picked up the book of poems that Elinor had given her. She stroked the binding, passed her hand over the curved spine, and traced the letters on the jacket with her forefinger. 'You know something, Mo?' she said hesitantly. 'I think I'd like to be able to do it too.'

'Do what?'

Meggie stroked the binding of the book again. She thought she could hear the pages whispering, very quietly. 'Read like that,' she said. 'Read aloud the way you do, and make everything come to life.'

Mo looked at her. 'You're out of your mind!' he said. 'That's what has caused all the trouble we're in.'

'I know.'

Mo closed his book, leaving his finger between the pages.

'Read me something aloud, Mo!' said Meggie quietly. 'Please. Just for once.' She offered him the book of poems. 'Elinor gave me this as a present. She said nothing much could happen if you did.'

'Oh, did she?' Mo opened the book. 'Suppose it does, though?' He leafed through the smooth white pages.

Meggie put her pillow close to his.

'Do you really have any idea how you might be able to read Dustfinger back into his story? Or were you making it up?'

'Nonsense. I'm useless at telling lies, as you know.'

'Yes, I do.' Meggie couldn't help smiling. 'Well, what's your idea?'

'I'll tell you when I know if it works.'

Mo was still leafing through Elinor's book. Frowning, he read a page, turned it over and read another.

'Please, Mo!' Meggie moved closer to him. 'Just one poem. A tiny little poem. Please. For me.'

He sighed. 'Just one?'

Meggie nodded.

Outside the noise of the cars had died down. The world was as quiet as if it had spun itself into a cocoon, like a moth preparing itself to slip out in the morning, young again and good as new.

'Please, Mo, read to me!' said Meggie.

So Mo began filling the silence with words. He lured them out of the pages as if they had only been waiting for his voice, words long and short, words sharp and soft, cooing, purring words. They danced through the room, painting stained-glass pictures, tickling the skin. Even when Meggie nodded off she could still hear them, although Mo had closed the book long ago. Words that explained the world to her, its dark side and its light side, words that built a wall to keep out bad dreams. And not a single bad dream came over the wall for the rest of that night.

Next morning, a bird flew down and perched on Meggie's bed, a bird as orange as the light of last night's moon. She tried to catch it, but it flew away to the window where the blue sky was waiting for it. It collided with the invisible glass again and again, bumping its tiny head, until Mo opened the window and let it out.

'Well, do you still wish you could do it?' asked Mo when Meggie had watched the bird fly away until it merged with the blue of the sky.

'It was beautiful!' she said.

'Yes, but will it like this world?' asked Mo. 'And what's gone to replace it in the world it came from?'

Meggie stayed by the window as Mo went downstairs to pay their bill. She remembered the last poem that Mo had read before she fell asleep. She picked up the book from her bedside table, hesitated for a moment – and opened it.

There is a place where the sidewalk ends
And before the street begins,
And there the grass grows soft and white,
And there the sun burns crimson bright,
And there the moon-bird rests from his flight
To cool in the peppermint wind.

Meggie whispered the words aloud as she read them, but no moon-bird flew down from the lamp. And she must be just imagining the smell of peppermint.

24

Fenoglio

You don't know about me, without you have read a book
by the name of *The Adventures of Tom Sawyer*, but that ain't
no matter. That book was made by Mr Mark Twain, and
he told the truth, mainly. There was things which he
stretched, but mainly he told the truth.

Mark Twain, *The Adventures of Huckleberry Finn*

Dustfinger and Farid were waiting for them in the car park
when they left the hotel. Over the nearby hills, a warm
wind was slowly driving rain-clouds towards the sea.
Everything seemed grey today, even the houses with their
bright colour-washed walls and the flowering shrubs in the
streets. Mo took the coastal road, which Elinor had said was
built by the Romans, and followed it further west.

All through the drive the sea lay to their left, its water
stretching to the horizon, sometimes hidden by houses, sometimes by trees, but this morning it didn't look half as inviting
as it had on the day when Meggie had come down from the
mountains with Elinor and Dustfinger. The grey of the sky

cast a dull reflection on the blue waves, and the sea-spray foamed like dirty dishwater. Several times, Meggie found her gaze wandering to the hills on her right. Capricorn's village was hidden somewhere among them. Once she even thought she saw its pale church tower in a dark fold of the hills, and her heart beat faster, although she knew that it couldn't possibly be Capricorn's church. Her feet remembered all too well how long that endless journey down the mountainside had been.

Mo was driving faster than usual, much faster. He could obviously hardly wait to reach their destination. After a good hour they turned off the coast road and followed a narrow, winding lane through a valley grey with buildings. Glasshouses covered the hills here, their panes painted white for protection against the sun that was now hidden behind clouds. Only when the road went uphill did the country on both sides turn green again. The buildings gave way to natural meadowland, and stunted olive trees lined the road, which forked unexpectedly a couple of times. Mo had to keep consulting the map he had bought, but finally the right name appeared on a sign.

They drove into a small village, little more than a square, a few dozen houses, and a church that looked very much like Capricorn's. When Meggie got out of the car she saw the sea far below. The waves were so rough on this overcast day that, even from this distance, she could see the breakers. Mo had parked in the village square beside the memorial for the dead of two world wars. The list of names was long for such a small place. Meggie thought there were almost as many names as the village had houses.

'You can leave the car unlocked. I'll keep an eye on it,' said

Dustfinger, as Mo was about to lock up. He threw his ruck-sack over his shoulder, put the sleepy Gwin on his chain, and sat on the steps in front of the war memorial. Farid sat down beside him without a word. Meggie looked uneasily at them both as she followed Mo.

'Remember, you promised not to mention me!' Dustfinger called after them.

'Yes, all right!' replied Mo.

Farid was playing with matches again. Meggie caught him at it when she looked round once more. By now he could extinguish the burning matches with his mouth quite well, but all the same Dustfinger took the box of matches away from him, and Farid looked sadly at his empty hands.

Meggie had met many people who loved books, sold them, collected them, printed them or, like her father, prevented them from falling apart, but she had never before met anyone who wrote the words that filled all a book's pages. She didn't even know the names of the authors of some of her favourite stories, let alone what they looked like. She had seen only the characters who emerged from the words to meet her, never the writer who had made them up. It was just as Mo had said: in general one thought of writers as dead or very, very old. But the man who opened the door to them, after Mo had rung the bell twice, was neither. That is, he was certainly quite old, at least in Meggie's eyes: in his mid-sixties or even older. His face was wrinkled like a turtle's, but his hair was black, with-out a trace of grey (she was to find out later that he dyed it), and he didn't look at all fragile. On the contrary: he planted himself so impressively in the doorway that Meggie was instantly tongue-tied. Luckily Mo was not.

'Signor Fenoglio?' he asked.

'Yes?' The face looked less forthcoming than ever. There was disapproval in every line of it. But Mo seemed undaunted.

'I'm Mortimer Folchart,' he introduced himself, 'and this is my daughter Meggie. I'm here about one of your books.'

A boy appeared at the door beside Fenoglio, a little boy of about five, and a small girl joined them on the other side of the doorway. She stared curiously, first at Mo, then at Meggie. 'Pippo's picked the chocolate chips out of the cake,' Meggie heard her whisper as she looked anxiously up at Mo. When his eyes twinkled at her she disappeared behind Fenoglio's back, giggling. But Fenoglio himself still looked anything but friendly.

'*All* the chocolate chips?' he growled. 'Very well, I'm coming. You go and tell Pippo he's in serious trouble.' The little girl nodded and ran away, obviously happy to be the bearer of bad news. The small boy clung to Fenoglio's leg.

'A very particular book,' Mo went on. '*Inkheart*. You wrote it quite a long time ago, and unfortunately I can't buy a copy anywhere now.' With the man's icy stare still resting on her father, Meggie could only marvel that the words didn't freeze on Mo's lips.

'Oh yes. So?' Fenoglio crossed his arms. The girl appeared on his left again. 'Pippo's hiding,' she said.

'That won't do him any good,' said Fenoglio. 'I can always find him.' The little girl scurried off again. Meggie heard her in the house, calling to the chocolate thief. Fenoglio, however, turned back to Mo. 'So what do you want? If you're planning to ask me clever questions of some kind about the book, forget it. I don't have time for that sort of thing. Anyway, as you said yourself, I wrote it ages ago.'

'No, there's only one question I was going to ask. I'd like to know if you still have any copies, and if so may I buy one from you?'

The old man's expression was no longer quite so forbidding as he inspected Mo. 'How extraordinary. You must be really keen on the book,' he murmured. 'I'm flattered. Although,' he added, and his face darkened again, 'I hope you're not one of those idiots who collect rare books just because they're rare, are you?'

Mo couldn't help smiling. 'No,' he said. 'I want to read it, that's all. I just want to read it.'

Fenoglio braced an arm against the door frame and looked at the house opposite as if he feared it might collapse at any moment. The street where he lived was so narrow that Mo could have touched both sides at once if he stretched his arms out. Many of the houses were built of coarse blocks of sandy grey stone, like the houses in Capricorn's village, but here there were flowers in window boxes and pots of plants on the steps, and many of the shutters looked as if they had been freshly painted. There was a pram outside one house, a moped leaning against the wall of another, and voices floated into the street from open windows. Capricorn's village probably looked like this once, thought Meggie.

An old woman passing by looked suspiciously at the strangers. Fenoglio nodded to her, murmured a brief greeting, and waited until she had vanished behind a green-painted front door. '*Inkheart*,' he said. 'That really is a long time ago. And it's odd that you should be asking about that one, of all my books.'

The girl came back. She tugged Fenoglio's sleeve and whispered something in his ear. Fenoglio's turtle face twisted in a smile. Meggie liked him better that way. 'Oh, that's where he always hides, Paula,' he told the little girl softly. 'Perhaps you should advise him to try a better hiding-place.'

Paula ran off for the fourth time, but not before gazing curiously at Meggie first.

'Well, you'd better come in,' said Fenoglio. Without another word he showed Mo and Meggie into the house, went down a dark, narrow passage ahead of them, limping because the little boy was still clinging to his leg like a monkey, and pushed open the door to the kitchen, where the ruins of a cake stood on the table. Its brown icing was as full of holes as the binding of a book when bookworms have been gnawing at it for years.

'Pippo?' Fenoglio bellowed so loud that even Meggie jumped, although she didn't feel guilty of any naughtiness. 'I know you can hear me. And I warn you I shall tie a knot in your nose for every hole in this cake. Understand?'

Meggie heard a giggle. It seemed to come from the cupboard next to the fridge. Fenoglio broke a piece off the cake with the holes still in it. 'Paula,' he said, 'give this girl a slice if she doesn't mind the missing chocolate.' Paula emerged from under the table and looked enquiringly at Meggie.

'I don't mind,' said Meggie, whereupon Paula took a huge knife, cut an enormous piece of cake, and put it on the table in front of her.

'Pippo, let's have one of the rose-patterned plates,' said Fenoglio, and a hand stuck out of the cupboard holding a plate in its chocolate-brown fingers. Meggie was quick to take the plate before it dropped, and put the piece of cake on it.

'What about you?' Fenoglio asked Mo.

'I'd prefer the book,' said Mo. He was looking rather pale.

Fenoglio removed the little boy from his leg and sat down. 'Go and find another tree to climb, Rico,' he said. Then he looked thoughtfully at Mo. 'I'm afraid I can't help you,' he said. 'I don't have a single copy left. They were stolen, all of them. I lent them to an exhibition of old children's books in Genoa: a lavishly illustrated special edition, a copy with a signed dedication by the illustrator, and the two copies that belonged to my own children with all their scribbled comments – I always asked them to mark the bits they liked best – and finally my own personal copy. Every last one of them was stolen two days after the exhibition opened.'

Mo ran a hand over his face as if he could wipe the disappointment off it. 'Stolen,' he said. 'Of course.'

'*Of course?*' Fenoglio narrowed his eyes and looked at Mo with great curiosity. 'You'll have to explain. In fact I'm not letting you out of my house until I find out why you're interested in this of all my books. In fact, I might set the children on you – and you wouldn't like that!'

Mo tried for a smile, without much success. 'My copy was stolen as well,' he said at last. 'And that was a very special edition too.'

'Extraordinary.' Fenoglio raised his eyebrows, which were like hairy caterpillars creeping above his eyes. 'Come on, let's hear your story.' All the hostility had vanished from his face. Curiosity, pure curiosity, had won out. In Fenoglio's eyes Meggie saw the same insatiable hunger for a good story that overcame her at the sight of any new and exciting book.

'There's not much to tell,' said Mo. Meggie heard in his voice that he didn't intend to tell the old man the truth. 'I restore books. That's how I make my living. I found yours in a second-hand bookshop some years ago, and I was going to give it a new binding and then sell it, but I liked it so much I kept it instead. And now it's been stolen and I've been trying in vain to buy another copy. A friend who knows a great deal about rare books and how to get hold of them finally suggested I might try the author himself. She was the person who found me your address. So I came here.'

Fenoglio wiped a few cake crumbs off the table. 'Fine,' he said, 'but that's not the whole story.'

'What do you mean?'

The old man scrutinised Mo's face until he turned his head away and looked out of the narrow kitchen window. 'I mean I can smell a good story miles away, so don't try keeping one from me. Out with it! And then you can have a piece of this magnificently perforated cake.'

Paula clambered up on to Fenoglio's lap, nestled her head under his chin, and looked at Mo as expectantly as the old man himself.

But Mo shook his head. 'No, I think I'd better say no more. You wouldn't believe a word of it anyway.'

'Oh, I'd believe all manner of things!' Fenoglio assured Mo, cutting him a slice of cake. 'I'd believe any story at all just so long as it's well told.'

The cupboard door opened a crack, and Meggie saw a boy's head emerge. 'What about my punishment?' he asked. Judging by the fingers, which were sticky with chocolate, this must be Pippo.

'Later,' said Fenoglio. 'I have something else to do now.'

Disappointed, Pippo came out of the cupboard. 'You said you were going to tie knots in my nose.'

'Double knots, seaman's knots, butterfly knots, any knots

you fancy, but I have to hear this story first. So go and fool about with something else until I have time for you.'

Pippo stuck his lower lip out sulkily and disappeared into the corridor. Rico, the little boy, ran after him.

Mo remained silent, pushing cake crumbs off the worn table-top, drawing invisible patterns on the wood with his forefinger. 'There's someone in this story, and I've promised not to tell you about him,' he said at last.

'Keeping a bad promise makes it no better,' said Fenoglio. 'Or at least so a favourite book of mine says.'

'I don't know if it was a bad promise.' Mo sighed, and looked up at the ceiling as if the answer might be found there. 'Very well,' he said. 'I'll tell you. But Dustfinger will murder me if he finds out.'

'Dustfinger? I once called a character that. Oh yes, of course, the poor trickster in *Inkheart*. I killed him off in the last chapter but one. A very touching scene. I cried while I was writing it.'

Meggie almost choked on the piece of cake she had just put in her mouth, but Fenoglio went on calmly. 'I haven't killed off many of my characters, but sometimes it just happens. Death scenes aren't easy to write – they can too easily get sentimental – but I thought I did pretty well with Dustfinger's death.'

Horrified, Meggie looked at Mo. 'He dies? Did – did you know that?'

'Yes, of course. I've read the whole story, Meggie.'

'But why didn't you tell him?'

'He didn't want to know.'

Fenoglio was following this exchange with a puzzled look on his face – and with great curiosity.

'*Who* kills him?' asked Meggie. 'Basta?'

'Ah, Basta!' Fenoglio smiled. Each of his separate wrinkles expressed self-satisfaction. 'One of the best villains I ever thought up. A rabid dog, but not half as bad as my other dark hero, Capricorn. Basta would let his heart be torn out for Capricorn, but his master is a stranger to such loyalty. He feels nothing, nothing at all, he doesn't even enjoy his own cruelty. Yes, I really did think up some pretty dark characters for *Inkheart*, and then there's the Shadow, Capricorn's hound, as I always called him to myself. Though of course that's far too friendly a name for such a monster.'

'The Shadow?' Meggie's voice was hardly more than a whisper. 'Does *he* kill Dustfinger?'

'No, no. I'm sorry, I'd quite forgotten your question. Once I begin talking about my characters it's hard to stop me. No, one of Capricorn's men kills Dustfinger. It was a very successful scene. Dustfinger has some kind of tame marten. Capricorn's man wants to kill it because he enjoys killing small animals, so Dustfinger tries to save his furry friend and dies in the attempt.'

Meggie said nothing. Poor Dustfinger, she thought. Poor, poor Dustfinger. She couldn't think of anything else. 'Which of Capricorn's men does it?' she asked. 'Flatnose? Or Cockerell?'

Fenoglio looked at her in surprise. 'Well, fancy that. You know all their names? I usually forget them soon after I've made them up.'

'It's neither of them, Meggie,' said Mo. 'The murderer's name isn't even mentioned in the book. A whole pack of Capricorn's men is hunting Gwin, and one of them draws a knife and uses it. A man who's probably still waiting for Dustfinger.'

'Waiting for him?' Fenoglio looked at Mo, confused.

'That's terrible!' whispered Meggie. 'I'm glad I didn't read any more.'

'What do you mean? Are you talking about my book?' Fenoglio's voice sounded hurt.

'Yes,' said Meggie. 'I am.' She looked at Mo, a question in her eyes. 'And Capricorn? Who kills him?'

'No one.'

'No one!'

Meggie stared at Fenoglio so accusingly that he rubbed his nose awkwardly. It was an impressive nose. 'Why are you looking at me like that?' he cried. 'Yes, I let him get away with it. He's one of my best villains. How could I kill him off? It's the same in real life: notorious murderers get off scot-free and live happily all their lives, while good people die – sometimes the very best people. That's the way of the world. Why should it be different in books?'

'What about Basta? Does he stay alive too?' Meggie remembered what Farid had said back in the ruined hovel: 'Why not kill them? That's what they were going to do to us!'

'Basta stays alive too,' replied Fenoglio. 'I remember toying for some time with the idea of writing a sequel to *Inkheart*, and I didn't want to do without those two. I was proud of them! And the Shadow was quite a success too, yes, he really was, but I'm always most attached to my human characters. You know, if you were to ask me which of those two I was prouder of, Basta or Capricorn, I couldn't tell you! Even though some critics said they were just *too* nasty!'

Mo stared out of the window again. Then he looked at Fenoglio. 'Would you like to meet them?' he asked.

'Meet who?' Fenoglio looked at him in surprise.

'Capricorn and Basta.'

'Good God, no!' Fenoglio laughed so loud that Paula, quite frightened, put her hand over his mouth.

'Well, we did,' said Mo wearily. 'Meggie and I – and Dustfinger.'

25

The Wrong Ending

Persons attempting to find a motive in this narrative will be
prosecuted; persons attempting to find a moral in it will be
banished; persons attempting to find a plot in it will be shot.

BY ORDER OF THE AUTHOR
per
G.G., CHIEF OF ORDNANCE

Mark Twain, *The Adventures of Huckleberry Finn*

Fenoglio said nothing for a long time after Mo had finished
his story. Paula had gone off long ago in search of Pippo
and Rico. Meggie heard them running over the wooden floorboards above her, back and forth, jumping, sliding, giggling
and squealing. But in Fenoglio's kitchen it was so quiet you
could hear the tick of the clock on the wall by the window.

'Does he have those scars on his face? I expect you know
what I mean? The fairies treated the cuts – that's why there
are only slight scars left, little more than three pale lines on
the skin, is that right?' Fenoglio looked enquiringly at Mo,

who nodded.

Fenoglio looked out of the window again, brushing a few crumbs off his trousers. 'Basta scarred him,' he said. 'They both fancied the same girl.'

Mo nodded. 'Yes, I know.'

A window was open in the house opposite, and you could hear a woman scolding a child inside. 'I suppose I ought to feel very, very proud,' murmured Fenoglio. 'Every writer wants to create lifelike characters – and mine are so lifelike they've walked straight off the page!'

'That's because my father read them out of the book,' said Meggie. 'He can do it with other books too.'

'Yes, of course.' Fenoglio nodded. 'A good thing you reminded me. Otherwise I might start taking myself for a minor god, mightn't I? But I'm sorry about your mother – although depending on how you look at it, that wasn't really my fault.'

'It's worse for my father,' said Meggie. 'I don't remember her.'

Mo looked at her, startled.

'Of course not. You were younger than my grandchildren,' said Fenoglio thoughtfully. 'I'd really like to see him,' he added. 'Dustfinger, I mean. Naturally I'm sorry now that I thought up such an unhappy ending for the poor fellow, but it somehow seemed right for him. As Shakespeare puts it so well, "Everybody plays his part, and mine is a sad one."' He looked out into the street. Something fell and broke on the floor above them, but Fenoglio didn't seem particularly interested.

'Are those your children?' asked Meggie, pointing up at the ceiling.

'Heaven help us, no. My grandchildren. One of my daughters lives in this village too. They're always visiting me, and I tell them stories. I tell half the village stories, but I don't feel like writing them down any more.' He turned to Mo with an enquiring look. 'Where is he now?'

'Dustfinger? I can't tell you. He doesn't want to see you.'

'He got quite a shock when my father told him about you,' added Meggie. But Dustfinger must be told what happens to him, she thought, he *must*. Then he'll understand why he really can't go back. And all the same, she thought next, he'll still be homesick. Homesick for ever.

'I must see him! Only once. Don't you understand?' Fenoglio looked pleadingly at Mo. 'I could just follow you, inconspicuously. How would he know who I am? I want to find out if he really looks the way I imagined him, that's all.'

However, Mo shook his head. 'I think you'd better leave him alone.'

'Nonsense. Surely I can see him whenever I like. After all, I invented him!'

'And you killed him off,' Meggie pointed out.

'Well.' Fenoglio raised his hands helplessly. 'I wanted to make the story more exciting. Don't you like exciting stories?'

'Only if they have happy endings.'

'Happy endings!' Fenoglio snorted scornfully, and then listened to what was going on upstairs. Something or someone had landed heavily on the wooden floorboards. Loud howls followed the thud. Fenoglio strode to the door. 'Wait here! I'll be back in a minute!' he called, disappearing into the corridor.

'Mo!' whispered Meggie. 'You've got to tell Dustfinger! You've got to tell him he can't go back.'

But Mo shook his head. 'He won't want to listen, I promise

you. I've tried more than a dozen times. Perhaps it wouldn't be a bad idea to bring him together with Fenoglio after all. He might well be more likely to believe his creator than me.' With a sigh, he brushed a few cake crumbs off Fenoglio's kitchen table. 'There was a picture in *Inkheart*,' he murmured, raising the palm of his hand over the table-top as if to conjure up the picture itself. 'It showed a group of women standing under an arched gateway, in splendid clothes as if they were going to a party. One of them had hair as fair as your mother's. You can't see the woman's face in the picture, she has her back turned, but I always imagined it was her. Crazy, isn't it?'

Meggie placed her hand on his. 'Mo, promise you won't go back to the village!' she said. 'Please! Promise me you won't try to get the book back.'

The second hand on Fenoglio's kitchen clock was dividing time into painfully small segments.

At last Mo answered. 'I promise,' he said.

'Look at me and say it!'

He did. 'I promise!' he repeated. 'There's just one more thing I want to discuss with Fenoglio, and then we'll go home and forget about the book. Happy now?'

Meggie nodded. Although she wondered what else there could be to discuss.

Fenoglio returned with a tearful Pippo on his back. The other two children followed their grandfather, looking crestfallen. 'Holes in the cake and now a dent in his forehead too. I think I ought to send the lot of you home!' Fenoglio told them crossly as he put Pippo down on a chair. Then he rummaged around in the big cupboard until he found a plaster, which he stuck none too gently on his grandson's cut forehead.

Mo pushed his chair back and stood up. 'I've changed my mind,' he said. 'I'll take you to Dustfinger after all.'

Fenoglio turned to him in surprise.

'Perhaps *you* can make it clear to him once and for all that he can't go back,' Mo continued. 'Goodness knows what he might do next! I'm afraid it could be dangerous for him – and I do have this idea, rather a weird idea, but I'd like to talk to you about it.'

'Weirder than what I've heard already? I'd say that's hardly possible!' Fenoglio's grandchildren had disappeared into the cupboard again. Giggling, they closed the doors. 'Very well, I'll listen to your idea,' said Fenoglio. 'But I want to see Dustfinger first!'

Mo looked at Meggie. It wasn't often that he broke a promise, and he clearly felt far from comfortable about it. Meggie could understand that only too well. 'He's waiting in the square,' said Mo hesitantly. 'But let me talk to him first.'

'In the square here?' Fenoglio's eyes widened. 'That's wonderful!' With one stride he was standing in front of the little mirror hanging next to the kitchen door, running his fingers through his black hair almost as if he were afraid Dustfinger might be disappointed by his creator's appearance. 'I'll pretend I don't see him until you call me,' he said. 'Yes, that's the thing to do.'

There was a clattering in the cupboard, and Pippo stumbled out in a jacket that came down to his ankles and a hat so large that it had slipped right over his eyes.

'Of course!' Fenoglio took the hat off Pippo's head and put it on his own. 'That's it! I'll take the children with me. A grandfather with three grandchildren – nothing about that sight to make anyone uneasy, is there?'

Mo just nodded and pushed Meggie out into the narrow passage.

As they walked down the street leading back to the square and their car, Fenoglio followed a few metres behind them, with his grandchildren running and jumping around him like three puppies.

26

Shivers Down the Spine and a Foreboding

And that's when she put her book down. And looked at me. And said it: 'Life isn't fair, Bill. We tell our children that it is, but it's a terrible thing to do. It's not only a lie, it's a cruel lie. Life is not fair, and it never has been, and it's never going to be.'

William Goldman, *The Princess Bride*

Dustfinger sat on the chilly stone steps, waiting. He felt sick with fear; but he wasn't quite sure of what. Perhaps the war memorial behind him reminded him too much of death. He had always been afraid of death, which he imagined as cold, like a night without fire. Now, however, he dreaded something else even more. Its name was sorrow, and it had been stalking him like a second shadow ever since Silvertongue lured him into this world. Sorrow that made his limbs heavy and turned the sky grey.

Beside him, the boy was running up and down the steps.

Up and down, tirelessly, with light feet and a cheerful face, as if Silvertongue had read him straight into Paradise. What could be making him so happy? Dustfinger looked round at the narrow houses, pale yellow, pink, peach, the dark green shutters at the windows and the rust-red tiles on the roofs, an oleander flowering in front of a wall as if its branches were on fire, cats stalking past the warm walls. Farid stole up to one of them, stroked its grey fur and put it on his lap, although it dug its claws into his thighs.

'You know what people do to keep the numbers of cats down around here?' Dustfinger stretched his legs and blinked up at the sun. 'When winter comes they take their own cats indoors for safety, then they put out dishes of poisoned food for the strays.'

Farid still fondled the grey cat's pointed ears. But his face was rigid and grim, not a trace left of the happiness that had just made it look so soft and open. Dustfinger glanced quickly aside. Why had he said that? Had the happiness on the boy's face upset him so much?

Farid let the cat go and climbed the steps to the memorial.

He was still sitting there on the wall, legs drawn up, when the other two came back. Silvertongue had no book with him, and he looked strained – his guilty conscience was clearly visible on his face.

Why? What could have made Silvertongue look so guilty? Dustfinger glanced suspiciously around without knowing quite what he was looking for. Silvertongue's face always showed his feelings; he was an open book that any stranger could read. His daughter was different. It wasn't so easy to make out what was going on in her mind. But now, as she came towards him, Dustfinger thought he saw something like concern in her eyes, perhaps even pity . . . What had that writer fellow said to make the girl look at him like that?

He got up and brushed the dust off his trousers.

'No copies left, am I right?' he asked, when the two of them had reached him.

'You're right. They've all been stolen,' Silvertongue replied. 'Years ago.'

His daughter never took her eyes off Dustfinger.

'Why are you staring at me like that, princess?' he snapped. 'Do you know something I don't?'

Bull's-eye. An accidental one, too. He hadn't wanted to score a bull's-eye at all, certainly not a direct hit on an uncomfortable truth. The girl bit her lip, still looking at him with that same mixture of pity and concern.

Dustfinger rubbed his hand over his face, feeling his scars on it like a picture postcard saying 'Greetings from Basta'. He could never forget Capricorn's rabid dog for a single day even if he wanted to. 'To help you please the girls even better in future!' Basta had hissed in his ear before wiping the blood off his knife.

'Oh, curse it all!' Dustfinger kicked the nearest wall so hard that he felt the pain in his foot for days to come. 'You've told that writer about me!' he accused Mo. 'And now even your daughter knows more about me than I do! Very well, out with it! I want to know now too. Tell me. You always wanted to tell me, after all. Basta hangs me, is that it? Strings me up and tightens the noose until I'm dead as a doornail, right? But why should that bother me? Basta's in this world now, isn't he? The story's changed – it must have changed. Basta can't hurt me if you just send me back there where I belong!'

Dustfinger took a step towards Silvertongue as if to grab

him, shake him, take out on him all that had been done to himself, but Meggie came between them. 'Stop it! It's not Basta!' she cried, pushing him away. 'It's one of Capricorn's men, and he's waiting for you in the book. They want to kill Gwin and you try to help him, so they kill you instead! Nothing about that has changed! It will simply happen and there's nothing you can do about it. Do you understand? You *must* stay here, you can't go back, ever!'

Dustfinger stared at the girl as if he could shut her up that way, but she held his gaze. She even tried to take his hand.

'You should be glad to be here!' she faltered as he retreated from her. 'You can escape from them here. You can go away, far away, and . . .' Her voice quivered. Perhaps she had seen the tears in Dustfinger's eyes. Angrily, he wiped them away with his sleeve, and looked round like an animal in a trap, searching for some way out. But there *was* no way out. No going forward and, even worse, no going back.

A trio of women standing at the bus stop glanced curiously in his direction. Dustfinger often attracted such glances; anyone could see he didn't belong here. A stranger for ever.

Three children and an old man were playing football with a tin can on the other side of the square. Farid looked at them. The Arab boy had Dustfinger's rucksack over his narrow shoulders, and grey cat hairs clung to his trousers. He was deep in thought, wriggling his bare toes into the gaps between the paving stones. He was always taking off the trainers Dustfinger had bought him and going about barefoot, even on hot tarmac, with his shoes tied to the rucksack like loot he was taking home.

Silvertongue looked at the playing children too. Had he given some sign to the old man with them? The old fellow left the children and came over. Dustfinger took a step back. A shiver ran down his spine.

'My grandchildren have been admiring the tame marten that boy has on a chain,' said the old man, as he approached.

Dustfinger took another step backwards. Why was the dark-haired man looking at him like that? In quite a different way from the women at the bus stop. 'The children say the marten can do tricks and the boy's a fire-eater. Perhaps we could come to the show and watch at close quarters?'

The cold shiver spread right through Dustfinger, although the sun was shining down on him. The way the old man looked at him – as if he were a dog who had run away long ago and was now back, tail between his legs, perhaps with lice in his coat, but definitely *his*, the old man's dog.

'Nonsense, we don't do tricks!' he managed to say. 'There's nothing to see here!' He retreated again, but the old man followed him – as if they were linked by an invisible thread.

'I'm sorry,' said the old man, raising a hand as if to touch Dustfinger's scarred face.

Dustfinger's back came up against a parked car. Now the old man was standing right in front of him, and still staring, staring—

'Go away!' Dustfinger pushed him roughly back. 'Farid, bring me my things!' The boy hurried to his side. Dustfinger snatched the rucksack from his hand, picked up the marten and stowed him in the rucksack, taking no notice of the animal's sharp, snapping teeth. The old man stared at Gwin's horns. Fingers flying, Dustfinger slung the rucksack over his shoulder and tried to push past him.

'Please. I only want to talk to you.' The old man barred his way, reaching for his arm.

'Well, I don't want to talk to *you*.' Dustfinger tried to free himself from the bony fingers. They were surprisingly strong, but Dustfinger had the knife, Basta's flick-knife. He took it out of his pocket, snapped it open and held it under the old man's chin. His hand was trembling, he had never enjoyed threatening anyone with a knife, but the old man let go. And Dustfinger ran.

He ignored whatever Silvertongue was calling after him. He just ran for it, as he had often done in the past. He could trust his legs even if he didn't yet know where they were taking him. He left the village and the road behind, dodged under some trees, ran through wild grass, plunged in among the mustard-yellow gorse bushes, let the silvery foliage of the olive trees hide him . . . he had to get away from the houses, away from the paved roads. Wild country had always protected him. Only when every breath he drew hurt him did he throw himself down into the long grass behind an abandoned cistern where frogs croaked and the rainwater that had collected among the grey stones steamed in the sun. He lay there gasping, listening to his own heartbeat and staring at the sky.

He jumped. 'Who's that?'

The boy stood there. Farid had followed him.

'Go away!' shouted Dustfinger.

The boy crouched down among the wild flowers that grew everywhere – blue and yellow and red splashes of bright colour in the grass.

'I don't want you!' snapped Dustfinger.

The boy said nothing, but picked a wild orchid and examined the bloom. It looked like a bumble-bee on the tip of a flower stem. 'What a strange flower!' he murmured. 'I've never seen one like that before.'

Dustfinger sat up and leaned against the side of the cistern. 'You'll be sorry if you keep running after me,' he said. 'I'm going back. You know where to.'

Only when he said it did he realise that he had made up his mind – long ago. Yes, he was going back. Dustfinger the coward was going back into the lion's den. Never mind what Silvertongue said, or what his daughter thought – there was only one thing he wanted. He had never wanted anything else. And if he couldn't have it now, then at least he could hope that one day his wish would come true.

The boy stayed sitting there.

'Go away, will you? Go back to Silvertongue! He'll look after you.'

Farid sat there unmoved, his arms round his knees. 'You're going back to that village?'

'Yes, the village where the devils and demons live. Believe me, they'll kill a boy like you and eat you for breakfast. They'll enjoy their coffee all the more afterwards.'

Farid stroked his cheeks with the orchid. He made a face as the petals tickled his skin. 'Gwin wants to get out,' he said.

He was right. The marten was biting the fabric of the rucksack and sticking his muzzle out of it. Dustfinger undid the straps and freed him. Gwin blinked up at the sun, chattered crossly, presumably complaining that it was the wrong time of day, and scurried over to the boy. Farid picked him up, put him on his shoulder, and looked earnestly at Dustfinger. 'I've never seen flowers like this,' he repeated. 'Or such green hills or such a clever marten. But I know a lot about the kind of men you mean. They're the same everywhere.'

Dustfinger shook his head. 'These are particularly bad.'

'No, not *particularly*.'

The defiance in Farid's voice made Dustfinger laugh; he himself didn't know why.

'We could go somewhere else,' said the boy.

'No, we couldn't.'

'Why not? What are you planning to do in that village?'

'Steal something,' said Dustfinger.

The boy nodded, as if stealing were the most natural plan in the world, and carefully put the orchid in his trouser pocket. 'Will you teach me a little more about fire first? Before we go there.'

'Before?' Dustfinger couldn't help smiling. The boy was a clever lad, and no doubt he knew there wouldn't be any *after*.

'Of course,' he said. 'I'll teach you everything I know. Before we go there.'

27

A Good Place To Stay

I keep six honest serving men (they taught me all I knew);
Their names are What and Why and When and How
and Where and Who.

Rudyard Kipling, *The Elephant's Child*

They did not set off to join Elinor after Dustfinger had left
them. 'Meggie, I know I promised we would,' said Mo,
as they stood in the square in front of the war memorial, feeling rather at a loss. 'But I'd like to leave the journey until
tomorrow. As I told you before, there's something else I have
to discuss with Fenoglio.'

The old man was still standing where he had been when he
spoke to Dustfinger, staring down the road. His grandchildren
were pulling at him and talking to him, but he didn't seem to
notice them.

'What exactly do you want to discuss with him?'

Mo sat on the steps in front of the memorial and made
Meggie sit down beside him. 'Do you see those names?' he

asked, pointing up at the chiselled letters listing people no longer alive. 'There's a family behind every name – a mother or father, brothers and sisters, perhaps a wife. If one of them were to find out that letters can be brought to life, that some-one who's only a name now could become flesh and blood again, don't you think he or she would do anything, anything at all, to make it happen?'

Meggie looked at the long list. Someone had painted a heart next to the name at the top, and there was a bunch of dried flowers on the stone steps in front of the memorial.

'No one can bring back the dead, Meggie,' Mo went on. 'Perhaps it's true that death is only the beginning of a new story, but no one has ever read the book in which it's written, and the writer of *that* book certainly doesn't live in a little village on the coast playing football with his grandchildren. Your mother's name isn't on a stone like this but hidden somewhere in a book, and I have an idea which just might make it possi-ble to alter what happened nine years ago.'

'You're going back!'

'No, I'm not. I gave you my word. Have I ever broken it?'

Meggie shook her head. You broke your word to Dustfinger, she thought, but she didn't say so out loud.

'There you are, then,' said Mo. 'I want to talk to Fenoglio. That's the only reason why I want to stay.'

Meggie looked at the sea. The sun had broken through the clouds, and all of a sudden the water was glistening and shin-ing as if someone had poured paint into it.

'It's not far from here,' she murmured.

'What isn't?'

'Capricorn's village.'

Mo looked eastward. 'Yes, it's odd that he felt drawn here

of all places, don't you think? As if he were looking for somewhere resembling the countryside of his own story.'

'Suppose he finds us?'

'Nonsense. Do you know how many villages there are along
this coast?'

Meggie shrugged her shoulders. 'He found you before,
even when you were far, far away.'

'He found me with Dustfinger's help, and you can be sure
Dustfinger isn't going to help him again.' Mo rose and drew
Meggie to her feet. 'Come on, let's go and ask Fenoglio where
we can stay the night. He looks as if he could do with some
company.'

Fenoglio did not tell them whether Dustfinger looked as he
had imagined him. He said very little as they walked back to
his house. But when Mo told him that he and Meggie would
like to stay there another day his face brightened slightly. He
even offered them a place to spend the night: an apartment he
sometimes rented out to tourists. Mo gratefully accepted.

He and the old man talked far into the evening, while
Fenoglio's grandchildren chased Meggie all over the nooks and
crannies of the house. The two men sat in Fenoglio's study.
It was next to the kitchen, and Meggie kept trying to listen at
the closed door, but Pippo and Rico always caught her in the
act and dragged her away to the next flight of stairs before she
had heard more than a few words. Finally, she gave up. She
let Paula show her the kittens scampering about with their
mother in the tiny garden behind the house, and followed the
three children to the house where they lived with their parents. They didn't stay long, just long enough to persuade their
mother to let them stay at their grandfather's for supper.

Supper was pasta with sage. Pippo and Rico picked the bitter-tasting green bits out of their sauce with disgusted expressions on their faces, but Meggie and Paula enjoyed the flavour of the leaves. After the meal Mo and Fenoglio drank a whole bottle of red wine between them, and when the old man finally saw Mo and Meggie to the door he said goodnight and added, 'So you'll look at my books as we agreed, Mortimer, and I'll get down to work first thing tomorrow.'

'What kind of work, Mo?' asked Meggie as they walked along the dimly lit alleys together. Night had hardly cooled the air at all; a strangely foreign wind blew through the village, hot and sandy, as if it were carrying the desert itself across the sea.

'I'd rather you didn't ask me that,' said Mo. 'Let's just act as if we were on holiday for a few days. This looks a good place for a holiday, don't you think?'

Meggie answered only with a nod. Mo really knew her very well – he could often tell what she was thinking before she put it into words – but he sometimes forgot she wasn't five years old any more, and these days it took rather more than a few kind words to distract her from her worries. Very well, she thought as she silently followed Mo through the sleeping village, if he doesn't want to tell me what Fenoglio's supposed to do for him I'll ask old turtle-face himself. And if *he* won't say either, then one of his grandchildren can find out for me! Paula was just the right size for a spy. It didn't seem all that long ago since Meggie herself had been able to hide unnoticed under a table.

Going Home

My library was dukedom large enough.
William Shakespeare, *The Tempest*

It was almost midnight by the time Elinor finally saw her garden gate beside the road. The lights down by the banks of the lake stood side by side like a caravan of glow-worms, trembling as they were reflected in the black water. It was good to be home again. Even the wind that blew on Elinor's face as she got out to open the gate felt familiar. It was all familiar, the scent of the hedges and the earth and the air, so much cooler and moister than in the south. It didn't taste of salt any more either. I might even miss that saltiness, thought Elinor. The sea always filled her with longing, though for what she was never sure.

The iron gate creaked quietly as she pushed it open, almost as if it were welcoming her home. But no other voice would greet her. 'What a silly notion, Elinor!' she muttered crossly as she got back into the car. 'Your books will welcome you home. That's good enough, surely.'

She had been in a strange mood even during the drive. She had taken her time on the way home, avoiding major roads, and had spent the night in a tiny place in the mountains, the name of which she had already forgotten. She had enjoyed being alone again, for that, after all, was what she was used to, yet the silence in her car had suddenly begun to trouble her, and she had gone into a café in a sleepy little town which didn't even have a bookshop, just to hear other human voices. She hadn't spent much time there, staying only long enough to gulp down a cup of coffee, because she was annoyed with herself. 'What's all this in aid of, Elinor?' she had muttered when she was back in the car. 'Since when did you long for human company? High time you were home again, before you go right round the bend.'

Her house looked so dark and deserted as she drove up to it that it seemed curiously strange to her. Only the scents of her garden made her feel a little better as she went up the steps to the front door. The light over the door which usually came on automatically at night wasn't working, and it took Elinor a ridiculous amount of time to get her key into the lock. As she pushed the door open and stumbled into the pitch dark hall she quietly cursed the man who usually kept an eye on the house and garden whenever she went away. She had tried phoning him three times before she set out, but she supposed he'd gone to see his daughter again. Didn't anyone realise what treasures this house contained? Of course, if they'd been made of gold . . . but they consisted only of paper and printer's ink.

It was very quiet, and for a moment Elinor thought she heard Mortimer's voice as it brought life into the church with the red walls. She could have listened to him for a hundred years. No, two hundred. At least. 'I must get him to read aloud to me when he arrives,' she murmured, taking the shoes off her tired feet. 'There must be some books he can read safely.'

Why had she never before noticed how quiet her house could be? It was silent as the grave, and the pleasure Elinor had expected to feel as soon as she was back within her own four walls was slow in coming.

'Hello, here I am again!' she cried into the silence, as she felt along the wall for the light switch. 'Now you shall all be dusted and tidied again, my dears!'

The ceiling light came on, very bright, and as Elinor stumbled back in alarm she fell over her own handbag, which she had put down on the floor. 'Oh heavens!' she whispered, getting to her feet again. 'Oh, dear heavens! Oh no!'

The custom-made bookshelves were empty. The books that had stood on them so safely, spine beside spine, now lay in untidy heaps on the floor, crumpled, dirty, and trampled underfoot, as if heavy boots had been performing a wild dance on them. Elinor began to tremble all over. She stumbled through her desecrated treasures as if she were wading through a muddy pond, pushed them aside, picked one up and let it drop, staggered on down the long corridor that led to her library.

The corridor was no better. Great disorderly piles of books were heaped so high that Elinor could hardly make her way through the ruins. At last she reached the library door. It had not been locked. Elinor stood there for an eternity, weak at the knees, before she finally dared to open it.

Her library was empty.

Not a book in sight, not a single book, not on the shelves or beneath the broken glass of the display cases. There wasn't a book on the floor either. They were all gone. Instead, a red rooster dangled from the ceiling, stone dead.

Elinor's hand flew to her mouth. The rooster's head was hanging down, its red comb flopped over its staring eyes. Its plumage was still glossy, as if all the life in it had fled there, into the fine russet breast feathers, the darkly patterned wings and the long deep-green tail feathers that shimmered like silk.

One of the windows was open. A black arrow had been drawn in soot on the white paint of the windowsill, and pointed the way to the garden outside. Elinor staggered towards the window, numb with fear. The night was not dark enough to hide what lay on the lawn outside: a shapeless mound of ashes, pale grey in the moonlight, grey as moth wings, grey as burnt paper.

There they were. Her most valuable books. Or all that was left of them.

Elinor knelt down on the floorboards, on the wood she had so carefully chosen. The wind wafted in through the open window and over her, the familiar wind, and it smelled almost like the air in Capricorn's church. Elinor wanted to scream, she wanted to curse, rage, cry out in fury, but not a sound came out of her mouth. All she could do was weep.

29

Only an Idea

'Don't have a mother,' he said. Not only had he no mother, but he had not the slightest desire to have one. He thought them very over-rated persons.

J.M. Barrie, *Peter Pan*

The apartment that Fenoglio rented to tourists was only two streets away from his own house. It had two rooms plus a tiny bathroom and kitchen. Since it was on the ground floor it was rather dark, and the beds creaked when you lay down in them. All the same, Meggie slept well or, anyway, better than on Capricorn's damp straw or in the hovel with the ruined roof.

Mo slept only fitfully. Meggie was woken twice on that first night by tom cats fighting out in the street, and both times she saw him lying there with his eyes open, arms folded behind his head, looking at the dark window.

He got up very early in the morning and went to buy food for breakfast in the little shop at the end of the street. The bread rolls were fresh and warm, and Meggie really did almost feel as if they were on holiday when Mo and she drove to the nearest town of any size to buy the basic tools of his trade: brushes, knives, fabric, stout cardboard – and truly gigantic ice-creams which they ate together in a café by the sea. Meggie still had the taste of the ice-cream in her mouth as they knocked on the door of Fenoglio's house. The old man and Mo drank another coffee in his green kitchen before he took Mo and Meggie up to the attic where he kept his books.

'I don't believe it!' said Mo, outraged, standing in front of Fenoglio's dusty bookshelves. 'They ought all to be removed from you on the spot! When did you last come up here? I could scrape the dust off their pages with a trowel.'

'I had to put them up here, said Fenoglio defensively, signs of a guilty conscience lurking among his wrinkles. 'I was getting so short of space downstairs with all those shelves, and anyway my grandchildren were always pulling them about.'

'They could hardly have done as much damage as the damp and dirt up here,' said Mo.

Fenoglio went downstairs again looking crestfallen. 'You poor child. Is your father always so strict?' he asked Meggie as they climbed down the steep staircase.

'Only about books,' she said.

Fenoglio disappeared into his study before she could ask him any questions, and his grandchildren were at school or playgroup, so she fetched the books that Elinor had given her and sat down with them on the flight of steps leading into Fenoglio's tiny garden. Wild roses grew so thickly there that you could hardly take a step without feeling their shoots twine round your legs, and from the top step you could see the sea, far away yet looking very close.

Meggie opened the book of poems. She had to narrow her

eyes because the sun was shining in her face so brightly, and before beginning to read she looked over her shoulder to make quite sure Mo hadn't followed her down. She didn't want him to catch her at what she was planning to do. She was ashamed of it, but the temptation was just too great.

When she was perfectly sure no one was coming she took a deep breath, cleared her throat – and began. She shaped every word with her lips the way she had seen Mo do it, almost tenderly, as if every letter were a musical note and any words spoken without love were a discord in the melody. But she soon realised that if she paid too much attention to every separate word the sentence didn't sound right any more, and the pictures behind it were lost if she concentrated on the sound alone and not the sense. It was difficult. So difficult. And the sun was making her drowsy, until at last she closed the book and held her face up to its warm rays. It was silly of her to try anyway. Very silly . . .

Later that afternoon Pippo, Paula and Rico came back and Meggie walked round the village with them. They bought things in the shop where Mo had gone in the morning, sat on a wall on the outskirts of the village, watched ants carrying pine needles and flower seeds over the rough stones, and counted the ships sailing by on the distant sea.

A second day passed like this. Now and then Meggie wondered where Dustfinger could be, and whether Farid was still with him, how Elinor was, and if she was beginning to wonder where they were.

There was no answer to any of these questions, and Meggie didn't find out what Fenoglio was doing behind his study door either. 'Chewing his pencil,' Paula told her when she had managed to hide under her grandfather's desk. 'Just chewing the end of his pencil and walking up and down.'

'Mo, when are we going to Elinor's house?' Meggie asked on their second night, when she sensed that, yet again, he couldn't sleep. She perched on the edge of his bed. The bed creaked just like hers.

'Soon,' he said. 'Go to sleep again now, OK?'

'Do you miss her – my mother, I mean?' Meggie herself didn't know why she asked that question out of the blue. All of a sudden it was there, on the tip of her tongue, and had to be spoken aloud.

It was a long time before Mo answered.

'Sometimes,' he said at last. 'In the morning, at midday, in the evening, at night. Almost all the time.'

Meggie felt jealousy digging its little claws into her heart. She knew that feeling; she felt it every time Mo had a new girlfriend. But how could she be jealous of her own mother? 'Tell me about her,' she said quietly. 'I don't mean the made-up stories you used to tell.'

She used to search her books for a suitable mother, but there were hardly any mothers in her favourite stories. Tom Sawyer? No mother. Huck Finn? Ditto. Peter Pan and the Lost Boys? Not a mother in sight. Jim Button was motherless too – and all you found in fairy tales were wicked stepmothers, heartless, jealous stepmothers . . . the list could go on for ever. That had often comforted Meggie in the past. It didn't seem particularly unusual not to have a mother, or at least not in the books she liked best.

'What do you want me to tell you?' Mo looked at the window. The tom cats were fighting outside again. Their yowls sounded like babies crying. 'You look more like her than me,

I'm glad to say. She laughs like you, and she chews a strand of hair while she's reading exactly the way you do. She's short-sighted, but too vain to wear glasses—'

'I can understand that.' Meggie sat down beside him. His arm hardly hurt him now. The bite from Basta's dog had almost healed up, but there would always be a scar, pale as the scar Basta's knife had left nine years ago.

'What do you mean? I like glasses,' said Mo.

'I don't. Go on.'

'She loves stones, flat, smooth stones that fit comfortably into the hand. She always has one or two of them in her pocket, and she weights down books with them, specially paperbacks. She doesn't like the covers to stick up in the air, but you were always taking the stones away and rolling them over the wooden floor.'

'And then she was cross.'

'Oh, I don't know. She tickled your fat little neck until you let go of the stones.' Mo turned round to look at her. 'Do you really *not* miss her, Meggie?'

'I don't know. Well, only if I'm feeling angry with you.'

'About a dozen times a day, then?'

'Don't be so silly!' Meggie dug her elbow into his ribs.

They both listened for any sounds in the night. The window was open just a crack, and it was quiet outside. The tom cats had fallen silent, probably licking their wounds For a moment Meggie thought she could hear the sea breaking in the distance, but perhaps it was only the traffic on the nearby motorway.

'Where do you think Dustfinger has gone?' The darkness enveloped them like a soft cloth. I'll miss this warmth, she thought, I really will.

'I don't know,' said Mo. His voice sounded absent. 'A long way off, I hope, but I'm not sure.'

Nor was Meggie. 'Do you think that boy's still with him?' Farid. She liked his name.

'I expect so. He was running after Dustfinger like a dog.'

'He likes Dustfinger. Do you think Dustfinger likes him?'

Mo shrugged his shoulders. 'I don't know who or what Dustfinger likes.'

Meggie rested her head against his chest, the way she always used to at home when he was telling her a story. 'He still wants the book, doesn't he?' she whispered. 'Basta will make mincemeat of him if he catches him. He must have got a new knife by now.'

Someone was coming along the narrow alley. A door opened and was closed again, a dog barked.

'If it wasn't for you,' said Mo, 'I'd go back too.'

30

Talkative Pippo

'We were told there was a village nearby that might enjoy
our skills.'

'You were misinformed,' Buttercup told him. 'There is
no one, not for many miles.'

'Then there will be no one to hear you scream,' the
Sicilian said, and he jumped with frightening agility toward
her face.

William Goldman, *The Princess Bride*

Next morning, at around ten o'clock, Elinor rang
Fenoglio's house. Meggie was sitting upstairs with Mo,
watching him remove a book from its mildewed binding as
carefully as if he were releasing an injured animal from a trap.

'Mortimer!' Fenoglio called up the stairs. 'Come down at
once, will you? There's some hysterical female on the phone,
shouting in my ear. I can't make head nor tail of it. Says she's
a friend of yours.'

Mo put the book to one side, minus its cover, and went
downstairs. Fenoglio handed him the receiver with a gloomy

expression on his face. Elinor's voice was pouring rage and despair into the peaceful study. Mo himself had some difficulty in making sense of what she was saying.

'But how did he know . . . oh, of course . . .' Meggie heard him saying. 'Burnt? All of them?' He passed a hand over his face and glanced in Meggie's direction, but she had a feeling that he was looking straight through her. 'All right,' he said. 'Yes, of course, though I'm afraid they won't believe a word of it. And the police down here aren't responsible for what's happened to your books . . . yes, of course. Naturally . . . I'll pick you up. Yes.'

Then he rang off.

Fenoglio could not conceal his curiosity. He scented a new story in the offing. 'What was all that about?' he asked impatiently as Mo just stood there staring at the telephone. Rico was clinging to Fenoglio's back like a little monkey. It was Saturday, but the other two children hadn't turned up yet. 'What's the matter, Mortimer? Aren't you talking to us any more? Look at your father, Meggie! Standing there like a stuffed dummy!'

'That was Elinor,' said Mo. 'Meggie's mother's aunt. I told you about her. Capricorn's men broke into her house. They swept the books off the shelves all over the house and trampled on them, and the books in Elinor's library . . .' He hesitated for a moment before going on. 'Her most valuable books – they took them out into the garden and burned them. All she found in her library was a dead rooster.'

Fenoglio let his grandson slide off his back. 'Rico, go and look for the kittens,' he said. 'This is not for your ears.' Rico protested, but his grandfather pushed him out of the room and closed the door after him. 'What makes you so sure Capricorn is behind this?' he asked, turning back to Mo.

'Who else would do such a thing? Anyway, as far as I remember the red rooster is his emblem. Forgotten your own story, have you?'

Fenoglio was looking downcast. 'No, no, I remember that,' he murmured.

'What about Elinor?' Meggie's heart beat anxiously as she waited for Mo's answer.

'Luckily, she wasn't back yet when it happened. She took her time going home. Thank heavens. But you can imagine how she feels. Her finest books – my God!'

Fenoglio was picking up some toy soldiers from his rug with trembling fingers. 'Yes, Capricorn likes fire,' he said huskily. 'If it was really his doing, your friend can think herself fortunate he didn't burn her too.'

'I'll tell her.' Mo picked up a matchbox lying on Fenoglio's writing-desk, opened it and slowly closed it again.

'What about my books?' Meggie hardly dared to ask. 'My book-box – I hid it under the bed.'

Mo put the matchbox back on the desk. 'That's the one piece of good news,' he said. 'No one touched your book-box. It's still under the bed. Elinor looked.'

Meggie took a deep breath. Was it Basta who had set fire to the books? No, Basta was afraid of fire; she remembered only too well how Dustfinger had mocked him for it. But in the last resort it made no difference which of the Black Jackets it had been. Elinor's treasures were gone, and not even Mo could bring them back.

'Elinor is flying back down here. I'm to pick her up at the airport,' said Mo. 'She's taken it into her head to set the police on Capricorn. I told her I didn't think she'd have much luck.

Even if she had evidence that it was his men who broke into her house, how can she prove he gave the order? But you know Elinor.'

Meggie nodded gloomily. Oh yes, she knew Elinor – and she understood her rage only too well.

But Fenoglio laughed. 'The police! You don't get anywhere by setting the police on Capricorn!' he said. 'He makes his own rules, his own laws—'

'Oh, be quiet! This isn't a book you're writing!' Mo interrupted him. 'Very likely it's amusing to invent a character like Capricorn, but believe you me, it's not in the least bit funny to cross his path. I'm off to the airport. I'll leave Meggie here. Look after her.'

And he was out of the door before Meggie could protest. She ran after him, but Paula and Pippo met her coming down the street. They caught hold of her, trying to make her play with them. They wanted her to be a cannibal, a witch, a six-armed monster – the characters from their grandfather's stories with which they populated their games. By the time Meggie had finally managed to shake off their little hands, Mo had long since gone. The place where he had parked the hire-car was empty, and Meggie stood in the square, alone with the war memorial and a few old men gazing out to sea with their hands in their trouser pockets.

Restlessly, she wandered over to the steps in front of the memorial and sat down. She didn't feel like chasing Fenoglio's grandchildren round his house or playing hide-and-seek with them. She just wanted to sit there and wait for Mo's return. The hot wind that had blown through the village overnight had left fine sand on all the windowsills. The air was cooler than it had been for the last few days. The sky above the sea was still clear, but grey clouds were forming above the hills, and every time the sun disappeared behind them a shadow fell over the village rooftops, making Meggie shiver.

A cat stalked towards her, stiff-legged, tail erect. It was a skinny little creature with ticks in its grey fur, and ribs showing through its thin coat like stripes. Meggie enticed it over, speaking to it gently, until it put its head under her arm and purred, asking to be petted. It didn't look as if it belonged to anyone: no collar, not an ounce of fat on it, nothing to suggest it had a caring owner. Meggie scratched its ears and chin and stroked its back as she looked down the road that went round a sharp bend as it left the village and disappeared from sight beyond the houses.

How far was it to the nearest airport? Meggie propped her chin on her hands. The clouds above her were massing more and more ominously. They loomed overhead, close-packed and grey with rain.

The cat rubbed against her knee, and as Meggie's fingers stroked its dirty fur an awful thought suddenly occurred to her. Suppose Elinor's house wasn't all Dustfinger had told Capricorn about? Suppose he'd told him where she and Mo had been living too? Would they find a heap of ashes waiting for them at the farmhouse? No, she wouldn't think about that. He doesn't know, she whispered. He has no idea! Dustfinger didn't tell him. She kept whispering it like a magic charm.

After a while she felt a raindrop on her hand, then another. She looked up at the sky. There wasn't so much as a speck of blue to be seen. How quickly the nearby sea could make the weather change! All right, I'll just wait in the apartment, she thought. We might even have some milk there for the cat. The poor thing weighed no more than a small damp towel. Meggie was afraid of breaking something when she picked it up.

It was pitch dark in the apartment. Mo had closed the shutters that morning so that the sun wouldn't make it too hot. Meggie was shivering and wet from the fine drizzle when she entered the cool bedroom. She put the cat down on her unmade bed, slipped on Mo's sweater, which was much too big for her, and went into the kitchen. The milk carton was almost empty, but if she diluted what was left with a little warm water there was just enough for a saucerful.

The cat jumped down so quickly when Meggie put the milk on the floor beside the bed that it almost fell over its own paws. Rain was falling harder and harder outside. Meggie listened to it drumming on the paving stones. She went over to the window and opened the shutters. The narrow strip of sky visible between the rooftops was as dark as if the sun were about to set. Meggie went over to Mo's bed and sat down on it. The cat was still licking the saucer, its little tongue greedily rasping over the flower-patterned china, hoping for a last delicious drop. Meggie heard footsteps out in the street, and then a knock at the door. Who was that? Mo couldn't possibly be back yet. Or had he forgotten something? The cat had disappeared, probably to hide under the bed. 'Who's there?' called Meggie.

'Meggie!' a child's voice called back. Of course, Paula or Pippo. Yes, it must be Pippo. They probably wanted to go looking for ants with her again, even though it was raining. A grey paw emerged from under the bed and patted her shoelace. Meggie went out into the tiny hall. 'I don't have time to play just now!' she called through the closed door.

'Please, Meggie!' begged Pippo's voice.

Sighing, Meggie opened the door – and found herself looking straight into Basta's face.

'Well, well, who do we have here?' he asked in a menacingly soft voice, his fingers around Pippo's thin little neck. 'What do you say to that, Flatnose? She doesn't have time to play.' Basta pushed Meggie roughly aside and came through the door with Pippo, followed, of course, by Flatnose, whose broad shoulders would hardly fit through the doorway.

'Let go of him!' Meggie snapped at Basta, although her voice shook. 'You're hurting him.'

'Am I indeed?' Basta looked down at Pippo's pale face. 'Not very nice of me, is it, especially since he showed us where you were hiding?' With these last words he squeezed Pippo's neck even more firmly.

'Do you know how long we lay in that filthy hovel?' he snarled at Meggie.

She took a step backwards.

'A *very* **long** time!' Basta emphasised the word, putting his foxy face so close to Meggie's she could see herself reflected in his eyes. 'Isn't that right, Flatnose?'

'Those damn rats almost nibbled my toes off,' growled the giant. 'Wouldn't I just love to twist this little witch's nose until it's pointing the wrong way round!'

'Later, maybe.' Basta pushed Meggie into the dark bedroom. 'Where's your father?' he asked. 'This little lad,' he said, letting go of Pippo's throat and prodding him in the back so roughly that he stumbled against Meggie, 'told us he's gone out. Gone out where?'

'Shopping.' Meggie could hardly breathe, she was so frightened. 'How did you find us?' she whispered, but instantly knew the answer. Dustfinger. Of course. Who else? But why had he betrayed them this time?

'Dustfinger,' replied Basta, as if he had read her thoughts. 'It's just too easy to find that fellow. There aren't so many crazy jugglers in this world who go around breathing fire and who have a tame marten, not to mention one with horns. So we only had to ask around a bit, and once we were on Dustfinger's trail we were also on your father's, of course. We arrived just in time to see you drive away from the hotel car park, and we'd certainly have paid you a visit before now if this fool,' he said, digging his elbow so hard into Flatnose's stomach he let out a grunt of pain, 'hadn't lost sight of you on our way here. We searched almost a dozen villages, wore our voices out asking questions, ran ourselves off our feet, until we finally got here, and one of those old fellows who spend all day staring out to sea remembered Dustfinger's scarred face. Where is he? Is he – er – out shopping too?' asked Basta, with a scornful twist of his mouth.

Meggie shook her head. 'He went away,' she replied tonelessly. 'Ages ago.' So Dustfinger hadn't given them away after all. Not this time. *And* he'd slipped through Basta's fingers. Meggie could almost have smiled.

'You burned Elinor's books!' she said, holding Pippo close. He was still speechless with terror. 'You'll be sorry you did that.'

'Oh, will we?' Basta smiled unpleasantly. 'I wonder why? As far as I know Cockerell had a lot of fun with those books. But that's enough talk. We don't have for ever. That boy,' he said, pointing at Pippo, who retreated as if Basta's forefinger were a knife, 'has told us some strange stories about a grandfather who writes books, and a book in which your father took a particular interest.'

Meggie swallowed. Stupid Pippo. Stupid, talkative little Pippo.

'Lost your tongue?' asked Basta. 'Shall I squeeze the boy's skinny neck again?'

Pippo began crying and buried his face in Mo's sweater. Meggie stroked his curly head comfortingly.

'His grandfather doesn't have the book you're thinking of any more,' she told Basta. 'You and your friends stole it long ago!' Her voice sounded hoarse with hatred, and her own thoughts sickened her. She wanted to kick Basta, hit him, stab him in the stomach with his own knife, the brand-new knife he wore stuck in his belt.

'Stole it. Just fancy!' Basta grinned at Flatnose. 'I think we'd better make sure of that for ourselves, don't you?'

Flatnose nodded distractedly, looking around him. 'Hey, hear that?'

There was a scratching sound under the bed. Flatnose knelt down, pushed the hanging edge of the sheet aside, and poked around under the bed with the barrel of his gun. Spitting, the grey cat shot out of hiding, and when Flatnose tried to grab it the cat raked his ugly face with its claws. He leaped to his feet with a yelp of pain. 'I'll wring its neck!' he bellowed. 'I'll break that cat's neck!'

Meggie was about to stand in his way as he lunged for the cat, but Basta got in first. 'You'll do no such thing!' he spat at Flatnose, as the grey cat disappeared under the wardrobe. 'Killing cats is unlucky. How often do I have to tell you?'

'Nonsense! Superstitious garbage! I've wrung several of the brutes' necks already!' said Flatnose angrily, pressing one hand to his bleeding cheek. 'And has my luck been worse than yours? You could send a man crazy, the way you carry on: don't walk in that shadow, it's unlucky; oh, watch out, you put your left boot on first, that's unlucky; oh my, someone yawned – mercy me, that means I'll fall down dead tomorrow!'

'Shut up!' snapped Basta. 'If anyone around here is talking nonsense it's you. Get those children to the door!'

Pippo clung to Meggie as Flatnose forced them out into the corridor. 'Why are you bawling like that?' he growled at the little boy. 'We're off to see your grandfather now.'

Pippo never let go of Meggie's hand once as they stumbled after Flatnose. He was clutching it so hard that his stubby fingernails dug into her skin. Oh, she thought, why didn't Mo listen to me? We could have gone home. It was still raining heavily. Raindrops ran over Meggie's face and down her neck. The streets were empty; there was no one around to help them. Basta was walking just behind her, and she heard him quietly cursing the rain. When they reached Fenoglio's house Meggie's feet were wet through, and Pippo's curls were plastered to his head. Perhaps he won't be at home, Meggie hoped. She was just thinking about what Basta would do then, when the red door opened and Fenoglio stood facing them.

'What on earth do you children think you're doing, running around in weather like this?' he said angrily. 'I was just going out to look for you. Come on in, and hurry up.'

'May we come in too?'

Basta and Flatnose had been standing either side of the door with their backs to the wall, so that Fenoglio wouldn't see them immediately, but now Basta moved up behind Meggie and put his hands on her shoulders. Fenoglio stared at him in surprise as Flatnose stepped forward and planted a foot in the open doorway. Pippo scurried past him, nimble as a weasel, and disappeared into the house.

'Who are these people?' Fenoglio looked at Meggie as crossly as if she had brought the two strangers there of her own free will. 'Friends of your father's?'

Meggie mopped the rain off her face and looked back at him with equal reproach. 'You ought to know them better than I do!' she said. Basta's fingers were digging into her shoulders.

'Know them?' Fenoglio looked at her blankly. Then he studied Basta. His face froze. 'Great heavens above!' he murmured. 'I don't believe it!'

Paula peered out from behind his back. 'Pippo's crying!' she announced. 'He's hidden in the cupboard.'

'Well, you go back to him,' said Fenoglio, never taking his eyes off Basta. 'I'll be with you in a minute.'

'How much longer are we going to stand out here, Basta?' growled Flatnose. 'Until we shrink in this rain?'

'Basta!' repeated Fenoglio without stepping aside.

'Yes, that's my name, old man.' Basta's eyes always narrowed when he smiled. 'We're here because you have something that interests us a great deal – a book.'

Of course. Meggie almost burst out laughing. He didn't know! Basta didn't know who Fenoglio was. How could he? How could he know that this old man had invented him, made him up out of paper and ink, made up his face, his knife, his evil nature?

'That's enough talk!' growled Flatnose. 'The rain's running into my ears.' He brushed Fenoglio aside like a troublesome fly as he pushed past him into the house. Basta followed, with Meggie. Pippo was still sobbing inside the kitchen cupboard. Paula was standing in front of it, talking to him soothingly through the closed door. When Fenoglio came into the kitchen with the strangers she spun round and looked at Flatnose's face nervously. It was as dark and dismal as ever.

Sitting down at the table, Fenoglio beckoned Paula over without a word.

'Well, where is it?' Basta was looking round, scanning the room, but Fenoglio was too deeply absorbed in the sight of his two creations to reply. He couldn't take his eyes off Basta in particular, as if he couldn't believe what he was seeing.

'I told you: there's no copy of it here!' Meggie replied for him.

Basta acted as if he hadn't heard her, and gestured impatiently to Flatnose. 'Look for it!' he ordered. Grumbling, Flatnose obeyed. Meggie heard him trampling up the narrow wooden staircase that led to the attic.

'Right, little witch, how did you and your father find the old man?' Basta prodded her in the back. 'How did you know he still has a copy?'

Meggie cast Fenoglio a warning glance, but unfortunately he was as ready to talk as Pippo, who had so willingly told Basta all about her and his grandfather.

'How did they find me? I wrote the book!' announced the old man proudly. Perhaps he expected that Basta would instantly fall on his knees before him, but Basta only gave a pitying smile.

'Oh yes, of course you did!' he said, taking the knife from his belt.

'He really did write it!' Meggie couldn't resist saying so. She wanted to see the fear that had turned Dustfinger pale when he heard about Fenoglio appear on Basta's face too, but Basta just smiled again and began carving notches in Fenoglio's kitchen table.

'Who thought up *that* story?' he asked. 'Your father? You think I look stupid? Everyone knows that stories in books are as old as the hills and were written by people dead and buried long ago.' He jabbed the blade of the knife into the wood, pulled it out and jabbed it in again. Flatnose was trampling about overhead.

'Dead and buried. How interesting.' Fenoglio sat Paula on his lap. 'Did you hear that, Paula? This young man believes all books were written in the distant past by dead people who picked up the stories from heaven knows where. Plucked straight from the air, maybe?' Paula couldn't help giggling. It had gone very quiet in the cupboard. Pippo was probably listening at the door, holding his breath.

'What's so funny about that?' Basta reared up like a snake when someone has trodden on its tail. Fenoglio ignored him. Smiling, he looked down at his hands – as if remembering the day when they had begun to write Basta's story. Then he looked straight at him.

'You always wear long sleeves, don't you?' he said. 'Shall I tell you why?'

Basta narrowed his eyes and looked up at the ceiling. 'Damn it all, why is it taking that idiot so long to find a book?'

Fenoglio looked at him, his arms folded. 'Easy: he can't read!' he said quietly. 'You can't read either – unless you've learnt by now? None of Capricorn's men can read, any more than Capricorn himself can.'

Basta drove the knife so far into the surface of the table that he had difficulty pulling it out again. 'Of course he can read. What are you going on about?' He leaned threateningly over the table. 'I don't like the way you talk, old man. Why don't I carve a few more wrinkles in your face?'

Fenoglio smiled. Perhaps he thought Basta couldn't hurt him because he, Fenoglio, had made him up. Meggie wasn't so sure of that. 'You wear long sleeves,' Fenoglio continued very slowly, as if giving Basta time to take in every single word, 'because your master likes playing with fire. You burned both arms right up to the shoulders when you obeyed his orders and set fire to the house of a man who had dared to refuse his daughter to Capricorn. Ever since then, someone else has laid the fire, and you confine yourself to playing games with knives.'

Basta jumped up so suddenly that Paula slid off Fenoglio's lap and hid under the table. 'Like to make yourself out clever, do you?' he growled, holding his knife under Fenoglio's chin. 'When all you've done is read the wretched book. Well?'

Fenoglio looked him in the eye. The knife under his chin didn't seem to scare him half as much as it did Meggie. 'Oh, I know all about you, Basta,' he said. 'I know you'd give your life for Capricorn any day, and you're always hungry for his praise. I know you were younger than Meggie when his men picked you up, and ever since you've loved him like a father. But shall I tell you something? Capricorn thinks you're stupid, and despises you for it. He despises you all, his devoted black-clad sons, although it's his own doing that you're still so ignorant. And he wouldn't hesitate to set the police on to any one of you if it was to his advantage. Are you quite clear about that?'

'Hold your filthy tongue, old man!' Basta's knife came alarmingly close to Fenoglio's face and, for a moment, Meggie thought he would slit his nose. 'You don't know anything about Capricorn. Only what you read in the stupid book. I think I ought to cut your throat – now!'

'Wait!'

Basta whirled round to look at Meggie. 'And you keep out

of this! I'll deal with you later, you little toad,' he said.

Fenoglio's hands were pressed to his own throat. He was staring blankly at Basta, having at last realised he was by no means safe from the man's knife.

'But you can't kill him. Really you can't!' cried Meggie. 'If you do—'

Basta's thumb stroked the blade of his knife. 'If I do, then what?'

Desperately, Meggie searched for the right words . . . what should she say? Oh, what? 'Because . . . because Capricorn would die too,' she managed. 'Yes. That's it. You'd all die, you and Flatnose and Capricorn. If you kill this old man you'll *all* die, because he made you up.'

Basta's lips twisted in a scornful smile, but he lowered his knife and, for a moment, Meggie even thought she saw a hint of fear in his eyes.

Fenoglio cast her a relieved glance.

Basta stepped back, examined the blade of his knife closely as if he had discovered a mark on it, and then rubbed it clean on the hem of his black jacket. 'I don't believe a word of it!' he said. 'But this is such a weird story, I think Capricorn might like to hear it too. So,' he added, giving the shiny blade a last polish before snapping the knife shut and putting it back in his belt, 'we won't take only the book and the girl, we'll take you too, old man.'

Meggie heard Fenoglio draw in a sharp breath. She herself was so scared she wasn't sure if her heart was beating at all. Take them away. Basta was going to take them away. No, she thought, oh please, no!

'Take us away where?' asked Fenoglio.

'Ask the girl here!' Basta pointed mockingly at Meggie.

'She and her father have had the honour of being our guests already. Bed and board thrown in.'

'But this is nonsense!' cried Fenoglio. 'I thought it was the book you wanted.'

'Then you thought wrong. We didn't even know there was supposed to be another copy. No, we were just sent to bring Silvertongue back. Capricorn doesn't like his guests to leave without saying goodbye, and Silvertongue's a very special guest, isn't that right, sweetheart?' Basta winked at Meggie. 'But he isn't here, and I have better things to do than hang around waiting for him. So I'll take his daughter – and he'll come chasing after her of his own accord.' Basta went up to Meggie and pushed her hair back behind her ears. 'She makes pretty bait, wouldn't you say?' he asked. 'Oh yes, old man, take it from me: if we have this little creature we'll have her father too. He'll come like a dancing bear led by a ring in his nose.'

Meggie struck his hand aside, trembling with fury.

'Don't you do that again!' Basta whispered in her ear.

Meggie was glad that Flatnose came trudging downstairs at this moment. He appeared in the kitchen doorway, breathless and with several books under his arm. 'Here!' he said, dumping them on the table. 'They all begin with this single upright stroke followed by the three up-and-down lines. Just the way you drew it.' He put a stained piece of paper down beside the books. The letters I and N were clumsily traced on it, and looked as if the hand that set them down had found the task very difficult.

Basta spread the books out on the table and pushed them apart from each other with his knife. 'These are no good,' he said, pushing two off the table so that they landed on the floor, with crumpled pages. 'Nor are these.' Two more landed on the floor, and finally Basta swept the rest off the table too. 'Are you quite sure there isn't another one beginning like that?' he asked Flatnose angrily.

'Yes, I'm sure!'

'You'd better not be wrong. Because I do assure you, you'll be the one to pay for it, not me!'

Flatnose cast a worried look over the books at his feet.

'Oh, and another little change of plan: we're taking *him* with us as well.' Basta pointed his knife at Fenoglio. 'So he can tell the boss his amazing stories. Very entertaining they are too, believe you me. And just in case he's hidden a book somewhere – well, we'll have plenty of time to ask him about that once we get back. You keep your eye on the old man and I'll watch the girl.'

Flatnose nodded, and hauled Fenoglio up from his chair. But Basta reached for Meggie's arm. Back to Capricorn – she had to bite her lip to stop herself bursting into tears as Basta dragged her to Fenoglio's kitchen door. No. Basta wouldn't see her weep, she wasn't going to give him that satisfaction. At least they haven't got Mo, she thought. And suddenly there was only one thought in her head: suppose he crossed their path before they left the village? Suppose he came to meet them, on his way back with Elinor?

All at once she couldn't wait to get away, but Flatnose had paused in the doorway. 'What about the little girl and that cry-baby in the cupboard?' he asked.

Pippo's sobs died away, and Fenoglio's face turned even whiter than Basta's shirt.

'Right, old man, what do you think I'm going to do with them?' asked Basta scornfully. 'You say you know all about me.'

Fenoglio couldn't utter a word. Every cruel deed with which he had ever credited Basta was probably going through his head. Basta relished the fear on his face for a few delicious minutes, then he turned to Flatnose. 'The other children stay behind,' he said. 'Our little madam here will do.'

With difficulty, Fenoglio recovered his powers of speech. 'Paula, go home!' he said as Flatnose forced him down the hall. 'Do you hear? Go home at once. Tell your mother I've gone away for a few days, all right?'

'We'll just look in at that apartment again,' Basta said as they were standing in the street outside. 'I quite forgot to leave a message for your father. I mean, he ought to know where you are, don't you think?'

What kind of message will it be, thought Meggie, when you can scarcely put two letters together? But of course she didn't say so out loud. She was terrified the whole time that Mo might come to meet them. But when they reached the front door of the apartment there was only an old lady walking down the street.

'One word out of you and I'll go back and wring both children's necks!' Basta whispered to Fenoglio as the old lady slowed down.

'Hello, Rosalia,' said Fenoglio huskily. 'Guess what – I have new tenants for my apartment. How about that, then?'

The suspicion vanished from Rosalia's face, and a moment later she had disappeared round a corner of the street. Meggie opened the door, and for the second time let Basta and Flatnose into the apartment where she and Mo had felt so safe.

In the hall she remembered the grey cat, and looked around anxiously, but it was nowhere to be seen. 'The cat has to go out,' she said when they were in the bedroom. 'Or it'll starve to death. That's unlucky.'

Basta opened the window. 'Right, it can get out now,' he said.

Flatnose snorted scornfully, but this time he made no comment on Basta's superstitious nature.

'Can I take some clothes?' asked Meggie.

Flatnose just grunted, and Fenoglio looked unhappily down at himself. 'I could do with a change of clothes too,' he said, but no one took any notice. Basta was busy with his message. Carefully, with the tip of his tongue between his teeth, he was gouging his name in the wood of the wardrobe with his knife. BASTA. Mo would understand that only too well.

Meggie hastily stuffed a few things in her rucksack. She kept Mo's sweater on. She was about to put Elinor's two books in with the clothes but Basta knocked them out of her hand.

'Those stay here,' he said.

Mo did not return in time to meet them as they walked to Basta's car. All that long, endless way, he didn't appear.

31

In the Hills

'Let him alone,' said Merlin. 'Perhaps he does not want to
be friends with you until he knows what you are like. With
owls, it is never easy-come and easy-go.'

T.H. White, *The Sword in the Stone*

Dustfinger looked across to Capricorn's village. It seemed
close enough to touch. Some of the windows reflected the
sky, and one of the Black Jackets was repairing a couple of
broken tiles on a roof. Dustfinger saw him wipe the sweat
from his brow. The fools never took their jackets off even in
this heat – as if they were afraid of falling apart without that
black uniform. Not that crows take off their feathers in the sun
either, and these men were just a flock of crows: robbers, car-
rion-eaters who liked to plunge their sharp beaks into dead
flesh.

The boy had been uneasy when he saw how close
Dustfinger's chosen hiding-place was to the village, but
Dustfinger had explained why there couldn't be anywhere
safer to lie low among the surrounding hills. The charred walls

were hardly visible, camouflaged as they were by the gorse and wild thyme that had taken root among the soot-blackened stones. Capricorn's men had set fire to the house soon after taking over the deserted village. The old woman who had lived there had refused to leave, but Capricorn wouldn't tolerate prying eyes so close to his new hideout and gave his followers a free hand. His crows, his black vultures, had set fire to the home-made chicken run and the one-roomed cottage. They had trampled over the carefully tended beds in the garden, and shot the donkey that was almost as old as its mistress. They came under cover of darkness as usual, and the moon, so one of Capricorn's maidservants had told Dustfinger, shone particularly brightly that night. The old woman had tottered out of the house, weeping and screaming. Then she'd cursed them. She cursed them all, but her eyes were turned on only one of them. Basta, who was standing a little way from the others because he feared the fire, his shirt very white in the moonlight. Perhaps she had hoped that shirt might conceal something like innocence or a kind heart. On Basta's orders, Flatnose had put his hand over her mouth to shut her up. The others had laughed – until, unexpectedly, she fell down dead and lay there lifeless among her trampled garden beds. Ever since that day, Basta had feared this place more than anywhere else in the hills. No, there could be nowhere better to keep watch on Capricorn's village.

Dustfinger spent most of the time perched in one of the oaks that had once given the old woman a shady place to sit outside her cottage. Its branches hid him from the curious eyes of anyone who might stray up the hillside. He perched there motionless for hour upon hour, watching the car park and the houses through his binoculars. He had told Farid to stay further away, in the hollow behind the house. The boy had reluctantly obeyed. He was sticking close to Dustfinger, close as a burr, and he didn't like the gutted cottage. 'Her ghost is still here, for sure,' he kept saying. 'That old woman's ghost. Suppose she was a witch?' But Dustfinger just laughed at him. There were no ghosts in this world, or if there were they never showed themselves. The hollow was so well sheltered that he had even risked lighting a fire the previous night. The boy had snared a rabbit; he was good at setting traps and more ruthless than Dustfinger. When Dustfinger caught a rabbit he didn't take it out of the trap until he was quite sure the poor thing had stopped wriggling. Farid had no such scruples. Perhaps he had gone hungry too often.

Above all he loved to watch with wonder and admiration whenever Dustfinger took a few little sticks and lit a fire. The boy had already burnt his fingers playing games with matches. The flames had bitten his nose and his lips, yet Dustfinger kept finding him making torches of cotton wool and thin twigs. Once he set light to the dry grass, and Dustfinger grabbed him and shook him like a disobedient dog until tears came into his eyes. 'Listen hard, because I'm not telling you again! Fire is a dangerous creature!' he had shouted at Farid. 'Fire is not your friend. It will kill you if you don't respect it. And its smoke will give you away to your enemies!'

'But it's *your* friend!' the boy had stammered defiantly.

'Nonsense! I'm not careless, that's all. I take note of the wind! You let it play with the fire. I've told you a hundred times: never light a fire when it's windy. Now go and look for Gwin.'

'It *is* your friend, though!' the boy had muttered before running off. 'Or anyway, it obeys you better than the marten does.'

He was right there, though that didn't mean much, for a marten obeys only itself, and even fire didn't obey Dustfinger in this world as well as in his own, where the flames turned to flower shapes whenever he told them to. They had forked up in the air for him, like trees branching in the night, and rained down sparks. They had roared and whispered with their crackling voices, they had danced when he said the word. The flames here were both tame and mutinous, strange, silent beasts which sometimes bit the hand that fed them. Only occasionally, on cold nights when there was nothing but the flames to stave off his loneliness, did he think he heard them calling to him, but they whispered words he didn't understand.

However, the boy was probably right. Yes, fire was his friend, but it was also the reason why Capricorn had summoned him back in that other life. 'Show me how to play with fire!' he had said when his men dragged Dustfinger before him, and Dustfinger had obeyed. He still regretted teaching him so much, for Capricorn loved to give fire free rein, catching it again only when it had eaten its fill of crops and stables, houses and anything that couldn't run fast enough.

'Is he still away?' Farid was leaning against the rough bark of the tree. The boy was as quiet as a snake. Dustfinger always jumped when he appeared so suddenly.

'Yes,' he said. 'Luck's on our side.' On the day they came to this hideout Capricorn's car had been standing in the parking place, but that afternoon two of the boys had begun polishing its silver paintwork until they could see their reflections in it, and shortly before it was dark it had driven off. Capricorn often had himself driven around the countryside, to the villages further down the coast or to one of his other bases, as he liked to call them, although these so-called bases were often little more than a hut in the woods with a couple of bored men guarding it. Like Dustfinger, he couldn't drive a car, but some of his men had mastered the art of it. Hardly any of them held a driving licence, though, because to pass the test they would have to be able to read.

'Yes, I'll go over there again tonight,' murmured Dustfinger. 'He won't be away much longer, and Basta is sure to be back soon too.' Basta's car had not been in the car park at all since they'd come here. It was unusual for it to be gone so long, because Basta didn't like to be away from the village for any length of time. Were he and Flatnose still lying in the ruined cottage, bound and gagged?

'Good! When do we start!' Farid sounded as if he wanted to get moving at once. 'After sunset? They'll all be in the church eating then.'

Dustfinger shooed a fly away from his binoculars. 'I'm going alone. You're to stay here and keep an eye on our things.'

'No!'

'Yes. This will be dangerous. There's someone I want to visit, and to do that I have to get into the yard behind Capricorn's house.'

The boy gazed at him with eyes full of astonishment. Eyes that sometimes looked as if they had seen too much already.

'Surprised, are you?' Dustfinger suppressed a smile. 'You wouldn't have thought I had any friends in Capricorn's house!'

The boy shrugged his shoulders and looked over to the village. A vehicle was driving into the car park, a dusty truck with two goats tethered on the open loading platform.

'Look at that – another farmer's lost his goats!' muttered

Dustfinger. 'Wise of him to give them up freely, or there'd have been a note pinned to his stable door this evening.'

Farid looked at him, an unspoken question in his eyes.

'*The red rooster crows tomorrow*, that's what the note would say. It's the only thing Capricorn's men know how to write. But sometimes they just hang a dead rooster above the door. Anyone can understand that.'

'Red rooster?' The boy shook his head. 'Is it a curse or something?'

'No! Good heavens, you sound like Basta.' Dustfinger laughed quietly. Capricorn's men were getting out of the truck. The smaller of them was carrying two plastic bags filled to bursting; the other was hauling the goats off the loading platform. 'The red rooster means fire, the fire they'll light in the farmer's outhouses or olive groves. And sometimes the rooster crows in the attic of the house or, if a farmer has been particularly stubborn, in his children's bedroom. We almost all have something we love dearly.'

The men were leading the goats into the village. Dustfinger knew by his limp that one of them was Cockerell. He had often wondered whether Capricorn knew about all the little deals his men did, or whether they were working for themselves on the side now and then.

Farid caught a grasshopper in the hollow of his hand and watched it through his fingers. 'I'm going with you all the same,' he said.

'No.'

'I'm not afraid!'

'That makes it worse.'

Capricorn had had floodlights installed after the escape of his captives – outside the church, on the roof of his house and in the car park. They didn't exactly make it easier to walk the streets unobserved. The first night after their arrival here Dustfinger had stolen into the village, his scarred face blackened with soot because it was too easily recognisable. Capricorn had also reinforced the guards on sentry duty, probably because of all the treasure Silvertongue had brought him. By now, of course, that treasure had disappeared into the cellars of his house and was carefully locked in the heavy safes that Capricorn had fitted there. He didn't care to spend money; like the dragons of legend, he hoarded it. Sometimes he placed a ring on his finger, or put a necklace round the neck of a maid who happened to take his fancy. Or he sent Basta out to buy him a new sporting gun.

'Who are you going to meet?'

'None of your business.'

The boy let the grasshopper go again. It hopped rapidly away on its spindly olive-green legs.

'A woman,' said Dustfinger. 'One of Capricorn's maids. She's helped me a couple of times before.'

'The one in the photo in your rucksack?'

Dustfinger lowered his binoculars. 'How do you know what's in my rucksack?'

The boy hunched his head down between his shoulders, like someone used to being beaten for every thoughtless remark. 'I was looking for matches.'

'If I catch you with your fingers in my rucksack again I'll tell Gwin to bite them off.'

The boy grinned. 'Gwin never bites me.'

He was right. The marten was crazy about Farid.

'Where is that faithless animal anyway?' Dustfinger peered through the branches. 'I haven't seen him since yesterday.'

'I think he's found a female.' Farid picked up a stick and poked at the dead leaves that lay everywhere under the trees. By night the rustling leaves would give away anyone trying to steal up to their camp in silence. 'If you don't take me with you tonight,' said the boy, without looking at Dustfinger, 'I'll just follow you anyway.'

'If you follow me I shall beat you black and blue.'

Farid lowered his head and gazed inscrutably at his bare toes. Then he glanced at the ruined walls where they had made their camp.

'And don't start on about the old woman's ghost again!' said Dustfinger crossly. 'How often do I have to tell you? All the danger is over in those houses. Light a fire in the hollow if you're afraid of the dark.'

'Ghosts don't fear fire.' The boy's voice was hardly more than a whisper.

Sighing, Dustfinger clambered down from his look-out post. The boy was almost as bad as Basta. He wasn't afraid of curses, ladders or black cats, but he saw ghosts everywhere, and not just the ghost of the old woman now sleeping buried somewhere in the hard ground. Farid saw other ghosts and spirits too, whole armies of them: malignant, all-powerful beings who tore the hearts out of poor mortal boys and ate them. He refused to believe it when Dustfinger told him they hadn't come with him, he had left them behind in a book along with the thieves who used to beat and kick him. He might well die of fear if he stayed here alone all night. 'Oh, very well then, you'd better come,' said Dustfinger. 'But not a squeak out of you, understand? The men down there aren't ghosts. They're real people, and they have knives and guns.'

Gratefully, Farid flung his thin arms around him.

'Yes, all right, that'll do!' said Dustfinger, pushing him away. 'Come on, let's see if you can stand on one hand yet.'

The boy immediately obeyed. Bright red in the face, he balanced first on his right hand and then on his left, bare legs up in the air. After three wobbly seconds he landed in the prickly leaves of a rockrose, but he promptly got up, pulled a few thorns out of his foot, and tried again.

Dustfinger sat down under a tree.

It was high time to get rid of the boy, but how? You could throw stones at a dog, but a boy . . . Why hadn't he stayed with Silvertongue, who knew more about looking after young people? And it was Silvertongue, after all, who had brought him here. But no, the boy had to run after him, Dustfinger.

'I'm going to look for Gwin,' said Dustfinger, getting to his feet.

Without a word Farid trotted after him.

32

Back Again

She spoke to the King, hoping he would forbid his son to go, but he said: 'Well, dear, it's true that adventures are good for people even when they are very young. Adventures can get into a person's blood even if he doesn't remember having them.'

Eva Ibbotson, *The Secret of Platform 13*

Capricorn's village didn't look like a dangerous place on the grey rainy day when Meggie set eyes on it again. The houses standing among the green hills were a miserable sight, with not a ray of sunlight to brighten their ruins. Meggie could hardly believe these same houses had looked so menacing on the night of their escape.

'Interesting,' whispered Fenoglio as Basta drove into the car park. 'Do you know, this village is very like one of the settings I thought up for *Inkheart*? Well, there's no fortress, but the landscape around is similiar, and the age of the village would be about right. Did you know that *Inkheart* is set in a world not unlike our own medieval times? Of course I added some things – the fairies and the giants.'

Meggie wasn't really listening to him now. She remembered how, after their flight from the sheds where Capricorn had held them captive, she had stumbled towards Elinor's car, and the man had shot at them. She had hoped she would never again have to see this car park, the church and these hills.

'Come on, get moving!' grunted Flatnose, opening the car door. 'I expect you remember the way.'

Oh yes, Meggie could remember – even though it did all seem rather different today. Fenoglio looked round the gloomy alleys like a tourist, staring at windows and open doors as if he'd paid for entry. 'I know this village!' he whispered to Meggie. 'I mean, I've heard of it. There's more than one sad story about the place. That earthquake in the last century, and then in the last war there was—'

'Save your tongue for later, scribbler!' Basta interrupted. 'I don't like whispering.'

Fenoglio shot him an angry glance but fell silent, and did not utter another sound until they had reached the church.

'Well, go on, open the door. What are you waiting for?' growled Flatnose.

With Fenoglio's help, Meggie opened the heavy wooden door. The cool air that met them smelled as musty as on the day she had entered the church with Mo and Elinor. Nothing much had changed inside. The red walls looked even more threatening on this overcast day, and the expression on the doll-like face of Capricorn's statue seemed rather more malevolent than before, if that were possible. The braziers in which the books had been burned still stood in the same place, but there was no sign of Capricorn's chair at the top of the steps. Two of his men were just carrying a new chair up them.

The old woman who looked like a magpie and whom Meggie didn't really like to remember was standing beside them, impatiently giving directions.

Basta pushed aside two women who were kneeling in the middle of the nave cleaning the floor, and strode towards the altar steps. 'Where's Capricorn, Mortola?' he called to the old woman as he approached. 'I have news for him. Important news.'

The old woman didn't even turn towards him. 'Further to the right, you fools!' she ordered the two men who were still struggling with the heavy armchair. 'Yes, there, that'll do.' Then she turned towards Basta, her face expressionless.

'We expected you back before this,' she said.

'What do you mean?' Basta had raised his voice, but Meggie caught the uncertainty it revealed. It sounded almost as if he were afraid of the old woman. 'Do you know how many villages there are down this damn coast? And we weren't even sure whether Silvertongue was still in the area. But I can rely on my nose, and as you see,' he said, nodding in Meggie's direction, 'I've done the job.'

'You have?' The Magpie looked past Basta to where Meggie and Fenoglio were standing with Flatnose. 'All I see is the girl and an old man. Where's her father?'

'He wasn't there, but he'll come after her. The girl's the best bait we could have.'

'And how will he know she's here?'

'I left him a message.'

'Since when can you write?'

Meggie saw Basta's shoulders tense with anger. 'I left him my name. He won't need more than that to know where to find his precious little daughter. Tell Capricorn I'm shutting her in one of the cages.' With these words he turned on his heel and stalked back to Meggie and Fenoglio.

'Capricorn's not here and I don't know when he'll be back!' Mortola called after him. 'But I'm in charge until then, and in my view you've not been doing your job recently as well as we expect.'

Basta swung round as if he had been bitten in the back of the neck, but Mortola continued unmoved.

'First, you let Dustfinger steal a set of keys from you, then you lose our dogs and we have to send a search party out into the mountains for you, and now this! Give me your keys.' The Magpie put out her hand.

'What?' Basta went white, like a boy being punished in front of the whole class.

'You heard. *I'm* going to look after them: the keys to the cages, the crypt and the fuel store. Bring them here.'

Basta didn't move. 'You've no right to them!' he snapped. 'Capricorn gave them to me, and he's the only one who can take them away again.' He turned away once more.

'And so he will!' Mortola called after him. 'And he'll expect your report as soon as he gets back. Maybe he'll understand better than I do why you didn't bring Silvertongue.'

Basta did not reply. Seizing Meggie and Fenoglio by the arm, he hauled them towards the church door. Mortola the Magpie called something after him, but Meggie couldn't make out what it was. And Basta did not turn back this time.

He locked her and Fenoglio in the shed marked number 5, the one where Farid had been imprisoned. 'Right, you can wait here till your father arrives!' he said before pushing Meggie inside.

She felt as if this were a nightmare and she was dreaming

it all over again. Only here there wasn't even musty straw to sit on, and the light bulb hanging from the ceiling didn't work. However, a little daylight did come in through a narrow hole in the wall.

'Oh, wonderful!' said Fenoglio, sitting down on the cold floor with a sigh. 'A cowshed. How unimaginative. I really would have expected Capricorn at least to have a proper dungeon for his prisoners.'

'Cowshed?' Meggie leaned her back against the wall. She heard the rain pattering against the locked door.

'Well, yes, what did you think it was? They always built houses like this in the old days: room for the livestock on the ground floor and living quarters for the family above them. They still keep their goats and donkeys like that in many mountain villages. Haven't you noticed when they've driven the animals out to pasture in the morning there are steaming heaps of dung left lying in the streets, and you tread in them when you go to buy your breakfast rolls?' Fenoglio plucked a hair from one nostril, looked at it as if he couldn't believe anything quite so bristly grew in his nose, and flicked it away. 'This is really rather uncanny,' he murmured. 'That's exactly how I imagined Capricorn's mother – that nose, the eyes set close together, even the way she folds her arms and her chin juts forward.'

Meggie looked at him incredulously. 'Capricorn's *mother*! The Magpie?'

'Magpie! Is that what you call her?' Fenoglio laughed softly. 'She has exactly the same nickname in my story. How amazing. Be careful of her. She's not a very pleasant character.'

'I thought she was his housekeeper.'

'That's probably what you're supposed to think. So keep

our little secret to yourself for now, all right?'

Meggie agreed, although she didn't really understand. What did it matter who the old woman was? It all came to the same thing. This time there was no Dustfinger to open the door in the night. It had all been for nothing – as if they had never run away at all. She went over to the locked door and pressed her hands against it. 'He'll come,' she whispered. 'Mo will come, and then they'll lock us up here for ever and ever.'

Fenoglio got up and went over to her. 'There, there!' he said, putting his arms round her and letting her bury her face in his jacket. It was made of rough fabric and smelled of pipe tobacco. 'I'll think of something!' he whispered to Meggie. 'After all, I invented these villains. It'll be an odd thing if I can't get rid of them. Your father had an idea, but . . .'

Meggie raised her face, wet with tears, and looked at him hopefully, but the old man shook his head. 'Later. Now, tell me what makes Capricorn so interested in your father. Is it something to do with the way he reads aloud?'

Meggie nodded and wiped the tears from her eyes. 'He wants Mo to read aloud to him here, to bring someone out of a book, an old friend.'

Fenoglio gave her a handkerchief. A few crumbs of tobacco fell from it when she blew her nose. 'A friend? Capricorn has no friends.' The old man frowned. Then Meggie felt him suddenly take a deep breath.

'Who is it?' she asked, but Fenoglio just mopped a tear off her cheek.

'Someone I hope you'll never meet except between the covers of a book,' he said evasively. Then he turned and began pacing up and down. 'Capricorn will be back soon,' he added. 'I must think how best to confront him.'

But Capricorn did not come. Darkness fell outside, and still no one had fetched them from their prison. They weren't even brought anything to eat. It grew cold when the night air came in through the hole in the wall, and they huddled side by side on the hard floor to keep warm.

'Is Basta still very superstitious?' Fenoglio asked at some time in the night.

'Yes, very,' replied Meggie. 'Dustfinger likes winding him up about it.'

'Good,' murmured Fenoglio. But he would say no more.

33

Capricorn's Maid

As I never saw my father or my mother . . . my first fancies regarding what they were like, were unreasonably derived from their tombstones. The shape of the letters on my father's gave me an odd idea that he was a square, stout, dark man with curly black hair. From the character and turn of the inscription 'Also Georgiana Wife of the Above' I drew a childish conclusion that my mother was freckled and sickly.

Charles Dickens, *Great Expectations*

Dustfinger set out when the night could grow no darker. The sky was overcast, with not a single star shining. Only the moon showed occasionally between the clouds, as thin as a slice of lemon.

Dustfinger was glad of such darkness, but the boy jumped whenever a twig brushed his face.

'For heaven's sake, I should have left you with the marten after all!' Dustfinger snapped as Farid clutched his arm in fright yet again. 'You'll give us away yet with your teeth chattering like that. Look ahead of you. That's what ought to scare you – guns, not ghosts.'

Before them, only a little way off now, lay Capricorn's village. The new floodlights poured light as bright as day over the grey houses.

'And they say that this electricity of theirs is a blessing!' whispered Dustfinger as they skirted the car park. A bored-looking guard was strolling round among the parked vehicles. Yawning, he leaned against the truck in which Cockerell had brought the goats back that afternoon, and put on a pair of earphones.

'Excellent! An army could march up now and he wouldn't hear it!' muttered Dustfinger. 'If Basta were here he'd discipline the man for that – shut him up in Capricorn's cowsheds for three days with nothing to eat.'

'Why don't we go over the rooftops?' All the fear had gone from Farid's face. The guard with his shotgun didn't alarm the boy half as much as his imaginary ghosts. Dustfinger could only shake his head over such foolishness. But the rooftop idea wasn't stupid. A vine that hadn't been pruned for years grew up one of the houses beside the car park. As soon as the guard wandered over to the other side of the area, swaying in time to the music that was filling his ears, Dustfinger clambered up its woody branches. The boy climbed even better than he did, and proudly offered him a hand once he was up on the roof. They moved on stealthily like stray cats, past chimneys, aerials and Capricorn's floodlights, which were angled downwards and left everything behind them in the cover of darkness. Once, a shingle came loose under Dustfinger's boots, but he managed to catch it just in time, before the terracotta tile could fall and break in the street below.

When they reached the square where the church and
Capricorn's house stood they let themselves down from a gut-
ter. For a few breathless moments Dustfinger ducked behind
a stack of empty fruit crates, looking out for guards. Both the
square itself and the narrow alley to one side of Capricorn's
house were bathed in light. A black cat was sitting on the edge
of the well outside the church. Basta's heart would probably
have missed a beat at the sight of it, but Dustfinger was much
more concerned about the guards outside Capricorn's house.
Two of them were lounging by the entrance. It was one of
these, a small, sturdy man, who had found Dustfinger four
years ago in a town up in the north, just as he was about to
give his last show. He and two companions had dragged the
fire-eater back here, where Capricorn had, in his own charac-
teristic way, questioned him about Silvertongue and the book.

The two guards were arguing, and as they were so absorbed
Dustfinger plucked up his courage, took a few rapid steps, and
disappeared down the alley beside Capricorn's house. Farid
followed him, as soundless as his own shadow come to life.

Capricorn's house was a large, bulky building which might
once have been the village hall, a disused monastery or a
school. All the windows were dark, and there were no other
guards to be seen in the alley. But Dustfinger remained watch-
ful. He knew the guards liked to lurk in dark doorways, invisible as ravens at night in their black suits. Indeed, Dustfinger
knew almost everything about Capricorn's village. He had
walked these streets often enough since Capricorn brought
him here to look for Silvertongue and the book. Whenever he
felt the sharp pangs of homesickness he had come back here
to his old enemies, where he didn't feel quite so out of place.
Even his fear of Basta's knife couldn't keep him away.

Dustfinger picked up a flat stone, beckoned Farid to his side, and threw the stone down the alley. Nothing moved. As he had hoped, the guard was doing his rounds. Dustfinger hurried to the high wall behind which Capricorn's garden lay: vegetable beds, fruit trees and herbs, protected by the wall from the cold wind that sometimes blew from the nearby mountains. Dustfinger had often entertained the maids as they hoed the beds. There were no floodlights in the garden, no guards either – who'd steal vegetables? – and only a door with a grating over it, a door that was locked at night, that led from the yard into the house. The dog kennels lay beyond the wall too, but when Dustfinger swung himself up and over they were empty. The dogs had not come back from the hills. They'd shown more sense than Dustfinger expected, and Basta obviously hadn't got new dogs yet. Stupid of him. Stupid Basta.

Dustfinger signalled to the boy to follow him, and stole past the carefully tended beds until he had reached the back door with the grating. The boy looked at him questioningly when he saw the solid bars, but Dustfinger just laid a finger to his lips and looked up at one of the windows on the second floor. The shutters, black as night, were open. Dustfinger mewed in so lifelike a fashion that several cats answered, but nothing moved behind the window. Dustfinger cursed under his breath, listened to the sounds of the night for a moment, then imitated the shrill cry of a bird of prey. Farid jumped and pressed close to the wall of the house. This time, something did move behind the upstairs window. A woman leaned out of it. When Dustfinger waved to her she waved back – and then quickly disappeared.

'Don't look like that!' whispered Dustfinger, seeing Farid's anxious glance. 'We can trust her. Quite a few of the women aren't too fond of Capricorn and his men – many of them didn't even come here of their own free will. But they're all afraid of him: afraid they'll lose their job, afraid he'll burn the roofs over the heads of their families if they talk about what goes on here, or perhaps send Basta to call on them with his knife. Resa doesn't have to worry about that kind of thing. She has no family.' Not any more, he added to himself silently.

The door behind the grating opened, and Resa's anxious face appeared behind the bars. It looked pale beneath her dark blonde hair.

'How are you?' Dustfinger went over to the grating and put his hand through the bars. Smiling, Resa pressed it, and nodded at the boy.

'This is Farid.' Dustfinger lowered his voice. 'You could say he's adopted me. But you can trust him. He doesn't care for Capricorn any more than we do.'

Resa nodded, looked at him reproachfully and shook her head.

'Yes, I know it wasn't sensible to come back. You heard what happened?' Dustfinger couldn't prevent something like pride creeping into his voice. 'They thought I'd put up with anything, but they were wrong. There's still one copy of the book left, and I'm going to get my hands on it. Don't look at me like that. Do you know where Capricorn keeps it?'

Resa shook her head. There was a rustling behind them and Dustfinger spun round, but it was only a mouse scurrying over the quiet yard. Resa took a pencil and a piece of paper out of her dressing-gown pocket. She wrote slowly and neatly, knowing that Dustfinger found it easier to read capital letters. She had taught him to read and write so that they could communicate with one another.

As usual, it took some time for the letters to make sense to Dustfinger. He felt a fresh sense of pride every time those spindly symbols finally fitted together into words and he could prise their secret out of them. *'I'll look around,'* he read softly. 'Good. But be careful. I don't want you risking your pretty neck.' He bent over the paper again. 'What do you mean, *The Magpie has Basta's keys now?'*

He gave her the note back. Farid watched Resa writing, as spellbound as if he were watching someone work magic. 'I think you'll have to teach him too!' Dustfinger whispered through the bars. 'See how he's staring at you?'

Resa looked up and smiled at Farid. Awkwardly, he looked away. Resa passed her finger round her face.

'You think he's a nice boy?' Dustfinger twisted his mouth in a teasing smile, while Farid felt so embarrassed he didn't know where to look. 'And what about me? Beautiful as the moon, am I? Hmm, what am I to make of that as a compliment? You mean I have almost as many craters?'

Resa pressed her hand over her lips. It was easy to amuse her; she laughed like a young girl. That was the only time you could hear her voice.

Shots rang out in the night. Resa clung to the bars, and Farid, terrified, crouched down at the foot of the wall. Dustfinger pulled him to his feet again. 'It's nothing!' he whispered. 'Just the guards taking pot-shots at cats. They always do that when they're bored.'

The boy looked at him with disbelief, but Resa went on writing. *'She took the keys away to punish him,'* Dustfinger read. 'Basta won't like that at all. The way he acted with those keys, you'd have thought he was looking after Capricorn's most treasured possession.'

Resa mimed taking a knife from her belt, looking so grim that Dustfinger almost laughed out loud. He quickly glanced around, but the yard was silent as the grave between its high walls. 'Oh yes, I can well imagine that Basta's furious,' he whispered. 'In that mood he'll do anything to please Capricorn – slit throats, gash faces open, anything.'

Resa reached for the paper again, and once more it took him a painfully long time to decipher her clear, neat writing. 'Oh, so you've heard about Silvertongue. You want to know who he is? Well, but for me he'd still be locked up in Capricorn's sheds. What else? Ask Farid. Silvertongue plucked the boy out of his own story, too, like a ripe apple. Luckily, he didn't bring out any of the ghouls the boy keeps carrying on about. Yes, he reads aloud very well indeed, much better than Darius. As you can see, Farid doesn't limp, his face probably always looked the way it does now, and he still has his voice too – even if you might not think so at the moment.'

Farid cast him a angry glance.

'What does Silvertongue look like? Well, I can at least tell you that Basta hasn't decorated *his* face yet.'

A shutter creaked above them. Dustfinger pressed close to the grating. Only the wind, he thought, nothing but the wind. Farid was staring at him, eyes wide with fear. No doubt the creaking sounded to him like a demon, but the figure who leaned out of the window above them was a creature of flesh and blood: Mortola, or the Magpie as she was secretly nicknamed. She was in charge of all the maids, and nothing was safe from the Magpie's eyes and ears, not even the secrets the women whispered to each other in their bedrooms at night.

Even Capricorn's strongboxes had better accommodation than his maidservants. They all slept in his house, four to a room, crammed in like sardines (except for those who had struck up a relationship with one of his men and moved to another house).

The Magpie leaned over the windowsill and breathed in the cool night air. She stayed there for what seemed an endless time, so long that Dustfinger could happily have wrung her neck, but finally she appeared to have filled every inch of her body with fresh air and closed the window.

'I must go, but I'll be back tomorrow evening. Maybe you'll have found out something about the book by then.' Dustfinger squeezed Resa's hand. Her fingers were rough from laundry work and cleaning. 'I know I've said it before, but all the same – be careful, and keep away from Basta.' Resa shrugged her shoulders. How else could she respond to such unnecessary advice? Almost all the women in the village kept away from Basta, but he didn't keep away from them.

Dustfinger waited outside the grating until Resa was back in her room. She signalled to him through the window with a candle.

The guard in the car park still had his earphones on. Deep in his own thoughts, he was dancing among the cars, shotgun in his outstretched arms as if he were dancing with a girl. By the time he finally looked their way, the night had already swallowed up Dustfinger and Farid.

They met no one on the way back to their hiding-place, only a fox who slunk away with hunger in his eyes. Gwin was eating a bird inside the walls of the burnt-out cottage. Its feathers were shadows in the darkness.

'Has she always been mute?' asked the boy as Dustfinger

lay down under the trees to sleep.

'As long as I've known her,' replied Dustfinger, turning his back to the boy. Farid lay down beside him. He had made this his habit from the first, and however often Dustfinger moved away the boy was always close beside him when he woke up.

'The photograph in your rucksack,' he said. 'It *is* her.'

'So?'

The boy did not reply.

'If you've taken a fancy to her,' Dustfinger mocked him, 'forget it. She's one of Capricorn's favourite maids. She's even allowed to take his breakfast and help him get dressed.'

'How long has she been with him?'

'Five years,' said Dustfinger. 'And in all that time Capricorn has never once let her leave the village. She can't even go out of the house very often. She ran away twice, but she never got far. One of those times a snake bit her. She never told me how Capricorn punished her, but I know she never tried to run away again.'

There was a rustling behind them. Farid jumped, but it was only Gwin. The marten was licking his muzzle as he leaped and landed on the boy's stomach. Laughing, Farid plucked a feather out of his fur. Gwin snuffled busily around the boy's chin and nose, as if he had missed him, and then he disappeared into the night again.

'He really is a nice marten!' whispered Farid.

'No, he's not,' said Dustfinger, pulling his thin blanket up to his chin. 'He probably likes you because you smell like a girl.'

Farid's only answer was a long silence.

'She looks like her,' he said at last, just as Dustfinger was dropping off to sleep. 'Silvertongue's daughter, I mean. She has the same mouth and the same eyes, and she laughs in the same way.'

'Nonsense!' said Dustfinger. 'There's not the slightest resemblance. They both have blue eyes, that's all. It's not unusual here. Hurry up and go to sleep.'

The boy obeyed. He wrapped himself in the sweater that Dustfinger had given him and turned his back to his companion. Soon he was breathing as peacefully as a baby. But Dustfinger lay awake all night, staring at the stars.

Capricorn's Secrets

'If I were to be made a knight,' said the Wart, staring dreamily into the fire, 'I should . . . pray to God to let me encounter all the evil in the world in my own person, so that if I conquered there would be none left, and, if I were defeated, I would be the one to suffer for it.'

'That would be extremely presumptuous of you,' said Merlin, 'and you would be conquered, and you would suffer for it.'

T.H. White, *The Sword in the Stone*

Capricorn received Meggie and Fenoglio in the church. About a dozen of his men were with him. He was sitting in the new black leather armchair they had installed under Mortola's supervision, and this time, for once, his suit was not red but pale yellow, like the morning daylight filtering in through the windows. He had them brought to him early, while the mist still hung above the hills, with the sun swimming in it like a ball floating in murky water.

'By all the letters of the alphabet!' whispered Fenoglio as

he and Meggie walked down the nave of the church with Basta close behind them. 'He really does look exactly the way I imagined him. "Colourless as a glass of milk." I think that's how I put it.'

He began walking faster, as if he couldn't wait to see his creation at close quarters. Meggie could hardly keep up with him, and Basta held him back before he had reached the steps. 'Here, what's the idea?' he hissed. 'Not so fast – and bow, understand?'

Fenoglio merely glanced scornfully at him and remained perfectly upright. Basta raised his hand, but when Capricorn almost imperceptibly shook his head he lowered it again like a rebuked child. Mortola was standing beside Capricorn's chair, her arms folded like wings behind her back.

'You know, Basta, I still wonder what you were thinking of not to bring her father too!' said Capricorn, letting his gaze wander from Meggie to Fenoglio's turtle-like face.

'He wasn't there. I told you.' Basta sounded injured. 'Was I supposed to sit about waiting for him like a toad beside a pond? He'll soon be here of his own accord! We all know how besotted he is with his daughter. I'll bet my knife he'll be here by tomorrow at the latest!'

'Your knife? But you've already mislaid your knife once recently.' The mockery in Mortola's voice made Basta grind his teeth.

'You're slipping, Basta!' remarked Capricorn. 'Your hot temper clouds your judgement. But let's move on to this other souvenir of yours.'

Fenoglio had never taken his eyes off Capricorn. He was looking at him like a painter seeing one of his pictures again after many long years, and judging by the expression on his face what he saw pleased him. Meggie couldn't see a trace of fear in his eyes, just incredulous curiosity, and satisfaction – with himself. She also saw that Capricorn did not care for that expression at all. He wasn't used to being inspected as fearlessly as this old man was scrutinising him now, not even by his men.

'Basta has told me some strange things about you, Signor . . .?'

'Fenoglio.'

Meggie was watching Capricorn's face. Had he ever read the name on the cover of *Inkheart* just below the title itself?

'Even his voice sounds the way I imagined!' Fenoglio whispered to her. She thought he was captivated, like a child looking at a caged lion – except that Capricorn wasn't in a cage. At a signal from him Basta jammed his elbow into the old man's back so roughly that Fenoglio was left gasping for air.

'I don't like whispering in my presence,' Capricorn said softly, while Fenoglio was still struggling to get his breath back. 'As I said, Basta has told me a strange story – he says you claimed to be the man who wrote a certain book – what was its name again?'

'*Inkheart*.' Fenoglio rubbed his aching back. 'Its title is *Inkheart* because it's about a man whose wicked heart is black as ink, filled with darkness and evil. I still like the title.'

Capricorn raised his eyebrows – and smiled. 'And how am I supposed to take that? As a compliment, maybe? After all, it's my story you're talking about.'

'No, no, it's mine. You just appear in it.'

Meggie saw Basta look enquiringly at Capricorn, but he shook his head again very slightly, and Fenoglio's back was spared for the time being.

'How interesting. So you're sticking to your lies.' Capricorn uncrossed his legs and rose from his chair. With slow strides, he came down the steps.

Fenoglio smiled conspiratorially at Meggie.

'What are you grinning for?' Capricorn's voice was as sharp as Basta's knife now. He stopped right in front of Fenoglio.

'Oh, I was only thinking that vanity is one of the qualities I gave you, vanity and –' Fenoglio paused for effect before continuing – 'and a few other weaknesses that I expect you'd rather I didn't mention in front of your henchmen.'

Capricorn examined him in silence, a silence that seemed to last an eternity. Then he smiled. It was a faint, thin smile, little more than a lift at the corners of his mouth, while his eyes scanned the church as if he had entirely forgotten Fenoglio. 'You're a shameless old man,' he said. 'And a liar into the bargain. But if you hope to impress me with your bare-faced lying and boasting the way you've impressed Basta, I must disappoint you. Your claims are ridiculous, just as you are, and it was more than stupid of Basta to bring you here, because now we have to get rid of you somehow.'

Basta turned pale. He hurried over to Capricorn, head lowered in submission. 'But suppose he isn't lying?' Meggie heard him whisper to Capricorn. 'They both say we shall all die if we touch the old man.'

Capricorn gave him a look of such contempt that Basta flinched backwards as if he had been struck.

Fenoglio, however, looked as if he were enjoying himself hugely. It seemed to Meggie that he was watching the whole scene as if it were a play performed especially for him. 'Poor Basta!' he said to Capricorn. 'You're doing him a great injustice again, for he's right. Suppose I'm not lying? Suppose I really did invent you both – you and Basta? Will you simply dissolve into thin air if you do anything to me? It seems very likely.'

Capricorn laughed, but Meggie sensed he was thinking over what Fenoglio had said, and it made him uneasy – even if he was taking great pains to hide his concern under a mask of indifference.

'I can prove that I'm what I say I am!' said Fenoglio, so quietly that apart from Capricorn only Basta could hear his words. 'Shall I do it here, in front of your men and those women? Shall I tell them about your parents?'

All was quiet in the church now. No one moved, neither Basta nor the other men waiting at the foot of the steps. Even the women cleaning the floor under the tables straightened up to look at Capricorn and the strange old man. Mortola was standing beside his chair, her chin jutting as if that would help her to hear what they were whispering about.

Capricorn inspected his cufflinks in silence. They were like drops of blood on his pale shirt. Then, at last, he turned his colourless eyes to Fenoglio's face again.

'Say what you like, old man! But if you value your life say it so that only I can hear.' He spoke softly, but Meggie heard the fury in his voice, suppressed with difficulty but lurking behind every word. She had never felt more afraid of him.

Capricorn signed to Basta, who reluctantly took a few steps backwards.

'I suppose the child can hear what I have to say?' asked Fenoglio, putting his hand on Meggie's shoulder. 'Or are you afraid of her too?'

Capricorn did not even look at Meggie. He had eyes only

for the old man who had invented him. 'Well, come on, let's hear you, even if you have nothing to say! You're not the first person to try saving his skin in this church with a few lies, but if you hedge your bets any longer I shall tell Basta to wrap a pretty little viper around your neck. I always keep a few around the place for such occasions.'

Even this threat didn't particularly impress Fenoglio. 'Very well,' he said, looking all round him as if sorry not to have a larger audience, 'where shall I begin? First, something basic: a storyteller never writes down everything he knows about his characters. There's no need for readers to know everything. Some of it is better kept secret between the author and his creations. Take him, for instance,' he added, pointing to Basta. 'I always knew he was a very unhappy boy before you picked him up. As it says in a another very fine book, it's terribly easy to persuade children that they are worthless. Basta was convinced of it. Not that you taught him any better, oh no! Why would you? But suddenly here was someone to whom he could devote himself, someone who told him what to do – he'd found a god, Capricorn, and if you treated him badly, well, who says that all gods are kindly? Most of them are stern and cruel, wouldn't you agree? I didn't write all this in the book. I knew it, that was enough. But never mind Basta now, let's move on to you.'

Capricorn's eyes did not move from Fenoglio. His face was as rigid as if it had turned to stone.

'*Capricorn.*' Fenoglio's voice sounded almost tender as he spoke the name. He gazed over Capricorn's shoulder as if he had forgotten that the man he was talking about was standing right in front of him, and no longer existed only in an entirely different world between the covers of a book. 'He has another name too, of course, but even he doesn't remember it. He has called himself Capricorn since he was fifteen, after the star sign under which he was born. Capricorn the unapproachable, unfathomable, insatiable, who likes to play God or the Devil as the fancy takes him. The Devil doesn't have a mother, though, does he?' Fenoglio then looked Capricorn in the eye. 'But *you* do.'

Meggie looked up at the Magpie. She had come to the edge of the steps, listening, her bony hands clenched into fists.

'You like to spread the rumour that she was of noble birth,' Fenoglio went on. 'Indeed, it sometimes even pleases you to say she was a king's daughter, and your father, you claim, was an armourer at her father's court. A very nice story too. Shall I tell you my version?'

For the first time, Meggie saw something like fear on Capricorn's face, a nameless fear without beginning or end, and behind it hatred rose like a vast black shadow.

Meggie felt sure that Capricorn wanted to strike Fenoglio to the ground, but his fear was too strong, leaving him helpless to act.

Did Fenoglio see that too?

'Go on, tell your story. Why not?' Capricorn's eyes were unblinking, like a snake's.

Fenoglio smiled as mischievously as one of his grandsons. 'Very well, let's go on. The tale of the court armourer was all lies, of course.' Meggie still had a feeling that the old man was enjoying himself enormously. He might have been teasing a kitten. Did he know so little about his own creation? 'Capricorn's father was an ordinary blacksmith,' he went on, refusing to let the cold rage in Capricorn's eyes distract him. 'He made his son play with hot coals, and sometimes he beat him almost as hard as he beat the iron he forged. There were blows if the boy ever showed pity, and more blows for shedding tears and for every time the lad said, "I can't" or "I'll never do it". "Power is all that counts," he taught his son. "Rules are made by the strongest, so be sure that you're the one who makes them." Capricorn's mother thought that was the only real truth in the world, and she told her son day in, day out that one day he would be the strongest of all. She was no princess but a serving maid, with coarse hands and roughened knees, and she followed her son like a shadow, even when he began to be ashamed of her and invented a new mother and new father for himself. She admired him for his cruelty; she loved to see the terror he spread abroad. And she loved his ink-black heart. Your heart is a stone, Capricorn, a black stone with about as much human sympathy as a lump of coal, and you are very, very proud of that.'

Capricorn went on playing with his cufflink, turning it round and looking at it as intently as if he were giving all his attention not to Fenoglio's words but to the little red piece of metal. When the old man fell silent, Capricorn carefully pulled the sleeve of his jacket down over his wrist and brushed a speck of fluff off his arm. With it, he seemed to have brushed off his anger – his pale, indifferent eyes no longer showed rage, hatred or fear.

'That really is an amazing story, old man,' he said in a quiet voice. 'I like it. You're a born liar, so I shall keep you here – for the time being – until I tire of your stories.'

'Keep me here?' Fenoglio stood very straight. 'I've no intention of staying here! What on earth—'

But Capricorn put a hand over his mouth. 'Not another word!' he hissed. 'Basta has told me about your three grandchildren. If you give me any trouble, or tell your lies not to me but to my men, I shall get Basta to gift-wrap a few young vipers and leave them outside your grandchildren's door. Do I make myself clear, old man?'

Fenoglio's head drooped as if Capricorn had broken his neck with nothing but a few softly spoken words. When he looked up again, fear showed in every wrinkle of his face.

With a satisfied smile, Capricorn put his hands in his trouser pockets. 'Yes, you all love something, soft-hearted as you are,' he said. 'Children, grandchildren, brothers and sisters, parents, dogs, cats, canary birds . . . There are no exceptions: farmers, shopkeepers, even policemen have families or at least keep a dog. You have only to look at her father!' Capricorn pointed at Meggie so suddenly, she jumped. 'He'll come here even though he knows I shan't let him go again, any more than I shall let his daughter go. He'll come all the same. Isn't this world an amazing place?'

'Amazing indeed,' murmured Fenoglio, and for the first time he looked at his creation with revulsion rather than admiration. Capricorn seemed to prefer that.

'Basta!' he called, beckoning him. Basta strolled over deliberately slowly. He was still looking sulky. 'Take the old man to the room where we once locked Darius,' Capricorn ordered. 'And post a guard outside the door.'

'You want me to take him into *your* house?' Basta sounded surprised.

'Yes, why not? After all, he claims to be almost like a father to me. Anyway, his tales amuse me.'

Basta shrugged and grasped Fenoglio's arm. Meggie looked at the old man, horrified. She would soon be all alone with nothing but the windowless walls and a locked door. But

Fenoglio reached for her hand before Basta could haul him away. 'Leave the girl with me,' he said to Capricorn. 'You can't shut her up in that hole again all by herself. And I promised her father I'd look after her.'

Capricorn turned his back, looking indifferent. 'As you like. Her father will be here soon in any case.'

Yes, Mo would come. Meggie could think of nothing else as Fenoglio led her away with him, his arm round her shoulders as if he really could protect her from Capricorn and Basta and all the others. But he couldn't. Would Mo be able to protect her? Of course not. He mustn't come, she thought. Please. Perhaps he won't be able to find the way again! He mustn't come. Yet there was nothing she wanted more, nothing in the whole wide world.

35

Different Aims

Faber sniffed the book. 'Do you know that books smell like nutmeg or some spice from a foreign land? I loved to smell them when I was a boy.'

Ray Bradbury, *Fahrenheit 451*

It was Farid who saw the car. Dustfinger was lying under the trees as it came along the road. He was trying to think clearly, but since learning that Capricorn was back he couldn't pull his thoughts together. He still didn't know where to look for the book. The leaves of the trees cast shadows on his face, the sun sent white-hot needles down through the branches, and his forehead felt feverish. Basta and Flatnose were back too, of course. What had he expected? Had he thought they'd stay away for ever? 'Why get so agitated, Dustfinger?' he whispered up at the leaves. 'You didn't have to come back here. You knew it would be dangerous.' Then he heard footsteps approaching, rapidly.

'A grey car!' Farid had run so fast that he was gasping for breath as he flung himself down on the grass beside

Dustfinger. 'I think it's Silvertongue!'

Dustfinger jumped up. The boy knew what he was talking about. He really could tell those stinking metal beetles apart from each other. He himself had never got the knack of it.

He quickly followed Farid to where there was a view of the bridge. The road wound away from it towards Capricorn's village like a slow-moving snake. They didn't have much time if they wanted to stop Silvertongue. At top speed, they stumbled down the hillside. Farid was the first to reach the road. Dustfinger had always been proud of his own agility, but the boy was far nimbler, fast as a deer and with legs just as agile. And he was getting better at playing with fire now too, as fascinated as a boy with a puppy.

Silvertongue braked sharply when he saw Dustfinger and Farid in the road. He looked tired, as if he had slept badly for the last few nights. Elinor was in the car beside him. Where had she sprung from? Hadn't she gone home to her book-lined tomb? And where was Meggie?

Silvertongue's face darkened when he saw Dustfinger. As he got out of the car he was rigid with anger. 'Of course! *You* told them!' he cried, coming towards him. 'You told them where we were! Who else? What did Capricorn promise you this time?'

'I told who what?' Dustfinger retreated. 'I never told anyone anything! Ask the boy.'

But Silvertongue didn't so much as glance at Farid. The bookworm woman had got out too. She stood beside the car looking grim.

'The only person who told anyone anything was you!' Dustfinger accused him. 'You told the old man about me even though you promised you wouldn't.'

Silvertongue stopped in his tracks. It was so easy to make him feel guilty.

'Better hide the car under the trees there.' Dustfinger pointed to the side of the road. 'One of Capricorn's men could pass at any time, and they don't like to see strange cars here.'

Silvertongue turned and looked down the road.

'Surely you don't believe him?' cried Elinor. 'Of course he's given you away, who else could? The man starts telling lies the moment he opens his mouth.'

'Basta took Meggie away.' Silvertongue sounded hoarse, quite unlike himself, as if when he lost his daughter he had lost the sound of his voice too. 'They took Fenoglio as well – yesterday morning when I went to meet Elinor at the airport. We've been looking for the wretched village ever since. I had no idea how many deserted villages there are in these hills. It wasn't until we came to the barrier over the road that I felt sure we were on the right track at last.'

Dustfinger said nothing, but looked up at the sky. A few birds as black as Capricorn's men were flying south. He had not seen them bringing the girl in, but then he hadn't spent the whole day watching that accursed village.

'Basta was gone for several days. I thought he must be looking for the two of you,' he said. 'You're lucky he didn't get hold of you too.'

'Lucky?' Elinor was still standing beside the car. 'Tell him to get out of the way!' she told Silvertongue. 'Or I'll run him down myself! He's been hand in glove with those miserable fire-raisers all along.'

Silvertongue was still looking at Dustfinger as if he could-n't decide whether or not to believe him. 'Capricorn's men broke into Elinor's house,' he said at last. 'They took all the books from her library into the garden and burned them.'

Dustfinger had to admit that for a split second he felt something almost like satisfaction. What had the silly bookworm woman expected? Did she think Capricorn would simply forget her? He shrugged his shoulders and looked at Elinor, his face unreadable. 'Only to be expected,' he said.

'Only to be expected!' Elinor's voice almost cracked. Belligerent as a bull terrier, she marched up to him. Farid tried to bar her way, but she pushed him aside so roughly that he fell on the hot asphalt of the road. 'Maybe you can fool the boy with your fire-breathing and your coloured balls, matchstick-eater!' she snapped at Dustfinger. 'But it won't work with me! There's nothing left of the books in my library but a load of ash. The police were full of admiration for what those villains had done. "At least they didn't burn your house down, Signora Loredan! Even your garden is all right except for the scorch mark on the lawn." What do I care for the house? What do I care for the wretched lawn? They burned my most valuable books!'

Dustfinger saw the tears in her eyes, although she quickly turned her face aside, and suddenly something like sympathy did awake in him. Perhaps she was more like him than he'd thought: her home too had consisted of paper and printer's ink. She probably felt as lost as he did in the real world. He didn't let her see his sympathy, of course, but hid it behind a mask of mockery and indifference, just as she hid her despair behind rage. 'What did you expect? Capricorn knew where you lived. Anyone could foresee that he'd send his men out when you've escaped him. He always takes revenge.'

'Oh yes, and who told him where I live? You did!' Elinor swung her arm back with her fist clenched, but Farid caught it. He had grazed his knee on the road. 'He didn't give any-thing away!' he cried. 'Nothing at all. He's only here to steal something.'

Elinor lowered her arm.

'So that's it!' Silvertongue went up to them. 'You're here to get hold of the book. That's crazy!'

'Well, how about you? What are *you* planning to do?' Dustfinger looked at him scornfully. 'You're just going to walk into Capricorn's church and ask for your daughter back, are you?'

Silvertongue did not reply.

'He won't hand her over and you know it!' Dustfinger went on. 'She's only the bait, and as soon as you've swallowed it the pair of you will be Capricorn's prisoners – for the rest of your lives, most likely.'

'*I* wanted to call the police!' Elinor freed her arm crossly from Farid's brown hands. 'But Mortimer was against it.'

'Sensible of him! Capricorn would have abandoned Meggie up in the mountains and you'd never have seen her again.'

Silvertongue looked up at the nearby mountains looming dark behind their foothills. 'Wait until I've stolen the book!' said Dustfinger. 'I'm going to creep into the village again tonight. I won't be able to get your daughter out the way I did last time, because Capricorn has trebled the guards, and the whole village is lit up at night now, brighter than a jeweller's shop window, but perhaps I can find out where they're keep-ing her prisoner. Then you can do what you like with the information. And in return for my trouble you could try read-ing me back into the book. What about it?'

Dustfinger considered this a very reasonable proposition, but Silvertongue thought it over only briefly before shaking his head. 'No,' he said. 'No, I'm sorry, I can't wait any longer. Meggie needs me.' With these words he turned and went back to the car, but before he could get in Dustfinger barred his way.

'I'm sorry too,' he said, snapping open Basta's knife. 'You know I don't like these things, but sometimes people have to be protected from their own stupidity. I'm not going to let you stumble into the village like a rabbit into a trap, just for Capricorn to shut you and your magic voice away. It won't help your daughter and it certainly won't help me.'

At Dustfinger's signal, Farid had drawn his knife too. Dustfinger had bought it for him in the village by the sea; it was a ridiculous little thing, but Farid pressed it into Elinor's ribs so hard that she grimaced. 'Good God, are you planning to slit me open, you little wretch?' she snapped at him. The boy jumped, but he did not remove his knife.

'Move the car off the road, Silvertongue!' ordered Dustfinger. 'And don't get any silly ideas: the boy will keep his knife pressed at your bookworm friend's chest until you're back here with us.'

Silvertongue obeyed. Of course. What else could he do? They tied him and Elinor to the trees just behind the burnt-out cottage, only a few paces from their own makeshift camp. Elinor scolded even louder than Gwin when he was pulled out of the rucksack by his tail.

'Stop that!' Dustfinger told her. 'It won't do any of us any good for Capricorn's men to find us here.' That worked. She fell silent at once, as if she had swallowed her tongue. Silvertongue had leaned his head back against the tree trunk and closed his eyes. Farid checked all the knots again carefully, but then Dustfinger beckoned him over.

'I want you to keep a watch on those two when I go down to the village tonight,' he whispered. 'And don't start carrying on about ghosts again. After all, you won't be alone this time.'

The boy looked at him with an injured expression, as if Dustfinger had taken his hand and thrust it into the fire. 'But they're tied up!' he protested. 'So what is there to watch? No one's ever managed to undo my knots. Word of honour. Please. I want to go with you! I can be your look-out or distract the guards. I can even get into Capricorn's house! I'm quieter than Gwin!'

But Dustfinger shook his head. 'No,' he said firmly. 'Tonight I'm going alone. If I want someone following me wherever I go I'll get myself a dog.' And with that he left the boy.

It was a hot day. The sky above the hills was blue and cloudless, and there were hours yet to pass before darkness fell.

36

In Capricorn's House

'It's the place that worries you,' said Hazel. 'I don't like it myself, but it won't go on for ever.'

Richard Adams, *Watership Down*

Two narrow metal bunks, one above the other against a whitewashed wall, a cupboard, a table by the window, a chair, an empty shelf with nothing but a candle on it. Meggie had hoped to be able to see the road or at least the car park through the window, but the only view was of the yard below. A couple of Capricorn's maids were bending over the vegetable patch pulling out weeds, and chickens were pecking about in a wire-netting run in one corner. The walls surrounding the kitchen garden were high enough for a prison.

Fenoglio was sitting on the lower bed, staring gloomily at the dusty floor. The wooden floorboards creaked whenever they stepped on them. Outside the door, Flatnose was protesting to Basta.

'You want me to do what? No, find someone else for the

job, dammit! I'd rather go over to the next village, put petrol-soaked rags outside someone's door or hang a dead rooster from the window-frame. Or run round outside the house with a devil mask on, like Cockerell had to do last month, but I'm not cooling my heels here just to keep watch on an old man and a little girl! Get one of the lads. They'll be glad to have a change from cleaning cars.'

But Basta wasn't open to persuasion. 'You'll be relieved after supper,' he said, and then he was gone. Meggie heard his footsteps retreating down the long corridor. There were five doors to pass, then go down the staircase, at the foot of the stairs turn left for the front door . . . She had carefully taken note of the way. But how was she to get past Flatnose? She went over to the window again and opened it. Just looking out made her feel dizzy. No, she couldn't climb down. She'd break her neck.

'Leave the window open,' said Fenoglio behind her. 'It's so hot in here I feel as if I might melt.'

Meggie sat down on the bed beside him. 'I'm going to run away,' she whispered. 'As soon as it gets dark.'

The old man looked at her incredulously, shaking his head very firmly. 'Are you mad? It's much too dangerous!'

Out in the corridor, Flatnose was still muttering angrily to himself.

'I'll say I have to go to the loo.' Meggie was clutching her rucksack. 'Then I'll just run off.'

Fenoglio took her by the shoulders. 'No!' he whispered emphatically. 'No, you won't! We'll think of something. Thinking up ideas is my job, remember?'

Meggie tightened her lips. 'Yes, all right,' she murmured, getting up to go back to the window. Dusk was already falling outside. I'm going to try, all the same, she thought as Fenoglio stretched out with a sigh on the narrow bed behind her. I'm not just going to sit here like bait! I shall run away before they catch Mo too.

And for the hundredth time, as she waited for darkness, she tried to push away the question that kept coming into her head: where was Mo? Why hadn't he come?

37

Carelessness

'You think this is a trap, then?' the Count asked.

'I always think everything is a trap until proven otherwise,' the Prince answered. 'Which is why I'm still alive.'

William Goldman, *The Princess Bride*

It was still hot when the sun had gone down. There was not a breath of wind in the darkness, and the glow-worms were dancing above the dry grass as Dustfinger crept back to Capricorn's village.

Two guards were strolling around the car park, and neither of them was wearing earphones, so Dustfinger took a different route to Capricorn's house this time. The streets at the far end of the village had been so utterly destroyed by the earthquake which drove out the last villagers that Capricorn had not had them rebuilt. These streets were still blocked by the rubble of ruined walls, and it wasn't very safe to walk there. Even after so many years, loose stones might fall. So Capricorn's men avoided that part of the village, where dirty dishes left by its

long-gone inhabitants still stood on many tables behind dilapidated front doors. There were no floodlights here, and even
the guards seldom came this way.

Tumbled heaps of broken tiles and stones stood more than
knee-high in the street that Dustfinger chose. They slipped
beneath his feet as he clambered over them, and when he
listened to the nocturnal sounds again, afraid the noise might
have attracted someone's attention, he saw a guard appear
among the ruined houses. His mouth was dry with terror as
he ducked behind the nearest wall. Swallows' nests clung to it,
one above another. The guard was humming as he came closer. Dustfinger knew him; he had been with Capricorn for
many years. Basta had recruited him from a village in another country. For Capricorn had not always lived among these
hills. There had been other places, remote villages like this
one, houses, abandoned farms, even a fortified castle once. But
a day had always come when the web of fear so expertly spun
by Capricorn tore, and the attention of the police was drawn
to his men and what they were up to. Eventually the same
thing would happen here.

The guard stood still to light a cigarette. Its smoke drifted
to Dustfinger's nostrils. Turning his head, he saw a thin white
cat perched among the stones. It sat there perfectly still, its
green eyes staring at him. 'Sssh!' he wanted to whisper. 'Do I
look dangerous? No, but that man there will shoot first you,
then me.' The green eyes went on staring. The white tail
began twitching back and forth. Dustfinger looked at his dusty
boots, at a twisted iron bar lying among the stones, anywhere
but at the cat. Animals don't like you to look them in the eye.
Gwin bared his sharp teeth whenever Dustfinger looked
straight at him.

The guard began humming again, the cigarette between his lips. At last, just as Dustfinger was beginning to feel he would be crouching behind this ruined wall for the rest of his life, the guard turned and strolled off. Dustfinger dared not move until the sound of his footsteps had died away. When he straightened up, feeling stiff, the cat raced away, spitting, and he stood there for a long time among the empty houses, waiting for his heartbeat to slow.

No other guard crossed his path, and soon he was vaulting over Capricorn's wall. The scent of thyme greeted him, a heavy scent that usually filled the air only by day. But everything seemed to be aromatic this hot night, even the tomato plants and lettuces. Poisonous plants grew in the bed just outside the house. These the Magpie tended herself. Many a dead body in the village had smelled of oleander or henbane.

The window of the room where Resa slept was open, as usual. When Dustfinger imitated Gwin's angry chattering a hand waved from the open window, and then quickly disappeared. He leaned against the grating over the door and waited. The sky above him was sprinkled with so many stars there hardly seemed to be any space left for the darkness. She's sure to have found out something, he thought, but suppose she tells me Capricorn has locked the book in one of his safes?

The door behind the grating opened. It always squealed, as if complaining of being disturbed at night. Dustfinger turned, and looked into a strange girl's face. She was young, perhaps fifteen or sixteen years old, her cheeks still chubby like a child's.

'Where's Resa?' Dustfinger clutched the grating. 'What's happened to her?'

The girl seemed to be transfixed by terror. She was staring

at him as if she had never seen a scarred face before.

'Did she send you down here?' Dustfinger wished he could put his hands through the grating and shake this silly little goose. 'Tell me! I don't have all night.' He ought not to have asked Resa to help him. He ought to have gone searching for the book himself. How could he have endangered her? 'Have they shut her up somewhere? Tell me!'

The girl looked at something over his shoulders, and took a step back. Dustfinger spun round, to see whatever she had seen – and found himself looking into Basta's face.

Dustfinger's mind raced. Why hadn't he heard anything? Basta was notorious for his silent tread, but Flatnose, who was with him, was no master of the art of stalking. And Basta had brought someone else too: Mortola was standing beside him. So it wasn't just fresh air that she had been enjoying last night. Or had Resa betrayed him to her? The idea hurt.

'I really didn't expect you to venture here again,' purred Basta, pushing him against the grating with the flat of his hand. Dustfinger felt the iron bars pressing into his back.

Flatnose was grinning as broadly as a child at Christmas. He always grinned like that when he was allowed to put the fear of death into someone.

'And what have you to do with the lovely Resa?' Basta snapped his knife open, and Flatnose's smile widened as fear brought out beads of sweat on Dustfinger's forehead. 'I always said so!' continued Basta as he slowly brought the tip of the knife closer to Dustfinger's chest. 'The fire-eater's in love with Resa, I said, he'd devour her with his eyes if he could, but the others wouldn't believe me. All the same – to think of a lily-livered coward like you venturing here!'

'Ah, but he's in love,' said Flatnose, laughing.

But Basta merely shook his head. 'No, our dirty-fingered friend wouldn't have come here for love, he's far too cold a fish. He's here for the book. Am I right? You're still homesick for those fluttering fairies and stinking trolls.' Almost tenderly, Basta ran the knife across Dustfinger's throat.

Dustfinger forgot how to breathe. The trick of it seemed to have escaped him.

'Back to your room!' the Magpie snapped at the girl behind him. 'Why are you still standing around?'

Dustfinger heard the rustle of a dress, and a door closed abruptly.

Basta's knife was still at his throat, but just as he was about to let the tip of it wander a little higher the Magpie seized his arm. 'That's enough!' she commanded. 'You can stop your little game now, Basta.'

'That's right, the boss said we were to bring him in uninjured.' Flatnose's voice made it clear how little he thought of this order.

Basta let the knife wander over Dustfinger's throat one last time. Then, with a swift movement, he snapped it shut again.

'What a shame!' said Basta.

Dustfinger felt the man's breath on his own skin. Basta's breath smelled of mint, fresh and sharp. Apparently a girl he'd once wanted to kiss had told him he had bad breath. The girl had regretted it, but ever since then Basta chewed peppermint leaves from morning to night. 'You've always given good sport, Dustfinger,' he said as he stepped back, still holding the closed flick-knife.

'Take him to the church!' Mortola ordered. 'I'll go and tell Capricorn.'

'Did you know the boss is very angry with your mute girlfriend?' whispered Flatnose to Dustfinger as he and Basta dragged him between them. 'She was always quite a favourite of his.'

For a split second Dustfinger felt almost happy.

So Resa hadn't given him away.

All the same, he never ought to have asked her for help. Never.

38

A Quiet Voice

She liked his tears so much that she put out her beautiful finger and let them run over it.

Her voice was so low that at first he could not make out what she said. Then he made it out. She was saying that she thought she could get well again if children believed in fairies.

J.M. Barrie, *Peter Pan*

Meggie did try her plan. As soon as it was dark she hammered on the door with her fist. Fenoglio woke with a start, but before he could stop her Meggie had called to the guard outside the door that she had to go to the loo. The man who had relieved Flatnose was a short-legged fellow with jug ears, who was amusing himself by swatting moths with a rolled-up newspaper. Over a dozen insects were already smeared on the white wall when he let Meggie out into the corridor.

'I need to go too!' cried Fenoglio, perhaps intending to dissuade Meggie from carrying out her plan, but the guard closed the door in his face. 'One at a time!' he grunted at the old man. 'And if you can't wait, you'll just have to pee out of the window.'

Taking his newspaper with him as he escorted Meggie to the lavatory, he killed three more moths and a butterfly that was fluttering helplessly from wall to bare wall. Finally, he pushed a door open, the last door before the staircase to the ground floor. Just a few more steps, thought Meggie. I'm sure I can run downstairs faster than he can.

'Please, Meggie, you must forget about running away!' Fenoglio had kept whispering in her ear. 'You'll get lost. There's nothing outside but wild country for miles! Your father would be furious if he knew what you were planning.'

Oh no, he wouldn't, Meggie had thought. But when she was in the little room which contained nothing but a lavatory and a bucket her courage almost failed her. It was so dark outside, so terribly dark. And it was still a long way to the door of Capricorn's house.

I must try, she whispered to herself before she opened the door. I must, I must!

The guard caught up with her on the fifth stair. He carried her back over his shoulder, like a sack of potatoes. 'And next time I'll take you to the boss!' he said before pushing her back into the room. 'He'll think up a good punishment for you.'

She cried for almost half an hour, while Fenoglio sat beside her staring unhappily into space. 'It's all right,' he kept murmuring, but nothing was all right, nothing at all.

'We don't even have a light in here,' she finally sobbed. 'And they've taken my books away.'

At that Fenoglio reached under his pillow and put a torch on her lap. 'I found it under my mattress,' he whispered.

'With a few books too. Who would have thought someone had hidden them there?'

Darius, the reader. Meggie could remember how the thin little man had come hurrying up the nave of Capricorn's church with his pile of books. The torch must surely be his. How long had Capricorn kept him prisoner in this bare little room?

'There was a blanket in the cupboard as well,' whispered Fenoglio. 'I put it on the top bunk for you. Can't get up there myself, I'm afraid – when I tried the whole thing swayed like a ship at sea.'

'I'd rather sleep in the top bunk anyway,' murmured Meggie, rubbing her sleeve over her face. She didn't want to cry any more. It was no good anyway.

Fenoglio had put some of Darius's books on the bunk along with the blanket for her. Meggie carefully laid them out side by side. They were almost all books for grown-ups: a well-worn thriller, a book about snakes, another about Alexander the Great, the *Odyssey*. The only books for children were a collection of fairy tales and *Peter Pan* – and she had read *Peter Pan* at least half a dozen times already.

Outside, the guard struck out with his newspaper again, and below her Fenoglio tossed and turned restlessly on the narrow bunk. Meggie knew she wouldn't be able to sleep, so there was no point even trying. Once again she looked at the strange books. Closed doors, all of them. Which should she open? Behind which of them would she forget all of this, Basta and Capricorn, *Inkheart*, herself, everything? She put aside the thriller and the book about Alexander the Great, hesitated – and picked up the *Odyssey*. It was a worn little volume; Darius must have liked it very much. He had even underlined some passages, one of them so hard that his pencil had almost gone through the paper: *But hard as he tried, he could not save his friends.* Undecidedly, Meggie leafed through the worn pages, then closed the book and put it down. No. She knew the story well enough to realise that she was almost as afraid of the Greek heroes as she was of Capricorn's men. She wiped a lingering tear away from her cheek, and let her hand hover over the other books. Fairy tales. She wasn't particularly fond of fairy tales, but the book looked attractive. The pages rustled as Meggie browsed through them. They were thin as tracing paper and covered with tiny print. There were wonderful illustrations of dwarves and fairies, and the stories told tales of mighty beings tall as giants, strong as bears, even immortal, but they were all malignant: the giants ate human beings, the dwarves were greedy for gold, the fairies were malicious and bore a grudge. No. Meggie turned the torch on the last book. *Peter Pan.*

The fairy in that book wasn't very nice either, but at least Meggie knew the world awaiting her between its covers very well. Perhaps it was just the thing for such a dark night. An owl screeched outside, but otherwise all was still in Capricorn's village. Fenoglio murmured something in his sleep and began to snore. Meggie snuggled down under the scratchy blanket, took Mo's sweater out of her rucksack and put it under her head.

'Please,' she whispered as she opened the book, 'please get me out of here just for an hour or so, please take me far, far away.' Outside, the guard muttered something to himself. He was probably bored to death. The floorboards creaked under his tread as he paced up and down outside the locked door.

'Take me away from here,' whispered Meggie, 'please take

me away from here.'

She let her finger run along the lines, over the rough, sandy paper, while her eyes followed the letters to another, colder place, in another time, to a house without locked doors and black-jacketed thugs. *A moment after the fairy's entrance the window was blown open,* whispered Meggie, hearing the sound of the window creaking as it opened, *blown open by the breathing of the little stars, and Peter dropped in. He had carried Tinker Bell part of the way, and his hand was still messy with the fairy dust.* Fairies, thought Meggie. I can see why Dustfinger misses the fairies. No, that was not allowed. She mustn't think of Dustfinger, only of Tinker Bell and Peter Pan, and Wendy lying in her bed, knowing nothing yet of the strange boy who had flown into her room dressed in leaves and cobwebs. *'Tinker Bell,' he called softly, after making sure that the children were asleep. 'Tink, where are you?' She was in a jug for the moment, and liking it extremely; she had never been in a jug before.* Tinker Bell. Meggie whispered the name twice; she had always liked the sound of it, you clicked your tongue against your teeth, and then there was the soft B sound slipping out of your lips like a kiss. *'Oh, do come out of that jug, and tell me, do you know where they put my shadow?' The loveliest tinkle as of golden bells answered him. It is the fairy language. You ordinary children can never hear it, but if you were to hear it you would know that you had heard it once before.* If I could fly like Tinker Bell, thought Meggie, I could simply climb out on the windowsill and fly away. I wouldn't have to worry about the snakes, and I'd find Mo before he gets here. He must have lost the way. Yes, that must be it. But suppose something had happened to him . . . Meggie shook her head as if to drive away the bad thoughts that had wormed their way into her mind yet again. *Tink said that the shadow was in the big box,* she whispered. *She meant the chest of drawers, and Peter jumped at the drawers, scattering their contents to the ground with both hands . . .*

Meggie stopped. There was something bright in the room. She switched the torch off, but the light was still there, *a thousand times brighter than the night-lights . . . and when it came to rest for a second,* whispered Meggie, *you saw it was a . . .* She did not speak the word aloud. She just followed the light with her eyes as it flew round the room, very fast, faster than a glow-worm and much larger.

'Fenoglio!' She couldn't hear any sound from the guard outside the door. Perhaps he'd gone to sleep. Meggie leaned over the side of the bunk until she could touch Fenoglio's shoulder. 'Fenoglio, look!' She shook him until he finally opened his eyes. Suppose the little creature flew out of the window?

Meggie slid down from the top bunk, and shut the window so quickly that she almost caught one of the shimmering wings in it. The fairy, alarmed, whirred away. Meggie thought she heard an indignant chirrup.

Fenoglio stared at the shining little creature, his eyes heavy with sleep. 'What is it?' he asked hoarsely. 'A mutated glow-worm?'

Meggie went back to the bed without taking her eyes off the fairy, who was darting faster and faster round the little room like a lost butterfly, up to the ceiling, back to the door, over to the window again. She kept returning to the window. Meggie put the book on Fenoglio's lap.

'*Peter Pan.*' He looked at the book, then at the fairy, then at the book again.

'I didn't mean to do it!' whispered Meggie. 'Really I didn't.'

The fairy kept colliding with the window again and again.

'No!' Meggie hurried over to her. 'You mustn't go out! You don't understand.' *It was a fairy, no longer than your hand, but still growing. It was a girl called Tinker Bell, exquisitely gowned in a skeleton leaf.*

'Someone's coming!' Fenoglio sat up in such a hurry that he hit his head on the top bunk. He was right. Out in the corridor footsteps were approaching, rapid, firm footsteps. Meggie retreated to the window. What did it mean? It was the middle of the night. Perhaps Mo's arrived, she thought, Mo is here. Although she didn't want to feel glad of it, her heart leaped with joy.

'Hide her!' whispered Fenoglio. 'Quick, hide her!'

Meggie looked at him, confused. Of course. The fairy. They mustn't find her. Meggie tried to catch Tinker Bell, but the fairy slipped through her fingers and whirred up to the ceiling, where she hovered like a light made of invisible glass.

The footsteps were very close now. 'Call that keeping watch?' It was Basta's voice. Meggie heard a hollow groan; he had probably woken the guard with a kick. 'Unlock that door, and get a move on. I don't have forever.'

Someone put a key in the lock. 'That's the wrong one, you dozy idiot! Capricorn wants to see the girl, and I shall tell him why he's had to wait so long.'

Meggie climbed up on her bed. The bunk swayed alarmingly as she stood on it. 'Tinker Bell!' she whispered. 'Please! Come here!' But as she reached out her hand, the fairy flew back to the window – and Basta opened the door.

'Hey, where did that come from?' he asked, standing in the

doorway. 'It's years since I saw one of those fluttery things.'

Meggie and Fenoglio said nothing – what was there to say?

'You needn't think you can wriggle out of telling me!' Basta took off his jacket and went slowly over to the window, holding it in his left hand. 'You stand in the doorway in case it gets away from me!' he told the guard. 'And if you let it get past you I shall slice off your ears.'

'Leave her alone!' Meggie slid hastily down from the bed again, but Basta moved faster. He threw his jacket. Tinker Bell's light disappeared, snuffed out like a candle. There was a faint twitching under the jacket as it fell to the floor. Basta picked it up carefully, holding it together like a sack, went over to Meggie and stopped in front of her. 'Well, sweetheart, let's hear your story,' he said in a menacingly quiet voice. 'Where did that fairy come from?'

'I don't know!' uttered Meggie without looking at him. 'She – she was just suddenly here.'

Basta looked at the guard. 'Ever seen anything like a fairy in these parts?' he asked.

The guard raised the newspaper, to which a couple of dusty moth wings were still clinging, and slapped the door frame with it, smiling broadly. 'No, but if I did I'd know what to do about it!' he said.

'You're right, those little creatures are as troublesome as midges. But they're supposed to bring luck.' Basta turned back to Meggie. 'Now then, out with it! Where did she come from? I'm not asking you again.'

Meggie couldn't help it: her eyes strayed to the book that Fenoglio had dropped. Basta followed her glance, and picked it up.

'Well, fancy that!' he murmured as he looked at the picture

on the cover. The artist had produced a good likeness of Tinker Bell. In real life she was a little paler and a little smaller than the picture suggested, but of course Basta still recognised her. He whistled softly through his teeth, then held the book close to Meggie's face. 'Don't try telling me the old man read her out of this!' he said. 'You did it. I'll bet my knife you did it. Did your father teach you how, or have you just inherited the knack from him? Well, it comes to the same thing.' He stuck the book in his waistband and grasped Meggie's arm. 'Come along, we're going to tell Capricorn about this. I was really supposed to fetch you just to meet an old acquaintance, but I'm sure Capricorn will have no objection to hearing such interesting news.'

'Has my father come?' Meggie did not resist as he forced her out of the door.

Basta shook his head and looked ironically at her. 'Him? No, he hasn't turned up yet,' he said. 'Obviously he thinks more of his own skin than yours. I wouldn't be best pleased with him if I were you.'

Meggie felt two emotions at once – disappointment as sharp as a prickle, and relief.

'I'll admit I'm rather disappointed in him,' Basta continued. 'I swore he'd come looking for you, but I guess we don't need him any more. Right?' He shook his jacket, and Meggie thought she heard a quiet, desperate tinkling.

'Lock the old man in,' Basta told the guard. 'And if you're snoring again when I get back it will be the worse for you!'

Then he hauled Meggie down the corridor.

39

The Punishment for Traitors

'What about you?' enquired Lobosch. 'You're not afraid, are you, Krabat?'

'More than you guess,' said Krabat. 'And not for myself alone.'

Otfried Preussler, *The Satanic Mill*

Meggie's shadow followed her like an evil spirit as she and Basta crossed the square outside the church. The glaring floodlights made the moon look faded.

It was not so bright inside the church. Capricorn's statue, looking down on them in the gloom, was pale and half swallowed up by the shadows. Between the columns it was as dark as if night had fled there to escape the floodlights. Only the place where Capricorn sat, leaning back in his armchair with a contemptuous expression and wrapped in a silk dressing gown that shimmered like peacock feathers, was illuminated by a single lamp. The Magpie stood behind him, appearing little more than a washed-out face above a black dress in the dim light. A fire was burning in one of the braziers at the foot of the steps. The smoke stung Meggie's eyes, and the flickering firelight danced on the red walls and columns as if the whole church were ablaze.

'Hang the rags outside his children's window as a final warning.' Capricorn's voice echoed in Meggie's ears, although he kept it lowered. 'And soak them with petrol until it's seeping out,' he told Cockerell, who was standing at the foot of the steps with two other men. 'When that smell reaches the fool's nostrils first thing in the morning, perhaps he'll finally realise that my patience is at an end.'

Cockerell received the order with a brief nod, turned on his heel and signalled to the other two to follow him. Their faces were blackened with soot, and each of the three wore a red rooster's feather in his buttonhole. 'Ah, Silvertongue's daughter!' growled Cockerell sarcastically as he limped past Meggie. 'Well, well, hasn't your father come for you yet? Doesn't seem very keen to see you, does he?' The other two laughed, and Meggie couldn't help the hot blood rising to her face.

'At last!' cried Capricorn, as Basta stopped at the foot of the steps with his prisoner. 'What kept you so long?' Something like a smile passed over the Magpie's face. She had pushed her lower lip out slightly, which gave her thin face a look of great satisfaction. It troubled Meggie much more than Capricorn's mother's usual dark looks.

'The guard couldn't find the right key,' replied Basta irritably. 'And then – well, I had to catch something.' The fairy began moving again as he held up his jacket, and its fabric bulged with her frenzied attempts to struggle free.

'What's that?' Capricorn's voice sounded impatient. 'Have

you taken to catching bats these days?'

Basta's lips quivered with annoyance, but he bit back his reply and, without a word, put his hand under the black cloth. Suppressing a curse, he produced the fairy. 'Devil take these flickery little things!' he said angrily. 'I'd quite forgotten how hard they can bite!'

One of Tinker Bell's wings was fluttering frantically, the other was held between Basta's fingers. Meggie couldn't watch. She was terribly ashamed of herself for luring this fragile little creature out of her book.

Capricorn looked at the fairy with an expression of distaste. 'Where did that come from? And what kind is it? I never saw one with wings like that before.'

Basta took *Peter Pan* out of his waistband and put the book down on the steps. 'I think it comes out of here,' he said. 'Look at the picture on the cover. There are more pictures of her inside. And guess who read her out of it.' He squeezed Tinker Bell so hard that she gulped silently for air, while he laid his other hand on Meggie's shoulder. She tried to shake his fingers off, but Basta merely tightened his grip.

'The girl?' Capricorn sounded incredulous.

'Yes, and it seems as though she's as good at it as her father. Look at this fairy.' Basta grabbed Tinker Bell's slender legs and dangled her up in the air. 'Seems perfectly all right, doesn't she? She can fly and scold and make tinkling sounds, all the things those stupid fairies do.'

'Interesting. Yes, very interesting indeed.' Capricorn rose from his chair, tightened the belt of his dressing gown and came down the steps. He stopped beside the book that Basta had put down on them. 'So it runs in the family!' he murmured as he bent to pick it up. Frowning, he looked at the cover. '*Peter Pan*,' he read. 'Why, that's one of the books my old reader Darius particularly liked. Yes, now I remember. He once read to me from it. The idea was to lure out one of those pirates, but he failed miserably. He fetched a load of stinking fish and a rusty grappling iron into my bedroom instead. Didn't we punish him by making him eat the fish?'

Basta laughed. 'Yes, but he was even more upset that you had his books taken away. He must have hidden this one.'

'So he must.' Capricorn went over to Meggie, looking thoughtful. She would have liked to bite his fingers when he put his hand under her chin, turning her face so that she had to look straight into his lifeless eyes. 'See how she looks at me, Basta?' he remarked mockingly. 'Just as obstinate as her father always was. Better save that look for him, sweetheart. You're very angry with your father, I'm sure. But I couldn't care less where *he* is. Because from now on I have you, my new, my wonderfully talented reader – whereas you, well, you must hate him for abandoning you, right? Don't be ashamed of it. Hatred can be very inspiring. I never liked my own father either.'

Meggie turned her head aside when Capricorn finally let go of her chin. Her face was burning with shame and fury, and she could still feel his fingers as if they had left marks on her skin.

'Did Basta tell you why he was to bring you here so late at night?'

'To meet someone.' Meggie tried to make her voice sound bold and unafraid, but she didn't succeed. The sobs in her throat would let only a whisper emerge.

'That's right!' Capricorn gave the Magpie a signal. She came down the steps and disappeared into the dark beyond the columns. A little later there was a creaking sound above Meggie's head, and when she looked up to the roof in alarm she saw something being lowered from the darkness: a net, no, two nets such as she had seen in fishing boats. They stopped and hung there about five metres above the floor, just over Meggie's head, and only then did she see human figures caught in the coarse ropes – like birds entangled in the netting over a fruit tree. Meggie was feeling dizzy just from looking up. What must it be like to be dangling there, held only by a few cords?

'Well, don't you recognise your old friend?' Capricorn put his hands in his dressing-gown pockets. Tinker Bell was still held in Basta's fingers like a broken doll. Her faint tinkling was the only sound to be heard. 'Yes, I see you do!' There was no mistaking the satisfaction in Capricorn's voice. 'That's what happens to filthy little traitors who steal keys and set prisoners free.'

Meggie refused to look at Capricorn. She had eyes only for Dustfinger.

'Hello, Meggie! You look rather pale!' he called down. He was trying very hard to sound light-hearted, but Meggie heard the terror in his voice. She knew what voices meant. 'I'm to give you love from your father! He'll come for you soon, he says, and he won't come alone.'

'You'll make a teller of fairy tales yet if you carry on like that, fire-eater!' Basta called up. 'But even the girl here doesn't believe that tale. You'll have to think up something better!'

Meggie stared up at Dustfinger. She so wanted to believe him.

'Basta, let go of that poor fairy!' he called to his old enemy.

'Send her up to me. It's far too long since I saw one of those.'

'Oh, I bet you'd like that. No, I'm keeping her for myself!' replied Basta, flicking Tinker Bell's tiny nose with his finger. 'I've heard that fairies keep bad luck away if you keep them in your house. I'll put her in one of those big glass wine jugs. You were always so keen on fairies – what do they eat? Do I feed her flies, or what?'

Tinker Bell braced her arms against his fingers and tried desperately to free her second wing. She managed it too, but Basta had a strong grip on her legs, and hard as she fluttered she couldn't break free. At last, with a quiet tinkle, she gave up. Her light was hardly any brighter now than a candle flickering out.

'Do you know why I had the girl brought here, Dustfinger?' Capricorn called up to his prisoner. 'She was to persuade you to tell us something about her father and where he is – if you really know anything, which I begin to doubt. But now I don't need the information any more. The daughter can take her father's place, and just at the right time too! For I've decided that we must think up something really special for your punishment. Something impressive, something memorable! After all, that's only right for a traitor, isn't it? Can you guess what my idea is? No? Then let me give you a clue. In your honour, my new reader will read aloud to us from *Inkheart*. It's your favourite book, after all, even though I know you're not very fond of the character I want her to bring out of it. Her father would have fetched that old friend for me long ago if you hadn't helped him to escape, but now his daughter will do it. Can you guess who it is I mean?'

Dustfinger laid his scarred cheek against the net. 'Oh yes, indeed I can. How could I ever forget him?' he said, so quietly that Meggie could hardly make out the words.

'Why are you talking only about the fire-eater's punishment?' The Magpie had appeared between the columns again. 'Have you forgotten our little mute pigeon Resa? Her treachery was at least as bad as his.' She looked up at the second net with a disdainful expression.

'Yes, to be sure!' There was something almost like regret in Capricorn's voice. 'Ah, what a waste – but there's nothing else for it.'

Meggie couldn't see the face of the woman dangling in the second net just beyond Dustfinger. She saw only the dark blonde hair, a blue dress, and slender hands clinging to the ropes.

Capricorn sighed heavily. 'It really is a shame,' he said, turning to Dustfinger. 'Why did you have to pick on her, of all people? Couldn't you have persuaded one of the others to go nosing around for you? I really have had a weakness for her, ever since that useless Darius read her out of the book for me. It never bothered me that she lost her voice in the process. No, far from it, I stupidly assumed that meant I could trust her more. Did you know her hair used to look like spun gold?'

'Yes, I remember that,' said Dustfinger hoarsely. 'But in your presence it's turned darker.'

'Nonsense!' Capricorn frowned with annoyance. 'Maybe we should try fairy dust. Sprinkled with a little fairy dust, they say, even brass will look like gold. Perhaps it works on a woman's hair as well.'

'Hardly worth the trouble!' said the Magpie mockingly. 'Unless you want her to look particularly beautiful for her execution.'

'Oh, never mind.' Capricorn turned abruptly and went

back to the steps. Meggie hardly noticed. She was looking up at the strange woman. Capricorn's words were working away feverishly in her mind: hair like spun gold . . . that useless reader Darius . . . no, it couldn't be true. She stared up, narrowing her eyes to see the face better through the ropes, but it was hidden in dark shadows.

'Good.' Capricorn dropped into his chair again with another heavy sigh. 'How long shall we need for the preparations? It all ought to be done properly, I think.'

'Two days.' The Magpie climbed the steps and took up her position behind him. 'If you want to summon the men from the other bases, that is.'

Capricorn frowned. 'Yes, why not? It's time to set everyone a little example. Discipline has left much to be desired recently.' He looked at Basta as he said this, and Basta bowed his head as if all the misdemeanours of the last few days weighed heavily on him. 'The day after tomorrow, then,' Capricorn went on. 'When darkness falls. I want Darius to carry out another experiment with the girl first. Get her to read something out of a book, anything – I just want to make sure that fairy didn't turn up by pure chance.'

Basta had wrapped Tinker Bell in his jacket again. Meggie wanted to put her hands over her ears so as not to hear the feeble tinkling sounds the fairy was making. She pressed her lips together to stop them trembling, and looked up at Capricorn.

'But I won't read aloud for you!' she said. Her voice rang out through the church at twice its usual volume. 'Not a word! I won't read you out any treasure, and I certainly won't read out some kind of – of executioner!' She spat the word into Capricorn's face.

But Capricorn only toyed with the belt of his dressing gown, looking bored. 'Take her away,' he told Basta. 'It's late. The child must get some sleep.'

Basta prodded Meggie in the back. 'You heard. Go on, get moving.'

Meggie looked up at Dustfinger one last time, and then walked uncertainly down the nave ahead of Basta. When she had passed below the second net she looked up again. The unknown woman's face was still hidden, but she thought she could make out her eyes, and a slender nose . . . and if she imagined the hair rather lighter in colour—

'Go on, I said!' snapped Basta.

Meggie obeyed, but she kept looking back. 'I won't do it!' she cried when she had almost reached the church porch. 'I swear! I won't read *anyone* here. Ever!'

'Oh, don't swear oaths you can't keep!' whispered Basta as he pushed the door open and led her out into the brightly floodlit square.

The Black Horse of
the Night

He bent down and lifted Sophie from his pocket . . . She
was still in her nightie and her feet were bare. She shivered
and stared around her at the swirling mists and ghostly
vapours.

'Where are we?' she asked.

'We is in Dream Country,' the BFG said. 'This is where
all dreams is beginning.'

Roald Dahl, *The BFG*

Fenoglio was lying on his bed when Basta pushed Meggie
in through the door.

'What have you done to her?' he demanded of Basta, swiftly getting to his feet. 'She's white as a sheet!'

But Basta had already closed the door behind him. 'You'll
be relieved in two hours,' Meggie heard him tell the guard.
Then he was gone.

Fenoglio put his hands on Meggie's shoulders and looked

into her face with concern. 'Come on, tell me. What did they want you for? Is your father here?'

Meggie shook her head. 'They've caught Dustfinger,' she said. 'And a woman.'

'What woman? Heavens, what a state you're in!' Fenoglio drew her over to the bed, and Meggie sat down beside him.

'I think she's my mother,' she whispered.

'Your mother?' Fenoglio looked at her in astonishment. His eyes were bloodshot from his sleepless night.

Distractedly, Meggie smoothed down her skirt. It was dirty and crumpled. No wonder, she'd been sleeping in it for days. 'Her hair's darker now,' she stammered, 'and of course Mo's photo of her is nine years old . . . Capricorn has her in a net, and Dustfinger too. He's going to have them both executed in two days' time, and I'm supposed to read someone out of *Inkheart* to do it – that friend, as Capricorn calls him. I told you. Mo was supposed to be going to do it. You wouldn't tell me who the friend was, but now you *must!*' She looked pleadingly at Fenoglio.

The old man closed his eyes. 'Merciful heaven!' he murmured.

Outside, it was still dark. The moon hung in the sky in front of their window, with a cloud drifting past it like a tattered dress.

'I'll tell you tomorrow,' said Fenoglio. 'That's a promise.'

'No! Tell me now.'

He looked at her thoughtfully. 'It's not a story for this hour of the night. You'll have bad dreams afterwards.'

'Tell me!' Meggie repeated.

Fenoglio sighed. 'Oh dear. I know that look from my grandchildren,' he said. 'Very well, then.' He helped her up to her bunk, put Mo's sweater under her head and pulled the blanket up to her chin. 'I'll tell it to you the way I wrote it in *Inkheart*,' he said quietly. 'I know that passage almost by heart. I was very proud of it at the time.' He cleared his throat before he began, whispering the words into the night. '*But one being was feared even more than Capricorn's men. He was known as the Shadow, and he appeared only when Capricorn called him. Sometimes he was red as fire, sometimes as grey as the ashes into which fire turns all that it devours. He leaped from the ground like flame flickering up from wood. His touch and even his breath brought death. He rose up at his master's feet, soundless and faceless, scenting the air like a dog on the trail, waiting to be shown his victim.*' Fenoglio swept a hand over his forehead and looked at the window. It was some time before he went on, as if he were recalling the words to mind from long ago. '*They say,*' he continued at last, '*that Capricorn had the Shadow made from his victims' ashes by a troll, or by the dwarves who know all that fire and smoke can do. No one was certain, for it was said that Capricorn had those who had brought the Shadow to life killed afterwards. But everyone knew one thing: the Shadow was immortal and invulnerable, and as pitiless as his master.*'

Fenoglio fell silent. And Meggie, her heart beating fast, gazed out at the night.

'Yes, Meggie,' Fenoglio said at last in a low voice. 'I think Capricorn wants you to fetch him the Shadow. And God have mercy on us if you succeed. There are many monsters in this world, most of them human and all of them mortal. I would not like to have an immortal monster on my conscience, a monster spreading fear and terror here for all time. Your father had an idea when he came to see me – I've already mentioned it to you, and it may be our only chance, but I just don't know how it will work yet. I must think hard. We don't have much time, and you ought to get some sleep now. When did you say this is to happen – the day after tomorrow?'

Meggie nodded. 'As soon as dusk falls,' she whispered.

Fenoglio passed a weary hand over his face. 'Don't worry about the woman,' he said. 'You may not want to hear this, but I don't think she can possibly be your mother, much as you may wish she were. How could she have come here?'

'It was Darius!' Meggie buried her face in Mo's sweater. 'The stupid man who can't read aloud well enough. Capricorn said so: he read her back out of *Inkheart* and she lost her voice coming out of the book. She's back, I'm sure she is, and Mo doesn't know! He thinks she's still stuck in the story.'

'Well, if you're right, then I wish she really were still there,' muttered Fenoglio, pulling the blanket up over her shoulders again with a sigh. 'I still think you're wrong, but believe what you like! And now go to sleep.'

But of course Meggie couldn't sleep. She lay there with her face to the wall, listening to her own heart. Fear and joy mingled there like two colours running into each other. Whenever she closed her eyes she saw the nets and the two faces there among the cords, Dustfinger's and the other face, blurred as an old photograph. Hard as she tried to see it more clearly, it always faded again.

Dawn was breaking outside by the time she finally fell asleep, but the nightmares hadn't finished with her yet. They grew especially fast in the grey time between night and day, spinning an eternity out of seconds. One-eyed ogres and giant spiders stole into Meggie's sleep, hounds of hell, witches who ate children, all the bugbears she had ever met in stories. They crept out of the box that Mo had made her and jumped from the pages of her favourite books. Even the monsters came out of the picture books that Mo had given her before she knew the alphabet. They danced through Meggie's dream, brightly coloured and shaggy, their wide mouths smiling, baring their pointed little teeth. There was the Cheshire Cat she had always been so afraid of, and here came the Wild Things that Mo liked so much he had hung a picture of them in his workshop. How huge their teeth were! Dustfinger would be crunched between those fangs like crispbread. But just as one of them was stretching out his claws, the one with eyes as big as saucers, a new figure came out of the grey void, hissing like a flame, ashen-grey and faceless, seized the Wild Thing and tore it into scraps of paper.

'Meggie!'

The monsters vanished, and the sun was shining on Meggie's face. Fenoglio was standing beside her bed. 'You were dreaming.'

Meggie sat up. The old man's face looked as if he hadn't closed his eyes all night and he had several new wrinkles. 'Where's my father, Fenoglio?' she asked. 'Oh, why doesn't he come?'

41

Farid

Ali Baba . . . was surprised to see a well-lighted and spacious chamber . . . filled with all sorts of provisions, rich bales of silks, embroideries, and valuable tissues, piled upon one another, gold and silver ingots in great heaps, and money in bags. The sight of all these riches made him suppose that this cave must have been occupied for ages by robbers, who had succeeded one another.

'The Story of Ali Baba and the Forty Thieves', from **The Arabian Nights' Entertainments**, tr. Edward William Lane

Farid stared at the dark until his eyes hurt, but Dustfinger did not return. Sometimes Farid thought he saw his scarred face among the low-growing branches. Sometimes he thought he heard his almost silent footsteps on the dead leaves, but he was always wrong. Farid was used to listening to the sounds of the night. He had spent endless hours doing so back in his other life, when the world around him was not green but brown and yellow; his eyes had often let him down, but he had always been able to rely on his ears.

All the same, Farid listened in vain that night, the longest night of his life. Dustfinger didn't come back. When day began to dawn above the hills Farid went to the two captives, gave them water, a little of the dry bread they still had left, and a few olives.

'Come on, Farid, untie us!' said Silvertongue as Farid put the bread in his mouth. 'Dustfinger should have been back by now, you know he should.'

Farid said nothing. He loved to hear Silvertongue's voice. It had lured him out of his old, wretched life, but it seemed that Dustfinger didn't like it any more, he didn't know why – and Dustfinger had told him to keep watch on the prisoners. He had said nothing about untying them.

'Look, you're a clever lad,' said the woman, 'so use your head for a moment, will you? Are you going to sit here until Capricorn's men come and find us? What a sight we'll be: a boy watching two captives who can't lift a finger to help him. They'll fall about laughing.'

What was she called again? Eli-nor. Farid had difficulty remembering the name. It was awkward as a pebble on his tongue, and sounded like the name of an enchantress from a far-distant land. He thought her unnatural; she looked at him as a man might look, without timidity or fear, and her voice could be very loud and as angry as a lion's roar.

'We have to get down to the village, Farid!' said Silvertongue. 'We must find out what's happened to Dustfinger – and where my daughter is.'

Yes, the girl – the girl with the clear, bright eyes, little pieces of sky fallen to the earth and caught in her dark lashes. Farid poked the ground with a stick. An ant was carrying a breadcrumb bigger than itself past his toes.

'Perhaps he doesn't understand what we're saying,' said Elinor.

Farid raised his head and cast her a glance of annoyance. 'Yes, I do. I understand everything.' And so he had, from the first moment, as if he had never heard any other language. He remembered the red church. Dustfinger had explained that it was a church, although Farid had never seen such a building before. He also remembered the man with the knife. There had been a great many such men in his old life. They loved their knives and did terrible things with them.

'You'll run off if I untie you.' Farid looked uncertainly at Silvertongue.

'No, I won't. Do you think I'd leave my daughter down there with Basta and Capricorn?'

Basta and Capricorn. Yes, those had been the names. The knife-man and the man with the eyes as colourless as water. A robber, a murderer . . . Farid knew all about him. Dustfinger had told him a great deal as they sat together by the fire in the evening. They had exchanged sad stories, although both of them longed for one with a happy ending.

Now this story, too, was growing darker with each day that passed.

'It'll be better if I go alone.' Farid dug the stick so hard into the ground that it broke in his fingers. 'I'm used to slinking into strange villages, strange palaces and houses – it was my job in the old days. If you know what I mean.'

Silvertongue nodded.

'They always sent me,' Farid went on. 'Who'd be afraid of a thin young boy? I could sniff around everywhere without arousing suspicion. When did the guards change? Which was the best way of escape? Where did the richest man in the village live? If all went well they gave me enough to eat. If it did not they beat me like a dog.'

'They?' asked Elinor.

'The thieves,' replied Farid.

The two adults fell silent. And Dustfinger still wasn't back. Farid looked towards the village and saw the first rays of the sun rising above its rooftops.

'Very well. You may be right,' said Silvertongue. 'You go down alone and find out what we need to know, but first untie us. If you don't we won't be able to help you if they do catch you. And I don't fancy sitting here tied up like this when the first snake wriggles past.'

The woman looked as frightened as if she already heard it rustling through the dead leaves. But Farid looked thoughtfully at Silvertongue's face, trying to decide whether his eyes could trust him as his ears already did. Finally he stood up without a word, took the knife Dustfinger had given him from his belt, and cut them both free.

'My God, I'm never letting anyone tie me up like that again!' said Elinor, rubbing her arms and legs. 'I feel as numb as a rag doll. How are you, Mortimer? Can you still feel your feet?'

Farid looked at her curiously. 'You don't look like his wife. Are you his mother?' he asked, nodding in Silvertongue's direction.

Elinor's face came out in more red blotches than a toadstool. 'Good Lord above, no! What makes you think that? Do I really look so old?' Glancing down at herself, she sighed. 'Yes, I probably do. All the same, I'm not his mother. I'm not Meggie's mother either, in case that's your next question. My children were all made of paper and printer's ink, and that man,' she said, pointing to the rooftops of Capricorn's village shining through the trees, 'that man down there destroyed a great many of them. Believe me, he'll regret it.'

Farid looked at her doubtfully. He couldn't imagine Capricorn being afraid of a woman, certainly not one who got out of breath when she climbed a hill and was scared of snakes. No, if the man with the pale eyes feared anything it would be what most people feared – death. And Elinor didn't look as if she knew much about killing. Nor did Silvertongue.

'The girl . . .' Farid hesitated before asking, 'Where is her mother?'

Silvertongue went over to the cold fireplace and took a piece of the bread lying among the soot-blackened stones. 'She went away long ago,' he said. 'Meggie was just three. What about your own mother?'

Farid shrugged his shoulders and looked up at the sky. It was as blue as if the night had never been. 'I'd better go now,' he said, putting his knife away and picking up Dustfinger's rucksack. Gwin was sleeping close to it, curled up between the roots of a tree. Farid picked him up and put him in the rucksack. The marten sleepily protested, but Farid tickled his head and strapped the rucksack up.

'Why are you taking that marten?' asked Elinor in surprise. 'The smell of him could give you away.'

'He may come in useful,' replied Farid, pushing the tip of Gwin's bushy tail into the rucksack too. 'He's clever. Cleverer than a dog or a camel, anyway. He understands what you say to him, and maybe he'll find Dustfinger.'

'Farid.' Silvertongue was searching his pockets, and took out a piece of paper. 'I don't know whether you'll be able to find out where they're keeping Meggie prisoner,' he said, hastily scribbling something with the stump of a pencil, 'but if possible can you try to see she gets this note?'

Farid took the piece of paper and looked at it. 'What does it say?' he asked.

Elinor took the note from his hand. 'Heavens above, Mortimer, what's this?' she asked.

Silvertongue smiled. 'Meggie and I have often sent secret messages in this writing – she's much better at it than I am. Don't you recognise it? It comes from a book. *We're not far away*, it says. *Don't worry. We'll soon get you out. Mo, Elinor and Farid*. Meggie will be able to read the message, but no one else will.'

'Aha!' murmured Elinor, giving Farid the note back. 'Yes, if it falls into the wrong hands it's better that way. After all, perhaps some of those fire-raisers can read.'

Farid folded the note until it was about the size of a coin, then put it in his trouser pocket. 'I'll be back when the sun is above those hills at the latest,' he said. 'Or if I'm not—'

'If you're not, I'll come and look for you,' Silvertongue ended the sentence.

'And so will I, of course,' added Elinor, looking fierce.

Farid did not think that was a good idea, but he didn't say so. He left, going the same way that Dustfinger had gone the night before, disappearing as if the ghosts who lurked in the darkness had eaten him alive.

A Furry Face on the
Windowsill

It's a poor sort of memory that only works backwards.
Lewis Carroll, *Through the Looking Glass*

Flatnose brought Meggie and Fenoglio their breakfast, and this morning it was more than bread and a few olives. He put a basket of fruit on the table for them, and a plate of small, sweet cakes. But Meggie didn't at all like the smile he served up at the same time.

'All for you, princess!' he grunted, pinching her cheek with his clumsy fingers. 'To strengthen your little voice. There's been a lot of excitement since Basta told us about the execution. Well, like I always said, there has to be more to life than hanging up a few dead roosters and shooting cats.'

Meggie exchanged a glance with Fenoglio. The old man was staring at Flatnose with an expression of disgust which suggested that he couldn't believe such a creature had slipped from his pen.

'Yes, to be sure, it's a terribly long time since we had a nice execution!' continued Flatnose, on his way back to the door. 'It'd attract too much attention, they always said. And when someone really had to disappear – well, the word was to go carefully! Make it look like an accident. Is that any fun? You bet it isn't. Not like it used to be, a good execution with eating and drinking and dancing and music, that's the way to do it in style! And so we will this time – just like we did back in the good old days!'

Fenoglio took a sip of the black coffee that Flatnose had brought him, and choked.

'Don't you fancy that kind of thing, grandpa?' Flatnose looked at him sneeringly. 'Take my word for it, Capricorn's executions are something to remember!'

'Who do you think you're telling?' muttered Fenoglio unhappily.

At that moment someone knocked on the door. Flatnose had left it ajar, and Darius the reader put his head round it.

'Sorry!' he breathed, looking at Flatnose as anxiously as a bird obliged to get close to a hungry cat. 'I – er – I'm to get the girl to read something aloud. Capricorn's orders.'

'Really? Well, let's just hope she reads something useful out of a book this time. Basta showed me the fairy. She doesn't even sprinkle any fairy dust, however hard you shake her.' Flatnose looked at Meggie with a mixture of dislike and respect. Perhaps he thought she was some kind of a witch. 'Knock when you want to come out again,' he grunted, pushing past Darius.

Darius nodded and stood there for a moment before sitting down at the table with Meggie and Fenoglio, looking embarrassed. He stared greedily at the fruit until Fenoglio pushed the basket over to him. Tentatively, he took an apricot, and put it into his mouth as if he thought he would never in his life taste anything so delicious again.

'Good heavens, it's only an apricot!' laughed Fenoglio. 'Not exactly a rare fruit in these latitudes.'

Darius spat the apricot stone out into his hand, still looking awkward. 'Whenever they shut me up in this room,' he said timidly, 'they gave me nothing but dry bread. And they took my books away too, but I managed to hide some of them, and when the hunger got too bad I looked at the pictures in them. The best was a picture of apricots. I sometimes sat for hours staring at the painted fruit with my mouth watering. Ever since then I just can't control myself when I see apricots.'

Meggie took another apricot from the basket and put it into his hand. 'Did they often shut you up?' she asked.

The thin little man shrugged. 'Yes, whenever I didn't read something out of a book properly,' he replied evasively. 'Well, that meant all the time, really. Then they finally gave up because they realised that my reading didn't exactly improve when they frightened me. On the contrary. Take Flatnose, for instance.' He lowered his voice, casting a nervous glance at the door. 'I read Flatnose out while Basta was standing beside me with his knife. Well . . .' He raised his narrow shoulders regretfully.

Meggie looked at him sympathetically. Then she asked, hesitantly, 'Did you ever read any women out of that story?'

Fenoglio looked at her uneasily.

'Certainly,' Darius replied. 'I read Mortola out of the book! She says I made her older, and rickety as a chair cobbled together badly, but I really don't think I got too much wrong with her. Luckily Capricorn agreed.'

'Any younger women?' Meggie was looking at neither

Darius nor Fenoglio.

'Oh yes,' Darius sighed. 'On the same day as I read Mortola out. I remember it very well. Capricorn was living up in the north then, at a lonely, half-ruined farm in the mountains, and there weren't many local girls around. I myself was living not far away, in my sister's house. I worked as a teacher, but in my free time I read aloud now and then in libraries and schools, or for children's parties, and sometimes on warm summer evenings, I even read in a square or café. I loved reading aloud.'

His gaze wandered to the window, as if he could catch a glimpse there of those long-forgotten, happier days. 'I think Basta noticed me when I was reading aloud at a party in the village – a passage from *Dr Dolittle* – and all of a sudden there was a bird flying around. I really didn't know I had the gift – perhaps it was something to do with Basta being there. Anyway, when I went home Basta caught me as if I were a stray dog and took me to Capricorn. First he made me read gold out of books, like your father did,' he said, smiling sadly at Meggie, 'but then I had to read Mortola out for him, and after that he told me to read his maidservants out too. It was terrible.' Darius pushed his glasses up on his nose with trembling fingers. 'I was so scared. How can you read aloud well when you're terrified? He made me try three times. Oh, I felt so sorry for them, I don't want to talk about it!' He buried his face in his hands, which were bony as an old man's. Meggie thought she heard him sob, and for a moment she hesitated to ask her next question, but then she did.

'The maid they call Resa,' she said, her heart beating in her mouth. 'Was she one of them?'

Darius took his hands away from his face. 'Yes, she came

out quite by chance,' he said huskily. 'Capricorn had really wanted another of them, but suddenly there was Resa, and at first I thought I'd got it right for once. She looked so beautiful, almost improbably beautiful with her golden hair and her sad eyes. But then we realised she couldn't speak. Well, that didn't bother Capricorn, in fact I think he liked it.' He searched his trouser pocket and brought out a crumpled handkerchief. 'I really could read better once,' he said, sniffing. 'But this constant fear . . . May I?' With a sad smile he took another apricot and bit into it. Then he wiped the juice from his mouth with his sleeve, cleared his throat, and gazed straight at Meggie. His eyes looked curiously large behind the thick lenses of his glasses.

'At the – er – festivities that Capricorn's planning,' he said, lowering his gaze and running his finger awkwardly along the edge of the table, 'the idea, as you probably know, is for you to read from *Inkheart*. The book's being kept in a secret place until that time comes. Only Capricorn knows where it is. So you won't see it before the – er – occasion. Which means that we're to use another book for the latest test Capricorn wants of your talents. Luckily, there are a few other books in this village, not many, but anyway I've been told to choose something suitable.' He raised his head again and gave a small, slight smile. 'Fortunately I didn't have to look for gold and such treasures this time. All Capricorn wants is proof of your skill, and so,' he said, pushing a small book over the table, 'so I chose this one.'

Meggie bent over the cover. '*Collected Fairy Tales of Hans Christian Andersen*,' she read aloud. She looked at Darius. 'They're beautiful stories.'

'Yes,' he breathed. 'Sad, but very, very beautiful.' Reaching over the table, he opened the book for Meggie at a place which he had marked with a couple of long blades of grass slipped between the yellowed pages. 'First I thought of my favourite story, the one about the nightingale. Maybe you know it?'

Meggie nodded.

'But the fairy you read out of the book yesterday isn't happy in the jug where Basta has put her,' Darius went on, 'so I thought it might be better if you tried the tin soldier.'

The tin soldier. Meggie did not reply at once. The brave tin soldier in his little paper boat . . . she imagined him suddenly appearing beside the fruit basket. 'No!' she said. 'No. I've told Capricorn already, I won't read anything out of a book for him, not even as a test. Tell him I can't do it any more. Just tell him I tried and nothing came out of the story!'

Darius gave her a sympathetic look. 'Oh, I would,' he said quietly. 'Really I would. But it's the Magpie—' he said, quietly putting his hand to his mouth as if he had said too much. 'Sorry, I mean the housekeeper, of course, Signora Mortola – it's *her* you have to read aloud to. I've only chosen the story.'

The Magpie. An image of her flashed into Meggie's mind, watching her with her birdlike eyes. Suppose I bite my tongue, she thought. Very hard. She had done that a few times by mistake, and once her tongue had swelled up so much she had to talk to Mo in sign language for two days. She looked at Fenoglio for help.

'Do it!' he said, to her surprise. 'Read aloud to the old woman, but make it a condition that you can keep the tin soldier. Tell her anything you like – say you want to play with him because you're bored to death – and then ask for something else: some sheets of paper and a pencil. Say you want to draw pictures, understand? If she agrees we'll take it from there.'

Meggie didn't understand a word of this, but before she could ask Fenoglio what he was planning the door opened, and there was the Magpie herself.

Darius leaped to his feet so quickly at the sight of her that he pushed Meggie's plate off the table. 'Oh, I'm sorry, so sorry!' he stammered, picking up the broken pieces in his bony fingers. He cut his thumb so deeply on the last piece that blood dripped to the wooden floorboards.

'Get up, you fool!' snapped Mortola. 'Have you shown her what she's to read from?'

Darius nodded, and looked unhappily at his bleeding thumb.

'Then get out. You can help the women in the kitchen. There are chickens to be plucked.'

Darius made a face, looking disgusted, but he bowed and disappeared into the corridor, but not without casting Meggie a last sympathetic glance.

'Right!' said the Magpie, waving to her impatiently. 'Start reading – and put your mind to it.'

Meggie read the tin soldier out of the story. It was as if he simply fell from the ceiling. *'He dropped down three storeys to the street and his bayonet stuck in the earth between two cobblestones.'* The Magpie reached for him before Meggie could, and stared at him as if he were just a painted toy, while he looked back at her with horror in his eyes. Then she put him in the pocket of her coarse-knit woollen jacket.

'Please can I have him?' stammered Meggie, just as the Magpie reached the doorway. Fenoglio placed himself behind her as if to cover her back, but the Magpie just looked at Meggie with her sharp-nosed gaze. 'I – I mean, there's nothing you'd want to do with him,' Meggie went on uncertainly, 'and I'm so bored. Please.'

The Magpie looked at her, unmoved. 'You can have him back when Capricorn has seen him,' she said, and then she was gone.

'The paper!' cried Fenoglio. 'You forgot to ask for paper and pencil!'

'I'm sorry,' murmured Meggie. She hadn't forgotten, it was just that she didn't dare ask the Magpie for anything else.

'Ah, well, I'll just have to get it by other means,' said Fenoglio. 'The only question is, how?'

Meggie went over to the window, rested her forehead on the pane and looked down at the garden, where a couple of Capricorn's maids were busy tying up tomato plants. What would Mo say, she wondered, if he knew I can do it too? 'Who did you read out, Meggie? Poor Tinker Bell and the Steadfast Tin Soldier?' . . . 'Yes,' murmured Meggie, tracing an invisible 'M' on the pane with her finger. Poor fairy, poor tin soldier, poor Dustfinger and – she thought again of the woman with the dark blonde hair. 'Resa,' she whispered. TeResa. Teresa was her mother's name.

She was about to turn away from the window when out of the corner of her eye she saw something appearing above the sill outside – a small furry face. Meggie retreated in alarm.

Do rats climb walls? Yes, but that wasn't a rat, the animal's muzzle wasn't pointed enough. She quickly ran back to the windowpane.

Gwin.

The marten was sitting on the narrow sill, looking in at her with sleepy eyes.

'Basta!' muttered Fenoglio behind her. 'Yes, Basta will get me the paper. That's a good idea.'

Meggie opened the window very slowly, so that Gwin wouldn't take fright and perhaps fall off the sill. Even a marten would break all his bones if he fell into the paved yard from this height. She put out her hand, still very slowly. Her fingers trembled as she stroked Gwin's back. Then she grabbed him before his little teeth could snap at her, and quickly lifted him into the room. She looked anxiously down, but none of the maids had noticed anything. They were all bending over the vegetable patch, their clothes drenched with perspiration from the heat of the sun burning down on their backs.

There was a note under Gwin's collar. It was dirty, and had been folded very small and tied in place with a piece of tape.

'Why are you opening the window? The air outside is even hotter than in here. We—' Fenoglio broke off and stared in amazement at the animal in Meggie's arms. She quickly put a warning finger to her lips. Then, holding the struggling Gwin tight, she removed the note from under his collar. The marten chattered crossly and snapped at her fingers again. He didn't like being held too long, and would even bite Dustfinger if he tried it.

'What have you got there – a rat?' Fenoglio came closer. Meggie let go of the marten, and Gwin immediately leaped back to the windowsill.

'A marten!' cried the astonished Fenoglio. 'Where did that come from?' Meggie looked anxiously at the door, but obviously the guard outside had heard nothing. Fenoglio pressed his hand to his mouth, and looked again at Gwin in such amazement that Meggie almost laughed. 'He's got horns!' he whispered.

'Of course! That's the way you wrote him!' she whispered back.

Gwin was still sitting on the windowsill, blinking uncomfortably at the sun. He didn't like bright light and preferred to sleep through the day. So how had he got here?

Meggie put her head out of the window, but there were still only the maids down in the yard. Hastily, she moved back into the room and unfolded the note.

'A message?' Fenoglio leaned over her shoulder. 'Is it from your father?'

Meggie nodded. She had recognised the writing at once, although it wasn't as steady as usual. Her heart began dancing inside her. She traced the letters with her eyes as longingly as if they were a path with Mo waiting for her at the end of it.

'What on earth does it say? I can't make out a word of it!' whispered Fenoglio.

Meggie smiled. 'It's elvish writing!' she whispered. 'Mo and I have been using it as our secret writing ever since I read *The Lord of the Rings*, but he's probably rather out of practice. He's made quite a lot of mistakes.'

'Well, what does it say?'

Meggie read it to him.

'Farid – who's he?'

'A boy. Mo read him out of *The Thousand and One Nights*, but that's another story. You saw him – when Dustfinger ran away from you Farid was with him.' Meggie folded the note up again and looked out of the window once more. One of the maids had straightened up. She was brushing the earth off her hands and looking up at the high wall as if she dreamed of flying away over it. Who had brought Gwin here? Mo? Or had the marten found his way by himself? That was most unlikely. He certainly wouldn't be wandering round in broad daylight unless someone else had a hand in it.

Meggie hid the note in the sleeve of her dress. Gwin was still sitting on the windowsill. Sleepily, he stretched his neck and sniffed at the wall outside. Perhaps he could smell the pigeons who sometimes settled outside the window. 'Feed him some bread so he won't run away!' Meggie whispered to Fenoglio, and then went over to the bed and got her rucksack down. Where was that pencil? She was sure she had a pencil. Yes, there it was, although it was only a small stump. Now, what about paper? She took one of Darius's books out from under the mattress and carefully tore out one of the endpapers. She had never done such a thing before – fancy tearing a page out of a book! – but now she had to. Kneeling on the floor, she began to write in the same curly script that Mo had used for his message. She knew the letters off by heart: *We're all right and I can do it too, Mo! I read Tinker Bell out of her book, and when it gets dark tomorrow Capricorn wants me to bring the Shadow out of 'Inkheart' to come and kill Dustfinger.* She didn't mention Resa. Not a word to show that she thought she had seen her mother, and if Capricorn had his way that she too had only two days to live. A message like that wouldn't fit on a piece of paper no matter how large it was.

Gwin was greedily nibbling the bread Fenoglio had given him. Meggie folded up the endpaper and tied it to his collar. 'Take care!' she whispered to Gwin, and then threw the rest of the bread down into Capricorn's yard. The marten scurried down the wall of the house as if it was the easiest thing in the world. One of the maids screamed as he scampered between her legs, and called out to the others. She was probably alarmed for Capricorn's chickens, but Gwin had already disappeared over the wall.

'Good. Excellent. So your father's here,' Fenoglio whispered to Meggie, standing beside her by the open window. 'Somewhere out there. Very good indeed. And you'll get the tin soldier back. Who was it said that *all's for the best in the best of all possible worlds*?' He rubbed the tip of his nose and blinked out at the dazzling sunlight. 'So the next thing to do,' he murmured, 'is to play on Basta's superstitions. What a good thing I gave him that little weakness. It was a clever move.'

Meggie had no idea what he was talking about, but that didn't matter to her. She had only one thought in her head: Mo was here.

43

A Dark Place

'Jim, old boy,' said Lukas . . . in a rough voice. 'That was a short journey. I'm sorry that you must share my fate now.'

Jim swallowed.

'We're friends,' he said quietly, biting his lower lip to keep it from trembling so hard.

The scribes chuckled again, and the bonzes nodded at each other, grinning.

'Jim Button,' said Lukas, 'you really are the best little fellow I ever met in all my life.'

'Take them to the place of execution!' commanded the Head Bonze, and the soldiers seized Lukas and Jim to drag them away.

Michael Ende, *Jim Button and Lukas the Engine Driver*

Dustfinger had expected Capricorn to leave him and Resa dangling in those dreadful nets until their execution, but they spent only a single if very long night there. In the morning, as soon as the sun cast its bright light on the red walls inside the church, Basta had them brought down. For a few horrible moments Dustfinger thought Capricorn had decided to put an end to them in some quick and inconspicuous way instead, and when he felt solid ground under his feet again he didn't know which made him weaker at the knees – that fear or his night in the net. Whichever it was, he could hardly stand upright.

Basta set his mind at rest for the time being, although that was certainly not his intention. 'Personally, I'd have liked to leave you dangling up there a while longer,' he said as his men dragged Dustfinger out of the net. 'But for some reason or other Capricorn's decided to lock the two of you in the crypt for what's left of your miserable lives.'

Dustfinger did his best to hide his relief. So death was still a little way off. 'I expect it bothers Capricorn to have an audience when he's discussing his filthy plans with the rest of you,' he said. 'Or perhaps he just wants us to be able to walk to our execution on our own two legs.' One more night in that net and Dustfinger wouldn't even have known he still *had* legs. His bones ached so much after that first night that he was moving like an old man as Basta took him and Resa down to the crypt. Resa stumbled once or twice on the stairs, and seemed to be feeling even worse than he was, but she made not a sound, and when Basta took her arm after she had slipped on one step she shook herself free, giving him such an icy look that he let her go on by herself.

The crypt below the church was a damp, cold place even on days like this when the sun was practically melting the tiles on the houses outside. It smelled of mould and mouse droppings and other things Dustfinger didn't want to think about. Soon after arriving in the deserted village Capricorn had had gratings fitted over the narrow niches where long-dead priests slept in their stone tombs. 'What could be more fitting than to make the condemned sleep on coffins?' he had said at the time, with a laugh. He had always had his own peculiar sense of humour.

Impatiently, Basta pushed them down the last few steps. He was in a hurry to get back to the light of day, away from the dead and their ghosts. His hand shook as he hung his lantern on a hook and opened the grating over the first cell. There was no electric light down here, no heating either, or any other comforts, only the quiet tombs and the mice scurrying over the cracked flagstones of the floor.

'Oh, aren't you going to give us the pleasure of your company a little longer?' asked Dustfinger as Basta pushed them into the cell. They had to duck. They couldn't stand upright under the old vaults here. 'We could tell ghost stories. I know some nice new ones.'

Basta growled like a dog. 'We won't be needing any coffin for you, dirtyfingers!' he said as he closed the grating again.

'No, indeed! An urn perhaps, a jam jar, but no coffin.' Dustfinger took a step back from the bars so as to be out of reach of Basta's knife. 'I see you have a new amulet,' he called. Basta had almost reached the steps. 'Another rabbit's foot, is it? Didn't I tell you they attract White Ladies? You could see the White Ladies in our old world. You don't see them here, which isn't very practical, but of course they're still around with their whispering and their icy fingers.'

Basta was standing at the foot of the steps with his fists clenched, his back still turned. Dustfinger was always surprised to find how easily you could scare the man with a few words. 'Remember how they come for their victims?' he went on softly. 'They whisper your name, "Bastaaa!" and next thing you know you're freezing cold, and then—'

'They'll soon be whispering *your* name, dirtyfingers!' Basta interrupted, his voice shaking. 'Yours and yours alone.' And he hurried up the steps as if the ghosts of the White Ladies were already after him.

The sound of his footsteps died away, and Dustfinger was alone – with the silence, with death, and with Resa. They were obviously the only prisoners. Now and then Capricorn had some poor fellow locked in the crypt just to give him a good fright, but most of those who came here and wrote their names on the tombs disappeared some dark night and were never seen again.

Their own departure from this world was going to be rather more spectacular.

My last performance, in a way, thought Dustfinger. Perhaps it will turn out that all this was only a bad dream, and I just had to die to get home again? A nice idea, if only he could have believed in it.

Resa had seated herself on a sarcophagus. It was a plain stone coffin, with a cracked lid, and the name that was once on it could no longer be deciphered. It didn't seem to frighten Resa to be so near the dead. Dustfinger felt differently. He was not afraid of ghosts and White Ladies, like Basta. If a White Lady had appeared he would have passed the time of day with her. No – he was afraid of death. He thought he heard death itself breathing down here, breathing so deeply that no air was left for anyone else. His chest felt as if a huge and ugly animal were sitting on it. Perhaps it hadn't been so bad up there in the net after all. At least they'd had air to breathe.

He sensed Resa watching him. She beckoned him over and

patted the lid of the coffin. Hesitantly, he sat down beside her. She put her hand into the pocket of her dress, brought out a candle and held it up to him with an enquiring look. Dustfinger had to smile. Yes, of course he had matches on him. It was child's play to conceal something as small as a few matches from Basta and the other idiots.

Resa fixed the flickering candle to the coffin with a little of its own wax. She loved candles – coloured candles and stones. She always had both in her pockets. But perhaps today she had lit the candle just for him, because she knew how he loved fire.

'I'm sorry. I should have looked for the book on my own,' he said, passing a finger through the bright flame. 'Forgive me.'

She put her fingers on his mouth. Presumably she was saying there was nothing to forgive. What a sweet, silent lie. She took her hand away, and Dustfinger cleared his throat. 'You – you didn't find it, did you?' Not that it would make any difference now, but he had to know.

Resa shook her head and shrugged her shoulders regretfully.

'That's what I thought.' He sighed. The silence was terrible, worse than a thousand voices. 'Tell me a story, Resa!' he said quietly, moving closer to her. Please, he added in his thoughts. Chase my fear away. It's crushing my chest. Take us somewhere else, somewhere better.

Resa could do that. She knew endless numbers of stories, just how she knew them she had never told him, but of course he knew. He knew exactly who had once read her those stories, for he had recognised her face the instant he first saw her in Capricorn's house. After all, Silvertongue had shown him the photograph often enough.

Resa took a piece of paper out of her inexhaustible pockets. They contained more than just candles and stones. Just as

Dustfinger always carried the means of lighting a fire, she always had a number of things with her: candle stumps, a few pebbles, some paper and a pencil – her wooden tongue, she called it. Obviously none of these things had seemed to Capricorn's men dangerous enough to be taken away from her. When Resa told one of her stories she sometimes wrote only half a sentence, and Dustfinger had to finish it. It went faster that way, and the story developed surprising twists and turns. But this time it seemed she didn't want to tell him a story, although he had never needed one so badly.

'Who is the girl?' wrote Resa.

Of course. Meggie. Should he lie? Why not? But he didn't, although he didn't know why not. 'She's Silvertongue's daughter – How old? – Twelve, I think.'

It was the right answer. He saw that in her eyes. They were Meggie's eyes. Perhaps rather wearier.

'What does Silvertongue look like? I think you've asked me that before. Well, he isn't scarred like me.' He tried to smile, but Resa remained grave. The candlelight flickered on her face. You know his face better than you know mine, thought Dustfinger, but I'm not going to say so. He's taken a whole world from me, why shouldn't I take his wife from him?

Rising to her feet, she put her hand in the air above her head.

'Yes, he's tall. Taller than you, taller than me.' Why didn't he lie to her? 'Yes, he has dark hair, but I don't want to talk about him now!' He heard the petulance in his own voice. 'Please!' Reaching for her hand, he drew her down beside him. 'Tell me a story. The candle will soon go out, and the light Basta's left us is enough to see these wretched coffins but not to read letters.'

She looked at him thoughtfully, as if she were trying to guess at his thoughts and uncover the words he didn't say. But Dustfinger could guard his face better than Silvertongue, much better. He could make it impenetrable, a shield to keep his heart from prying eyes. What business was it of anyone else to know what was in his heart?

Resa bent over the paper again and began to write.

'*Hear and attend and listen; for this befell and behappened and became and was, O my Best Beloved, when the Tame animals were wild,*' she wrote.

Dustfinger smiled. '*The Dog was wild,*' he whispered. '*And the Horse was wild, and the Sheep was wild, and the Pig was wild – as wild as wild could be – and they walked in the Wet Wild Woods by their wild lones. But the wildest of all wild animals was the Cat. He walked by himself, and all places were alike to him.*'

Resa always knew what story he needed at any given moment. She was a stranger in this world, just like him. It couldn't be that she belonged to Silvertongue.

Farid's Report

'All right,' said Spiff. 'Now this is what I say, anyone who thinks they've got a better plan can say so afterwards.'
Michael de Larrabeiti, *The Borribles Go for Broke*

When Farid came back Silvertongue was waiting for him. Elinor was asleep under the trees, her face flushed by the midday heat, but Silvertongue was still standing where Farid had left him. Relief spread over his face as he saw the boy coming up the hill.

'We heard shots!' he called. 'I thought we'd never see you again.'

'They were shooting at cats,' replied Farid, letting himself drop on to the grass. Silvertongue's concern made Farid feel awkward. He wasn't used to people being concerned for his safety. *What kept you? Where have you been all this time?* That was the kind of reception he was used to. Even Dustfinger's face had always been closed to him, as uncommunicative as a barred door. But with Silvertongue's face it was different.

Anxiety, joy, anger, pain, love – it was all plain to see, written on his brow, even when he tried to hide it, just as he was now trying not to ask the question that must have been on the tip of his tongue ever since he saw Farid approaching.

'Your daughter's all right,' said Farid. 'And she got your message, though she's shut up on the top floor of Capricorn's house. But Gwin is a wonderful climber, even better than Dustfinger, and that's saying something.' He heard Silvertongue breathe a sigh of relief, as if all the cares in the world had been lifted from his shoulders.

'I've even brought an answer.' Farid took Gwin out of the rucksack, held him firmly by the tail and untied Meggie's note from his collar. Silvertongue unfolded the paper as carefully as if he feared his fingers might wipe away the words. 'An endpaper,' he murmured. 'She must have torn it out of a book.'

'What does she say?'

'Have you tried to read it?'

Farid shook his head and took a piece of bread out of his trouser pocket. Gwin had earned a reward. But the marten had disappeared, probably to catch up on his long overdue daytime sleep.

'You can't read, is that it?'

'No.'

'Well, not many people could read this anyway. It's the same secret writing that I used. As you saw, not even Elinor can decipher it. 'Silvertongue smoothed out the paper. It was a dull yellow like desert sand. He read – and then suddenly raised his head. 'Good heavens!' he murmured. 'Imagine that!'

'Imagine what?' Farid bit into the bread he had been keeping for the marten. It was stale; they'd have to steal some more soon.

'Meggie can do it too!' Silvertongue shook his head incredulously and stared at the note in his hand.

Farid propped one elbow on the grass. 'I know. They're all talking about it – I heard them. They say she can work magic like you, and now Capricorn doesn't have to wait for you any more. He doesn't need you now.'

Silvertongue looked at him as if this idea hadn't yet crossed his mind. 'True,' he murmured. 'Now they'll never let her go. Not of their own accord.' He stared at the words his daughter had written on the paper. To Farid they looked like the tracks left by snakes slithering across the sand.

'What else does she say?'

'They've caught Dustfinger, and Meggie is to read someone out of the book to come . . . and kill him. Tomorrow, when it gets dark.' He lowered the note and ran his hand through his hair.

'Yes, I heard about that too.' Farid pulled up a blade of grass and tore it into tiny pieces. 'It seems they've locked him in the crypt under the church. What else is in that note? Doesn't your daughter say who it is she's to fetch out for Capricorn?'

Silvertongue shook his head, but Farid saw that he knew more about it than he was saying.

'Come on, you can tell me! Some kind of executioner, am I right? A man who knows all about cutting off heads.'

Silvertongue acted as if he hadn't heard him.

'I saw something like that once,' said Farid, 'so it's all right for you to tell me about it. If the executioner is good with a sword it's all over quite fast.'

Silvertongue looked at him for a moment, astonished, and then shook his head. 'It's not an executioner,' he said. 'At least, not a man with a sword. Not a man at all.'

Farid turned pale. 'Not a man?'

Silvertongue shook his head. It was some time before he went on. 'They call him the Shadow,' he said in an expressionless voice. 'I don't remember the exact words describing him in the book, all I know is that I pictured him to myself as a figure made completely of burning ashes, red and grey. And without a face.'

Farid stared at him. For a moment he wished he hadn't asked.

'They – they're all looking forward to this execution,' he said in a faltering voice. 'Those Black Jackets are in a really good mood. They're going to kill the woman Dustfinger was visiting as well. Because she tried to find the book for him.' He burrowed his bare toes into the earth. Dustfinger had tried to get him used to wearing shoes because of the snakes, but when you wore shoes you felt as if someone was pinching your toes, so in the end he'd thrown them on the fire.

'What woman? One of Capricorn's maids?' Silvertongue looked at him with a gleam in his eyes.

Farid nodded. He rubbed his toes. They were covered with ant bites. 'She can't talk. Dumb as a sand-fly. Dustfinger has a photo of her in his rucksack. She's probably helped him quite often. And I think he's in love with her.'

It hadn't been difficult for Farid to explore the village. There were lots of boys there no older than him. They washed the cars for the Black Jackets, cleaned their boots and their guns, delivered love letters. He'd delivered love letters himself in that other life. He hadn't had to clean boots, but weapons, yes – and he'd had to shovel camel dung. Polishing cars was much lighter work.

Silvertongue looked up at the sky. Tiny clouds were drifting by, pale as a heron's feathers, ruffled like acacia flowers. Clouds often passed across this sky. Farid liked that. The desert sky he had known before was always empty.

'Tomorrow,' murmured Silvertongue. 'What am I to do? How am I going to get her out of Capricorn's house? Perhaps I can get in somehow by night. I'd need one of those black suits the—'

'I've brought you one.' Farid took first the jacket, then the trousers out of the rucksack. 'Stole them off a washing line. And a dress for Elinor.'

Silvertongue looked at him with such obvious admiration that Farid blushed. 'What an extraordinary fellow you are! Perhaps I should ask *you* how I'm going to get Meggie out of this village?'

Farid smiled awkwardly and looked at his toes. Ask him? No one had ever asked him for his ideas before. He had always been the scout, the tracker dog. Others had made the plans for robberies, raids, revenge. You didn't ask the dog's opinion. You beat the dog if he didn't obey. 'There are only two of us, and there are at least twenty of them down there,' he said. 'It won't be easy . . .'

Silvertongue looked over at their camp site and the woman asleep under the trees. 'Aren't you counting Elinor? You should! She's much fiercer than I am, and just at the moment she is very, very angry.'

Farid had to smile. 'All right, three!' he said. 'Three against twenty.'

'Yes, I know, that doesn't sound good.' Silvertongue stood up, sighing. 'Come on, let's tell Elinor what you've found out,' he said, but Farid stayed where he was in the grass. He picked up one of the dry branches lying everywhere. First-class fire-wood. There was any amount of it here. In his old life, people would have gone a long, long way for wood like this. They'd have given good money for it. Farid looked at the wood, rubbed his finger over the rough bark, and looked at Capricorn's village.

'We could get fire to help us,' he said.

Silvertongue looked at him blankly. 'What do you mean?'

Farid picked up another stick, and another. He heaped them all up, all the dry twigs and branches. 'Dustfinger showed me how to tame fire. It's like Gwin: it bites if you don't know how to handle it, but if you treat it properly it does as you want. That's what Dustfinger taught me. If we use it at the right time, in the right place . . .'

Silvertongue bent down, picked up one of the branches and weighted it in his hand. 'And how are you going to control it once you've got a fire going? It hasn't rained for ages. The hills will be ablaze before you know it.'

Farid shrugged. 'Only if the wind blows the wrong way.'

But Silvertongue shook his head. 'No,' he said firmly. 'I won't play with fire in these hills unless I can't think of anything else. Let's steal into the village tonight. Maybe we can get past the guards. Maybe they know each other so little they'll think I'm one of them. After all, we managed to slip through their fingers once, so maybe we can do it again.'

'That's a lot of *maybes*,' said Farid.

'I know!' replied Silvertongue. 'I know.'

45

Telling Lies to Basta

'If ye see the laird, tell him what ye hear; tell him this makes the twelve hunner and nineteen time that Jennet Clouston has called down the curse on him and his house, byre and stable, man, guest and master, wife, miss, or bairn – black, black be their fall.'

Robert Louis Stevenson, *Kidnapped*

It took Fenoglio only a few words to persuade the guard outside the door that he had to speak to Basta at once. The old man was a gifted liar. He could spin stories out of thin air faster than a spider spins its web.

'What do you want, old man?' asked Basta when he was standing in the doorway. He had brought the tin soldier. 'Here, little witch!' he said to Meggie, handing her the soldier. '*I'd* have thrown it on the fire, but nobody here listens to me these days.'

The tin soldier started at the word 'fire'. His moustache bristled, and his eyes looked so alarmed it touched Meggie's heart. When she put her hands protectively round him she

420

thought she felt his heart beating. She remembered the end of his story: *The soldier melted. The next day when the maid emptied the stove, she found a little tin heart, which was all that was left of him.*

'That's right, no one listens to you any more. I can see that for myself!' Fenoglio looked sympathetically at Basta, as a father might look at his son – which in a way he was. 'And that's why I wanted a word with you.' He lowered his voice and spoke in a conspiratorial whisper. 'I'm offering you a deal.'

'A deal?' Basta scrutinised him with a mixture of wariness and arrogance.

'Yes, a deal,' repeated Fenoglio softly. 'I'm bored here! I'm a scribbler, as you so aptly put it. I need paper to live on much as other people need bread and wine and so forth. Bring me some paper, Basta, and I'll help you to get those keys back. You remember – the keys that the Magpie took away from you.'

Basta took out his knife. When he snapped it open the tin soldier began trembling so much that the bayonet slipped from his tiny hands. 'How?' asked Basta, cleaning his finger-nails with the tip of the knife.

Fenoglio bent down to him. 'I'll write you a magic charm to put a hex on Mortola. A hex that will keep her in bed for weeks and give you time to show Capricorn you are the rightful keeper of the keys. Of course that kind of charm doesn't work instantly, it needs time, but believe you me, when it does start to take effect . . .' Fenoglio raised his eyebrows meaningfully.

But Basta only wrinkled his nose in scorn. 'I've already tried with spiders. And parsley and salt. The old woman's proof against them all.'

'Parsley and spiders!' Fenoglio laughed quietly. 'What a fool you are, Basta! I'm not talking about children's magic. I mean the magic of the written word. Nothing is more powerful for good or evil, I do assure you.' Fenoglio lowered his voice to a whisper. 'I made you yourself out of words and letters, Basta! You and Capricorn.'

Basta flinched. Fear and hatred are closely linked, and Meggie saw both on his face. He believed the old man. He believed every word of it. 'You're a sorcerer!' he muttered. 'You and the girl alike – you both ought to be burned like those accursed books, and her father too.' He quickly spat three times at the old man's feet.

'Ah, spitting! What's that supposed to prevent? The Evil Eye?' Fenoglio mocked him. 'That notion of burning us isn't a very new idea, Basta, but then you never were fond of new ideas. Well, are we in business or aren't we?'

Basta stared at the tin soldier until Meggie hid him behind her back. 'Very well!' he growled. 'But I shall check what you've been scribbling every day, understand?'

How are you going to do that, thought Meggie, when you can't read? Basta looked at her as if he had heard her thoughts. 'I know one of the maids,' he said. 'She'll read it to me, so don't try any tricks, right?'

'Of course not!' Fenoglio nodded energetically. 'Oh yes, and a pen would be a good idea too. A black one if possible.'

Basta brought the pen and a whole stack of white typing paper. Fenoglio sat down at the table with a purposeful look, put the first sheet of paper in front of him, folded it and then tore it neatly into nine parts. He wrote five letters on each piece. They were ornate, barely legible, and always the same. Then he carefully folded these notes, spat once on each, handed them to Basta and told him to hide them as he told him. 'Three where she sleeps, three where she eats, and three where she works. Then, after three days and three nights, the desired effect will set in. But should the accursed woman find even one of the notes, the magic will instantly turn against *you*.'

'What's that supposed to mean?' Basta stared at Fenoglio's notes as if they would strike him with plague on the spot.

'Best to hide them where she won't find them!' was all that Fenoglio replied as he propelled Basta towards the door.

'If it doesn't work, old man,' growled Basta before he closed the door behind him, 'I shall decorate your face to match Dustfinger's.' Then he was gone, and Fenoglio leaned against the closed door with a satisfied smile.

'But it won't work!' whispered Meggie.

'So? Three days are a long time,' replied Fenoglio, sitting down at the table again. 'And I hope we shan't need that long. After all, we want to prevent an execution tomorrow evening, don't we?'

He spent the rest of the day alternately staring into space and writing like a man possessed. More and more of the white sheets were covered with his large handwriting, scrawled impatiently over the paper. Meggie didn't disturb him. She sat by the window with the tin soldier, looking at the hills and wondering exactly where Mo was hiding among all the branches and leaves there. The tin soldier sat beside her, his leg stretched straight out in front of him, looking with fear in his eyes at the world that was so entirely new to him.

Perhaps he was thinking of the paper ballerina he loved so much, or perhaps he wasn't thinking at all. He said not a single word.

46

Woken in the Dead
of Night

'Let us use our magic and enchantments to conjure up a
woman out of flowers.' . . . Math and Gwydyon took the
flowers of oak and broom and meadowsweet and from these
conjured up the loveliest and most beautiful girl anyone
had seen; they baptized her with the form of baptism that
was used then, and named her Blodeuedd.

'Math Son of Mathonwy', from *The Mabinogion*,
translated by Jeffrey Gantz

Night had fallen long ago, but Fenoglio was still writing.
Under the table lay the sheets of paper he had crumpled
up or torn. He had discarded many more pages than he had laid
aside, collecting those few pages very carefully, as if the words
themselves might slip off the paper. When one of the maids, a
skinny little thing, brought their supper Fenoglio hid the written sheets he had kept beneath the covers of his bed. Basta did
not return that evening. Perhaps he was too busy hiding

Fenoglio's magic charms.

Meggie did not go to bed until everything outside was so dark that she couldn't distinguish the hills from the sky. She left the window open. 'Good-night,' she whispered into the dark, as if Mo could hear her. Then she took the tin soldier and clambered up to her bed. She put the little soldier by her pillow. 'You're better off than Tinker Bell, honestly!' she whispered to him. 'Basta has her in his room because he thinks fairies bring good luck, and if we ever get out of here I promise I'll make you a ballerina just like the one in your story.'

The tin soldier said nothing in reply to that either. He just looked at her with his sad eyes, then, barely perceptibly, he nodded. Has he lost his voice too, wondered Meggie, or could he never speak? His mouth did look as if he had never once opened it. If I had the book here, she thought, I could read the story and find out, or I could try to bring the ballerina out of it for him. But the Magpie had the book. She had taken all the books away.

The tin soldier leaned back against the wall and closed his eyes. No, the ballerina would only break his heart, thought Meggie before she fell asleep. The last sound she heard was Fenoglio's pen scribbling over the paper, writing word after word as fast as a weaver's shuttle turning threads into colourfully patterned cloth . . .

Meggie did not dream of monsters that night – not even a spider scurried through her dream. Even though she dreamed of a room that appeared to be the bedroom in Elinor's house, she knew that she was at home. Mo was there, too, and so was her mother. She looked like Elinor, but Meggie knew she was the woman who had been in the net hanging beside Dustfinger in Capricorn's church. You know a great many things in dreams, often despite the evidence of your eyes. You just *know* them. She was about to sit down next to her mother on the old sofa surrounded by Mo's bookshelves when someone suddenly whispered her name. 'Meggie!' Again and again: 'Meggie!' She didn't want to hear it, she wanted the dream to go on and on, but the voice kept calling to her. Meggie recognised it. Reluctantly, she opened her eyes. Fenoglio was standing by her bed, his ink-stained fingers as black as the night beyond the open window.

'What's the matter? Let me sleep.' Meggie turned her back to him. She wanted to return to her dream. Perhaps it was still somewhere there behind her closed eyelids. Perhaps a little of its happiness still clung like gold dust to her lashes. Don't dreams in fairy tales sometimes leave a token behind? The tin soldier was still asleep, with his head sunk on his chest.

'I've finished!' Fenoglio whispered. Even with the guard's snores reverberating through the door, she couldn't ignore it.

Meggie yawned and sat up.

A thin pile of handwritten sheets of paper lay on the table in the light of the flickering candle.

'We're going to try an experiment!' whispered Fenoglio. 'Let's see whether your voice and my words can change what happens in a story. We're going to try to send the little soldier back.' He quickly picked up the hand-written sheets and put them on her lap. 'It's not the best of ideas to try the experiment with a story I didn't write myself, but that can't be helped. What do we have to lose?'

'Send him back? But I don't want to send him back!' said Meggie, horrified. 'He'll die if he goes back. The little boy throws him into the stove and he melts. And the ballerina burns up.' *Among the ashes lay the metal spangle from the ballerina's dress; it had been burned as black as coal.*

'No, no!' Fenoglio impatiently tapped the sheets of paper on her lap. 'I've written him a new story with a happy ending. *That* was your father's idea: changing what happens in stories! He just wanted to get your mother back, he wanted *Inkheart* rewritten to give her up again. But if the idea really works, Meggie – if you can change the fate of a character you read out of a book by adding new words to his story, then maybe you can change everything about it: who comes out, who goes in, how it ends, who's happy and who's unhappy afterwards. Do you understand? It's just a trial run, Meggie! If the tin soldier disappears, then believe me, we can change *Inkheart* too! I still have to work out just how, but for now, will you read this aloud. Please!' Fenoglio took the torch out from under the pillow and put it in Meggie's hand.

Hesitantly, she turned the beam on the first densely written page. Suddenly her mouth went dry. 'Does it really end well?' She ran her tongue over her lips and looked at the sleeping tin soldier. She thought she heard a tiny snore.

'Yes, yes, I've written a truly sentimental happy ending.' Fenoglio nodded impatiently. 'He moves into the toy castle with the ballerina and they live happily ever after – no melted heart, no burnt paper, nothing but their blissful love.'

'Your writing is difficult to read.'

'What? I went to endless trouble!'

'It's difficult all the same.'

The old man sighed.

'Oh, all right,' said Meggie. 'I'll try.'

Every letter, she thought, every single letter matters! Let the words echo, ring out, whisper and rustle and roll like thunder. Then she began to read.

At the third sentence the tin soldier sat bolt upright. Meggie saw him out of the corner of her eye. For a moment she almost lost the thread of the story, stumbled over a word and re-read it. After that she dared not look at the little soldier again – until Fenoglio put his hand on her arm.

'He's gone!' he breathed. 'Meggie, he's gone!'

He was right. The bed was empty.

Fenoglio squeezed her arm so hard that it hurt. 'You truly are a little enchantress!' he whispered. 'And I didn't do so badly myself, did I? No, definitely not.' He looked with some awe at his ink-stained fingers. Then he clapped his hands and danced round the cramped room like an old bear. When he finally stopped beside Meggie's bed again he was rather breathless. 'You and I are about to prepare a most unpleasant surprise for Capricorn!' he whispered, a smile lurking in every one of his wrinkles. 'I'll set to work at once! Oh yes, he'll get what he wants: you'll read the Shadow out of the book for him. But his old friend will be slightly changed! I guarantee that! I, Fenoglio, master of words, enchanter in ink, sorcerer on paper. I made Capricorn and I shall destroy him as if he'd never existed – which I have to admit would have been better! Poor Capricorn! He'll be no better off than the magician who conjured up a flower maiden for his nephew. Do you know that story?'

Meggie was staring at the place where the tin soldier had been. She missed him. 'No,' she muttered. 'What flower maiden?'

'It's a very old story. I'll tell you the short version. The long one is better, but it will soon be light. Well – there was once a magician called Gwydyon who had a nephew. He loved his nephew better than anything in the world, but his mother had put a curse on the young man.'

'Why?'

'It would take too long to tell that part now. Anyway, she cursed him. If he ever touched a woman he would die. This broke the magician's heart – must his favourite nephew be condemned to being sad and lonely for ever? No. Was he not a magician? So he shut himself up in the chamber where he worked magic for three days and three nights and made a woman out of flowers – the flowers of oak and broom and meadowsweet, to be precise. There was never a more beautiful woman in the world, and Gwydyon's nephew fell in love with her at first sight. But Blodeuedd, for that was her name, was his undoing. She fell in love with another man, and the two of them killed the magician's nephew.'

'Blodeuedd!' Meggie savoured the name like an exotic fruit. 'How sad. What happened to her? Did the magician kill her too as a punishment?'

'No. Gwydyon turned her into an owl, and to this day all owls sound like a weeping woman.'

'That's beautiful! Sad and beautiful,' murmured Meggie. Why were sad stories often so beautiful? It was different in real life. 'Right, so now I know the story of the flower maiden,' she said. 'But what does it have to do with Capricorn?'

'The point is that Blodeuedd didn't do what was expected of her. And that's our own plan: your voice and my words, beautiful, brand-new words, will see to it that Capricorn's Shadow does *not* do what's expected of him!' Fenoglio looked as pleased as a tortoise who has found a fresh lettuce leaf somewhere entirely unexpected.

'Then what exactly *is* he to do?'

Fenoglio wrinkled his brow. His satisfaction was all gone.

'I'm still working on that,' he said crossly, tapping his fore-head. 'In here. It takes time.'

Voices were raised outside – men's voices. They came from the other side of the wall. Meggie slipped quickly off her bed and ran to the open window. She heard footsteps, rapid, stumbling, fleeing footsteps – and then shots. She leaned out of the window so far that she almost fell out, but she could see nothing. The noise seemed to come from the square outside the church.

'Careful!' whispered Fenoglio, grasping her shoulders. More shots were heard. Capricorn's men were calling to each other. Their voices sounded angry and excited – oh, why couldn't she make out what they were saying? She looked at Fenoglio, her eyes full of fear. Perhaps he had been able to understand some of the shouting – words, names?

'I know what you're thinking, but it certainly wasn't your father,' he soothed her. 'He wouldn't be crazy enough to creep into Capricorn's house at night!' Gently, he drew her back from the window. The voices died away. The night became still again as if nothing had happened.

Her heart beating fast, Meggie went back to bed. Fenoglio helped her up.

'Make him kill Capricorn!' she whispered. 'Make the Shadow kill him.' Her own words frightened her, but she did not take them back.

Fenoglio rubbed his forehead. 'Yes, I suppose I must, mustn't I?' he murmured.

Meggie took Mo's sweater and held it close. Doors slammed somewhere in the house; the sound of footsteps echoed up to them. Then all was silent again. It was a *menacing* silence. A deathly silence, thought Meggie. The word kept going through her mind.

'Suppose the Shadow doesn't obey you?' she asked. 'Like the flower maiden. Then what?'

'We had better not even think of that,' replied Fenoglio slowly.

47

Alone

'Why, O why did I ever leave my hobbit-hole!' said poor
Mr Baggins bumping up and down on Bombur's back.

J.R.R. Tolkien, *The Hobbit*

When Elinor heard the shots she jumped up so fast that
she stumbled over her blanket in the dark and fell full
length in the coarse grass. It pricked her hands as she got up.
'Oh God, oh God, they've caught them!' she stammered,
groping round in the night looking for the stupid dress the boy
had stolen for her. It was so dark that she could scarcely see
her own feet. 'Oh, it serves them right,' she kept repeating to
herself. 'Why didn't they take me with them, the stupid
idiots? I could have kept watch, I'd have been on the alert.'
But when she had finally found the dress and pulled it over
her head with trembling fingers she suddenly stood still.

How quiet it was. Deathly quiet.

They've shot them, something whispered inside her. That's
why it's so quiet. They're dead. Dead as mutton. They're

lying bleeding in that square outside the house, both of them. Oh, my God! Now what? She sobbed. No, Elinor, no tears now. What use are tears? You must look for them, come on. She stumbled off. Was she going the right way?

'No, you can't come too, Elinor,' Mortimer had said. He had looked so different in the black suit Farid had stolen for him – like one of Capricorn's men, which of course was the point of the masquerade. The boy had even found him a shot-gun.

'Why not?' she had replied. 'I'll even put that silly dress on!'

'A woman would be conspicuous, Elinor! You've seen for yourself – there are never any women in the streets at night. Only the guards. Ask the boy.'

'I don't want to ask him! Why didn't he steal a suit for me too? Then I could have disguised myself as a man.'

They had no answer to that.

'Elinor, please, we need someone to stay with our things!'

'Our things? You mean Dustfinger's dirty rucksack?' She was so angry she had kicked it. How clever they'd thought themselves, but their disguise had done them no good! Who had recognised them? Basta, Flatnose, the man with the limp? 'We'll be back by dawn, Elinor, with Meggie,' Mo had said. Liar! She could tell from his voice that he didn't believe it himself. Elinor stumbled over a tree root, grabbed at something prickly, and fell to her knees sobbing. Murderers! Murderers and fire-raisers. What had she to do with people like that? She should have known better when Mortimer suddenly turned up at her door, asking her to hide the book. Why hadn't she just said no? Hadn't she thought instantly that the matchstick-eater looked like someone with the word *trouble* written all over him in red? But the book – ah, the book. Of course she hadn't been able to resist the book.

They took that stinking marten with them, she thought as she picked herself up again, but not me. And now they're dead. 'Let's go to the police!' How often she'd said that! But Mortimer had always given the same answer. 'No, Elinor, Capricorn would get Meggie well out of the way as soon as the first police officer set foot in the village. And believe me, Basta's knife is faster than all the police in the world.' As he spoke she had seen that little frown above his nose, and she knew him well enough to know what it meant.

What was she going to do? She was alone, after all.

Don't make such a fuss, Elinor, she told herself. You've always been alone, remember. Now, use your head. Whatever's happened to her father, you must help the girl – get her out of this thrice-accursed village. There's no one left but you to do it. If you don't, she'll end up as one of those timid maidservants who scarcely dare to raise their heads and whose only purpose is to clean and cook for their ghastly master. Perhaps she'll be allowed to read aloud to Capricorn now and then, when he feels like it, and then, when she's older . . . she's a pretty little thing. Elinor felt sick. 'I need a shotgun,' she whispered, 'or a knife, a big sharp knife. I'll slip into Capricorn's house with it. Who's going to recognise me in this unspeakable dress?' Mortimer had always thought she couldn't cope with the world except between the covers of a book, but she'd show him!

Just how will you do that? asked the little whispering voice inside. He's gone, Elinor, gone like your books.

She wept, so loudly that she alarmed even herself and put a hand to her mouth. A twig cracked under her feet, and the light went out behind one of the windows in Capricorn's village. She had been right. The world was a terrible place, cruel, pitiless, dark as a bad dream. Not a good place to live in. Only in books could you find pity, comfort, happiness – and love. Books loved anyone who opened them, they gave you security and friendship and didn't ask anything in return, they never went away, never, not even when you treated them badly. *Love, truth, beauty, wisdom and consolation against death.* Who had said that? Someone else who loved books, she couldn't remember the author's name, only the words. Words are immortal – until someone comes along and burns them.

She stumbled on, getting closer all the time. Pale light seeped from Capricorn's village, like milky water running into the night. Three of the murderers were standing among the vehicles in the car park with their heads together. 'Talk away!' whispered Elinor. 'Boast, why don't you, with your blood-stained fingers and black hearts – you'll be sorry yet for killing them.' Would it be better to go down straight away or wait until daylight? Both were mad ideas; she wouldn't get beyond the third house in the village. One of the three men looked round, and for a moment Elinor thought he could see her. She scrambled back, slipped, and grabbed at a branch before she lost her footing again. Then came a rustling behind her, and a hand covered her mouth before she could look round. She wanted to scream, but the fingers were pressing so hard on her lips that she couldn't utter a sound.

'So here you are. Any idea how long I've been looking for you?'

It couldn't be true. She had been so sure she would never hear that voice again.

'Mortimer!'

'Sorry, but I knew you'd scream! Come on!' Mortimer took his hand away from her mouth and gestured to her to follow him. She wasn't sure which she wanted to do most, fling her arms round his neck or hit him hard enough to hurt.

Only when the houses of Capricorn's village were almost out of sight behind the trees did he stop. 'Why didn't you stay at the camp? Staggering round here in the dark – have you any idea how dangerous it is?'

This was too much. He had walked so fast that Elinor was still gasping for breath. 'Dangerous?' In her fury she found it difficult to keep her voice down. 'You're a fine one to talk about danger! I thought you were both dead! I thought they'd stabbed you or shot you or . . .'

He rubbed a weary hand over his face. 'Some of them are pretty poor shots,' he said. 'Luckily.'

His calm tone made Elinor want to shake him. 'Really? And what about the boy?'

'He's all right too, except for a scratch on his forehead. When they started firing the marten ran away and Farid went after him. That's when a ricochet caught him. I've left him up at the camp.'

'The marten? Is that all you can think about, that vicious, stinking animal? Tonight has aged me by ten years!' Elinor's voice was rising again, and she forced herself to lower it. 'I put on this horrible dress,' she hissed. ' And I could see you in my mind's eye, lots of blood and terrible wounds . . . oh, must you look at me like that?' she snapped. 'It's a wonder you're not both dead. I should never have listened to you. We should have gone to the police. This time they must believe us, they—'

'It was bad luck, Elinor, that's all,' Mo interrupted.

'Honestly. It just happened to be Cockerell on guard outside the house. The others wouldn't have recognized me.'

'And what about tomorrow? Perhaps it'll be Basta or Flatnose then. How's it going to help your daughter if you're dead?'

Mo turned his back to her. 'But I'm not dead, Elinor,' he said evenly. 'And I'm going to get Meggie out of there before she has to play the leading role at an execution.'

When they reached their camp Farid was asleep. The bloodstained bandage Mortimer had tied round his head looked almost like the turban he had been wearing when he first appeared among the columns of Capricorn's church.

'It looks worse than it is,' Mo whispered. 'But if I hadn't held him back he'd have chased half-way round the village after that marten. And if they hadn't caught us I expect he'd have slipped into the church too, to see how Dustfinger was doing.'

Elinor only nodded and wrapped her blanket round her. It was a mild night; anywhere else it could have been called peaceful.

'How did you shake them off?' she asked.

Mortimer sat down beside the boy. Only now did Elinor see that he was carrying the shotgun Farid had stolen for him. He took it off his shoulder and put it down in the grass beside him. 'They didn't follow us for long,' he said. 'Why bother? They know we'll be back. All they have to do is wait.'

And this time Elinor would be with them, she promised herself. She never again wanted to feel as utterly deserted as she had this night. 'What are you planning to do next?' she asked.

'Farid's idea was to start a fire. I thought that would be too dangerous, but we're running short of time.'

'Fire?' Elinor felt as if the word would burn her tongue. Ever since she had found the ashes of her books, the mere sight of a matchstick had caused her to panic.

'Dustfinger's taught the boy something about handling fire, and anyway, as we know, even the biggest fool can start one. If we were to send Capricorn's house up in flames—'

'Are you crazy? Suppose it spreads to the hills?'

Mo bowed his head and stroked his hand over the barrel of the gun. 'I know,' he said, 'but I can't see any other way. The fire will create a diversion, Capricorn's men will be kept busy putting it out, and in all the confusion I'll try to get through to Meggie while Farid releases Dustfinger.'

'You're mad!' This time Elinor couldn't help her voice rising. Farid muttered something in his sleep, put his hand nervously to the bandage round his head, then turned over.

Mo straightened the boy's blanket and leaned back against the tree trunk. 'That's our plan, all the same, Elinor,' he said. 'Believe me, I've been racking my brains till I thought I'd go crazy. But there's no other way. And if none of that is any use I'll set fire to his damn church as well. I'll melt down his gold and reduce his whole damned village to dust and ashes, but I'll have my daughter back.'

Elinor had no answer to that. She lay down and pretended to be asleep even though she couldn't sleep a wink. When day dawned, she persuaded Mortimer to get a little rest himself while she kept watch. Before long he was fast asleep. As soon as his breath sounded peaceful and regular, Elinor took off the stupid dress, got into her own clothes, combed her tousled hair and wrote him a note. *Gone to get help. Back around midday. Please don't do anything until then. Elinor.*

She put the note into his half-opened hand, so that he would see it as soon as he woke up. As she tip-toed past the boy she saw that the marten was back. He was curled up beside Farid, licking his paws. His black eyes stared at Elinor as she bent over the boy to adjust his bandage. Uncanny little beast, she could never take to him, but Farid loved him like a dog. Sighing, she straightened up. 'Look after them both, will you?' she whispered, then set off. The car was still where she had hidden it under the trees. It was a good hiding-place; the branches hung so low that she missed the car herself at first. The engine caught immediately. Elinor listened anxiously to the sounds of the morning for a moment, but there was nothing to be heard apart from the birds greeting the day as exuberantly as if it were their last.

The nearest village, the last village through which she and Mortimer had driven, was scarcely half an hour's drive away. There was sure to be a police station there.

48

The Magpie

But they woke him with words, their cruel, bright weapons.
T.H. White, *The Book of Merlin*

It was still quite early when Meggie heard Basta's voice out in the corridor. She hadn't touched the breakfast one of the maids brought them. When she had asked what had happened last night, what the shots meant, the girl had just stared at her, terrified, shook her head and scurried out of the door. She probably thought Meggie was a witch.

Fenoglio hadn't eaten any breakfast either. He was writing. He wrote and wrote without stopping, filling sheet after sheet of paper, tearing up what he'd written, beginning again, putting one sheet aside and starting another, frowning, crumpling up the paper – and starting once more. Hours and hours passed like this, until there were only three sheets of paper he hadn't torn up. Just three. At the sound of Basta's voice he hastily hid them under his mattress, kicking the crumpled pieces of paper under the bed with his foot. 'Quick, Meggie!

Help me get them under the bed!' he whispered. 'He mustn't find any – not a single one.' Meggie obeyed, but all she could think about was why Basta was here. Was he going to tell her something? Did he want to see her face when he told her not to expect Mo any more?

Fenoglio had sat down at the table again in front of a blank sheet of paper and was rapidly scribbling a few words on it when the door opened.

Meggie held her breath as if that would hold back the words which were about to come out of Basta's mouth and stab her in the heart. Fenoglio put down his pen and went to stand beside her. 'What is it?' he asked.

'I'm to fetch her,' said Basta. 'Mortola wants to see her.' He sounded angry, as if it were beneath his dignity to carry out such a trivial task.

Mortola? The Magpie? Meggie looked at Fenoglio. What did this mean? But the old man only shrugged his shoulders, at a loss.

'This little pigeon's to take a look at what she's to read this evening,' Basta explained. 'So she won't stumble over the words like Darius and spoil everything.' He beckoned impatiently to Meggie. 'Come on.'

Meggie took a step towards him but then stopped. 'First, I want to know what happened last night,' she asked. 'I heard shots.'

'Oh, that!' Basta smiled. His teeth were almost as white as his shirt. 'I've an idea your father was planning to visit you, but Cockerell wouldn't let him in.'

Meggie stood there as if rooted to the spot. Basta took her arm and pulled her roughly away with him. Fenoglio tried to follow them, but Basta slammed the door in his face. Fenoglio called something after her, but Meggie couldn't hear what it was. There was a rushing sound in her ears as if she were listening to her own blood running far too fast through her veins.

'He managed to get away, if that makes you feel any better,' said Basta, shoving her towards the staircase. 'Not that that means much, come to think of it. When Cockerell shoots at the cats, they seem to dodge the bullets too. He's such a useless shot. But they're usually found dead in a corner somewhere later.'

Meggie kicked his shin with all her might, and raced away down the stairs, but Basta soon caught up with her. His face distorted with pain, he grabbed her by the hair and hauled her back in front of him. 'Don't you try that again, sweetheart!' he hissed. 'You can think yourself lucky you're the main attraction at our festivities this evening, or I'd wring your skinny little neck here and now.'

Meggie did not try it again. Even if she had wanted to she wouldn't have had the chance. Basta kept hold of her hair, pulling her along behind him as if she were a disobedient dog. The pain brought tears to Meggie's eyes, but she kept her face turned away so that Basta couldn't see them. He took her down to the cellars. She hadn't been in this part of Capricorn's house before. The ceiling was even lower than the one in the shed where she, Mo and Elinor had first been imprisoned. The walls were whitewashed, like the walls in the upper storeys of the house, and there were just as many doors. Most of them looked as if it was a long time since they'd been opened, and heavy padlocks hung in front of some of them. Meggie thought of the safes Dustfinger had talked about, and the gold Mo had brought tumbling into Capricorn's church. They didn't get him, she thought. Of course not. The man with the limp doesn't shoot well. Basta said so himself.

At last, they stopped outside a door. It was made of different wood from the other doors down here, wood with a beautiful grain like a tiger's coat that shimmered with a tinge of red under the naked electric bulbs that lit the cellars.

'And let me tell you,' Basta whispered to Meggie before he knocked on the door, 'if you're as impertinent to Mortola as you are to me she'll sling you in one of those nets in the church until you're so hungry you'll be gnawing at the ropes. Compared to her heart, mine's as soft as a little girl's cuddly toy.' His peppermint-scented breath wafted into Meggie's face. She would never again be able to eat anything smelling of peppermint.

The Magpie's room was large enough to hold a dance in. The walls were red, like the walls in the church, but you couldn't see much of them. They were covered with photographs in gold frames, photographs of houses and people crammed close together on the walls like a crowd in a space too small for it. In the middle, framed in gold like the photos but much larger, hung a portrait of Capricorn. Even Meggie could see that whoever had painted it was no more skilled at his trade than the sculptor who had carved the statue in the church. Capricorn's features in the picture were rounder and softer than in real life, and his curiously feminine mouth lay like a strange fruit below the nose, which was a little too short and broad. It was only his eyes that the painter had caught perfectly. As cold as they were in the flesh, they looked down on Meggie like the eyes of a man examining a frog he is about to slit open to see what it looks like inside. No face, she had learned in Capricorn's village, is as terrifying as a face without pity.

The Magpie sat, curiously rigid, in a green velvet armchair directly below her son's portrait. She looked unaccustomed to sitting down – like a constantly busy woman who resented having to stop, but whose body forced her to rest. Meggie saw that the old woman's legs were swollen above her ankles. They bulged formlessly below her bony knees. Noticing her glance, the Magpie pulled her skirt well down over those knees.

'Have you told her what she's here for?' She found standing up difficult. Meggie watched her support herself with one hand on a little table, her lips pressed together. Basta seemed to enjoy her frailty; a smile played round his mouth until the Magpie looked at him, wiping it away with a single icy glance. Impatiently, she beckoned Meggie over. Basta prodded her in the back when she didn't move.

'Come here. I want to show you something.' With slow but firm steps, the Magpie walked over to a chest of drawers that looked much too heavy for its gracefully curved legs. Two lamps stood on it, their shades patterned with flowery tendrils. Between them was a wooden casket, decorated all the way round with a pattern of tiny holes. When the Magpie opened its lid Meggie flinched back. Two snakes, thin as lizards and not much longer than Meggie's lower arm, lay in the casket.

'I always keep my room nice and warm so that this pair don't get too sleepy,' explained the Magpie, opening the top drawer of the chest and taking out a glove. It was made of stout black leather, and was so stiff that she had difficulty forcing her gnarled hand into it. 'Your friend Dustfinger played a nasty trick on poor Resa when he asked her to look for that book,' she continued, reaching into the box and grasping one of the snakes firmly behind its flat head.

'Come here!' she ordered Basta, and held the wriggling

snake out to him. Meggie saw from his face that everything in him felt revulsion, but he came closer and took the creature. He held the scaly body well away from him as it wound and twisted in the air.

'As you see, Basta doesn't care for my snakes!' said the Magpie, with a smile. 'He never did, not that that means much. As far as I know Basta doesn't like anything but his knife. He also believes that snakes bring bad luck, which of course is pure nonsense.' Mortola handed Basta the second snake. Meggie saw the viper's tiny poison fangs when it opened its mouth. For a moment, she almost felt sorry for Basta.

'Well, don't you think this is a good hiding-place?' asked the Magpie, reaching into the casket yet again. This time she brought out a book. Meggie would have known what book it was even if she hadn't recognised the coloured jacket. 'I've often kept valuables in this casket,' continued the Magpie. 'No one knows about it and its contents apart from Basta and Capricorn. Poor Resa searched high and low for this book – she's a brave creature – but she didn't get as far as my casket. As it happens, she likes snakes. I've never met anyone who feels less fear of them than Resa, although she's been bitten now and then, isn't that so, Basta?' The Magpie took off her glove and looked scornfully at him. 'Basta likes to use snakes to scare women who reject his advances. It didn't work with Resa. How did it go exactly – didn't she finally put the snake outside *your* door, Basta?'

Basta did not reply. The snakes were still twisting and turning in his hands. One of them had wound its tail around his arm.

'Put them back in the casket,' the Magpie ordered. 'But be

careful not to hurt them.' Then she returned to her armchair with the book. 'Sit down!' she said, pointing to the footstool beside her.

Meggie obeyed. Surreptitiously, she looked around her. Mortola's room reminded her of a fairy-tale treasure chest filled to the brim. But there was too much of everything – too many golden candlesticks, too many lamps, rugs, pictures, vases, china ornaments, silk flowers, gilded bells.

The Magpie looked at her smugly. In her plain black dress she sat there like a cuckoo that has forced its way into another bird's nest. 'A fine room for a domestic servant, don't you think?' she said with satisfaction. 'Capricorn knows how to value me.'

'But he still makes you live in the cellar!' replied Meggie. 'Even though you're his mother.' If only words could be swallowed – caught and slipped quickly back between your lips.

The Magpie looked at her with such hatred that Meggie almost felt the woman's bony fingers on her throat. But Mortola just sat there, her birdlike eyes looking fixedly at Meggie. 'Who told you that? The old sorcerer?'

Meggie clamped her lips together and looked at Basta. He probably hadn't heard a word; he was just putting the second snake back in the casket. Did he know Capricorn's little secret? Before she could wonder about that any more Mortola put the book on her lap.

'A word about this to anyone here, or indeed anywhere else,' hissed the Magpie, 'and I personally shall prepare your next meal. A little extract of monkshood, a few shoots of yew or perhaps a couple of hemlock seeds in the sauce, how do you fancy that? I can assure you you'd find it a hard meal to digest. Now, start reading.'

Meggie stared at the book on her lap. When Capricorn held it up in the church she hadn't been able to make out the picture on the jacket. Now she had a chance to see it at close quarters. There was a landscape in the background that looked like a slightly different version of the hills surrounding Capricorn's village. But the foreground showed a heart, a black heart surrounded by red flames.

'Go on, open it!' snapped the Magpie.

Meggie obeyed. She opened the book at the page beginning with the N and the horned marten perched on it. How long ago was it since she had stood in Elinor's library looking at the same page? An eternity, a whole lifetime?

'Wrong page. Go on,' the Magpie told her. 'Find the page with the corner turned down.'

Wordlessly, Meggie obeyed. There was no picture on that page or the one opposite it. Without thinking she smoothed the corner out with her thumbnail. Mo hated to see dog-eared pages.

'What's the idea? Do you want to make it difficult for me to find the place again?' hissed the Magpie. 'Begin with the second paragraph, but mind you don't read aloud. I don't want to find the Shadow here in my room.'

'How far shall I go? I mean, how far am I to read this evening?'

'How should I know?' The Magpie leaned over and rubbed her left leg. 'How long does it usually take you to read your fairies and tin soldiers and so forth out of their stories?'

Meggie lowered her head. Poor Tinker Bell. 'I can't say,' she murmured. 'It depends. Sometimes it happens soon, sometimes not until after many pages, or not at all.'

'Well, read the whole chapter, that ought to be enough!

And you can leave out the "not at all" business.' The Magpie rubbed her other leg. They were both wrapped in bandages that could be seen through the dark stockings she wore. 'What are you staring at?' she hissed at Meggie. 'Can you read me something out of a book to do my legs good? Do you know a story with a cure for old age and death in it, little witch that you are?'

'No,' whispered Meggie.

'Then don't gawp so stupidly, look at the book. Mind you notice every word. I don't want to hear you stumble once tonight, no stammering, no mispronunciations, understood? This time Capricorn is to get exactly what he wants. I shall see to that.'

Meggie let her eyes wander over the letters. She wasn't taking in a word of what she read; she could think of nothing but Mo and the shots fired in the night. But she pretended to be reading, on and on, while Mortola never took her eyes off her. Finally, she raised her head and closed the book. 'Finished,' she said.

'What, already?' The Magpie looked at her suspiciously.

Meggie did not reply. She glared at Basta. He was leaning on Mortola's armchair looking bored. 'I'm not going to read that aloud this evening,' she said. 'You shot my father last night. Basta told me. I won't read a word.'

The Magpie turned to Basta. 'What was the idea of that?' she asked angrily. 'Do you think the child will read better if you break her silly heart? Tell her you missed him and get on with it.'

Basta lowered his head like a boy caught doing wrong by his mother. 'I did tell her, well...almost,' he growled. 'Cockerell's a terrible shot. Your father didn't suffer so much as a scratch.'

Meggie closed her eyes with relief. She felt warm and wonderful. Everything was all right, or at least what wasn't all right soon would be.

Happiness made her bold. 'There's something else,' she said. Why should she be afraid? They needed her. She was the only one who could read their wretched Shadow out of the book for them, no one else could do it – except Mo, and they hadn't caught him yet. They would never catch him now, ever.

'What is it?' The Magpie smoothed her sternly pinned-up hair. What had she looked like when she was Meggie's age? Had her lips been so mean even then?

'I shall only read if I can see Dustfinger again. Before he . . .' She did not end the sentence.

'What for?'

Because I want to tell him we're going to try to save him, and because I think my mother is with him, thought Meggie, but naturally she did not say so out loud. 'I want to tell him I'm sorry,' she replied instead. 'After all, he helped us.'

Mortola's mouth twisted mockingly. 'How touching!' she said.

I only want to see her once, close to, thought Meggie. Perhaps it isn't her after all. Perhaps . . .

'Suppose I say no?' The Magpie was watching her like a cat playing with a young and inexperienced mouse.

But Meggie had been expecting that question. 'Then I shall bite my tongue!' she said. 'I shall bite it so hard that it swells right up and I won't be *able* to read aloud this evening.'

The Magpie leaned back in her chair and laughed. 'Hear that, Basta? The child is no fool!' Basta only grunted. But

Mortola studied Meggie, almost benevolently. 'I'll tell you something: yes, you can have your silly little wish. But about this evening: before you read, I want you to have a good look at my photographs.'

Meggie glanced round.

'Look at them closely. Do you see all those faces? Every one of those people made an enemy of Capricorn, and none of them was ever heard of again. The houses you see in the photographs are no longer standing either, not one of them, they have all been burnt down. Think of those photos when you're reading, little witch. Should you stumble over the words, or get any silly notions about simply holding your tongue, then your face will soon be looking out of one of these pretty gold frames too. But if you do well we'll let you go back to your father. Why not? Read like an angel tonight, and you'll see him again! I've been told that his voice clothes every word in silk and satin, turns it into flesh and blood. And that's how you are to read aloud, not uncertainly and stammering like that fool Darius. Do you understand?'

Meggie looked at her. 'I understand!' she said quietly, although she knew for certain that the Magpie was lying.

They would never let her go back to Mo. He would have to come and fetch her.

451

49

Basta's Pride and Dustfinger's Cunning

'Still, I wonder if we shall ever be put into songs or tales. We're in one, of course; but I mean: put into words, you know, told by the fireside, or read out of a great big book with red and black letters, years and years afterwards. And people will say: "Let's hear about Frodo and the Ring!" And they'll say: "Yes, that's one of my favourite stories."'

J.R.R. Tolkien, *'The Two Towers'* from
The Lord of the Rings

Basta was grumbling to himself non-stop as he escorted Meggie over to the church. 'Bite her tongue, would she? Since when has the old woman fallen for that kind of thing? And who has to take this little madam to the crypt? Basta, of course! What am I supposed to be – the only male maidservant in the place?'

'Crypt?' Meggie had thought the prisoners were still in the nets, but she could see no trace of them when she and Basta entered the church, and Basta had impatiently pushed her past the columns.

'Yes, the crypt,' he spat. 'Where we put the dead and those who soon will be. Down here. Get on with it. I've got better things to do today than baby-sit Miss Silvertongue.'

The stairs to which he was pointing were steep and led down into darkness. The treads were worn, and so uneven that Meggie stumbled at every other step. Down below it was so dark that at first she didn't realise the staircase had come to an end, and she was feeling for the next step with her foot when Basta pushed her roughly forward. 'What's the idea now?' she heard him say, with a curse. 'Why's the damn lantern out again?' A match flared, and Basta's face appeared out of the darkness.

'Visitor for you, Dustfinger,' he announced derisively as he lit the lantern. 'Silvertongue's little girl wants to say goodbye. Her father brought you into this world and his daughter will make sure you leave it again tonight. I wouldn't have let her come, but the Magpie's going soft in her old age. The child actually seems fond of you. It can hardly be your pretty face, can it?' Basta's laugh echoed unpleasantly back from the damp walls.

Meggie went up to the grating behind which Dustfinger stood. She looked at him only briefly, and then gazed over his shoulder. Capricorn's maid was sitting on a stone coffin. The lantern Basta had lit gave only a dim light, but it was enough for Meggie to recognise her face. It was the face from Mo's photograph, except that the hair surrounding it was darker now, and there was no sign of any smile.

As Meggie came closer to the grating her mother lifted her head, and was now looking at her as if nothing else in the world existed.

'Mortola let her come here?' said Dustfinger. 'That's hard to believe.'

'The girl threatened to bite her own tongue.' Basta was still standing on the stairs, playing with the rabbit's foot he wore round his neck as a lucky charm.

'I wanted to say I'm sorry.' Meggie was speaking to Dustfinger, but as she spoke she looked at her mother, who was still sitting on the stone coffin.

'What for?' Dustfinger smiled his strange smile.

'For what I must do this evening. For reading aloud from the book.' If only she could have let the two of them know Fenoglio's plan.

'Right, now you've said your piece!' barked Basta impatiently. 'Come on, the air down here could make your voice hoarse.'

But Meggie did not turn. She clung to the bars of the grating as firmly as she could. 'No,' she said, 'I want to stay a bit longer.' Perhaps she could think of some way to tell them, some apparently innocent remark. 'I read something else out of a story,' she told Dustfinger. 'A tin soldier.'

'Did you, though?' Dustfinger was smiling again. It was odd, but this time his smile seemed to her neither mysterious nor supercilious. 'Well, nothing can go wrong this evening, then, can it?'

He was looking at her thoughtfully, and Meggie tried to tell him with her eyes: We're going to rescue you. It won't work out the way Capricorn expects, believe me! Dustfinger was still looking at her, trying to understand. He raised his eyebrows enquiringly, and then turned to Basta.

'And how's that fairy, Basta?' he asked. 'Still alive, is she, or has your company done for her?'

Meggie saw her mother get up and come towards her, walking tentatively, as if she were treading on broken glass.

'She's still alive,' said Basta sullenly. 'Tinkling all the time. I can't get a wink of sleep. If she carries on like that I'm going to tell Flatnose to wring her neck, the way he does the pigeons when they poo on his car.' Meggie saw her mother take a piece of paper from the pocket of her dress and surreptitiously press it into Dustfinger's hand.

'That would mean at least ten years' bad luck for you both,' said Dustfinger. 'Take my word for it – I know about fairies. Oh, watch out, what's that in front of you?'

Basta leaped back as if something had bitten his toes. Quick as a flash, Dustfinger's hand came through the grating and gave Meggie the note.

'Dammit, there's nothing there!' swore Basta. 'Don't try that again, you hear me?' He turned just as Meggie's fingers were closing round the paper. 'A note, eh? Well, well!'

Meggie tried in vain to keep her hand closed, but it was easy enough for Basta to prise her fingers apart. Then he stared at her mother's tiny writing.

'Read it, go on!' he growled, holding the note in front of her eyes.

Meggie shook her head.

'Read it!' Basta's voice was dangerously low. 'Or do you want me to carve a pretty pattern on your face like your friend's here?'

'Go on, read it, Meggie,' said Dustfinger. 'He knows I like a good drop of wine anyway.'

'Wine?' Basta laughed. 'You wanted the child to get you some wine? How did you think she'd do that?'

Meggie stared at the real note. She concentrated on every word until she knew it by heart.

Nine years are a long time. I celebrated all your birthdays. You're even lovelier than I imagined you.

She heard Basta laughing.

'Just like you, Dustfinger!' he said. 'You think you could drown your fears in drink, but a whole cask of wine wouldn't be enough for that.'

Dustfinger shrugged his shoulders. 'It was worth a try.'

Perhaps he looked a little too pleased when he said that, for Basta frowned and looked thoughtfully at his scarred face. 'On the other hand,' he said slowly, 'you always were a crafty dog. And there are rather a lot of letters there just for a bottle of wine. What about it, sweetheart?' He held the note in front of Meggie again. 'Are you going to read it to me now, or shall I show it to the Magpie?'

Meggie snatched the note from him so fast that she had crumpled it behind her back while Basta was still wondering where it had gone.

'Give it here, you little brat!' he hissed at her. 'Give me that note or I'll cut off your fingers.'

But Meggie retreated from him until her back was up against the grating. 'No!' she said, clinging to the bars with one hand and pushing the note through them with the other. Dustfinger caught on at once. She felt him taking the paper from her fingers.

Basta hit her in the face so hard that her head struck the grating. Immediately, a hand stroked her hair, and when she looked round, dazed, she was gazing into her mother's face. He'll notice any moment, she thought, he'll understand it all, but Basta had eyes only for Dustfinger, who was waving the

note back and forth behind the grating as if he were brandishing a worm in front of a hungry bird's beak.

'Well, how about it?' enquired Dustfinger, taking a step
back. 'Do you dare come in here with me, or would you rather
go on hitting little girls?'

Basta stood there motionless, like a child whose ears have
suddenly and unexpectedly been boxed. Then he seized
Meggie's arm and dragged her towards him. She felt something cold on her throat. She didn't have to see it to know
what it was. Her mother screamed and pulled at Dustfinger's
hand, but he only held the note higher in the air. 'I knew it!'
he said. 'What a coward you are, Basta! You'd rather put a
knife to a child's throat than venture in here. Of course if
Flatnose were here to back you up, too, with his broad back
and his great fat fists – but he isn't. Come along, you're the
one with the knife! I've got nothing but my hands, and you
know how I hate to misuse them for fighting.'

Meggie felt Basta's grip relax. The blade was no longer
pressing into her skin. She swallowed, and put a hand to her
throat. She almost expected to feel warm blood, but there was
none. Basta pushed her away so hard that she stumbled and
fell on the damp, cold floor. Then he put his hand into his
trouser pocket and brought out a bunch of keys. He was panting with rage like a man who had run too far and too fast.
Fingers trembling, he put a key into the lock of the cell.
Dustfinger watched him, his face impassive. He gestured to
Meggie's mother to step back from the grating, and retreated
himself, nimble as a dancer. You couldn't tell from his scarred
face whether he was afraid or not, but the scars looked darker than usual.

'What's that for?' he said, when Basta came into the cell

and held out his knife. 'You might as well put it away. If you kill me you'll spoil Capricorn's fun. He won't forgive you for that in a hurry.'

Yes, he *was* afraid. Meggie could hear it in his voice. The words were spilling out of his mouth a little too fast.

'Who said anything about killing?' growled Basta as he closed the cell door behind him.

Dustfinger retreated as far as the stone coffin. 'Ah, you were thinking of adding a few more decorations to my face?' He was almost whispering. There was something else in his voice now – hatred, scorn, rage. 'Don't expect it to be so easy this time,' he said softly. 'I've learned a few useful tricks since then.'

'Have you indeed?' Basta was standing barely a pace away from him. 'And what may they be? Your friend fire isn't here to help you. You don't even have that stinking marten.'

'It was words I had in mind.' Dustfinger placed a hand on the coffin. 'You see, the fairies have taught me how to lay a curse on someone. They were sorry for my cut face, and they knew how bad I am at fighting. So . . . I curse you, Basta – I curse you by the bones of the dead man lying in this coffin. I'll bet there's no old priest in it now, but someone you disposed of. Isn't that right?'

Basta did not answer, but his silence was more eloquent than any words.

'Of course. An old coffin like this makes a wonderful hiding-place.' Dustfinger caressed the cracked lid with his fingers as if trying to call the dead back to life with the warmth of his hand. 'May his spirit haunt you, Basta!' he said in a solemn voice. 'May he breathe my name in your ear at every step you take, may he—'

Meggie saw Basta's hand leap to his rabbit-foot.

'That thing won't help you!' Dustfinger's hand was still on the coffin. 'Poor Basta! Are you feeling hot already? Do your limbs begin to tremble?'

Basta lunged at him with the knife, but Dustfinger, light on his feet as he was, avoided the blade. 'Fire is faster than you, Basta!' he whispered. 'Much faster.'

'Give me the note you handed her!' Basta screamed in his face.

Dustfinger just put the note in his trouser pocket.

Meggie stood motionless as a doll. Out of the corner of her eye she saw her mother put her hand in the pocket of her dress. When she brought it out again she was holding a stone in it, a grey stone not much bigger than a bird's egg.

Dustfinger passed his hands over the lid of the coffin, then held them out to Basta. 'Shall I touch you?' he asked. 'What happens when you touch a murdered man's coffin? Tell me. You know all about such things.'

He took another step aside, like a dancer circling round his partner.

'I'll cut your filthy fingers off if you try to touch me!' yelled Basta, his face red with rage. 'Every one of them, and your tongue into the bargain.' He lunged with the knife again, cutting through the air with the bright blade, but Dustfinger avoided it. He was leaping around Basta faster and faster, ducking, retreating, advancing, but suddenly he found that his fearless dance had trapped him. He had only the bare wall behind him now, the grating cut off his retreat to the right – and Basta was coming straight at him.

At that moment Meggie's mother raised her hand. The stone hit Basta on the head. Astonished, he spun round, looked at her as if trying to remember who she was, and put his hand to his bleeding face. She never knew how Dustfinger did it, but suddenly he had Basta's knife in his hand. Basta was staring at its familiar blade in amazement, as if he couldn't grasp the fact that the faithless thing was pointing at his own chest.

'Well, how's this, then?' Dustfinger slowly brought the tip of the knife close to Basta's stomach. 'Do you feel how soft your flesh is? The human body is a fragile thing, and you can't get a new one. What is it you and your friends do to cats and squirrels? Flatnose likes describing it—'

'I don't hunt squirrels.' Basta's voice cracked. He was trying not to look at the blade, now scarcely a hand's breadth from his snow-white shirt.

'No, so you don't. I remember now. It doesn't amuse you as much as it does the others.'

Basta's face was white. All the furious red had ebbed out of it. Fear is not red. Fear is pale as a dead man's face. 'What are you going to do now?' he gasped. He was breathing hard, as if he were drowning. 'You don't think you'll get out of this village alive, do you? They'll shoot you down before you're across the square.'

'Well, I'd prefer that to a meeting with the Shadow,' replied Dustfinger. 'Anyway, none of you are very good shots.'

Meggie's mother came up to him, and mimed writing with her finger in the air. Dustfinger put his hand in his trouser pocket and gave her the note. Basta followed the paper with his eyes as if the strength of his gaze would draw it to him. Resa wrote something on it and handed it back to Dustfinger, who read what she had written, frowning. 'Wait until dark? No, I won't wait. But perhaps the girl had better stay here.'

He looked at Meggie. 'Capricorn won't harm her. After all, she's his new Silvertongue, and some time her father will try to rescue her.' Dustfinger put the note away again and ran the tip of the knife down Basta's shirt buttons. They clinked as the metal touched them. 'You go to the stairs, Resa,' he said. 'I'll finish this business off, and then we'll stroll across Capricorn's square and walk away like an innocent pair of lovers.'

Cautiously, Resa opened the cell door. She came out past the grating and took Meggie's hand. Her fingers were cold and rather rough, a stranger's fingers, but her face was familiar, although it had looked younger and less anxious in the photograph.

'Resa! We can't take her with us!' Dustfinger seized Basta's arm and forced him back against the wall. 'Her father will murder me if she gets shot out there. Now, turn round and cover her eyes, unless you want her to watch . . . .' The knife was trembling in his hand. Resa looked at him, horrified, and shook her head vigorously, but Dustfinger acted as if he didn't see her.

'You must thrust hard, Dirtyfingers!' hissed Basta as he pressed his hands against the stone behind him. 'Killing isn't easy. You have to practise to do it well.'

'Nonsense!' Dustfinger grabbed him by the jacket and held the knife under his chin, the way Basta had pulled his knife on Mo that time in the church. 'Any fool can kill. It's easy – as easy as throwing a book on the fire, breaking down a door, or frightening a child.'

Meggie began to tremble, she didn't know why. Her mother took a step back towards the grating, but when she saw Dustfinger's stony face she stopped. Then she turned, drew

Meggie's face against her breast, put her arms round her and held her tight. Her smell seemed familiar to Meggie, like something long forgotten; she closed her eyes and tried not to think of anything, not Dustfinger or the knife or Basta's white face. And then, for a terrible moment, there was only one thing in the world she wanted – to see Basta lying dead on the floor, limp as a doll thrown away, an ugly, stupid toy which always seemed a little scary.

The knife was barely a finger's breadth from Basta's white shirt, but suddenly Dustfinger plunged his hand into Basta's trouser pocket, took out the keys to the cells and stepped back. 'No, you're right, I don't know much about killing,' he said as he made his way backwards out of the cell, 'and I'm not about to learn just for you.'

A scornful smile spread over Basta's face, but Dustfinger paid no attention. He locked the barred door, took Resa's arm and led her to the stairs. ' Let go of her!' he begged, when he saw that she was still holding Meggie tightly. 'Believe me, nothing will happen to her, and we can't take her with us!'

But Resa just shook her head and put her arm round Meggie's shoulders.

'Hey, Dustfinger!' called Basta. 'I knew you couldn't do it. Give me my knife back. You don't know what to do with it anyway!'

Dustfinger ignored him. 'They'll kill you if you stay,' he told Resa, but he let go of her hand.

'Hey, you up there!' bellowed Basta. 'Help! Help! The prisoners are escaping!'

Meggie looked at Dustfinger in alarm. 'Why didn't you gag him?'

'What with, princess?' asked Dustfinger. Resa held Meggie

close and stroked her hair.

'They'll shoot you, they'll shoot you!' Basta's voice rang out. 'Hey there! Help!' he shouted again, shaking the bars of the grating.

Footsteps were heard overhead. Dustfinger swore quietly, cast Resa one last glance, then turned and ran up the worn steps. Meggie couldn't hear whether or not he got the door open at the top. She could hear nothing but Basta's shouting, and she ran back towards him, helpless but wanting to strike him through the bars, right in his bellowing face. Once again, she heard footsteps overhead, muffled cries. What were they to do? Someone came crashing down the stairs. Was Dustfinger coming back? No, it wasn't his face but Flatnose's that emerged from the darkness. Another of Capricorn's men was stumbling down the stairs behind him. He looked very young, round-faced and beardless, but he immediately pointed his gun at Meggie and her mother.

'Hello there, Basta! What are you doing behind those bars?' asked Flatnose, surprised.

'Open up, you damn fool!' snapped Basta through the grating. 'Dustfinger's gone.'

'Dustfinger?' Flatnose wiped his face on his sleeve. 'Then the lad here was right. Came to me just now and said he'd seen the fire-eater up there behind a column.'

'And you didn't give chase? Are you really as big a fool as you look?' Basta pressed his face to the bars as if he could make his way through them.

'Hey, watch what you say, right?' Flatnose came up to the grating and studied Basta with obvious pleasure. 'So that dirty-fingered fellow has outwitted you again! Capricorn won't like that.'

'Send someone after him!' roared Basta. 'Or I'll tell Capricorn it was you who let him go!'

Flatnose took a handkerchief out of his trouser pocket and noisily blew his nose. 'Oh yes? So who's behind bars, you or me? He won't get far. There are two guards in the car park, another three in the square, and his face is easy to recognise, you made good and sure of that, right?' His laughter sounded like a dog barking. 'Tell you what, I could really get used to this sight! Your face looks good behind bars. They're just the thing to stop you waving your knife about under anyone's nose.'

'Will you unlock this damn door?' bellowed Basta. 'Or I'll cut off your ugly nose. Open up!'

Flatnose folded his arms. 'Sadly, I can't,' he smirked in a mock-serious voice. 'Our dirty-fingered friend seems to have taken the keys. Or do *you* see them anywhere?' he enquired of the boy who was still pointing his gun at Meggie and her mother. When he shook his head, Flatnose grinned all over his squashed-in face. 'No, he can't see them either. Well, I suppose I'll just have to go to Mortola. Maybe she has a master key.'

'Wipe that grin off your face!' shouted Basta. 'Or I'll carve it off!'

'You don't say! I can't see your knife anywhere. Has Dustfinger stolen another one? If this goes on he'll soon have a whole collection.' Flatnose turned his back on Basta and pointed to the cell next to him. 'Shut the woman in there and guard her till I get back with the keys,' he said. 'I'll just take little Miss Silvertongue back to her room first.'

Meggie resisted as he pulled her away, but Flatnose simply picked her up and threw her over his shoulder. 'What was the girl doing down here anyway?' he asked. 'Does Capricorn know about it?'

'Ask the Magpie!' spat Basta.

'No fear!' Flatnose muttered as he marched towards the stairs with Meggie. She had time to see the boy push her mother into the other cell with the barrel of his gun, then she saw only the steps and the floor of the church and the dusty square as Flatnose carried her across it like a sack of potatoes.

'Let's hope your voice isn't as thin as you,' he grunted as he put her down on her feet outside the room. 'Or the Shadow will be rather narrow-chested if he really does turn up this evening.'

Meggie did not answer.

When Flatnose unlocked the door, she walked past Fenoglio without a word, climbed up on her bed and buried her head in Mo's sweater.

50

No Luck for Elinor

Having described the precise situation of the office, and accompanied it with copious directions how he was to walk straight up the passage, and when he got into the yard take the door up the steps on the right-hand side, and pull off his hat as he went into the room, Charley Bates bade him hurry on alone, and promised to bide his return on the spot of their parting.

Charles Dickens, *Oliver Twist*

Elinor had been driving for more than an hour before she finally reached a town with its own police station. The sea was still some way off, but the hills were lower, and vines covered the slopes rather than the undergrowth and trees that grew on the hills around Capricorn's village. It was terribly hot, even hotter than the day before, and when Elinor got out of the car she heard a distant rumble of thunder that sounded as if a great beast were lurking somewhere beyond the hills. The sky above the houses was a blue as dark as deep water – an ominous blue . . .

Don't be silly, Elinor, she told herself as she made for the pale yellow building which was the police station. There's a storm coming, that's all. Not getting as superstitious as that man Basta, are you?

There were two officers in the small police station. They had hung their uniform jackets over their chairs. Despite the big fan whirring round under the ceiling, the air was so muggy it could have been bottled.

The younger of the two men, who was broad and snub-nosed like a pug dog, laughed at Elinor when she told her story, and asked whether she looked so red in the face, perhaps, because she liked the local wine a little too much. Elinor would have tipped him off his chair if his companion hadn't calmed her down. The second officer was a tall, thin man with a melancholy expression and dark hair thinning above his forehead. 'Stop that,' he told the other policeman. 'At least let her finish her story.' He listened unmoved as Elinor told them about Capricorn's village and the Black Jackets, frowned when she started talking about fire-raising and dead roosters, and when she came to Meggie and the planned execution he raised his eyebrows. She said nothing, of course, about the book and just how the execution was to be carried out. Only two weeks ago she wouldn't have believed a word of it herself.

When she had finished, the tall man said nothing for a while. He rearranged the pencils on his desk, tidied some papers, and finally looked at her thoughtfully. 'I've heard about that village before,' he said.

'Naturally, everyone's heard of it!' mocked the other officer. 'The Devil's village, the accursed village, even the snakes avoid it. The walls of the church are painted with blood and Black Jackets, who are really ghosts and carry fire in their pockets, haunt the streets. You only have to get near them and you go up in smoke – whoosh!' He raised his hands and clapped them above his head.

Elinor looked at him icily. His colleague smiled, but then rose with a sigh, laboriously put on his jacket and signed to Elinor to follow him. 'I'm going to take a look at this,' he said over his shoulder.

'Might as well, if you've nothing better to do!' the other man called after him, laughing so uproariously that Elinor felt like going back to tip him off his chair after all. A little later she was in the passenger seat of a police car, and the road along which she had come was winding its way through the hills. Why on earth, she kept thinking, didn't I do this before? Everything will be all right now, everything. No one will be shot or executed, Meggie will get her father back and Mortimer will be reunited with his daughter. Yes, everything will be all right, thanks to Elinor! She could have sung and danced (not that she was much of a dancer, and she was sitting in a car). She had never in her life felt so pleased with herself. Now who could say she didn't know how to cope with the real world?

The policeman beside her said nothing. He just kept his eyes on the road, taking bend after bend at a speed that made Elinor's heart beat painfully fast. Occasionally, he absent-mindedly kneaded his right earlobe. He seemed to know the way, and never hesitated when the road branched or passed any turning. Elinor could not help thinking how long it had taken her and Mo to search for the village. Suddenly a disturbing thought came into her mind.

'There are quite a lot of them,' she said in an uncertain voice, just as they were taking another bend so fast that they came alarmingly close to the abyss yawning on her left. 'I mean, this Capricorn has rather a lot of men. And they're armed, even if they're not particularly good shots. Might it be a good idea to ask for reinforcements?' That was what people did in stupid films about cops and robbers – the police were always asking for reinforcements.

The policeman here with her ran his hand through his sparse hair and nodded as if he had already thought of that. 'Yes, of course,' he said, reaching for his radio. 'Reinforcements won't hurt, but they'd better keep in the background. The first thing is to ask a few questions.'

Over the radio, he asked for five men. Not many against Capricorn's Black Jackets, thought Elinor, but better than nothing, certainly better than a desperate father, a boy, and an overweight book collector.

'There it is!' she said as Capricorn's village appeared in the distance, grey and insignificant-looking amidst all the dark green.

'Yes, that's what I thought,' replied the policeman, after which he was silent again. When he just nodded to the guard in the car park Elinor simply refused to believe the worst. Only when they were standing in front of Capricorn, and he was handing her over like lost property being restored to its rightful owner, was she forced to admit to herself that nothing was going to turn out well after all. Everything was ruined now – and oh, how stupid she had been, how dreadfully stupid.

'She's spreading slander about you,' he heard the policeman tell Capricorn, avoiding Elinor's eyes. 'Something about child abduction. And there was talk of fire-raising . . .'

'All nonsense!' replied Capricorn, answering the unspoken

question in a bored voice. 'I love children – as long as they don't come too close to me. Children and business don't mix.'

The policeman nodded, and looked unhappily at his hands. 'And she said something about an execution . . .'

'Did she indeed?' Capricorn looked Elinor up and down as if amazed by such fantasies. 'Well, as you know, I have no call for anything of that nature. People do as I say without my having to resort to such drastic measures.'

'Of course,' murmured the policeman, nodding. 'Of course.'

He couldn't wait to leave. As his rapid, clipped footsteps died away Cockerell, who had been sitting on the steps, laughed. 'He has three small children, right? It ought to be compulsory for all policemen to have small children. That one was a pushover! Basta just had to stand outside the school twice. What about it – should we pay him another visit, to refresh his memory?'

Capricorn shook his head. 'I don't think that will be necessary. Let's just think what to do with our guest here. How should we deal with someone who tells such shocking lies about us?'

Elinor felt weak at the knees as he turned his colourless eyes on her. If Mortimer offered to read me into some book now, any book, she thought, I'd accept. I wouldn't even want to pick and choose.

Three or four black-clad men were standing behind her, so trying to run away was pointless. All you can do is submit to your fate with dignity, Elinor, she told herself. But reading about such a thing was much easier than doing it.

'The crypt or the sheds?' asked Cockerell, strolling up to her. The *crypt*, thought Elinor. Dustfinger said something about that. And it was nothing nice.

'The crypt? Why not? We have to dispose of her, or who might she bring here next?' Capricorn hid a yawn behind his hand. 'Very well, we'll give the Shadow a little more work to do this evening. He'll like that.'

Elinor wanted to say something – something bold and heroic – but her tongue wouldn't work. It just lay there in her mouth, numb. Cockerell had already hauled her as far as that ridiculous statue when Capricorn called him back.

'I quite forgot to ask her about Silvertongue!' he cried. 'Ask her if she happens to know where he is at the moment.'

'Well, come on, out with it!' growled Cockerell, seizing her by the nape of the neck as if to shake the answer out of her. 'Where is he?'

Elinor tightened her lips. Quick, Elinor, quick, she told herself, think of a good answer. And suddenly her tongue was working again.

'Why ask me?' she said to Capricorn, who was still sitting in his chair as pale as if he had been left in the wash too long, or the sun burning down out in the square had bleached him. 'You should know! He's dead. Your men shot him – and the boy.' Look at him, Elinor, she thought. Look him straight in the face the way you used to look at your father when he caught you with the wrong book. A few tears would come in useful too. Go on, just think of your books, all your burnt books! Think of last night, the fear, the despair – and if none of that works pinch yourself!

Capricorn was gazing at her thoughtfully.

'There!' Cockerell called to him. 'I knew we'd hit him!'

Elinor was still looking at Capricorn, a blurred sight through the veil of her false tears.

'We'll see,' he said slowly. 'My men are searching the hills for an escaped prisoner. I don't suppose you're going to tell me where they should look for the two bodies?'

'I buried them, and I'm certainly not saying where.' Elinor felt a tear running down her nose. By all the letters of the alphabet, Elinor, she told herself, there's a great actress lost in you!

'Buried them. Well, well.' Capricorn played with the rings on his left hand. He was wearing three at once, and he adjusted them, frowning, as if they had got out of line without his permission.

'That's why I went to the police,' said Elinor. 'To avenge them. And my books.'

Cockerell laughed. 'You didn't have to bury those books, right? They burned beautifully, like the very best firewood, and their pages – ah, they quivered like pale little fingers.' He raised his hands and imitated the movement. Elinor hit him in the face with all her might, and she was quite strong. Blood flowed from Cockerell's nose. He wiped it away with his hand, and looked at it as if he were surprised to see something so red coming out of him. 'Look at that!' he said, showing Capricorn his bloodstained fingers. 'You wait, she'll give the Shadow more trouble than Basta.'

When he led her away Elinor walked beside him with her head held high. Only when she saw the steep stairway disappearing into a bottomless black hole did her courage forsake her for a moment. The crypt, of course, now she remembered – the place where they put the condemned. That was what it smelled like, anyway, damp and mouldy, just as one imagines the odour of death.

At first Elinor couldn't believe her eyes when she saw

Basta's wiry figure pressed up against the iron bars. She had thought she must have misheard Cockerell's last remark, but sure enough, there was Basta shut up in the cage like an animal, with all the fear and hopelessness of a trapped beast in his eyes. Even the sight of Elinor did not cheer him. He looked straight through her and Cockerell, as if they were two of the ghosts he feared so much.

'What's *he* doing here?' asked Elinor. 'Have you taken to locking each other up now?'

Cockerell shrugged. 'Shall I tell her?' he asked Basta, who responded with nothing but the same glazed stare. 'First he let Silvertongue escape, and now Dustfinger. That's a sure way to ruin your chances with the boss, even if you do think you're his personal pet. And of course it's years since you managed to light a decent fire.' He smiled maliciously at Basta.

Signora Loredan, it's time to think about making a will, Elinor told herself as Cockerell pushed her further into the crypt. If Capricorn intends to kill his most faithful dog, he's certainly not going to stop short at you.

'Hey, you might look a bit more cheerful!' Cockerell told Basta as he fished a bunch of keys out of his jacket pocket. 'You've got two women for company now!'

Basta pressed his forehead against the grating. 'Haven't you caught the fire-eater yet?' he croaked. His voice sounded as if he had shouted himself hoarse.

'No, but the fat woman here says we did hit Silvertongue. Says he's dead as a doornail. Sounds like I winged him after all. Well, I have had plenty of practice on the cats.'

Behind the door with the grating that Cockerell unlocked for her something moved. A woman was sitting there in the dark, leaning back against something that looked suspiciously like a stone coffin. Elinor could not see the woman's face, but then the figure straightened up.

'Company for you, Resa!' called Cockerell as he pushed Elinor through the open door. 'You two can have a nice chat!'

He was laughing uproariously as he trudged away.

As for Elinor, she didn't know whether to laugh or cry. She would rather have seen her favourite niece again anywhere but here.

51

A Narrow Escape

'I don't know what it is,' answered Fiver wretchedly. 'There isn't any danger here, at this moment. But it's coming – it's coming.'

Richard Adams, *Watership Down*

Farid heard footsteps just as they were making the torches.

The torches had to be larger and more solid than those Dustfinger used in his shows, for they would have to burn a long time. Farid had already cut Silvertongue's hair with the knife Dustfinger had given him. It was short and bristly now, and at least that made Silvertongue look slightly different. Farid had also shown him the kind of earth he needed to rub on his face to darken his skin. No one must recognise them, not this time— but then he heard the footsteps

And voices: one was speaking angrily, the other laughed and called out. But they were still too far away for him to make out the words.

Silvertongue picked up the torches, and Gwin snapped at

Farid's fingers as the boy pushed him roughly into the rucksack. 'Where can we hide, Farid? Where?' whispered
Silvertongue.

'I know a place.' Farid threw the rucksack over his shoulder and led Silvertongue over to the charred wall. He climbed
over the blackened stones where there had once been a window, jumped down in the dry grass behind the wall, and
crouched low. The metal cover he now pushed aside had
buckled in the fire and was overgrown by alyssum. Its tiny
white flowers rambled like snow over the opening. Farid had
found the metal plate while he was exploring during the long
hours he spent here with the silent and ever-reserved
Dustfinger. He had jumped off the wall and noticed the hollow sound. Perhaps the space under it had originally been a
store for perishable foodstuffs, but at least once before it had
also been used as a hiding-place.

Silvertongue recoiled when he touched the skeleton in the
darkness. It looked small, scarcely big enough for an adult,
and it lay there in the cramped, underground space quite
peacefully, curled up as if it had lain down to sleep. Perhaps
it was because it looked so peaceful that Farid was not afraid
of it. If there was a ghost down here, he felt sure, it could be
only a sad, pale creature, nothing to be frightened of.

There wasn't much space when Farid drew the metal cover
across again. Silvertongue was tall, almost too tall to hide here,
but it was reassuring to have him close, even if his heart was
beating just as fast as Farid's own. The boy could feel every
single beat of it as they crouched there side by side, listening
for sounds from above.

The voices were coming closer, but it was difficult to make
them out, for the ground muffled them as if they came from

another world. Once a foot stepped on the metal cover, and Farid dug his fingers into Silvertongue's arm and wouldn't let him go until all was quiet again overhead. It was a long time before they dared trust the silence, such a very long time that once or twice Farid turned his head because he imagined that the skeleton had moved.

When Silvertongue cautiously raised the metal cover and looked out it did seem as if they really had gone. Only the grasshoppers were chirping tirelessly, and a bird, startled, flew up from the charred wall.

Whoever it was had taken everything with them: the blankets, the sweater that Farid had curled up in at night like a snail going into its shell, even the bloodstained bandages that Silvertongue had tied round the boy's forehead the night they'd been shot at.

'Never mind,' said Silvertongue, as they stood beside their cold fireplace. 'We shan't be needing our blankets tonight.' Then he ran his fingers through Farid's dark hair. 'What would I do without you, master scout, rabbit-catcher, finder of hiding-places?' he asked.

Farid stared at his bare toes and smiled.

52

A Fragile Little Thing

When she expressed a doubtful hope that Tinker Bell would be glad to see her, he said, 'Who is Tinker Bell?'

'O Peter,' she said, shocked; but even when she explained he could not remember.

'There are such a lot of them,' he said. 'I expect she is no more.'

I expect he was right, for fairies don't live long, but they are so little that a short time seems a good while to them.

J.M. Barrie, *Peter Pan*

Capricorn's men were looking for Dustfinger in the wrong place. He hadn't left the village. He hadn't even tried. Dustfinger was in Basta's house.

It was in an alley just behind Capricorn's yard, surrounded by empty houses inhabited only by cats and rats. Basta did not want neighbours. Indeed, he wanted no other company but Capricorn's. Dustfinger knew Basta would have slept on the threshold of Capricorn's room if he had been allowed to, but none of the men lived in the main house. They stood guard there, that was all. They ate in the church and slept in one or other of the many abandoned houses in the village, that was the rule and it could not be broken. Most of the men kept moving round, living in one house and going on to another when the roof began to leak. Only Basta had lived in the same place ever since they came to the village. Dustfinger suspected he had chosen that house because St John's wort grew beside the door, and there is no other plant with such a reputation for keeping away evil – leaving aside the evil in Basta's own heart.

Like most of the buildings in the village the house was built of grey stone, with black-painted shutters that Basta usually kept closed and on which he had painted the signs he believed would keep bad luck away, just like the yellow flowers of St John's wort. Sometimes Dustfinger thought Basta's constant fear of curses and sudden disaster probably arose from his terror of the darkness within himself, which made him assume that the rest of the world must be exactly the same.

Dustfinger had been lucky to make it as far as Basta's house. He had run into a whole crowd of Capricorn's men almost as soon as he stumbled out of the church. Of course they had recognised him instantly, Basta had long ago made that a certainty. But their surprise had given Dustfinger just enough time to disappear down one of the alleys. Fortunately, he knew every nook and cranny of this accursed village. He had meant to make for the car park and go on into the hills, but then he'd thought of Basta's empty house. He had forced his way through holes in walls, crawled through cellars, and ducked down behind the parapets of balconies that were no longer used. When it came to hiding, even Gwin had nothing to teach Dustfinger. A strange sense of curiosity had always driven him to explore the hidden, forgotten corners of this and any other place, and all that knowledge had now come in useful.

He was out of breath when he finally reached Basta's house. Basta was probably the only man in Capricorn's village who locked his front door, but the lock was no great obstacle to Dustfinger. He let himself in and hid in the attic until his heart had slowed down, even though the wooden planks were so rotten that he feared he would go through the floor at every step. Downstairs, he found enough food in Basta's kitchen to quell the hunger that had been gnawing like a worm at the walls of his stomach. Neither he nor Resa had been given anything to eat since they were put in those nets, so it was doubly satisfying to fill his belly with Basta's food.

When he had partially satisfied his hunger he opened one of the shutters just a crack, so that he could have warning in good time of any approaching footsteps, but the only sound that met his ears was a tinkling, so faint that he could hardly hear it. Only then did he remember the fairy that Meggie had read into this world that normally had no fairies.

He found her in Basta's bedroom. The room contained nothing but a bed and a chest of drawers on which a number of bricks lay carefully arranged side by side, all of them covered with soot. They said in the village that whenever Capricorn had a house set on fire Basta took away a brick or stone, even though he feared fire at other times, and clearly that story was true. On one of the bricks stood a glass jug with a faint light coming from it, not much brighter than a glowworm would have made. The fairy was lying at the bottom of the glass, crumpled up like a butterfly just out of the cocoon. Basta had put a plate over the top of the jug, but the fragile little thing didn't look as if she had the strength to fly.

When Dustfinger took the plate away the fairy didn't even raise her head. Dustfinger put his hand into her glass prison and carefully took the little creature out. Her limbs were so delicate he was afraid his fingers would break them. The fairies he knew had looked different, smaller but stronger, with fair blue skin and four shimmering wings. This one had skin the same colour as a human, a very pale human, and her wings were more like butterfly than dragonfly wings. But would she like the same things to eat as the fairies he knew? It was worth a try. She looked half dead.

Dustfinger took the pillow off Basta's bed and put it on the kitchen table, which was scrubbed clean. (Everything in Basta's house was scrubbed clean, as spotless as his snow-white shirt.) He laid the fairy on the pillow, then filled a dish with milk and put it on the table beside her. She immediately opened her eyes – so in having a good sense of smell and a taste for milk she seemed no different from the fairies he knew. He dipped his finger in the milk and let a white drop fall on her lips. She licked it up like a hungry little cat. Dustfinger trickled drop after drop into her mouth until she sat up and feebly beat her wings. Her face had a little colour in it now, but although he spoke three fairy languages he understood not a word of what she finally said in her faint tinkling voice.

'What a pity!' he whispered, as she spread her wings and flew, rather unsteadily, up to the ceiling. 'That means I can't ask you if you could make me invisible, or so small that you could carry me to Capricorn's festivities.'

The fairy looked down at him, tinkled something that he couldn't understand, and settled on the side of the kitchen cupboard.

Dustfinger sat down on the only chair by Basta's kitchen table and looked up at her. 'All the same,' he said, 'it's good to see someone like you again. If only the fire in this world had more of a sense of humour, and a troll or a glass man would look out of the trees now and then – well, perhaps I could get used to the rest of it after all, the noise, the speed, the crowds – and the way the nights are so much lighter . . .'

He sat there in his worst enemy's kitchen for quite a long time, watching the fairy flying round the room investigating everything, for fairies are naturally inquisitive, and this one was obviously no exception. Every now and then she stopped to sip her milk, and he filled the dish a second time. Once or twice, footsteps approached, but each time they passed by the house. What a good thing Basta had no friends. The air that came in through the window was sultry; it made Dustfinger drowsy. The narrow strip of sky showing above the houses would stay light for many hours yet – long enough for him to make up his mind whether or not to go to Capricorn's festivities.

Why should he go? He could get hold of the book later, some time when all the excitement in the village had died down and everything was back to normal. And what about Resa? What was going to happen to her? The Shadow would come for her. There was nothing to be done about that, not by anyone, not even Silvertongue if he were really so mad as to try. But Silvertongue didn't know about her, or about his daughter, and at least there was no need to worry about Meggie – not now that she was Capricorn's favourite toy. Capricorn wouldn't let the Shadow hurt *her*.

No, I won't go, thought Dustfinger, I'll hide here for a while. Tomorrow, there'll be no more Basta, that's one good thing. And perhaps I shall go away from here, go away for ever . . . No. He knew he wouldn't do that. Not while the book was here.

The fairy had flown over to the window, and was peering curiously out at the alley.

'Forget it. Stay here,' said Dustfinger. 'Please. Believe me, it's no place for you out there.'

She looked at him quizzically, then folded her wings and knelt on the windowsill. And there she stayed, as if she couldn't decide between the hot room and the strange freedom on offer outside.

53

The Right Words

*This was the shocking thing; that the slime of the pit seemed to
utter cries and voices; that the amorphous dust gesticulated and
sinned; that what was dead, and had no shape, should usurp
the offices of life.*

Robert Louis Stevenson,
The Strange Case of Dr Jekyll and Mr Hyde

Fenoglio wrote and wrote, but the number of pages he had
hidden under the mattress was no greater. He kept taking
them out, fiddling with them, tearing up one and adding
another. 'No, no, no!' Meggie heard him muttering crossly to
himself. 'No, that's not it yet.'

'It will be dark in a few hours,' she said at last, anxiously.
'Suppose you don't finish it in time?'

'I have finished!' he snapped, irritated. 'I've finished a
dozen times already, but I'm not happy with it.' He lowered
his voice to a whisper before he went on. 'There are so many
questions. Suppose the Shadow turns on you or me or the prisoners once he's killed Capricorn? And is killing Capricorn

really the only solution? What's going to happen to his men afterwards? What do I do with them?'

'What do you think? The Shadow must kill them all!' Meggie whispered back. 'How else are we ever going to get home or rescue my mother?'

Fenoglio did not like this reply. 'Good heavens, what a heartless creature you are!' he whispered. 'Kill them all! Haven't you seen how young some of them are?' He shook his head. 'No! I'm not a mass murderer, I'm a writer! I'm sure I can think of some less bloodthirsty ending.' And he began writing again . . . and crossing words out . . . and writing more, while outside the sun sank lower and lower until its rays were gilding the hilltops.

Every time steps came along the corridor Fenoglio hid what he had been writing under his mattress, but no one came in to see what the old man kept scribbling on his blank sheets of paper. For Basta was down in the crypt.

The bored guards on duty outside their door had several visitors that afternoon. Men had obviously come into the village from Capricorn's outposts to watch the execution. Putting her ear to the door, Meggie eavesdropped on their conversations. They laughed a lot, and their voices sounded excited. They were all looking forward to the night's spectacle. Not one of them seemed to feel sorry for Basta. Far from it. Knowing Capricorn's former favourite was to die that night just seemed to add to their fun. Of course they discussed Meggie too. That little witch, they called her, that little madam the enchantress, and not all of them seemed to be convinced of her powers.

As for Basta's executioner, Meggie learned no more than what Fenoglio had already told her and what she remembered of the passage that the Magpie had made her read. It wasn't much, but she heard the fear in those voices outside the door, and the horrified awe that overcame them all at the mention of his name, which was not a real name at all. Only those who, like Capricorn himself, had come out of Fenoglio's book had ever seen the Shadow – but they had all obviously heard about him – and they painted pictures in the darkest tones of the way he would deal with the prisoners. There were evidently several opinions about how he actually killed his victims, but the suggestions Meggie overheard grew more and more horrible the closer evening came, until she could bear it no longer. She went to sit by the window with her hands over her ears.

It was six o'clock – the church clock was just beginning to strike – when Fenoglio suddenly put down his pen and looked over what he had written with a satisfied expression. 'Got it!' he whispered. 'Yes, that's it. That's how it will be. It will turn out splendidly.' Impatiently, he beckoned Meggie over and gave her the paper.

'Read it!' he whispered, glancing nervously at the door. Out in the corridor, Flatnose was just boasting of the way he had poisoned a farmer's stocks of olive oil.

'Is that all?' Meggie looked incredulously at the single sheet of paper.

'Yes, that's all. No more is needed. As you'll see. The words just have to be the right ones. Go on, read it!'

Meggie did as he said.

The men outside were laughing, and she found it difficult to concentrate on Fenoglio's words. Finally, she did it. But she had no sooner finished the first sentence than the men outside fell utterly silent. The Magpie's voice echoed down the corridor. 'What's all this? A coffee morning?'

Fenoglio hastily took the precious paper and put it under his mattress. He was just readjusting the bedspread when the Magpie opened the door.

'Your supper,' she told Meggie, putting a steaming plate down on the table.

'What about me?' enquired Fenoglio in a deliberately cheerful voice. The mattress had slipped slightly when he hid the paper under it, and he had to lean against his bed to hide it from Mortola, but luckily she had no eyes for him. Meggie felt sure she thought he was merely a liar, and very likely it annoyed her that Capricorn did not agree with her.

'Eat it all up!' she ordered Meggie. 'And then get changed. Your clothes look dreadful, and stiff with dirt too.' She signalled to the maid who had come with her, a young girl at most only four or five years older than Meggie herself. The rumours of Meggie's supposed powers of witchcraft had obviously reached this girl's ears too. A snow-white dress was draped over her arm, and she avoided looking at Meggie as she made her way past her to hang it in the wardrobe.

'I don't want that dress!' Meggie spat at the Magpie. 'I want to wear this.' She took Mo's sweater off her bed, but Mortola snatched it from her hands.

'Nonsense. Do you want Capricorn to think we've been keeping you in a sack? You'll wear that dress. Either you put it on yourself or we'll put it on you. I shall come for you as soon as darkness falls. Wash your face and comb your hair. You look like a stray cat.'

The maid scurried past Meggie again, looking as frightened as if any contact might burn her. The Magpie impatiently pushed the girl out into the corridor.

'Lock the door,' she told Flatnose. 'And send your friends

away. You're supposed to be on guard.'

Flatnose strolled casually towards the door. Meggie saw him make a face at the Magpie behind her back before he closed it.

She went over to the dress and touched the white material. 'White!' she murmured. 'I don't like white things. Death has white hounds. Mo once told me a story about them.'

'Ah yes, the white, red-eyed hounds of Death.' Fenoglio came over to her. 'Ghosts are white too, and the thirst of the ancient gods for blood was quenched only by white sacrificial animals, as if the gods liked the taste of innocence best. Oh no, no!' he added quickly, seeing Meggie's terrified eyes. 'No, believe me, Capricorn certainly wasn't thinking of any such thing when he sent you that dress. How would he know such stories? White is the colour of the beginning too, and of the end. And,' he added, lowering his voice, 'remember, both you and I, Meggie, are going to make sure it is Capricorn's end and not ours.' Gently, he led Meggie to the table and made her sit down. The smell of roast meat rose to her nostrils.

'What do you think it is?' she asked.

'Looks like veal. Why?'

Meggie pushed the plate away. 'I'm not hungry,' she murmured.

Fenoglio looked at her with great sympathy. 'You know, Meggie,' he said, 'I think I ought to write a story about you next, you and how you save us all with your voice. It would be a very exciting story.'

'But would it have a happy ending?' Meggie looked out of the window. Only another hour, two at the most, and it would be dark. Suppose Mo came then? Suppose he made another attempt to free her? He didn't know what she and Fenoglio were planning. Suppose they shot at him again? Suppose they really did hit him last time? Meggie put her arms on the table and buried her face in them.

She felt Fenoglio stroking her hair. 'It will be all right, Meggie!' he whispered. 'Believe me, my stories always have happy endings. If I want them to.'

'That dress has very tight sleeves!' she whispered. 'How am I to hide the paper in my sleeve without the Magpie noticing?'

'I'll distract her attention. Don't worry.'

'But later? They'll all see me take the paper out.'

'Nonsense, you'll manage.' Fenoglio put a hand under her chin. 'It will be all right, Meggie!' he said again, wiping a tear off her cheek with his forefinger. 'You're not alone, even if you may feel you are tonight. I'm here, and Dustfinger is somewhere out there. I know him as well as I know myself, and I can assure you he'll come, if only to see the book and perhaps get it back – and then there's your father, and that boy who was looking at you in such a lovesick way back in the square in front of the memorial when I first saw Dustfinger.'

'Oh, stop it!' Meggie dug her elbow into his stomach, but she had to laugh, even though her tears were still blurring everything, the table, her hands, Fenoglio's wrinkled face. She felt as if she had used up enough tears for a whole lifetime in these last few weeks.

'Why? He's a good-looking lad. I'd put in a good word for him with your father like a shot.'

'I said stop it!'

'Only if you'll eat something.' Fenoglio pushed the plate back towards her. 'And that lady, your friend, what was her name?'

'Elinor.' Meggie put an olive in her mouth and chewed it

until she could feel the stone between her teeth.

'Exactly. Perhaps she's out there too, with your father. Good Lord, when I come to think of it we're almost in the majority.'

Meggie almost choked on the olive stone. Fenoglio smiled, pleased with himself. Mo always raised his eyebrows when he had managed to make her laugh, looking both surprised and serious as if he had no idea what she was laughing at. Meggie could see his face before her so clearly that she might almost have reached out to touch it.

'You'll soon see your father again!' whispered Fenoglio. 'And then you can tell him how you found your mother along the way and rescued her from Capricorn. That's quite something, don't you think?'

Meggie just nodded.

The dress felt scratchy on her throat and arms. It was more like a dress for a grown-up than a child, and it was rather too big for Meggie. When she took a few steps in it she trod on the hem. The sleeves fitted tightly, but she had no difficulty in pushing the sheet of paper up inside one of them; it was as thin as a dragonfly's leg. She practised a couple of times – pushing it in, pulling it out. Finally, she left it up her sleeve. It crackled slightly when she moved her hands or raised that arm.

The moon hung pale in the sky above the church tower, and the night wore a veil of moonlight when the Magpie came back to fetch Meggie.

'You haven't combed your hair!' she said crossly. This time she had another maid with her, a stocky woman with a red face and red hands who was obviously not afraid of Meggie's powers of witchcraft. She pulled the comb so brutally through Meggie's hair that she almost cried out.

'Shoes!' said the Magpie, seeing Meggie's bare toes peep out from under the hem of the dress. 'Didn't anyone think of shoes?'

'She could put those on.' The maid pointed to Meggie's worn-out trainers. 'The dress is long enough, no one will see them. Anyway, don't witches always go barefoot?'

The Magpie gave her such a look that her voice died on her lips.

'Exactly!' cried Fenoglio, who had been watching the two women get Meggie ready, with an ironic expression on his face. 'That's what they do, they always go barefoot. Do I have to change for this festive occasion too? What does one wear to attend an execution? I imagine I shall be sitting beside Capricorn?'

The Magpie stuck her chin out. It was a small, soft chin and looked as if it came from another, gentler face.

'You can stay as you are,' she said, putting a slide set with pearls in Meggie's hair. 'Prisoners don't have to change.' The mockery dripped from her voice like poison.

'What do you mean, prisoners?' Fenoglio pushed his chair back.

'I mean *prisoners*, what else?' The Magpie stepped back and looked critically at Meggie. 'That will have to do,' she said. 'It's odd, but with her hair back she reminds me of someone.' Meggie quickly lowered her head, and before the Magpie could give this observation more thought Fenoglio diverted her attention.

'But I am no ordinary prisoner, madam, let's get that quite clear!' he roared. 'Without me none of this would exist at all,

491

your own less than delightful self included.'

The Magpie cast him a final contemptuous glance and took hold of Meggie's arm, luckily not the one with Fenoglio's precious words inside its sleeve. 'The guard will come for you when it's time,' she said to Fenoglio, leading Meggie to the door.

'Remember what your father told you!' called Fenoglio when Meggie was out in the passage. 'Words don't come to life until you can taste them on your tongue.'

The Magpie nudged Meggie in the back. 'Get moving!' she said, and closed the door behind them.

54

Fire

'And then – I have it!' said Bagheera, leaping up. 'Go thou down quickly to the men's huts in the valley, and take some of the Red Flower which they grow there, so that when the time comes thou mayest have even a stronger friend than I or Baloo or those of the Pack that love thee. Get the Red Flower.'

By Red Flower Bagheera meant fire, only no creature in the jungle will call fire by its proper name. Every beast lives in deadly fear of it.

Rudyard Kipling, *The Jungle Book*

They set out when dusk fell over the hills, leaving Gwin at their camp. After what had happened on their last night-time visit to Capricorn's village, even Farid could see it was better that way. Silvertongue made him go first. He knew nothing of the boy's fear of ghosts and other nocturnal terrors. Farid had hidden it from him more successfully than he had from Dustfinger. Silvertongue did not mock his fear of the dark either, as Dustfinger had, and curiously enough that made the fear less, shrinking it as only daylight usually did. But now Farid was going to use something else that Dustfinger thought him too foolhardy to handle.

Fire. They had decided to start a fire next to Capricorn's house, so that it would not spread to the hills so fast but would threaten the only thing Capricorn cared about: his treasure chambers.

This time, the village was not quiet and empty as it had been on the previous nights, but was buzzing like a wasps' nest. Four armed guards were patrolling the car park, and cars were parked all round the wire-netting fence that surrounded the former football field. Their headlights bathed the area in glaring light, as if a bright cloth had been spread out in the dark.

'So that's where the show's to take place,' whispered Silvertongue as they approached the houses. 'Poor Meggie.'

A kind of rostrum had been set up in the middle of this arena with a cage opposite it, perhaps for the monster that Silvertongue's daughter was to read out of the book, perhaps for the prisoners. On the left-hand side of the field, facing away from the wire fence and the village, stood long wooden benches. A few of the Black Jackets were already sitting on them, like ravens that had found a bright, warm place to spend the night.

They had thought of stealing into the village from the car park. With so many strangers around, perhaps no one would notice them. But then they decided on a longer, darker route. Farid went ahead again, using every tree as cover, always keeping uphill from the houses until they were above the uninhabited part of the village that looked as if a giant had trodden on it. Even there, more guards than usual were patrolling. They had to keep retreating into the shadows of a gateway, ducking down behind a wall, or climbing through a window and waiting with bated breath for the guard to pass by. Luckily there were many dark corners in Capricorn's village, and the guards strolled through the alleys with an air of boredom, as men do when they are sure there is no threat of danger.

Farid had Dustfinger's rucksack with him, containing all they would need to kindle a quick, hot fire. Silvertongue carried the wood they had collected, in case the flames did not find enough to feed on among the stones. And there were Capricorn's stocks of petrol too. Farid still had the smell of it in his nostrils from the night when they had shut him up in the sheds. The tanks were seldom guarded, but they might not need them. It was a windless night; the flames would burn quietly and steadily. Farid remembered Dustfinger's warning: 'Never light a fire when it's windy. The wind will catch hold of it and it will forget you, it will fan the flames until they leap up and bite you and lick the skin from your bones.' But the wind was sleeping tonight, and still air filled the alleyways, like warm water in a bucket.

They had hoped to find the square outside Capricorn's house empty, but as they were about to enter it from one of the alleys they saw half a dozen men standing outside the church.

'Why are they still here?' whispered Farid, as Silvertongue drew him into the shadow of a doorway. 'The festivities are about to begin.'

Two maids came out of Capricorn's house, each with a pile of plates. They were taking them to the church. Obviously the successful execution was to be celebrated there later. When the maids passed the guards the men whistled at them. One of the women almost dropped the crockery when one of them tried to lift her skirt with the barrel of his gun. It was the man who had recognised Silvertongue when they slipped into the village the night before. Farid touched his forehead, which was still bloodstained, and cursed him with the worst curses he knew. Why did *he* have to be the one there? But even if they got past him unrecognised, how were they going to start a fire while the others were still standing around?

'Take it easy!' Silvertongue whispered to him. 'They'll soon go away. The first thing we have to do is make sure Meggie really has left the house.'

Farid nodded, looking at the big house. There were still lights on in two of the windows, but that didn't necessarily mean anything. 'I'll sneak down to the football field and see if she's there,' he whispered to Silvertongue. Perhaps they had already fetched Dustfinger from the church, perhaps he was in the cage they had set up, and he could whisper to him that they had brought his best friend, fire, to save him.

Night shadows filled many of the nooks and crannies among the houses, despite the brightness of the street lights. Farid was about to set off, using their shelter, when the door of Capricorn's house opened. The old woman with a face like a vulture came out. She was dragging Silvertongue's daughter along behind her. Farid hardly recognised Meggie in the long white dress she wore. After them, gun in hand, came the man who had shot at him and Silvertongue. He looked round, took a bunch of keys from his pocket, locked the door, and beckoned to one of the men standing outside the church. He was obviously telling him to guard the house. So only one man would stay on guard when the others went off to see the show.

Farid felt Silvertongue tensing every muscle – as if he wanted to run to his daughter, who looked almost as pale as her dress. The boy clutched his arm in a warning gesture, but Silvertongue seemed to have forgotten him. He had eyes only for the girl. One reckless step and he would be out of the shelter of the shadows.

'Don't!' Farid pulled him back in alarm – as best he could, for he scarcely came up to Silvertongue's shoulder. Luckily, Capricorn's men were watching the old woman as she crossed the square, walking so fast the girl stumbled over the hem of her dress a couple of times.

'She looks so pale!' whispered Silvertongue. 'Heavens, do you see how frightened she is? Perhaps she'll look this way, perhaps we can give her a signal—'

'No!' Farid was still hanging on to him with both hands. 'We must start the fire. That's the only way we can help her. Please, Silvertongue – they'll see you!'

'Don't keep calling me Silvertongue. It gets on my nerves.'

The old woman disappeared among the houses with Meggie. Flatnose was following them, lumbering like a bear in a black suit, and at last the other men left too. They went down the street, laughing, looking forward to what the night promised them: death spiced with fear, and the appearance of a new terror in this accursed village.

Only the guard outside Capricorn's house was left. He watched the others go, his face gloomy as he kicked an empty cigarette packet and struck the wall with his fist. He was the only one who was going to miss the fun. Even the guard at the top of the church tower could at least watch the show from a distance.

They had expected a guard to be posted outside the house.

Farid had explained the best way to get rid of him, and Silvertongue had nodded and agreed to the plan. When the footsteps of Capricorn's men had died away and they could hear nothing but the noise from the direction of the car park, they moved out of the shadows, acting as if they had only just emerged from the alley, and openly approached the guard side by side. He looked at them suspiciously, pushed himself away from the wall against which he had been leaning, and took the gun from his shoulder. Alarmed, Farid involuntarily put his hand to his forehead, but at least the guard was not one of the men who might have recognised them, not the man with the limp, or Basta, or any of Capricorn's other personal henchmen.

'Hey, lend us a hand!' called Silvertongue, ignoring the gun. 'Those fools forgot Capricorn's armchair. We've been sent to fetch it.'

The guard was holding his gun in front of his chest. 'Oh, for heaven's sake! That thing's so heavy it'd break your back. Where are you from?' He scrutinised Silvertongue's face, as if trying to remember whether he had seen it before. He took no notice of Farid at all. 'You from the north, then? I heard you have a lot of fun up there.'

'That's right.' Silvertongue went so close to the guard that the man took a step back. 'Come on, you know Capricorn doesn't like to be kept waiting.'

The guard nodded sullenly. 'Yes, yes, all right,' he muttered, looking over to the church. 'There's no point standing guard here anyway. What do they think will happen? Do they expect the fire-eater to come and steal the gold? That fellow was always lily-livered, he'll be well away by now, he—' But suddenly, while the guard was still looking at the church,

Silvertongue seized the gun and hit him on the head with the butt. Then he dragged him round behind Capricorn's house where it was pitch dark.

'Did you hear what he said?' Farid had quickly gagged the guard and was expertly tying a rope round the man's legs. 'Dustfinger must have escaped! He said "he'll be well away". He can't have meant anyone else!'

'Yes, I heard. But my daughter is still here.' Silvertongue gave him the rucksack and looked round, but the square was now so deserted and quiet it was as if they were the only people left in Capricorn's village. Not a sound was heard from the guard up in the church tower. No doubt tonight he had eyes for nothing but the events taking place on the brightly lit football field.

Farid took two torches and the bottle of inflammable liquid from Dustfinger's rucksack. He got away, he was thinking, he got away! He could almost have laughed out loud.

Silvertongue went back to Capricorn's house, peered into several windows, and finally broke one of them, taking off his jacket and pressing it against the glass to muffle the sound when it broke. Laughter and music drifted up from the car park.

'The matches! I can't find them!' Farid rummaged among Dustfinger's things until Silvertongue took the rucksack from his hand.

'Give it to me!' he whispered. 'You get the torches ready.'

Farid did as he was told. He carefully soaked the cotton wool in the acrid-smelling spirits. Dustfinger will come back, he thought, he'll come back to look for Gwin, and then he'll fetch me. Voices came from one of the alleys. Men's voices. For a few terrible moments they seemed to be coming closer, but they died away again, swallowed up by the music coming from the car park and filling the night like a foul smell.

Silvertongue was still looking for the matches. 'Ugh!' he said, swearing softly and removing his hand from the rucksack. Marten droppings were smeared over his thumb. He wiped them off on the nearest wall, put his hand in the rucksack again and threw Farid a box of matches. Then he took something else out – the little book that Dustfinger kept in a side pocket he had sewn inside. Farid had often looked at it. It had pictures stuck in it, cut-out pictures of fairies and witches, trolls and dragons, brownies, nymphs and ancient trees. Silvertongue flicked through it while Farid was soaking the second torch. A photograph was lying between the pages – the photograph of Capricorn's maid, the woman who had tried to help Dustfinger and was to die for it tonight! Or had she escaped with him? Silvertongue was staring at the photograph and suddenly it was as if nothing else in the world existed.

'What's the matter?' Farid put the match to the dripping torch. The flame flared up, hissing and hungry. How beautiful it was! Farid licked his finger and passed it through the flame. 'Here, take this.' He held the torch out to Silvertongue. It would be best for him, as the taller of them, to throw it through the window. But Silvertongue just stood there gazing at the photo.

'That's the woman who helped Dustfinger,' said Farid. 'The one they caught too. I think he's in love with her. Here.' Once again he held the burning torch out to Silvertongue. 'What are you waiting for?'

Silvertongue looked at him as if he had been woken from a dream. 'In love . . . in love,' he murmured as he took the torch from Farid's hand. Then he put the photograph in the breast pocket of his shirt, cast another glance at the empty square, and threw the torch through the broken window into Capricorn's house.

'Give me a leg up! I want to see it burning!'cried Farid. Silvertongue did as he asked. The room seemed to be some kind of office. Farid saw paper, a desk, a picture of Capricorn on the wall. Someone here could write after all. The burning torch lay among the sheets of paper covered with writing, it licked and gulped, it whispered with delight at such a feast, flared up and leaped on, from the desk to the curtains at the window. Greedily, it consumed the dark fabric. The whole room was filled with red and yellow. Smoke billowed out of the broken window, stinging Farid's eyes.

'I must go!' Silvertongue put him down abruptly. The music had stopped. Suddenly it was eerily quiet. Silvertongue ran off along the street leading down to the car park. Farid watched him go. He had something more to do. He waited until the flames were shooting out of the window, then he began shouting. 'Fire! Capricorn's house is on fire!' His voice echoed over the empty square.

Heart thudding, he ran to the corner of the big house and looked up at the church tower. The guard there had leaped to his feet. Farid lit the second torch and threw it at the church porch. The air began to smell of smoke. The guard froze, turned, and – at last – he rang the bell.

And Farid ran off to follow Silvertongue.

55

Treachery, Loose Talk, and Stupidity

Then he said, 'Without a doubt, I must perish; there is no way I can get out of this narrow prison.'

Tales from the Thousand and One Nights

Elinor thought she was showing considerable courage. Of course she still did not know exactly what fate awaited her – and if her niece knew more than she did, she hadn't told her – but she could be sure it would be nothing pleasant. Nor did Teresa give the men who came to take them up from the crypt the satisfaction of seeing her shed tears. She couldn't curse them or shout at them anyway; her voice was gone, like a garment she no longer wore. Luckily, she had two pieces of paper with her, crumpled, dirty scraps, much too small for all the words unspoken over nine years. She had filled the paper with tiny writing until there wasn't space for a single word more. She didn't want to say anything about herself and what had happened to her, and just waved Elinor's whispered questions impatiently away. There were questions of her own she wanted to ask, question after question about her daughter and her husband. Elinor whispered the answers into her ear, very quietly so Basta in the adjoining cell would not realise that the two women who were about to die with him had known each other ever since the younger one had learned to walk holding on to Elinor's endless bookshelves.

Basta was not in a good way. Whenever they looked at him they saw his hands clinging to the bars, knuckles white under his sun-tanned skin. Once, Elinor thought she heard him weeping, but when they were taken out of the cells his face was as vacant as a dead man's, and when their guards locked them up in that unspeakable cage he crouched on the floor in a corner, and sat as motionless as a doll that no one wants to play with.

The cage smelled of dogs and raw meat, and indeed it did look like a dog pound. Several of Capricorn's men ran the butts of their shotguns along the silvery grey bars before sitting down on the benches that had been made ready for them. Basta in particular was the object of enough scorn and derision for ten men, and from his failure to react at all one could only guess at the depths of his despair. All the same, Elinor and Teresa kept as far away from him as they could in the same cage. They also kept away from the bars, from all the fingers poking through, the faces the men made at them, and the burning cigarettes flicked at them. They stood close together, both glad and sorry to be with one another.

On the outskirts of the arena, right beside the entrance and carefully segregated from the men, sat the women who worked for Capricorn. They showed none of the men's ghastly excitement. Most of their faces were downcast, but again and again their glances strayed to Resa with expressions of pity – and dread.

Capricorn arrived when the long benches were full. There were no seats for the boys, so they squatted on the ground in front of the Black Jackets. His face emotionless, Capricorn strode past them all as if they were nothing but a flock of crows that had assembled at his command. Only in front of the cage containing his prisoners did he slow his pace to examine each of the three with a small, satisfied glance. For the fraction of a second, life came back into Basta as his former lord and master stopped by the bars; he raised his head, his eyes pleading silently, like a dog begging for forgiveness, but Capricorn walked on without a word. When he had seated himself in his black leather armchair Cockerell placed himself behind it, legs planted wide apart. Obviously, he was the new favourite now.

'For heaven's sake, stop looking at him like that!' Elinor snapped at Basta when she realised that his eyes were still following Capricorn. 'He's planning to feed you to his friend like a fly to a frog, so how about a little indignation? You were always so ready with a choice selection of threats: "I'll cut your tongue out, I'll slice you to pieces . . ." What's happened to all that, then?'

But Basta only bowed his head and stared at the floor beneath his boots. Elinor thought he looked like an oyster with the flesh and life sucked out of it.

When Capricorn was sitting down the blaring music fell silent, and they brought Meggie forward. They had put a horrible dress on her, but she held her head high, and the old woman whom they all called the Magpie had difficulty dragging her up on to the rostrum which the Black Jackets had set up in the middle of the field. A single chair stood on the rostrum, looking as forlorn as if someone had left it there and forgotten it. Elinor thought a gallows and a rope would have looked more suitable. Meggie looked down at them as the Magpie forced her up the wooden steps.

'Hello, darling!' called Elinor when Meggie's frightened gaze recognised her. 'Don't worry, I'm only here because I didn't want to miss hearing you read!'

Everything had fallen so still on Capricorn's arrival that her voice echoed over the whole arena. It sounded brave and fearless. Fortunately, no one could hear how hard her heart was hammering against her ribs. Nor did anyone notice that she was almost choking with fear, for Elinor had put on her armour, the impenetrable and extremely useful armour behind which she had always hidden at times of need. It had become a little harder with every grief she felt, and lately there had been grief enough in Elinor's life.

One of the Black Jackets laughed at her words, and a faint smile even flitted over Meggie's face. Elinor put her arm round Teresa's shoulders and held her close. 'Look at your daughter,' she whispered. 'As brave as . . . as . . .' She wanted to compare Meggie to a hero from some story, but all the heroes she could think of were men, and anyway none of them seemed to her brave enough for a comparison with the girl standing there perfectly straight, scrutinising Capricorn's Black Jackets with her chin jutting defiantly.

The Magpie had brought not only Meggie but an old man. Elinor guessed that this was the writer who had caused them so much trouble – Fenoglio, the creator of Capricorn, Basta and all the other monsters, including the terrible creature Meggie was to bring to life tonight. Elinor had always thought more of books than their authors, and she looked at the old man without much goodwill as Flatnose led him past their cage. There was a seat ready for him only a little way from Capricorn's armchair. Elinor wondered whether that meant Capricorn had found a new friend, but when Flatnose placed himself behind the grim-faced old man she concluded that Fenoglio was more likely a prisoner himself.

Capricorn rose as soon as the old man was seated. Without a word, he let his gaze pass slowly over the long line of his men, as if recalling every one of them, remembering what good and what bad service each had done him. The silence in the arena smelled of fear. All the laughter had died away, and not a whisper could be heard.

'There is no need,' Capricorn finally began, raising his voice, 'for me to explain to most of you why the three prisoners you see here are to be punished. For the rest, it is enough for me to say it is for treachery, loose talk, and stupidity. One may argue, of course, over whether or not stupidity is a crime deserving of death. I think it is, for it can have exactly the same consequences as treachery.'

As he said this there was a restless stir on the benches. At first Elinor thought Capricorn's words had set it off, but then she heard the bell. Even Basta raised his head as its tolling sounded through the night. At a sign from Capricorn, Flatnose beckoned to five men and strode off with them. Those left behind put their heads together uneasily, and some even jumped up and turned to look at the village. However, Capricorn raised his hand to quell the murmur that had arisen. 'It is nothing!' he called in so loud and cutting a tone that everything immediately fell still again. 'A fire, that's all. And we know how to deal with fire, don't we?'

There was laughter, but some of the crowd, both men and women, were still looking anxiously at the houses.

So they'd done it. Elinor bit her lips so hard that they hurt. Mortimer and the boy had started a fire. No smoke yet showed above the rooftops, and, reassured, all the faces turned back to Capricorn who was saying something about deceit and falsehood, discipline and negligence, but Elinor only half heard him. She kept looking at the houses of the village, though she knew it was dangerous to do so.

'So much for the prisoners we have here!' cried Capricorn. 'Now for those who got away.' Cockerell picked up a sack that had been lying behind Capricorn's chair and gave it to him. Smiling, Capricorn put his hand into it and held something up: a piece of fabric from a shirt or dress, torn and blood-stained.

'They are dead!' called Capricorn to his audience. 'I'd rather have seen them here, of course, but unfortunately there was nothing for it: they were trying to escape and had to be shot. Well, no one will miss the treacherous little fire-eater – almost all of you knew him – and fortunately Silvertongue has left us his daughter, who has inherited his gifts.'

Teresa looked at Elinor, her eyes glazed with horror.

'He's lying!' Elinor whispered to her, although she too could not take her eyes off the bloodstained rags. 'He's using my lies, my tricks! That's not blood, it's paint, or some kind of dye.' But she saw that her niece did not believe her. She believed in the bloodstained cloth, just as her daughter did. Elinor could read this on Meggie's face, and she longed to call out to her that Capricorn was lying, but she wanted him to believe his own story for a little longer – to believe that they were all dead, and no one would come to disturb his festivities.

'That's right, boast of a bloodstained rag, you miserable fire-raiser!' she shouted through the bars. 'That's really something to be proud of. Why do you need another monster? You're all monsters! Every one of you sitting there! You murder books, you abduct children . . . !'

No one took any notice of her. A couple of the Black Jackets laughed. Teresa moved closer to the bars, clutching their cold metal with her fingers, never taking her eyes off Meggie.

Capricorn left the bloodstained fabric lying over the arm of his chair. I know that rag, thought Elinor. I've seen it somewhere before. They're not dead. Who else would have started the fire? The matchstick-eater, something inside her whispered, but she refused to listen. No, the story must have a happy ending. It wouldn't be right otherwise! She had never liked sad stories.

56

The Shadow

My heavens are brass my earth is iron my moon a clod of
clay
My sun a pestilence burning at noon & a vapour of death
in the night.

William Blake, *Enion's Second Lament*

In books hatred is often described as hot, but at Capricorn's
festivities Meggie discovered it was cold – an ice-cold hand
that stops the heart and presses it like a clenched fist against
the ribs. Hatred made her freeze, in spite of the mild air waft-
ing around her telling her that the world was a good, safe place.
She knew it was *not* – as the bloody cloth on which the smiling Capricorn had laid his ringed hand showed all too clearly.

'Well, so much for that!' he cried. 'And now for the real
reason we are all gathered here tonight. Not only are we about
to punish the traitors but we're also going to celebrate a
reunion with an old friend. Some of you may remember him,
and as for the others, I promise that once you have met him
you will never forget him.'

Cockerell twisted his thin face into a sour smile. He was obviously not looking forward to the reunion and, at Capricorn's words, alarm showed on several other faces.

'But that's enough talking. Now let's hear something read aloud to us.'

Capricorn leaned back in his chair and nodded to the Magpie. Mortola clapped her hands, and Darius came hurrying across the arena with the casket that Meggie had last seen in the Magpie's room. He clearly knew what it contained. His face was even more haggard than usual as he opened the casket and held it out to the Magpie, his head bowed humbly. The snakes seemed to be drowsy, and this time Mortola did not put on a glove before she lifted them out. She even draped them over her shoulders while she took the book out of its hiding-place. Then she put the snakes back as carefully as if they were precious jewels, closed the lid, and handed the casket back to Darius. He stayed on the rostrum, looking awkward. Meggie caught him looking sympathetically at her as the Magpie made her sit down on the chair and placed the book on her lap.

Here it was again, the unlucky thing, in its brightly coloured paper jacket. What colour was the binding under it? Raising the dust-jacket with her finger, Meggie saw the dark red cloth, as red as the flames surrounding the ink-black heart. Everything that had happened had begun between the pages of this book, and only the words of its author could save them now. Meggie stroked its binding as she always did before opening a book. She had seen Mo doing the same. Ever since she could remember she had known that movement – the way he would pick up a book, stroke the binding almost tenderly, then open it as if he were opening a box full to the brim with precious things. Of course, the marvels you hoped to find might not be waiting inside the covers, so then you closed the book, sorry that its promise had not been kept. But *Inkheart* was not a book of that kind. Badly told stories never come to life. There are no Dustfingers in them, not even a Basta.

'I am told to tell you something!' The Magpie's dress smelled of musty lavender, its fragrance enveloping Meggie in a suffocating threat. 'Should you fail to do what Capricorn asks, should it occur to you to stumble over the words on purpose, or distort them so that the guest Capricorn is expecting does not come, then . . .' Mortola paused and Meggie felt the old woman's breath on her cheek, 'then Cockerell will cut the old man's throat. Capricorn may not give the order himself, because he believes the stupid lies the old man told him, but I don't, and Cockerell will do as I say. Understand me, my little cherub?' She pinched Meggie's cheek with her bony fingers. Meggie shook off her hand and looked at Cockerell. He moved up behind Fenoglio, smiled at her, and ran a finger across the old man's throat. Fenoglio pushed him away, and looked at Meggie as if one look could convey everything he wanted to say to her and give her: encouragement, comfort, and maybe even a little amusement in the face of all the horrors surrounding them.

Whether or not their plan worked depended on him and his words – and Meggie's reading.

Meggie felt the paper in her sleeve, scratching her skin. Her hands seemed like the hands of a stranger as she leafed through the pages of the book. The place where she was to begin was no longer marked by a folded corner. A bookmark as black as charred wood lay between the pages. 'Push your hair back from your forehead,' Fenoglio had told her. 'That will be the signal to me.' But just as she raised her left hand the crowd on the benches became restless again.

Flatnose was back, with soot marks on his face. He hurried to Capricorn's side and whispered something to him. Capricorn frowned and looked towards the houses. Now Meggie saw two plumes of smoke rising into the sky from behind the church tower.

Capricorn rose quickly from his chair. He tried to sound composed, ironic, like a man amused at some childish prank, but his face told a different story. 'I am sorry to have to spoil the fun for a few more of you, but tonight the red rooster is crowing here too. A feeble little rooster, but its neck must be wrung all the same. Flatnose, take another ten men back with you.' Flatnose obeyed and marched off with his reinforcements. The benches now looked a good deal emptier. 'And don't any of you show your faces back here before you've found the fire-raiser!' Capricorn called after them. 'Whoever it is, we'll teach him not to start fires in the Devil's own domain – we'll teach him a lesson, right here and now!'

Someone laughed, but most of those who had stayed behind were looking uneasily in the direction of the village. Some of the maids had actually risen to their feet, but the Magpie called their names in a sharp voice, and they were quick to sit back down with the others, like schoolchildren unfairly slapped on the hand. Nonetheless, the restlessness persisted. Scarcely anyone was looking at Meggie, almost all the members of her audience had turned their backs to her, and were pointing at the smoke and whispering to one another. A red glow was creeping up the church tower, and grey smoke formed a dense cloud above the rooftops.

'What is all this? Why are you staring at that little wisp of smoke?' There was no missing the anger in Capricorn's voice now. 'A bit of smoke, a few flames – so what? Are you going to let that spoil our festivities? Fire is our best friend, have you forgotten?'

Meggie saw the doubting faces turn back towards him. Then she heard a name. Dustfinger. A woman's voice had called it out.

'What does that mean?' Capricorn's voice was so sharp that Darius almost dropped the casket of snakes. 'There is no Dustfinger any more. He's lying up there in the hills with his mouth full of earth and that marten of his on his breast. I never want to hear his name again. He is forgotten as if he had never been—'

'That's not true.'

Meggie's voice rang out over the arena so loud and clear that she herself was alarmed. 'He's here!' She held up the book. ' Never mind what you do to him. Everyone who reads this story will see him – you can even hear his voice, and see the way he laughs and breathes fire.'

All went perfectly quiet. A few feet scraped uneasily on the red clinkers of the old football field – then, suddenly, Meggie heard something behind her. It was a ticking like the sound of a clock, yet not quite the same; it sounded like a human tongue imitating a clock: *tick-tick, tick-tick, tick-tick.*

The sound was coming from among the cars parked behind the wire fence with their dazzling headlights on. Meggie couldn't help it – she looked round, in spite of the Magpie and all the suspicious eyes turned on her. She could have kicked herself for being so stupid. Suppose they had seen it too – the thin figure rising among the cars and quickly ducking down again. But no one seemed to have noticed her glance any more than the ticking.

'A very fine speech!' said Capricorn slowly. 'But you're not here to make funeral orations for dead traitors. You're here to read aloud, and I am not going to tell you so again.'

Meggie forced herself to look at Capricorn. She mustn't look at the cars again. Suppose that really had been Farid? Suppose she hadn't imagined the ticking?

The Magpie was watching her suspiciously. Perhaps she had heard it too, that soft, harmless ticking, nothing but a tongue clicking against someone's teeth. What did it mean, unless you knew the story of Captain Hook and his fear of the crocodile with the ticking clock inside it? The Magpie wouldn't have read it, but Mo knew that Meggie would understand his signal. He had woken her up often enough with that ticking sound, right beside her ear, so close that it tickled. 'Breakfast time, Meggie!' he used to whisper. 'The crocodile's here!'

That was it. Mo knew she would recognise the ticking that helped Peter Pan to go aboard Captain Hook's ship and rescue Wendy. He couldn't have given her a better signal.

Wendy, thought Meggie. What had happened next? For a moment she almost forgot where she was, but the Magpie reminded her. She slapped Meggie's face with the flat of her hand.

'Start reading, will you, little witch!' she hissed.

And so Meggie obeyed.

Hastily, she removed the black bookmark from the pages where it lay. She must hurry, she must read before Mo did anything silly. He didn't know what she and Fenoglio were planning.

'I'm going to start now, and I don't want anyone disturbing me!' she cried. '*Anyone*! Is that understood?' Oh please, let

Mo understand, she thought, please!

A few of Capricorn's remaining men laughed, but Capricorn himself leaned back and folded his arms in anticipation. 'Yes, just you take heed of what the girl said!' he called. 'Anyone who disturbs her will be given to the Shadow to welcome him here.'

Meggie put two fingers up her sleeve. There they were, Fenoglio's words. She looked at the Magpie. 'Well, *she's* disturbing me!' she said out loud. 'I can't read with her standing so close behind me.'

Capricorn gestured impatiently to the Magpie. Mortola's face looked sour, as if he had told her to eat a bar of soap, but she took two or three reluctant steps back. That would have to do.

Meggie raised her hand and pushed the hair back from her forehead.

The signal for Fenoglio.

He instantly launched into his performance. 'No, no, no! She's not to read!' he cried, moving towards Capricorn before Cockerell could stop him. 'I can't allow it! I am the author of this story, and I didn't write it to be misused for purposes of violence and murder!'

Cockerell tried to put his hand over Fenoglio's mouth, but Fenoglio bit his fingers and side-stepped him with more agility than Meggie would ever have expected of the old man.

'I invented you!' he bellowed as Cockerell chased him round Capricorn's chair. 'And I'm sorry I did, you stinking devil of a villain.' Then he ran off. Cockerell didn't catch up with Fenoglio until he reached the cage containing the prisoners, and in revenge for the mockery and laughter coming from the benches he twisted the old man's arm behind his back so viciously that Fenoglio let out a cry of pain. Yet when Cockerell dragged him back to Capricorn's side Fenoglio was looking quite pleased, because he knew he had given Meggie plenty of time. They had rehearsed it often enough. Her fingers had been shaking as she took the sheet of paper out of her sleeve, but no one noticed anything when she slipped it into the pages of the book. Not even the Magpie.

'How the old man boasts!' cried Capricorn. 'Do I look as if an old fellow like that invented me?'

There was more laughter. The smoke above the rooftops seemed to have been forgotten. Cockerell put his hand over Fenoglio's mouth.

'Once again, and I hope this will be the last time,' said Capricorn to Meggie, 'start reading! The prisoners have waited long enough for their executioner.'

Silence fell again, and once more it smelled of fear.

Meggie bent over the book on her lap. The letters seemed to dance on the pages.

Come out, thought Meggie, come out and save us! Save us all: Elinor and my mother, Mo and Farid. Save Dustfinger if he's still alive, and save Basta too for all I care.

Her tongue felt like a little animal that had found refuge in her mouth, and was now butting its head against her teeth.

'*Capricorn had many men,*' she began. '*And every one of them was feared in the surrounding towns and villages. They stank of cold smoke, they stank of sulphur and everything that reminds you of fire. Whenever one of them passed by, people closed their doors and hid under the stairs with their children. They called them Firefingers and Bloodhounds; Capricorn's men had many names. They were feared by day, and by night they made their way into dreams and poisoned them. But there was one who*' *was feared even more than Capricorn's villains.'* Meggie felt as if her voice was growing stronger with every word she read. It seemed to grow until it filled the arena. *'Folk called him the Shadow.'*

Two more lines at the bottom of the page, then turn it over. Fenoglio's words were waiting. 'Look at this, Meggie!' he had whispered when he showed her the sheet of paper. 'What an artist I am, eh? Is there anything in the world better than words on the page? Magic signs, the voices of the dead, building blocks to make wonderful worlds better than this one, comforters, companions in loneliness. Keepers of secrets, speakers of the truth . . all those glorious words.'

Taste every word, Meggie, whispered Mo's voice inside her, savour it on your tongue. Do you taste the colours? Do you taste the wind and the night? The fear and the joy? And the love. Taste them, Meggie, and everything will come to life. *'Folk called him Capricorn's Shadow.'* How the *sh* hissed as it passed her lips, how darkly the sound of the *'o'* formed in her mouth.

'He came only when Capricorn called him,' she read. *'Sometimes he was red as fire, sometimes grey as the ash to which fire turns all that it devours. He darted out of the earth as fast as flames lick their way up wood. His fingers and even his breath brought death. He rose before his master's feet, soundless, faceless, scenting his way like a hound on the trail and waiting for his master to point to the victim. It was said that Capricorn had commanded one of the trolls who understand the whole art of fire and smoke to create the Shadow from the ashes of his victims. No one was sure, for it was also said that Capricorn had ordered those who called the Shadow to life to be killed. All that everyone knew was that he was immortal, invulnerable and pitiless, like his master.'*

Meggie's voice died away as if the wind had blown it from her lips.

Something was rising from the gravel that covered the football pitch. It grew taller, it stretched its ashen limbs. The night air suddenly stank of sulphur. That stench burned Meggie's eyes so that the letters blurred, but she must go on reading while the eerie creature grew taller and taller.

'Yet one night, a mild and starlit night, the Shadow heard not Capricorn's voice when it was called forth, but the voice of a girl, and when she called his name he remembered; he remembered all those from whose ashes he was made, all the pain and all the grief—'

The Magpie reached over Meggie's shoulder. 'What's this? What are you reading?' But Meggie jumped up and backed away before the old woman could snatch the sheet of paper from her. 'He remembered,' she read on in a loud, clear voice, 'and he determined to be avenged – avenged upon those who were the cause of all this misfortune, whose cruelty poisoned the whole world.'

'Make her stop!'

Was that Capricorn's voice? Meggie almost fell off the rostrum as she tried to keep away from the Magpie. Darius stood there, staring at her in astonishment, the casket in his hands. Then suddenly but deliberately, as if he had all the time in the world, he put down the casket and wrapped his thin arms firmly around the Magpie from behind. Nor did he let go, no matter how hard she struggled and cursed. And Meggie read on as the Shadow stood, watching her. The figure had no face, that was true, but it had eyes, terrible eyes, red as the embers of a hidden fire.

'Get the book away from her!' shouted Capricorn. He was standing in front of his chair, bent double as if he feared his legs would refuse to obey him if he took so much as a step towards the Shadow. 'Get it away from her!'

But none of his remaining men moved, none of the boys and none of the women came to his aid. They had eyes for nothing but the Shadow as he stood there listening to Meggie's voice, as if she were telling him a long-forgotten tale.

'*Indeed, he wanted revenge,*' Meggie read on. If only her voice weren't shaking so much, but it wasn't easy to kill, even if someone else was going to do it for her. '*So the Shadow went to his master, and reached out to him with ashen hands . . .*'

How soundlessly it moved, that terrible, gigantic figure!

Meggie stared at Fenoglio's next sentence. *And Capricorn fell down on his face, and his black heart stopped beating*— She couldn't say it. She couldn't. It had all been in vain.

Then, suddenly, someone else was standing behind her. She hadn't even noticed him climbing up on to the rostrum. The boy was there too, holding a shotgun aimed at the benches – but no one sitting there stirred. No one so much as lifted a finger to save Capricorn. And Mo took the book from Meggie's hands, ran his eyes over the lines Fenoglio had added, and in a firm voice read to the end of what the old man had written.

'*And Capricorn fell down on his face, and his black heart stopped beating, and all those who had gone burning and murdering with him disappeared – blown away like ashes in the wind.*'

57

A Deserted Village

In books I meet the dead as if they were alive,
in books I see what is yet to come . . .
All things decay and pass with time . . .
all fame would fall victim to oblivion
if God had not given mortal men the book to aid them.

Richard de Bury, *The Philobiblon*

So Capricorn died, just as Fenoglio had written, and
Cockerell disappeared at the same moment as his master
fell to the ground, and with him more than half the men left
on the benches. The rest ran away, all of them, the boys and
women too. Those heading towards the village met some of
Capricorn's men running back from extinguishing the fire.
Their faces were smeared with soot and full of horror, and not
because of the flames that had been licking around Capricorn's
house, for they had put these out. No. They had seen Flatnose
and several other men vanish into thin air before their very
eyes. They were *gone*, as if the darkness had swallowed them
up, as if they had never existed. And perhaps that was the

truth of it. The man who had made them had now destroyed them, erased them like mistakes in a drawing, like marks on white paper. They were *gone*, and the others, the men who had not been born of Fenoglio's words, were hurrying back to tell Capricorn what had happened. But Capricorn lay on his face with gravel clinging to his red suit, and never again would anyone tell him anything – about fire and smoke, about fear and death. Never again.

Only the Shadow still stood there, a figure so tall that the men running across the car park saw him from afar, grey before the black night sky, his eyes two blazing red stars, and they forgot the master they had been going to serve. Every one of them ran for the cars. They wanted only to get away, far away, before the being who had been summoned like a dog turned and devoured them all.

Meggie did not come to her senses properly until they had all gone. She had nestled her head under Mo's arm, as she always did when she simply didn't want to see the world. Mo put the book under the jacket which had almost made him look like one of Capricorn's henchmen. And he held her tight while all about them people were running and screaming. Only the Shadow stood perfectly still, as if killing his master had sapped all his power.

'Farid,' Meggie heard Mo say, 'can you get that cage open?'

Only then did she bring her head out from under Mo's arm, and saw that the Magpie was still there. Why hadn't she disappeared too? Darius was still holding on to her as if he were afraid of what would happen if he let go. But she was no longer kicking and struggling. She was just looking at Capricorn, with tears running down her sharp-boned face, over her small soft chin, and falling like rain on her dress.

Agile as Gwin, Farid jumped down from the rostrum and ran over to the cage, without once taking his eyes off the Shadow. However, the Shadow just stood there frozen, as if he would never move again.

'Meggie,' whispered Mo. 'Let's go over to the prisoners, shall we? Poor Elinor looks exhausted, and there's someone else I want to introduce to you.' Farid was already busy with the door of the cage, but the two women inside were watching them.

'You don't need to introduce her,' said Meggie, squeezing his hand. 'I know who she is. I've known for ages. I wanted so much to tell you, but you weren't here, and now there's something else we have to read first. The last few sentences.' She took the book out from under Mo's jacket and leafed through it until she found Fenoglio's sheet of paper still among the pages. 'He wrote them on the other side, there wasn't any space left on the first page,' she said. 'He just can't make his handwriting small.'

Fenoglio!

Meggie lowered the sheet of paper and looked round, searching for him, but she couldn't see him anywhere. Had Capricorn's men taken him with them, or—?

'Mo, he's gone!' she said, dismayed.

'I'll go and look for him in a moment,' Mo reassured her. 'But now read the rest, quick! Or shall I do it?'

'No, I will.'

The Shadow was beginning to move again. He took a step towards the dead Capricorn, staggered back and turned as clumsily as a dancing bear. Meggie thought she heard a groan. Farid ducked down behind the cage when the red eyes looked his way. Her mother and Elinor flinched, too, but Meggie read in a firm voice:

'*There stood the Shadow, and his memories hurt so much that they almost tore him apart. He heard them in his head, all those screams and sighs, he thought he could feel tears on his grey skin. Their fear burned his eyes like smoke. Then, quite suddenly, he felt something different, something that made him shudder and forced him to his knees. Then his whole terrible figure disintegrated, and suddenly they were all back again, all the beings from whose ashes the Shadow had been made: men, women and children, dogs and cats, brownies, fairies, and many others as well.*'

Meggie saw the arena filling up with them. More and more of them were gathering in a throng where the Shadow had collapsed, all looking around as if they'd just woken from a deep sleep. She read Fenoglio's last sentence.

'*They woke as if from a bad dream and then, at last, everything was all right again.*'

'He isn't here any more!' said Meggie when Mo took Fenoglio's sheet of paper from her and put it back in the book. 'Fenoglio's gone, Mo! He's in the story now. I know he is.'

Mo looked at the book and tucked it back under his jacket. 'Yes, I think you're right,' he said. 'But if so, there's nothing we can do about it for the moment. Perhaps the story now goes on beyond the book.' He led Meggie away with him down from the rostrum, past all the people and the strange creatures crowding into the arena outside Capricorn's village as if they had always been there. Darius followed them. He had finally let go of the Magpie, who was now standing with her bony hands gripping the back of the chair where Meggie had been sitting. She was weeping soundlessly, her face crumpled, as if her whole being were made of tears.

A tiny, blue-skinned fairy apologised profusely when it fluttered into Meggie's hair as she and Mo went towards the cage containing her mother and Elinor. Then a shaggy creature who looked half human, half animal stumbled across her path, and finally she almost trod on a tiny little man who seemed to be made entirely of glass. Capricorn's village had acquired some strange new inhabitants.

Farid was still trying to get the lock open when they reached the cage. He was picking at it, looking angry, and muttering something to the effect that Dustfinger had shown him just how to do it and this must be a very special sort of lock.

'Oh, wonderful!' said Elinor sarcastically, pressing her face to the bars from inside. 'So the Shadow didn't eat us after all, but we'll be left to starve in a cage. Well, well! What do you think of your daughter, Mo? Isn't she a brave little thing? I couldn't have uttered a word myself, not a single word. My God, my heart almost stopped when that old woman tried to get the book away from her.'

Mo put his hand on Meggie's shoulder and smiled, but he was looking at someone else. Nine years are a long, long time.

'I've done it! I've done it!' cried Farid, pulling the door of the cage open. But before the two women could take a step, a figure rose in the darkest corner of their prison, leaped towards them, and seized the first person he could lay his hands on – Meggie's mother.

'Wait!' spat Basta. 'Stop, stop, not so fast. Where are you off to, then, Resa? To join your beloved family? You think I didn't understand all that whispering down in the crypt? Well, I did.'

'Let go of her!' cried Meggie. 'Let go of her!' Why hadn't

she noticed the dark heap lying so still in the corner? She had just assumed Basta was as dead as Capricorn. And indeed, why wasn't he? Why hadn't he disappeared like Flatnose and Cockerell and all the others?

'Let her go, Basta!' Mo spoke very quietly, as if he had no strength for anything else. 'You won't get out of here, even by using her as a shield. No one will help you. They're all gone.'

'Oh, I'll get out!' replied Basta unpleasantly. 'I shall choke her if you don't let me pass. I'll break her scrawny neck. Did you know she can't talk? She can't make a sound because that useless Darius read her out of the book. She's as silent as a fish, a pretty, mute fish. But if I know you, you'll want her back all the same, am I right?'

Mo made no reply, and Basta laughed.

'Why aren't you dead?' Elinor shouted at him. 'Why didn't you fall down dead like your master, or vanish? Why not?'

Basta merely shrugged. 'How should I know?' he growled, keeping his hand round Resa's neck. She tried to kick him, but he only tightened his grip. 'After all, the Magpie's still here too, but she always made other people do her dirty work for her, and as for me – perhaps I'm one of the good characters in the story now because they put me in the cage? Perhaps I'm still here because it's a long time since I set fire to anything, and Flatnose got much more fun out of killing people? Perhaps, perhaps, perhaps . . . but anyway here I am, so let me pass, you old book-bag!'

But Elinor did not budge.

'No,' she said. 'You don't get out of here until you let her go! I'd never have expected this story to have a happy ending, but it has – and a creature like you isn't going to spoil that at the last moment, as sure as my name's Elinor Loredan!'

Looking very determined, she placed herself in front of the cage door. 'You don't have your knife with you this time,' she went on in a dangerously soft voice. 'You have nothing but your filthy tongue, and believe you me, that'll be no use to you now. Poke your fingers into his eyes, Teresa! Kick him, bite him, the beast!'

But before Teresa could do as she said Basta thrust her away from him so violently that she fell against Elinor and brought her down – her and Mo, for both of them had been coming to her aid. As for Basta, he raced for the open door of the cage, pushed the startled Farid and Meggie aside – and ran away past all the people and creatures still wandering like sleepwalkers around the scene of Capricorn's festivities. Before Farid or Mo could give chase he had disappeared.

'Oh, great!' muttered Elinor, stumbling out of the cage with Teresa. 'Now that wretched fellow will haunt me in my dreams, and every time I hear something rustling out in my garden at night I shall feel his knife at my throat.'

Not only had Basta gone, but the Magpie also disappeared without trace that night. And when, wearily, they set off to find a vehicle of some kind to get them away from Capricorn's village, they found that all the cars had gone too. Not a single one was left in the car park, which was dark now.

'Oh no, tell me it isn't true!' groaned Elinor. 'Does this mean we have to go the whole wretched way on foot again?'

'Unless you happen to have a mobile phone with you,' said Mo. He had not moved from Teresa's side since Basta had made his escape. He had looked with concern at her neck, where the red marks left by Basta's fingers were still visible, and he had run a strand of her hair through his fingers and said he almost liked it better now it was darker. But nine years are a long time, and Meggie saw how careful they were with each other, like people on a narrow bridge crossing a wide, wide void.

Of course Elinor did not have her mobile. Capricorn had had it taken away from her, and although Farid immediately offered to go and search Capricorn's fire-blackened house for it, it did not turn up. So they finally decided to spend one last night in the village, along with all the creatures that Fenoglio had brought back to life. It was still a beautiful, mild night, and sleeping under the trees would be quite comfortable. Meggie and Mo found plenty of blankets in the now deserted houses. But they did not go back into Capricorn's house. Meggie never wanted to set foot inside it again, not because of the acrid smell of burning seeping out of its windows, or the charred doors, but because of the memories that leaped out at her like fierce animals at the mere sight of the place.

Sitting between Mo and her mother under one of the old oaks surrounding the car park, Meggie thought for a moment of Dustfinger, and wondered whether perhaps Capricorn had been telling the truth after all. Maybe he really was dead and buried somewhere in the hills. I may never find out what's happened to him, she thought, as one of the blue fairies rocked back and forth on a twig above her, its face bland and happy.

The whole village seemed to be enchanted that night. The air was full of buzzing and murmuring, and the figures wandering round the car park looked as if they had escaped from the dreams of children and not the words of an old man. That was something else Meggie kept asking herself during the night: where was Fenoglio now, and did he like it in his own story? She so much hoped so. But she knew he would miss his grandchildren and their games of hide-and-seek in his kitchen cupboard.

Before Meggie's eyes closed, she saw Elinor walking about among the trolls and fairies, looking happier than she had ever seen her. And her own parents were sitting to the left and right of Meggie, her mother was writing and writing, on leaves from the trees, on the fabric of her dress, in the sand. There were so many words, so many tales to tell.

58

Homesickness

Yet Bastian knew he couldn't leave without the book. It was clear to him that he had only come to the shop because of this book. It had called him in some mysterious way, because it wanted to be his, because it had somehow always belonged to him.

Michael Ende, *The Neverending Story*

Dustfinger watched it all from a rooftop far enough from the scene of Capricorn's festivities for him to feel safe from the Shadow, but close enough for him to see everything through the binoculars he had found in Basta's house. At first he had meant to stay in hiding. He had seen the Shadow kill too often already. Yet a strange feeling, as irrational as Basta's good-luck charms, had driven him out: a feeling that he could protect the book just by his presence. When he slipped into the alley he felt something else too. He didn't like to admit it to himself, but he wanted to see Basta die through the same binoculars that Basta himself had so often turned on his future victims.

So he sat on the tiles of a dilapidated roof, his back against the cold chimney, his face blackened with soot (for the face is treacherously pale by night), and watched smoke rise into the sky from Capricorn's house. He saw Flatnose set out with several men to extinguish the fire. He saw the Shadow emerge from the ground, he saw the old man disappear with an expression of infinite amazement on his face, and he saw Capricorn die the death he himself had summoned. Unfortunately Basta did not die as well, which was really annoying. Dustfinger saw him running away. And he saw the Magpie follow him.

He, Dustfinger the spectator, saw it all.

He had often been just a spectator, and this was not his story. What were they to him, Silvertongue and his daughter, the boy, the bookworm, and the woman who was another man's wife once more? She could have escaped with him, but she had stayed in the crypt with her daughter, so he had thrust her out of his heart as he always did with anyone who tried to stay there too long. He was glad that the Shadow hadn't taken them all, but they were none of his business any more. From now on Resa would be telling Silvertongue all the wonderful stories that drove away loneliness and homesickness and fear again. Why should it bother him?

But what about the fairies and the brownies suddenly stumbling around the scene of Capricorn's festivities? They were as out of place in this world as he was – and they too wouldn't let him forget that he was still here for one reason alone. He was interested only in the book, nothing but the book, and when he saw Silvertongue hide it under his jacket he decided to get it back. The book at least would be his. It must be his. He would stroke the pages, and if he closed his eyes at the same time he would be home again.

The old man was there now, the old man with the wrinkled face. Crazy. If only you hadn't been so afraid, Dustfinger, he thought bitterly. But you're a coward and you always will be. Why wasn't it *you* standing beside Capricorn? Why didn't you venture down? Then perhaps *you* would have disappeared back into the book instead of the old man.

The fairy with the butterfly wings and milky white face had flown after him. She was a vain little thing. Whenever she caught sight of her reflection in a window she lingered, smiling in front of it, oblivious to all else. She turned and preened in the air, ran her fingers through her hair and examined herself as if delighted by her own beauty all over again. The fairies he had known had not been particularly vain. On the contrary, sometimes they positively enjoyed smearing their tiny faces with mud or pollen, and then asked him, giggling, to guess which of them it was behind all the muck.

Perhaps I ought to catch myself one, thought Dustfinger. They could make me invisible. It would be wonderful to be invisible now and then. Or a troll – I could make him part of my show. Everyone would think he was just a little human being in a furry suit. No one can stand on his head as long as a troll, no one can make faces so well either, and those funny little dances they do – yes, why not?

When the moon had travelled half-way across the sky and Dustfinger was still sitting on the roof, the fairy with the butterfly wings grew impatient. Her tinkling sounded shrill and angry as she flew round him. What did she want? Did she want him to take her back where she came from, back to the place where all fairies had butterfly wings and people understood their language?

'You've picked the wrong man here,' he told her quietly. 'See that girl down there, and the man beside the woman with the dark blonde hair? They're what you need, but I might as well warn you: they're very good at luring people into their world, and not so good at sending them home again. Still, you can try! Maybe you'll have better luck than me.'

The fairy turned in the air, looked down, cast him a final injured glance and flew away. Dustfinger saw her brightness mingle with the light of the other fairies flying around and chasing each other through the branches of the trees. They were so forgetful. No grief or sorrow lived longer than a day in their little heads – and, who knows, perhaps the mild night air had already made them forget that this was not their own story.

Faint light was coming into the sky by the time they were all asleep down there. Only the boy kept watch. He was a suspicious boy, always on his guard, always careful except when he played with fire. Dustfinger couldn't help smiling when he thought of Farid's eager face, and the way he had burned his lips when he secretly took the torches from his rucksack. The boy would be no problem, no, none at all.

Silvertongue and Resa were asleep under a tree with Meggie between them, sheltered like a young bird in a warm nest. Elinor was sleeping not far away, and smiling in her sleep. Dustfinger had never seen her look so happy. One of the fairies was lying curled up like a caterpillar on her breast, with Elinor's hand around it. The fairy's face was not much bigger than the ball of her thumb, and her fairy light shone between Elinor's strong fingers like the light of a captive star.

Farid stood up as soon as he saw Dustfinger coming. He had a shotgun in his hand. It must have belonged to one of Capricorn's men.

'You— you're not dead?' Farid breathed incredulously. He still wore no shoes, which was hardly surprising, for he had always been falling over the shoelaces, and tying a bow had presented him with problems.

'No, I'm not.' Dustfinger stopped beside Silvertongue and looked down on him and Resa. 'Where's Gwin?' he asked the boy. 'I hope you've been looking after him!'

'He ran away after they shot at us, but he came back.' There was pride in the boy's voice.

'Ah.' Dustfinger crouched down beside Silvertongue. 'Well, he always knew when it was time to run, just like his master.'

'We left him at our camp up by the burnt-out cottage last night, because we knew it was going to be dangerous,' the boy went on. 'But I was going to fetch him as soon as I came off watch.'

'Well, I can do that now. Don't worry, he's sure to be all right. A marten like Gwin will always survive.' Dustfinger reached out his hand and put it under Silvertongue's jacket.

'What are you doing?' The boy's voice sounded uneasy.

'Just taking what's mine,' replied Dustfinger.

Silvertongue did not stir as Dustfinger slipped the book out. He was sleeping well and soundly, and what was there now to disturb his sleep? He had everything his heart desired.

'It's not yours!'

'Yes, it is.' Dustfinger stood up. He looked up at the branches. There were three fairies asleep up there. He'd always wondered how they could sleep perched in the trees without falling to the ground. Carefully, he took two of them off the spindly branch where they were lying, blew gently into their faces as they opened their eyes and yawned, and put them in his pocket.

'Blowing at them makes them sleepy,' he explained to the boy. 'Just a little tip in case you ever have anything to do with fairies. But I think it only works on the blue sort.'

He didn't bother to wake a troll. They were an obstinate lot; it would take a long time to persuade one of them to go with him, and very likely it would disturb Silvertongue.

'Let me come too!' The boy barred his way. 'Here, I've got your rucksack.' He held it up, as if to buy Dustfinger's company with it.

'No.' Dustfinger took the rucksack from him, slung it over his shoulders and turned his back on the boy.

'Yes!' Farid ran after him. 'You must let me come too! Or what am I going to tell Silvertongue when he realises the book is gone?'

'Tell him you fell asleep. It happens to a lot of sentries keeping watch.'

'Please!'

Dustfinger stopped. 'What about her?' he pointed to Meggie. 'You like the girl, don't you? Why not stay with her?'

The boy blushed, and stared at the girl for a long time, as if to commit the sight of her to memory. Then he turned back to Dustfinger. 'I don't belong with them.'

'You don't belong with me either.' Dustfinger walked away again, but when he was a good way from the car park the boy was still behind him. He was trying to walk so quietly that Dustfinger wouldn't hear him, and when Dustfinger turned he stopped like a thief caught in the act.

'What's the idea? I'm not going to be here much longer anyway!' snapped Dustfinger. 'Now I have the book I shall look for someone who can read me into it again, even if it's a stammerer like Darius who sends me home with a lame leg or a squashed face. What will you do then? You'll be left alone.'

The boy shrugged his shoulders and looked at him with his black eyes. 'I can breathe fire well now,' he said. 'I practised and practised while you were gone. But I'm not so good at swallowing it yet.'

'That's more difficult. You go at it too fast. I've told you so a thousand times.'

They found Gwin in the ruins of the burnt-out house, sleepy and with feathers round his muzzle. He seemed pleased to see Dustfinger, and even licked his hand, but then he ran after the boy. They walked until it was light, always heading south towards the sea. At last, they stopped for a rest and ate the food Dustfinger had brought from Basta's larder: some red spicy sausage, a piece of cheese, bread, olive oil. The bread was rather hard, so they dipped it in the oil, ate in silence sitting side by side on the grass, and then went on. Blue and dusty-pink wild sage flowered among the trees. The fairies moved in Dustfinger's pocket – and the boy walked behind him like a second shadow.

59

Going Home

And [he] sailed back over a year
and in and out of weeks
and through a day
and into the night of his very own room
where he found his supper waiting for him
and it was still hot.

Maurice Sendak, *Where the Wild Things Are*

In the morning, when Mo found that the book had gone,
Meggie's first thought was that Basta had taken it, and she
felt sick with fear at the thought of his prowling round them
while they slept. But Mo had a different explanation.

'Farid has gone too, Meggie,' he said. 'Do you think he'd
have gone with Basta?'

No, she didn't. There was only one person Farid would
have gone with. Meggie could well imagine Dustfinger emerging from the darkness, just as he had on the night when it all
began.

'But what about Fenoglio?' she said.

Mo only sighed. 'I don't know whether I'd have tried to read him back anyway, Meggie,' he said. 'So much misfortune has come from that book already, and I'm not a writer who can make up the words he wants to read aloud for himself. I'm only a kind of book doctor. I can give books new bindings, rejuvenate them a little, stop the bookworms eating them, and prevent them losing their pages over the years like a man loses his hair. But inventing the stories in them, filling new, empty pages with the right words – I can't do that. That's a very different trade. A famous writer once wrote, "An author can be seen as three things: a storyteller, a teacher or a magician – but the magician, the enchanter is in the ascendant." I always thought he was right about that.'

Meggie didn't know what to say. She only knew that she missed Fenoglio's face. 'And Tinker Bell,' she said. 'What about her? Will she have to stay here too now?' When she'd woken up, the fairy had been lying in the grass beside her. Now she was flying around with the other fairies. If you didn't look too closely they might have been a cloud of moths. Meggie couldn't imagine how she had escaped from Basta's house. Hadn't he been planning to keep her in a jug?

'As far as I remember, Peter Pan himself once forgot she'd ever existed,' said Mo. 'Am I right?'

Yes, Meggie remembered it too. 'All the same!' she murmured. 'Poor Fenoglio!'

But as she said that, her mother shook her head vigorously. Mo searched his pockets for paper, though all he could find was a shopping receipt and a felt-tip pen. Teresa took both from him, smiling. Then, while Meggie crouched in the grass beside her, she wrote: *Don't be sorry for Fenoglio. It's not a bad story he's landed in.*

'Is Capricorn still in it? Did you ever meet him there?' asked Meggie. How often she and Mo had wondered that. After all, he was one of the main characters in *Inkheart*. But perhaps there really was something behind the printed story, a world that changed every day just like this one.

I only heard of him there, her mother wrote. *They spoke of him as if he had gone away for a while. But there were others just as bad. It's a world full of terror and beauty* (here her writing became so small that Meggie could hardly make it out) *and I could always understand why Dustfinger felt homesick for it.*

The last sentence worried Meggie, but when she looked anxiously at her mother, Teresa smiled and reached for her hand. *I was far, far more homesick for you two*, she wrote on the palm of it, and Meggie closed her fingers over the words as if to hold them fast. She read them again and again on the long drive back to Elinor's house, and it was many days before they faded.

Elinor hadn't been able to reconcile herself to the idea of another walk all the way down through the thorny hills where the snakes lived. 'Do you think I'm crazy?' she said crossly. 'My feet hurt at the mere thought of it.' So she and Meggie had set off again in search of a telephone. It was a strange feeling to walk through the village – a truly deserted village now – past Capricorn's smoke-blackened house and the half-charred church porch. Water lay in the square outside. The blue sky was reflected in it, and made it look almost as if the square had turned into a lake overnight. The hoses Capricorn's men had used to save their master's house lay like huge snakes in the pools of water. In fact the fire had ravaged only the ground floor, but all the same Meggie would not go in, and when they had searched over a dozen other houses in vain Elinor bravely went through the charred door on her own. Meggie told her where to find the Magpie's room, and Elinor took a gun just in case the old woman had come back to save what she could of her own and her robber son's treasures. But the Magpie was long gone, just like Basta, and Elinor came back with a triumphant smile on her lips, carrying a cordless phone.

They called a taxi. It was rather difficult to persuade the driver that he must ignore the road barrier when he came to it, but luckily he had never believed any of the sinister stories that were told of the village. They arranged to wait for him by the roadside, so he wouldn't see any of the fairies and trolls. Meggie and her mother stayed in the village while Mo and Elinor went in the taxi to the nearest town, and came back a few hours later driving the two small buses they had hired. For Elinor had decided to offer a home, or 'asylum', as she put it, to all the strange creatures who had landed in her world. 'After all,' she said, 'many people here have little enough patience or understanding for their fellow human beings who are only superficially different to them – so how would it be for little people with blue skins who can fly?'

It took some time for them all to understand Elinor's offer – which was, of course, also made to the men, women and children out of the book – but most of them decided to stay in Capricorn's village. It obviously reminded them of a home that their earlier death had almost made them forget, and of course they could use the treasure that Meggie told the children must still be lying in the cellars of Capricorn's house. It would probably be enough to keep them all for the rest of their lives. The birds, dogs and cats who had emerged from the

Shadow had not hung about, but had long ago disappeared into the surrounding hills, while a few fairies and two of the little glass men, enchanted by the broom blossoms, the scent of rosemary, and the narrow alleys where the ancient stones whispered their stories to them, decided to make the once sinister village their home.

In the end, however, forty-three blue-skinned fairies with dragonfly wings fluttered into the buses and settled on the backs of the grey-patterned seats. Capricorn had obviously swatted fairies as carelessly as other people swat flies. Tinker Bell was among those who didn't come, which did not particularly trouble Meggie, for she had realised that Peter Pan's fairy was very self-centred. Her tinkling really got on your nerves, too, and she tinkled almost all the time if she didn't get what she wanted.

In addition to four trolls who looked like very small and hairy human beings, thirteen little glass men and women climbed into Elinor's buses – and so did Darius, the unhappy stammering reader. There was nothing to keep him in the village with its new inhabitants, and it held too many painful memories for him. He offered to help Elinor build up her library again, and she accepted. Meggie suspected that she was secretly toying with the idea of getting Darius to read aloud again, now that Capricorn's malevolent presence no longer left him tongue-tied.

Meggie looked back for a long time as they left Capricorn's village behind them. She knew she would never forget the sight of it, just as you never forget many stories even though – or perhaps because – they have scared you.

Before they left Mo had asked her, with concern in his voice, whether she minded if they drove to Elinor's first.

Meggie did not mind at all. Oddly enough, she felt more homesick for Elinor's house than for the old farmhouse where she and Mo had lived for the last few years.

The scar left by the bonfire was still to be seen on the lawn behind the house, where Capricorn's men had piled up the books and burned them. But before Elinor had the ashes taken away, she had filled a jam jar with the fine grey dust, and it stood on the bedside table in her room.

Many of the books that Capricorn's men had only swept off the shelves were already back in their old places, others were waiting on Mo's workbench to be rebound, but the library shelves were empty, and as they stood looking at them Meggie saw the tears in Elinor's eyes, even though she was quick to wipe them away.

Elinor did a great deal of buying over the next few weeks. She bought books. She travelled all over Europe in search of them. Darius was always with her, and sometimes Mo went with them too. But Meggie stayed in the big house with her mother. They would sit together at a window looking out at the garden where the fairies were building themselves nests, gently glowing globes that hung among the branches of the trees. The glass men and women settled into Elinor's attic, and the trolls dug caves among the big old trees which grew in abundance in Elinor's garden. She told them all that if possible they should never leave her property, warning them urgently of the dangers of the world beyond the hedges that enclosed it, but soon the fairies were flying down to the lake by night, the trolls were walking along its banks and stealing into the sleeping villages, and the little glass people would disappear into the tall grass that covered the slopes of the mountains around the lake.

'Don't worry too much,' said Mo, whenever Elinor bewailed their stupidity. 'After all, the world they came from wasn't without its dangers.'

'But it was different!' cried Elinor. 'There were no cars – suppose the fairies fly into a windscreen? And there were no hunters with rifles shooting at anything that moves, just for the fun of it.'

By now Elinor knew everything about the world of *Inkheart*. Meggie's mother had needed a great deal of paper to write down her memories of it. Every evening Meggie asked her to tell more stories, and then they sat together while Teresa wrote and Meggie read the words, and sometimes even tried to paint pictures of what her mother described.

The days went by, and Elinor's shelves filled up with wonderful new books. Some of them were in poor condition, and Darius, who had begun to draw up a catalogue of Elinor's printed treasures, kept interrupting his own work to watch Mo at his. He sat there wide-eyed as Mo freed a badly worn book from its old cover, fixed loose pages back, glued the spines in place and did whatever else was necessary to preserve the books for many more years to come.

Long after all this, Meggie couldn't have said exactly when they had decided to stay on with Elinor. Perhaps not for many weeks, or perhaps they had known from the first day they were back. Meggie was given the room with the bed that was much too big for her, and which still had her book-box standing under it. She would have loved to read aloud to her mother from her own favourite books, but of course she understood why Mo very seldom did so, even now. And one night when she couldn't get to sleep, because she thought she saw Basta's face out in the dark, she sat down at the desk in front of her window and began to write, while the fairies played in Elinor's garden and the trolls rustled in the bushes. For Meggie had a plan: she wanted to learn to make up stories like Fenoglio. She wanted to learn to fish for words so that she could read aloud to her mother, without worrying about who might come out of the stories and look at her with homesick eyes. So Meggie decided that words would be her trade.

And where better could she learn that trade than in a house full of magical creatures, where fairies built their nests in the garden and books whispered on the shelves by night? As Mo had said: writing stories is a kind of magic, too.

The Author and Publisher would like to thank the following for the permission to use copyright material:

Richard Adams: from *Watership Down* (Penguin Books, 1974), reprinted by permission of David Higham Associates

Hans Christian Andersen: from *Hans Andersen: His Classic Fairy Tales*, translated by Erik Haugaard (Gollancz, 1976)

J. M. Barrie: from *Peter Pan* (Penguin Popular Classics, 1995), reprinted by permission of Great Ormond Street Hospital Children's Charity

Lucy M. Boston: from *The Children of Green Knowe* (Puffin Books, 1975)

Ray Bradbury: from *Fahrenheit 451* (Flamingo Modern Classics, 1993)

Roald Dahl: from *The BFG* (Jonathan Cape, 1982) and *The Witches* (Jonathan Cape, 1983), reprinted by permission of David Higham Associates

Richard de Bury: from *Philobiblon* (Blackwell, 1970), reprinted by permission of the publisher

Michael de Larrabeiti: from *The Borrible Trilogy* (Macmillan, 2002), reprinted by permission of the publisher

J. Doraston: from *A Passion for Books* (Three River Press, New York)

Solomon Eagle: from *A Gentle Madness* by Nicholas Basbanes (Henry Holt & Co. 1995)

Michael Ende: from *Jim Button and Luke the Engine Driver* (Penguin Books, 1990) and *The Never Ending Story* (Penguin Books, 1984)

William Goldman: from *The Princess Bride* (Bloomsbury Publishing, 1990)

Kenneth Grahame: from *The Wind in the Willows* (Puffin Books, 1994)

Eva Ibbotson: from *The Secret of Platform 13* (Macmillan Children's Books, 2001)

Rudyard Kipling: from *The Jungle Book* (Puffin Classics, 1994), reprinted by permission of A. P. Watt Ltd on behalf of The National Trust for Places of Historical Interest or Natural Beauty

Edward William Lane (translator): from *The Arabian Nights' Entertainments* (East-West Publications, 1982)

C. S. Lewis: from *The Lion, the Witch and the Wardrobe* (Collins, 1987)

Otfried Preussler: from *Satanic Mill* (Peter Smith Publishers, 1985)

Maurice Sendak: from *Where the Wild Things Are* (The Bodley Head, 1967)

Shel Silverstein: from *Where the Sidewalk Ends: The Poems & Drawings of Shel Silverstein* (HarperCollins Publishers, 1974), (c) 1974 by Evil Eye Music, Inc.

Isaac Bashevis Singer: from *Naftali the Storyteller and His Horse, Sus, & Other Stories* (Oxford University Press, 1977)

J. R. R. Tolkien: from *The Hobbit* (HarperCollins, 1994) and *The Lord of the Rings* (HarperCollins, 1994), reprinted by permission of the publisher

Evangeline Walton: from *The Mabinogion Tetralogy* (Overlook Press, 2002)

T. H. White: from *The Sword in the Stone* (Harper & Row, 1973) and *The Book of Merlyn: The Unpublished Conclusion to The Once and Future King* (Univerisity of Texas Press, 1988)

Every effort has been made to trace or contact all copyright holders. The publishers would be pleased to rectify any omissions brought to their notice at the earliest opportunity.

*Want to know what happens next to
Meggie, Dustfinger and Farid?*

*Turn the page for two exciting
preview chapters from*

INKSPELL

BY CORNELIA FUNKE

*The captivating second book in the
Inkheart trilogy*

Fool's Gold

For plainly this miscreant had sold himself to Satan, and it would be fatal to meddle with the property of such a power as that.

Tom Sawyer, *Mark Twain*

'No!' Farid heard the horror in his own voice. 'No! What have you done? Where has he gone?'

Orpheus rose ponderously from the wall, still holding that wretched piece of paper, and he smiled. 'Home. Where else?'

'But what about me? Go on reading. Go on!' Everything was blurred by the tears in his eyes. He was alone again, alone as he had always been before he found Dustfinger. Farid began trembling so hard that he didn't even notice Orpheus taking the book from his hands.

'And here's the proof of it once again,' he heard the man murmur. 'I bear my name by right. I am the master of *all* words, both written and spoken. No one can compete with me.'

'Master of words? What are you talking about?' Farid

shouted in such a loud voice that even the hell-hound flinched. 'If you know so much about your trade, then why am I still here? Go on, start reading again! And give me that book back!' He reached for it, but Orpheus avoided him with surprising agility.

'The book? Why should I give it to you? You probably can't even read. Let me tell you something! If I'd wanted you to go with him, then you'd be there now, but you have no business in his story, so I just left out what I'd written about you. Understand? And now, be off before I set my dog on you. Boys like you threw stones at him when he was a puppy, and he's enjoyed chasing your sort ever since!'

'You brute! You liar! You traitor!' Farid's voice broke. Hadn't he known it? Hadn't he told Dustfinger? Cheeseface was as false as fool's gold.

Something made its way between his bare feet, something furry and round-nosed with tiny horns between its ears. The marten. He's gone, Gwin, thought Farid. Dustfinger's gone. We'll never see him again!

The hell-hound lowered its bulky head and took a hesitant step towards the marten, but Gwin bared his needle-sharp teeth, and the huge dog withdrew its nose in astonishment. Its fear gave Farid fresh courage.

'Come on, give it to me!' He rammed his thin fist into Orpheus's chest. 'That piece of paper, and the book too! Or I'll slit you open like a carp. I swear I will!' But he couldn't help sobbing, which made the words sound nothing like as impressive as he had intended.

Orpheus patted his dog's head as he stowed the book away in the waistband of his trousers. 'Dear me, that really scares us, Cerberus, doesn't it?'

Gwin pressed close to Farid's ankles, his tail twitching uneasily back and forth. Even when the marten ran across the road and disappeared into the trees on the other side, Farid thought it was because of the dog. Deaf and blind, he kept thinking later, you were deaf and blind, Farid. But Orpheus smiled, like someone who knows more than his opponent.

'Let me tell you, my young friend,' he said, 'it gave me a terrible fright when Dustfinger wanted the book back. Luckily he handed it to you, or I couldn't have done anything for him. It was hard enough persuading my clients not to just kill him, but I made them promise. Only on that condition would I act as bait ... bait for the book, because in case you haven't caught on yet, this is all about the book. The book and nothing else. They promised not to hurt a hair of Dustfinger's head, but I'm afraid no one said a word about you.'

And before Farid realized what Cheeseface was talking about, he felt the knife at his throat – sharp as the edge of a reed, colder than mist among the trees.

'Well, well, who have we here?' a well-remembered voice murmured in his ear. 'Didn't I last see you with Silvertongue? It seems you helped Dustfinger to steal the book for him, isn't that so? What a fine little fellow you are!' The knife scratched Farid's skin, and the man breathed peppermint into his face. If he hadn't known Basta by his voice, then that stinking breath would have identified the man. His knife and a few mint leaves – Basta was never without them. He chewed the leaves and then spat out what remained. He was dangerous as a rabid dog, and not too bright, but how did he come to be here? How had he found them?

'Well, how do you like my new knife?' Basta purred into Farid's ear. 'I'd have liked to introduce the fire-eater to it too, but Orpheus here has a weakness for him. Never mind, I'll find Dustfinger again. Him and Silvertongue, and Silvertongue's witch of a daughter. They'll all pay....'

'Pay for what?' said Farid. 'Saving you from the Shadow?'

But Basta only pressed the blade more firmly against his neck. 'Saving me? They brought me bad luck, nothing but bad luck!'

'For heaven's sake put that knife away!' Orpheus interrupted, sounding sickened. 'He's only a boy. Let him go. I have the book as we agreed, so—'

'Let him go?' Basta laughed aloud, but the laughter died in his throat. A snarling sound came from the woods behind them, and the hell-hound laid its ears back. Basta spun round. 'What the devil ...? You damned idiot! What have you let out of the book?'

Farid didn't want to know the answer. He felt Basta loosen his grip for a moment. That was enough: he bit the man's hand so hard that he tasted blood. Basta screamed and dropped the knife. Farid jerked back his elbows, rammed them into the man's narrow chest and ran. But he had entirely forgotten the little wall by the roadside; he stumbled on it and fell to his knees, so hard that he was left gasping for breath. As he picked himself up he saw the paper lying on the asphalt, the sheet of paper that had carried Dustfinger away. The wind must have blown it into the road. With quick fingers, he reached for it. *I just left out what I'd written about you. Understand?* Orpheus's words still rang in his head, mocking him. Farid clutched the sheet of paper to his chest and ran on, over the road and towards the dark trees waiting on the other side. The hell-hound was growling and barking behind him. Then it howled. Something snarled again, so fiercely that

Farid ran even faster. Orpheus screamed, fear making his voice shrill and ugly. Basta swore, and then the snarl came again, wild as the snarling of the great cats that had lived in Farid's old world.

Don't look round, he thought. Run, run! he told his legs. Let the cat eat the hell-hound, let it eat them all, Basta and Cheeseface included, just keep running. The dead leaves lying under the trees were damp and muffled the sound of his footsteps, but they were slippery too, and made him lose his balance on the steep slope. Desperately he caught hold of a tree-trunk, pressed himself against it, knees trembling, and listened to the sounds of the night. Could Basta hear him gasping?

A sob escaped his throat. He pressed his hands to his mouth. The book, Basta had the book! He'd been supposed to look after it – and how was he ever going to find Dustfinger again now? Farid felt the sheet of paper that held Orpheus's words. He was still holding it tight. It was damp and dirty – and now it was his only hope.

'Hey, you little bastard! Bite me, would you?' Basta's voice reached him through the quiet night air. 'You can run but I'll get you yet, do you hear? You, the fire-eater, Silvertongue and his hoity-toity daughter – and the old man who wrote those accursed words! I'll kill you all! One by one! The way I've just slit open the beast that came out of the book.'

Farid hardly dared to breathe. Go on, he told himself. Go on! He can't see you! Trembling, he felt for the next tree trunk, sought a handhold, and was grateful to the wind for blowing through the leaves and drowning out his footsteps with their rustling. *How many times do I have to tell you? There aren't any ghosts in this world. One of its few advantages.* He heard Dustfinger's voice as clearly as if he were still following the fire-eater. Farid kept repeating the words as the tears ran down his face and thorns gashed his feet: *There are no ghosts, there are no ghosts!*

A branch whipped against his face so hard that he almost cried out. Were they following him? He couldn't hear anything except the wind. He slipped again, and stumbled down the slope. Nettles stung his legs, burrs caught in his hair. And something jumped up at him, furry and warm, pushing its nose into his face.

'Gwin?' Farid felt the little head. Yes, there were the tiny horns. He pressed his face into the marten's soft fur. 'Basta's back, Gwin!' he whispered. 'And he has the book! Suppose Orpheus reads him over again? He's sure to go back into the book some time, don't you think? How are we going to warn Dustfinger about him now?'

Farid twice found himself back at the road that wound down the mountain, but he dared not walk along it, and instead made his way on through the prickly undergrowth. Soon every breath he drew hurt, but he did not stop. Only when the first rays of the sun made their way through the trees, and Basta still hadn't appeared behind him, did he know that he had got away.

Now what? he thought as he lay in the damp grass, gasping for breath. Now what? And suddenly he remembered another voice, the voice that had brought him into this world. Silvertongue. Of course. Only Silvertongue could help Farid now, he or his daughter. Meggie. They were living with the bookworm woman these days. Farid had once been there with Dustfinger. It was a long way to go, particularly with the cuts on his feet. But he had to get there before Basta did. ...

Meggie's Decision

The idea hovered and shivered delicately, like a soap bubble, and she dared not even look at it directly in case it burst. But she was familiar with the way of ideas, and she let it shimmer, looking away, thinking about something else.

Philip Pullman, *Northern Lights*

Mo came home just as they were all sitting down to breakfast, and Resa kissed him as if he'd been away for weeks. Meggie hugged him harder than usual too, relieved that he had come back safe and sound, but she avoided looking him straight in the eye. Mo knew her too well. He would have spotted her guilty conscience at once. And Meggie's conscience was very guilty.

The reason was the sheet of paper hidden among her school books up in her room, closely written in her own hand, although the words were by someone else. Meggie had spent hours copying out what Orpheus had written. Every time she got something wrong she had begun again from the beginning, for fear that a single mistake could spoil everything. She had added just three words – where the passage mentioned a boy, in the sentences left unread by Orpheus, Meggie had added 'and the girl'. Three nondescript, perfectly ordinary words, so ordinary that it was overwhelmingly likely that they occurred somewhere in the pages of *Inkheart*. She couldn't check, however, because the only copy of the book she would have needed to do that was now in Basta's hands. Basta ... the mere sound of his name reminded Meggie of black days and black nights. Black with fear.

Mo had brought her a present to make peace between them, as he always did when they had quarrelled: a small notebook bound by himself, just the right size for her jacket pocket, with a marbled paper cover. Mo knew how much Meggie liked marbled patterns; she had been only nine when he had taught her how to colour them for herself. Guilt went to her heart when he put the notebook down by her plate, and for a moment she wanted to tell him everything, just as she had always done. But a glance from Farid prevented her. That glance said, 'No, Meggie, he won't let you go there – ever.' So she kept quiet, kissed Mo, whispered, 'Thank you,' and said no more, quickly bending her head, her tongue heavy with the words she hadn't spoken.

Luckily no one noticed her sad expression. The others were still anxious about Farid's news of Basta. Elinor had gone to the police, on Mo's advice, but her visit to them had done nothing to improve her mood.

'Just as I told you,' she said crossly, working away at the cheese with her knife as if it were the cause of all this trouble. 'Those fools didn't believe a word I said. A couple of sheep in uniform would have listened better. You know I don't like dogs, but maybe I ought to get some after all ... a couple of huge black brutes to tear Basta apart the moment he comes through my garden gate. A Dobsterman dog, yes. A Dobsterman or two. Isn't a Dobsterman the dog that eats people?'

'You mean a Dobermann.' Mo winked across the table at Meggie.

It broke her heart. There he was winking at her, his deceitful daughter who was planning to go right away, to somewhere he probably couldn't follow her. Perhaps her mother would understand, but Mo? No, not Mo. Never.

Meggie bit her lip so hard that it hurt, while Elinor, still in a state of agitation, went on. 'And I could hire a bodyguard. You can do that, can't you? One with a pistol – no, not just a pistol, armed to the teeth: knives, guns, everything, and so big that Basta's black heart would stop at the mere sight of him! How does that sound?'

Meggie saw Mo suppress a smile with difficulty. 'How does it sound? As if you'd been reading too many thrillers, Elinor.'

'Well, I *have* read a lot of thrillers,' she said, injured. 'They're very informative if you don't usually mix much with criminals. What's more, I can't forget seeing Basta's knife at your throat.'

'Nor can I, believe me.' Meggie saw his hand go to his throat as if, just for a moment, he felt the sharp blade against his skin again. 'All the same, I think you're worrying unnecessarily. I had plenty of time to think it all over on the drive back, and I don't believe Basta will come all the way here just to get revenge. Revenge for what? For being saved from Capricorn's Shadow – and by us? No. He'll have had this Orpheus read him back by now. Back into the book. Basta never liked our world half as much as Capricorn did. Some things about it made him very nervous.'

He spread jam on top of his bread and cheese. Elinor watched this, as usual, with horror, and Mo, also as usual, ignored her disapproving glance.

'So what about those threats he shouted after the boy?'

'Well, he was angry that he'd got away, wasn't he? I don't have to tell you the kind of thing Basta says when he's angry. I'm only surprised he was actually clever enough to find out that Dustfinger had the book. And I'd like to know where he found this man Orpheus too. He seems to be better than me at reading aloud.'

'Nonsense!' Elinor's voice sounded cross, but relieved too. 'The only one who may be as good at it as you are is your daughter.'

Mo smiled at Meggie and put another slice of cheese on top of the jam. 'Thanks, very flattering. But, however that may be, our knife-happy friend Basta has gone! And I hope he's taken the wretched book with him, and put an end to that story for ever. There'll be no more need for Elinor to jump when she hears something rustling in the garden at night, and Darius won't have to dream of Basta's knife – which means that the news Farid has brought is in fact very good news! I hope you've all thanked him warmly!'

Farid smiled shyly as Mo raised his coffee cup to him, but Meggie saw the anxiety in his black eyes. If Mo was right, then by now Basta was in the same place as Dustfinger. And they all thought Mo *was* right. You could see the relief in Darius's and Elinor's faces, and Resa put her arms around Mo's neck and smiled as if everything was fine again.

Elinor began asking Mo questions about the books he had so shockingly abandoned to answer Meggie's phone call. And

Darius was trying to tell Resa about the new system of classification he had thought up for Elinor's library. But Farid looked at his empty plate. Against the background of its white china, he was probably seeing Basta's knife at Dustfinger's neck.

Basta. The name stuck in Meggie's throat like a pebble. She kept thinking the same thing: if Mo was right, Basta was now where she soon hoped to be herself. In the Inkworld.

She was going to try it that very night, she would try to use her own voice and Orpheus's words to make her way through the thicket of written letters, into the Wayless Wood. Farid had pleaded with her to wait no longer. He was beside himself with anxiety for Dustfinger, and Mo's remarks had certainly done nothing to change that. 'Please, Meggie!' He had begged her again and again. 'Please read it!'

Meggie looked across the table at Mo. He was whispering something to Resa, and she laughed. You heard her voice only when she laughed. Mo put his arm round her, and his eyes sought Meggie. When her bed was empty tomorrow morning he wouldn't look as carefree as he did now. Would he be angry, or merely sad? Resa laughed when, for her and Elinor's benefit, he mimicked the horror of the collector whose books he had abandoned so disgracefully when Meggie had phoned, and Meggie had to laugh too when he imitated the poor man's voice. The collector had obviously been very fat and breathless.

Elinor was the only one who didn't laugh. 'I don't think that's funny, Mortimer,' she said sharply. 'Personally, I'd probably have shot you if you'd simply gone off leaving my poor books behind, all sick and dirty.'

'Yes, I expect you would.' Mo gave Meggie a conspiratorial

look, as he always did when Elinor lectured him or his daughter on the way to treat books or the rules of her library.

Oh Mo, if only you knew, thought Meggie, if only you knew ... She felt as if he would read her secret in her face any minute now. Abruptly, she pushed her chair back, muttered, 'I'm not hungry,' and went off to Elinor's library. Where else? Whenever she wanted to escape her own thoughts, she went to books for help. She was sure to find something to keep her mind occupied until evening finally came and they all went to bed, suspecting nothing.

Looking at Elinor's library, you couldn't tell that scarcely more than a year ago it had contained nothing but a red rooster hanging dead in front of empty shelves, while Elinor's finest books burnt on the lawn outside. The jar that Elinor had filled with some of their pale ashes still stood beside her bed.

Meggie ran her forefinger over the backs of the books. They were ranged side by side on the shelves again now, like piano keys. Some shelves were still empty, but Elinor and Darius were always out and about, visiting second-hand bookshops and auctions, to replace those lost treasures with new and equally wonderful books.

Orpheus ... where was the story of Orpheus?

Meggie was on her way over to the shelf where the Greeks and Romans whispered their ancient stories when the library door opened behind her, and Mo came in.

'Resa says you have the sheet of paper that Farid brought with him in your room. Can I see it?' He was trying to sound as casual as if he were just asking about the weather, but he'd never been any good at pretending. Mo couldn't pretend, any more than he could tell lies.

'Why?' Meggie leant against Elinor's books as if they would strengthen her backbone.

'Why? Because I'm curious, remember? And what's more,' he added, looking at the backs of the books, as if he could find the right words there, 'and what's more, I think it would be better to burn that sheet of paper.'

'Burn it?' Meggie looked at him incredulously. 'But why?'

'I know it sounds as if I'm seeing ghosts,' he said, taking a book off the shelf, opening it and leafing absent-mindedly through it, 'but that piece of paper, Meggie … I feel it's like an open door, a door that we'd be well advised to close once and for all. Before Farid tries disappearing into that damn story too.'

'What if he does?' Meggie couldn't help the cool note that crept into her voice. As if she were talking to a stranger. 'Why can't you understand? He only wants to find Dustfinger! To warn him against Basta.'

Mo closed the book he had taken off the shelf and put it back in its place. 'So he says. But suppose Dustfinger didn't actually want to take him along, suppose he left him behind on purpose? Would that surprise you?'

No. No, it wouldn't. Meggie said nothing. It was so quiet among the books, so terribly quiet among all those words.

'I know, Meggie,' said Mo at last, in a low voice. 'I know you think the world that book describes is much more exciting than this one. I understand the feeling. I've often imagined being right inside one of my favourite books. But we both know that once imagination turns to reality things feel quite different. You think the Inkworld is a magical place, a world of wonders – but believe me, your mother has told me a lot about it that you wouldn't like at all. It's a cruel, dangerous place, full of darkness and violence, ruled by brute force, Meggie, not by justice.'

He looked at her, searching her face for the understanding he had always found there before, but did not find now.

'Farid comes from a world like that,' said Meggie. 'And he didn't choose to get into this story of ours. You brought him here.'

She regretted her words the moment they were out. Mo turned away as if she had struck him. 'Yes. You're right, of course,' he said, going back to the door. 'And I don't want to quarrel with you again. But I don't want that paper lying about your room either. Give it back to Farid. Or else, who knows, there could be a giant sitting on your bed tomorrow morning.' He was trying to make her laugh, of course. He couldn't bear the two of them to be on bad terms again. He looked so depressed. And so tired.

'You know perfectly well nothing like that can happen,' said Meggie. 'Why do you always worry so much? Things don't just come out of the words on the page unless you call them. You should know that better than anyone!'

His hand was still on the door-handle.

'Yes,' he said. 'Yes, no doubt you're right. But do you know what? Sometimes I'd like to put a padlock on all the books in this world. And as for that very special book ... I'd be glad, now, if Capricorn really had burnt the last copy back there in his village. That book brings bad luck, Meggie, nothing but bad luck, even if you won't believe me.'

Then he closed the library door after him.

Meggie stood there motionless until his footsteps had died away. She went over to one of the windows looking out on to the garden, but when Mo finally came down the path leading to his workshop he didn't look back at the house. Resa was with him. She had put her arm round his shoulders, and her other hand was tracing words, but Meggie couldn't make them out. Were they talking about her?

It was sometimes an odd feeling suddenly to have not just a father, but two parents who talked to each other when she wasn't with them. Mo went into his workshop alone, and Resa strolled back to the house. She waved to Meggie when she saw her standing at the window, and Meggie waved back.

An odd feeling …

Meggie sat among Elinor's books for some time longer, looking first at one, then at another, searching for passages to drown out her own thoughts. But the letters on the pages remained just letters, forming neither pictures nor words, and finally Meggie went out into the garden, lay down on the grass and looked at the workshop. She could see Mo at work through its windows.

I can't do it, she thought, as the wind blew leaves off the trees and whirled them away like brightly painted toys. No. I can't! They'll all be so worried, and Mo will never, ever say a word to me again.

Meggie thought all those things, she thought them over and over again. And at the same time she knew, deep down inside her, that she had made up her mind long ago.